RED SKY IN THE MORNING

A young girl stands alone in the cobbled marketplace of a small Lincolnshire town, bedraggled, soaked through and very afraid. No one knows or cares who she is or where she has come from. Only kindly farmer Eddie Appleyard recognises something in the girl that touches his heart. In a drunken haze Eddie takes her home. His wife Bertha accuses him of infidelity and turns Anna out into the cold, wet night. Eddie hides the girl in a tumbledown shepherd's cottage that becomes her new home. Anna's arrival will change their lives: Eddie's, Bertha's and even that of their young son Tony, torn between his warring parents and the mysterious stranger. It will take years for the secrets of Anna's former life to be revealed, but Bertha bides her time and awaits her moment, little realizing the tragedy her vengeance will unleash.

RED SKY IN THE MORNING

Margaret Dickinson

WINDSOR

PARAGON

First published 2004
by
Pan Books
This Large Print edition published 2004
by
BBC Audiobooks Ltd by arrangement with
Pan Macmillan Ltd

ISBN 1 4056 1012 3   (Windsor Hardcover)
ISBN 1 4056 2008 0   (Paragon Softcover)

British Library Cataloguing in Publication Data available

Printed and bound in Great Britain by
Antony Rowe Ltd., Chippenham, Wiltshire

For Zoë and Scott,
my daughter and son-in-law

ACKNOWLEDGEMENTS

My grateful thanks to Graham and Liz Jarnell for answering all my questions about sheep. Any errors, of course, are mine and not theirs! As always, my love and thanks go to my family and friends, especially my husband, Dennis, and those who read the script in the early stages: Robena and Fred Hill, David and Una Dickinson, Linda and Terry Allaway and Pauline Griggs. Your constant support and encouragement mean more to me than you can ever know.

Special thanks to the best agent any writer could have—Darley Anderson. Thank you, too, to all the 'team' at Macmillan, headed by my lovely editor, Imogen Taylor. You're all absolutely wonderful.

1946

CHAPTER ONE

The girl was standing in the middle of the cobbled marketplace. She had been there for hours whilst the busy market bustled around her. All day the raucous shouts of the stallholders had rung out, each vying with the others to attract the attention of the shoppers, but they had not gained hers. It was two weeks before Christmas and the stalls were laden with holly wreaths and mistletoe, bringing colour to a drab, wet day.

Now it was growing dark and the traders were packing up and going home. Home to a warm fire and a hot drink, no doubt liberally laced with whisky to drive out the chill and to thaw frozen hands and feet. The rain had been falling steadily since early morning and the girl, just standing there so quiet and still, staring ahead of her and looking neither to right nor left, was soaked to her skin. Her long black hair was plastered against her head. The bottom button of the shapeless coat she wore was missing and the garment flapped open, revealing the swelling mound of her belly. Yet she didn't seem to care about her condition, or even about the discomfort she must be feeling. She seemed unaware of everything and everyone around her. Her thin face was white and pinched with cold, and devoid of expression. Her blue eyes, so dark they were almost violet, were lifeless.

'A' ya goin' to stand there all night, lass?' The last market trader to load his wares into the back of an old van shouted across the wet cobblestones, shining now in the pale glow from the street lamp.

3

She did not even glance in his direction. It was as if she hadn't heard him. The man wiped the back of his hand across his face and shrugged. 'Please ya'sen,' he muttered and turned away. He looked longingly towards the public house, the Shepherd's Crook. Even out here in the cold and the wet, the buzz of conversation could be heard through the open door. A haze of pipe and cigarette smoke drifted out into the night air. The market trader hesitated for a moment, seemingly torn between the inviting hospitality the place offered and the thought of home, where his wife would be waiting with a hot meal and warm slippers. The pull of home won and he bent to swing the starting handle of his battered van. The engine spluttered into life and he moved to the driver's side of the vehicle, slinging the starting handle into the well in front of the passenger seat. He glanced across at the girl, then shrugged again and climbed into the van.

When the noise of the motor had died away the marketplace was deserted, except for the girl. The only other living creature was a pony, harnessed to an old-fashioned trap and tethered outside the Shepherd's Crook. It looked as wet and miserable as the girl felt. Just once she licked her lips, tasting the rain.

The laughter and the noise from the pub spilled into the street as three men came out, lurching along the pavement, bumping into one another, laughing and joking and filled with the merriment of the festive season. They didn't even notice her. More men left the pub in twos and threes, yet the pony still stood there, occasionally pawing the ground, his metal-clad hoof scraping the cobbles. He shook his head and water droplets showered from his rain-soaked mane.

'Time to go home, Eddie. You can't stay here all night.' There was a disturbance in the doorway of the pub and, for the first time, the girl's glance focused on the two men there. One was very unsteady, reeling from side to side and being steered towards the waiting pony and trap by the other. 'Come on. Your pony'll tek you home. Good job he knows the way better'n you when you're in this state, in't it?'

For a moment the drunken man leant against the trap, then he grasped the side and, with the aid of the other man, heaved himself into the back. The pony lifted his head, perking up at once now his warm stable was almost in sight.

'On you go, then.' The publican raised his hand, about to untether the pony and slap its rump to send it on its way, when the man in the back mumbled, 'Wait. Wait a mo'.'

Through the blur of drink and the steadily falling rain, he had caught a glimpse of the girl standing in the middle of the square. He raised a shaking finger and pointed. 'Who's that?'

'Eh?' The landlord glanced over his shoulder. 'Oh, her. Bin there hours. Some tramp beggin', I 'spect. Well, she needn't think she's goin' to get a bed at my place.'

Eddie was scrambling out of the trap again.

'Now, now,' the other man remonstrated. 'On you go home, Eddie. You're goin' to be in enough trouble with your missis as it is. Don't be bothering yourself with the likes of that little trollop.'

Eddie shook off the man's restraining hand. 'You can't leave a poor lass standing there in this weather,' he mumbled and began to shamble

5

towards the girl. The landlord shrugged. 'Have it your way, then. I've better things to do with me time. Goodnight to you, Eddie Appleyard.'

The landlord went inside and slammed the heavy door of the public house. The sound of the bolts being shot home echoed in the silence.

Still the girl had not moved as Eddie reached her and stood before her, swaying slightly. He peered at her through the gloom. 'Nowhere to go, lass?' His voice was gentle and caring and the girl, who had thought she was empty of all emotion, felt tears prickle behind her eyelids. It was the first kind word she had heard in weeks, months even. Slowly, she shook her head.

He touched her arm lightly. 'Then you'd best come home with me.' Without waiting for any sign of agreement or otherwise from her, Eddie turned and reeled back towards the trap. But before he reached it, he stumbled and fell to the cobbles. The girl watched for a moment and then, when he made no attempt to rise, she moved at last. Her limbs were stiff with cold and for the first few steps she hobbled like an old woman. She bent and grasped his arm. He grunted and, leaning heavily on her, struggled to his feet. They staggered towards the trap. The man scrambled into the back and then turned, holding out his hand towards her. 'Come on, lass. You can't stay out here all night.'

She hesitated and then put her hand into his. When she was sitting beside him on the floor he said, 'Giddup, Duke.' The pony moved and, as the trap swayed, the girl clung on to the side, but the man merely shifted himself into a more comfortable position. Curling his body to fit into the confined space, he lay down. With a satisfied grunt, he rested his head on her lap and, almost at once, began to snore.

The pony bent its head against the driving rain as it plodded up the steep hill, leaving the lights of the town behind them. Beneath the slight shelter the sides of the trap afforded and with the warmth of the man close to her seeping into her chilled being, the girl's eyelids closed. Her head drooped forward and soon, draped across the man, she too slept.

CHAPTER TWO

'Who the hell's this?'

A woman's strident voice startled the girl awake. The pony and trap had come to a halt in the middle of a farmyard. Farm buildings and a house loomed through the darkness. The woman, a raincoat over her head, was standing at the back of the trap, poking the sleeping man with her forefinger.

'Eddie—wake up. Who's this, I'd like to know? Some trollop you've picked up at the market?' She prodded him viciously. 'You've a nerve and no mistake. Come on.' She began to pull at him. 'Stir ya'sen. I want an explanation. And it'd better be good.'

The man grunted and lifted his head. His face now on a level with the woman's, he murmured, 'Bertha, my dearly beloved wife.' He grinned foolishly, but even in his drunken state the girl could detect the sarcasm in his tone.

'I'll "beloved wife" you,' the woman shrilled as she dragged him from the trap. He fell to the

7

ground on his hands and knees, but she made no effort to help him up. Instead she pushed him with her toe. 'Get up, ya daft beggar. And as for you,' she added, glaring up at the girl still sitting on the floor of the trap, 'you can be on ya way—'

'No—no.' Hanging on to the back of the trap, the man dragged himself upright. He swayed slightly, but his voice was less slurred now. 'No, she's stayin'. She's nowhere to go.'

'What's that to do with you? Who is she?'

The man shrugged. 'Dunno. She was standing in the marketplace getting soaking wet, so I brought her home.'

'Oh, a real knight in shining armour, aren't ya? Get on inside.' The woman pushed him again. Then she jabbed her finger towards the girl. 'And you. You'd better come inside an' all. Only for a minute, mind. I want to get to the bottom of this.'

The woman, small and very overweight, nevertheless marched towards the back door of the farmhouse with surprising agility.

'Come on, lass,' Eddie said. 'We'd better do as she says.' He held out his hand to her and, stiffly, she climbed out of the trap. As they began to walk towards the house, the girl spoke for the first time. Her voice was low and husky.

'What about the pony?'

'Eh?' Eddie blinked. 'Oh aye.' He lurched back towards the animal, still waiting patiently, and patted its neck. 'Poor old Duke. You always get the rough end of the stick, don't you?' His voice was low as he muttered, 'Reckon we both do.'

The man began to grapple with the harness and the girl moved to help him. As soon as the pony felt himself released from the shafts, he trotted towards

8

the building on the right-hand side of the yard. The man gave a wry laugh. 'He knows his way home all right.'

They left the trap in the middle of the yard and went towards the house.

'If she—if she won't let you stay in the house, lass, the hayloft above Duke's stable is dry and in the morning—' He wiped his hand across his face and then shook his head as if trying to clear it. 'I'm not thinking too straight, but I'll sort summat out for you in the morning.' They stepped into a scullery and through that into a warm kitchen, where the smell of freshly baked mince pies still lingered. 'I'll see if I can get her to—'

'So? What's all this about?' Bertha was standing with her fat arms folded across her bosom. Her mousy coloured hair was straight and roughly cut into an untidy bob. Parted on one side, the long section of hair was held back from her face by a grip. Her florid cheeks were lined with tiny red veins and her mouth was small, the thin lips lost in the fatness of her face. Only in her mid-thirties, yet already she had a double chin. As she stood awaiting her husband's explanation, her pale hazel eyes sparked with anger.

Behind the woman, in the doorway leading further into the house, stood a young boy in striped flannelette pyjamas. He was no more than ten years old and his large brown eyes were darting from one to the other between his parents, but they seemed oblivious to his presence.

The girl shivered and glanced towards the glowing fire, longing to kneel before it and hold out her hands to its heat.

'Well? I'm waiting.' The woman's glance raked

the girl, taking in her bedraggled state. Then her mouth turned down in disgust. 'I might 'ave known. She's in the family way. Is it yours, Eddie Appleyard?'

'Don't talk daft, woman.' Her accusation brought a brief spark of retaliation. 'I ain't even seen her afore tonight.'

'Huh! Expect me to believe that.' She stepped towards the girl. 'Well, you can be on your way, whoever you are.'

The man said nothing, but he made a motion with his head as if to remind the girl of his earlier offer for her to sleep in the hayloft.

'I saw that. Ee, there's more going on here than you're letting on. I can tell.'

Eddie ran his hand agitatedly through his thick brown hair. He was a tall, thin man in his mid-thirties, yet slightly stooping, as if the years of farm work were already bending his back. His face was weather-beaten and there were lines around his brown eyes.

'There's nothing going on, as you put it,' he said wearily. 'She's just a poor lass who's got nowhere to go. Surely, you can show a bit of—'

'And why's she got nowhere to go?' Bertha flung her arm out, pointing at the girl's stomach. 'Because 'er family—if she's got any—has slung the little slut out, that's why.'

Eddie sighed. 'You don't know that.' They were talking about the girl as if she was not there. 'You don't know anything about her. No more than I do.'

'Aye, but I can guess.'

'It's the truth I'm telling you,' he said quietly, yet there was a note in his tone that implied he knew

10

she wouldn't believe him.

Bertha turned towards the girl. 'What's your name then?'

The violet eyes regarded the woman steadily. 'Anna,' the girl said softly.

'Anna what?'

The girl hesitated and looked away, avoiding Bertha's probing, hostile eyes. She ran her tongue nervously round her lips. 'Anna Woods.'

But Bertha had noticed the hesitation. She sniffed in disbelief. 'Oh aye. Well then, Anna Woods—or whatever your name is—you'd better take yourself off, 'cos we don't want the likes of you hanging around here. Go on.' She flapped her hand. 'Be off with you. And don't come round here again.'

'She can sleep in the stable,' Eddie put in. 'You can't turn the lass out, specially when it's nearly Christmas.' Sadly, he added, 'No room at the inn, eh, Bertha? Now look, love, why don't you find her a blanket and—?'

'I aren't finding the little trollop owt.' Bertha whipped round on him. 'And as for you, Eddie Appleyard, you ain't heard the last of this.' At that moment she noticed the boy still standing in the doorway. Instantly Bertha's whole demeanour changed. She stepped towards him and put her arm around his shoulders. 'What are you doing down here, Tony? Go back to bed, there's a good boy.'

Anna saw the boy glance briefly at his father as he murmured, 'Yes, Mam,' and then he scuttled out of sight. She heard his light footsteps on the stairs and then the sound of his bare feet pattering across the floor above.

'There.' The woman rounded on her husband

11

again. 'See how you upset him? He can't sleep till he knows you're safely home. He's the same every week. Though why he should bother himself after the way you carry on beats me.'

Sickened by the woman's ranting, Anna turned and stepped out of the warm kitchen and through the scullery. As she opened the back door, she shivered again as the coldness of the wet night hit her once more. She bent her head against the rain and hurried towards the barn door through which the pony had disappeared. Halfway across the yard, she jumped as a dog, chained outside its kennel, barked and tried to run towards her. She couldn't see it clearly in the darkness, but she made soothing sounds in her throat. The dog ceased its barking, whined and then returned to its shelter. *Even he doesn't like the wet*, she thought wryly.

Inside the barn, it was cold but dry. As her eyes became accustomed to the dark, Anna felt her way around, her icy fingers touching the brick walls. She heard the sound of the pony and her fingers touched a coarse blanket thrown over the boarding at the side of his stall.

'Sorry, Duke,' she murmured and stroked his rump, 'but my need is greater than yours tonight.'

Hugging the blanket, which smelled strongly of horse, she felt her way up a ladder and into the hayloft. She removed her wet coat and wrapped herself in the blanket, then lay down on the hay, burrowing beneath it to find what warmth she could.

Exhausted, she was asleep in seconds.

*   *   *

Anna was awakened by the sound of someone climbing the ladder to the loft. She stretched and raised herself on one elbow. It was not the man whose head appeared, but the young boy's. They stared at each other for several moments in the pale light of a cold dawn, before Anna lay down again and closed her eyes. She hoped he would go away once his curiosity had been satisfied. She had not yet made up her mind what to do next. She wished she could stay here for ever. She was warm and snug for the first time in weeks.

In fact, she thought, *this would be a nice place to die.*

She was about to drift off into sleep again when she heard the boy climb the rest of the ladder and creep, on hands and knees, across the hay towards her. There was a long silence before he whispered, 'I've brought you something to eat.' Another pause and then he added, 'And some milk.'

She opened her eyes again and looked up at him. He was holding a roughly wrapped parcel and had a small milk can hooked over his wrist. 'It's only bread and cheese.' He was apologetic. 'It's all I could take without me mam finding out.'

Now Anna sat up, reaching out thankfully to take the food. She had been ready to give up, to succumb at last to an overwhelming desire to close her eyes and never wake up, but the physical ache of hunger revived her instinct to survive.

The boy watched her as she ate ravenously, his brown eyes large in his thin face. 'Are you going to have a baby?' The question was innocent enough, but the girl scowled at him and did not answer. Yet it was the first time her face had registered any kind of emotion. 'Where have you come from?'

13

Again, no answer. 'Where are you going?' To this she replied only with a vague lift of her shoulders. 'Haven't you got a home? A mam and dad?'

Anna lay down again. 'Thanks for the food,' she said flatly, deliberately ignoring his questions. Her words were a dismissal, yet the boy did not move. He sat quietly beside her and she could feel him watching her.

They heard a noise below and, startled, the boy scrambled away towards the ladder. Anna raised her head. He was peering down the open hatch, his eyes wide and fearful. Then she saw him relax, the sudden tension in his limbs drain away.

'Hello, lad.' Eddie Appleyard's voice drifted up. 'Come to see if our visitor's still here, have you?'

The boy nodded as the man began to climb up towards him. 'I brought her some bread an' cheese, Dad. And some milk. But don't tell Mam, will you?'

Eddie appeared at the top of the ladder. Even through the poor light, Anna could see that he was smiling. He reached out and ruffled his son's hair. 'No, son, course I won't.' His grin broadened and Anna had the feeling it was not the first secret that father and son had shared. 'As long as you don't tell her I've raided the larder an' all.' He handed up a blue-and-white-check cloth bundle as he glanced across to where the girl lay. The boy took it and moved back to her side. 'Me dad's brought you something too.'

The man levered himself up the last rungs of the ladder and stepped into the loft, bending his head to avoid the low rafters. He dropped to his haunches beside her as, now, Anna sat upright.

'It's very kind of you,' she said huskily as she

14

unwrapped the cloth. There was a slice of pork pie, two cold sausages and two slices of bread, spread thickly with butter.

'And here's a couple of apples,' the man said, fishing in his pocket. 'From our own orchard. We lay 'em out on newspaper in the loft to last us through the winter.'

Now they both sat and watched her eat. When she had finished, the man said kindly, 'Now, lass, what can we do to help you? Are you heading for somewhere? I could mebbe take you there, if it's not too far away?'

There was a long silence whilst the girl seemed to be struggling inwardly. She saw the man and his young son exchange a glance, but they waited patiently for her answer. At last she said haltingly, 'No, I'm not going anywhere.'

'Are you looking for work?' Eddie asked. 'Is that it?'

'I suppose so, though—' She hesitated, before adding bitterly, 'I won't be able to work for very long.'

'Do you know owt about farm work?' Eddie asked, carefully ignoring her brief reference to her condition.

The girl regarded him steadily, seeming to weigh up the consequences of her answer before uttering it. Guardedly, she said, 'A bit.'

'Can you milk cows?'

She shook her head, her eyes downcast. Her reluctance was obvious, but at last she admitted, 'Sheep. I know about sheep.'

The boy clapped his hands excitedly. 'We've got sheep. Lincolnshire Longwools,' he added with a note of pride. 'And it'll be lambing time soon. She

15

could help with the sheep, Dad, couldn't she?'

'Well—' Now the man was doubtful. 'I wasn't thinking so much of her staying with us.' His expression was both apprehensive and apologetic at the same time. 'I was just wondering if we could find her a place on a farm hereabouts.'

The boy's face fell.

'It's all right, Mister.' Anna moved to get up from her warm nest in the hay. 'I don't want to cause you any bother.' She glanced at him shrewdly as, remembering the previous night, she added softly, 'No more than I have already.' In a shaft of early morning light slanting through the rafters, she could see that Eddie had a scratch on his left cheekbone. A scratch that had not been there the previous evening.

Eddie made a dismissive gesture with his hand, but she could see the wariness deep in his eyes. The boy was still glancing from one to the other, biting his lip. Suddenly, his expression brightened again. 'What about the cottage, Dad? Couldn't she stay there?'

The man looked at him, at the girl and then back to his son. 'But it's nearly falling down, lad. It's hardly weatherproof.'

'You could mend it, Dad.' The boy's face was alight with eagerness. 'You could do the walls.' He glanced at Anna. 'They're only mud.' Now he looked back again to his father. 'And Mr Wainwright could do the roof.' Once more he explained to Anna, 'It's a thatched roof and Mr Wainwright does thatching. He mended the corner shop in the village. It's got a thatched roof an' all. Oh Dad, do let her stay. Please. She's got nowhere else to go.'

16

'Is that right, lass?' the man asked her quietly and when she nodded, he sighed.

His brow furrowed, he sat deep in thought for several minutes until a shout made them all jump. It was Bertha's shrill voice in the barn below them.

'Eddie? Where are you?'

The boy made a sudden movement like a startled fawn, but his father put his finger to his lips.

Bertha was at the bottom of the ladder. 'Are you up there, Eddie Appleyard? 'Cos if you are—'

It sounded as if the woman suspected that Anna had spent the night in the hayloft. Like statues the three of them were motionless, the boy holding his breath, his father looking guilty. Anna watched the man with detached curiosity. *He's afraid of her*, she thought with a flicker of surprise. Never before had she seen a man fearful of a woman. The other way about, yes, oh yes . . .

She closed her mind against thoughts that threatened to overwhelm her.

Bertha's voice, still calling her husband's name, was further away now. 'She'll be gone in a minute,' the man said in a low voice, 'then you can go down, Tony.'

'What if she asks where I've been?'

Eddie's smile flickered briefly. 'Well, I wouldn't tell her you've been up here with this lass. Don't worry, I don't think she'll ask you. It's me she's after.' He looked at Anna. 'She'll be wanting the trap harnessed. She always goes into the town on a Thursday to see her sister and do a bit of shopping.' He chuckled, a deep rumbling sound, and his face looked suddenly much younger, laughter lines wrinkling around his eyes. 'For all

17

the things I've forgotten to bring from the market the day before when I've had one too many.'

He stood up and brushed the hay from his clothes. 'Come on, Tony. Time you were getting ready for school.' He turned back to Anna and smiled down at her. 'You stay here. When the wife's gone, I'll come back and take you down to the cottage.' He pulled a wry expression. 'But it's not much to look at.'

The man descended the ladder first and the boy followed, pausing briefly to smile back at her. Anna raised her hand and curled her fingers in a kind of wave, but could not summon an answering smile.

CHAPTER THREE

'It's not much of a place,' Eddie said again as they walked up the slope away from the farm, 'but it's in a good spot near the woods. Sheltered, but very isolated.' Anna felt his glance. 'It'll be lonely for you.'

That'll suit me, she thought, though she said nothing.

She had waited in the hayloft until she heard the trap rattle out of the yard, the sound of its wheels on the roadway receding into the distance. Only a moment later she had heard the man calling softly from below. 'Coast's clear, lass.'

They walked on, but near the top of the hill Anna paused and looked back towards the farm where the man and his family lived. Cackle Hill Farm, for she had seen the name on the gate as they left, was set against a background of trees, beyond which was the rolling countryside of the Lincolnshire Wolds. She turned and followed the man, who was still plodding to the top of the rise. When they reached it, they both paused to take in the view below them. The land sloped away again and at the bottom of the track on this side of the hill Anna could see the outline of a cottage nestling against a wooded area on the right from where she was standing. The land was cold and stark, the trees naked against the grey sky, but in spring and summer she guessed the view would be idyllic. Just beyond the cottage she could see a stream bubbling down the hillside and disappearing round the far side of the wood. Sheep dotted the sloping fields and, for the first time in weeks, Anna smiled.

'You like it?' Eddie asked gently. Anna jumped. For a moment she had forgotten he was there.

'Oh! Oh yes.' She nodded. 'It was the sheep. I—I like sheep,' she added diffidently.

Eddie nodded. 'Mek you feel at home, d'they?'

Her smile faded and at once her face took on a closed look. 'Something like that,' she murmured and the man knew he had said the wrong thing. Silently, he vowed not to mention her home, nor question her about her background. But he liked this lass. He wanted to help her. She was like a lost sheep herself and his tender heart reached out to her. He sighed. If only his wife would be as kindly disposed towards her.

They were nearing the cottage now and Anna could see that it was as tumbledown as he had said. It was a small, lime-washed, mud-and-stud, thatched building with a central front door and a window on either side. To the left of the door, there was a gaping hole where the mud had

19

crumbled away, leaving the wooden slats of the framework exposed. On the same side of the cottage the thatched roof was badly in need of repair. Several of the windowpanes were broken and the front door leant drunkenly on its hinges. When Eddie pushed it open, it scraped the mud floor.

'This place is only used at lambing time. I stay here, specially if the weather's bad. My lad comes too—if his mam'll let him.' The last few words were murmured, almost as if he did not intend the girl to hear them.

The door opened into a tiny hallway with steep stairs, more like a ladder than a proper staircase, leading to the upper floor.

'It's two up and two down, but I only ever use this room,' Eddie said, leading her into the room to the right. He laughed as he jerked his thumb over his shoulder towards the other room. 'I put the sheep in yon one.' He stood looking about him. 'But it's not too bad in here. At least it's weatherproof. We'll get a fire going in there.' He nodded towards the grate, beside which, built into the brickwork, was a bread oven.

Anna glanced around. It was like stepping back into the last century—or maybe even the one before that. There were no rugs to clothe the coldness of the beaten-earth floor. In one corner there was a rusty iron bedstead, but there was no mattress on it. A wooden rocking chair stood near the fireplace, and in the centre of the room there was a table and one kitchen chair. But to the girl, who had lived rough for months in barns and outhouses, the promise of somewhere dry and warm was heaven-sent.

'It's a bit sparse.' Eddie smiled apologetically. 'But we don't need much when we stay here. Anyway, I'll fetch you the feather mattress I use. It's in our loft at the moment.' He pointed. 'That door there's the pantry. I'll soon get that stocked up for you. And this one'—he opened another door that led directly out of the kitchen at the side of the cottage—'goes outside to the privy. It's down the path there. And you'll have to fetch your water from the stream, I'm afraid. But it's fresh and clean. Comes from a spring up the hill.'

Anna nodded.

'Like Tony said,' Eddie went on, 'I can repair the walls and the windows. I'll rehang the front door and I'll ask Joe Wainwright if he—'

'I can't pay for work to be done,' Anna said at once. Then, realizing she might have sounded ungrateful, she gestured with her hand and added, 'It's—it's very kind of you, but I—I have nothing.'

Gently, Eddie said, 'I wouldn't expect you to pay, lass. The cottage belongs to me and it's high time I got it repaired up.'

'But I can't afford to pay you rent, at least not at the moment.'

The man dismissed the idea. 'Don't you worry about that, love. Besides, you're going to help me with the lambing.' He paused significantly, as if he realized he was forcing her to make up her mind, before adding quietly, 'Aren't you?'

They regarded each other steadily for several moments before she nodded slowly.

*   *   *

When Tony arrived home from school it was

already dusk. He rushed into the kitchen and skidded to a halt, surprised to see his mother standing behind the table unpacking her shopping. Before he could bite back the words, he said, 'You're home early. I didn't think you'd be back from Auntie Lucy's yet.'

Bertha smiled. 'I couldn't wait to get back to show you what I've bought you. Here'—she held out a brown paper bag towards him—'open it.'

Tony sat at the table. 'But it's not Christmas yet.'

His mother smiled at him. 'Oh, that's just a little extra one from your mam.'

Inside the bag was the usual bar of chocolate she always brought him after her trip to town, but today there was another present. A Dinky toy.

'Aw, Mam—thanks! It's that tractor I wanted.' He opened the box and ran the toy along the table, imitating the sound of a real vehicle. 'Chugger-chugger-chugger.'

Bertha watched him fondly. 'That's all right, love.' She sat down opposite him and rested her arms on the table. 'Now, tell me,' she said, 'what you've been doing at school today.'

'We had writing this morning and sums and then we played footie this after.' The boy reeled off the events of his day.

With deceptive mildness, Bertha asked, 'And did you enjoy the piece of pork pie and the cold sausages as well as the sandwiches I packed for you?'

The boy sat very still. His eyes were still on his new toy, but now he was not moving the tractor or imitating its sounds.

'You can tell your mam, Tony love. I won't be cross. I just want you to tell me if you took them.

That's all.'

The boy's lower lip trembled. He opened his mouth once, then twice, but no sound came out. The back door opened and closed and there was the sound of Eddie removing his boots in the scullery.

He appeared in the doorway into the kitchen and stood there for a few moments, glancing between the two seated on either side of the table. 'What's up?'

'Nothing.' Bertha snapped. 'Me an' Tony are just having a little chat. That's all.'

'Oh aye. What've you been up to now, lad? Not in trouble at school, are you?' Eddie moved into the room and went to stand beside his son's chair. He smiled down at the boy and ruffled his hair. Tony shook his head but still did not speak. Instead he stared miserably at his new toy as if all the joy had been taken out of the gift. Eddie looked across the table at his wife, a question in his eyes.

'I was just asking him if he'd enjoyed the pork pie and sausages that's gone missing out of my meat safe in the larder. That's all. Simple enough question, I'd've thought, but it seems as if he doesn't want to answer me.'

'Ah.' Eddie let out a long sigh. 'Now I get it.' Heavily, he said, 'Go out and feed the hens, there's a good boy. Me and ya mam need to talk.'

Tony scrambled from his chair, leaving his new toy on the table. Quietly he closed the door from the kitchen into the scullery, but he did not leave the house. Instead, he stood with his ear pressed to the closed door. He could hear every word clearly.

'You know very well the lad didn't take the food, but it's your way of trying to find out. You shouldn't

23

use him, Bertha. It isn't his fault you an' me don't get on nowadays.'

'And whose fault is it, I'd like to know? *I* don't disappear off to market every week and come home rolling drunk, after being with goodness knows how many trollops in the town. And then you have the gall to bring one of 'em home with you. Into my house.' She beat her chest with her fist.

Wearily, Eddie said, 'Bertha, I don't go with trollops, as you put it. In fact, I don't go with other women at all—'

Bertha snorted. 'Spect me to believe that. I know what men are like.'

Eddie regarded her with pity and shook his head slowly. 'Bertha love, I wish you'd believe me. We're not all the same. Just because your dad was a ladies' man—'

'Don't you say things about my dad, Eddie Appleyard. You're no saint.'

'The whole town knew about your dad and his carryings on, love.'

'I aren't sitting here listening to you calling my dad names just to mek ya'sen feel better.' She wagged her finger in his face. 'He didn't get drunk and come home and knock his wife about.'

Appalled, Eddie stared at her. 'Bertha, I've never—'

'Oh 'aven't you? How do you know what you do when you're sow drunk?'

Eddie dropped his head into his hands. He couldn't believe it. He was not a violent man. Never had been. And though things were not right between him and his wife, he couldn't imagine that he would ever attack her physically. But then, he

24

had to admit, he did get 'sow drunk' as the locals called it, a state that resembled a snoring, snorting pig. And, to his eternal shame, Eddie had to admit that he could not remember what he had done when he was in that state.

He couldn't even remember having brought the girl home from the town until Bertha pulled him from the trap and there the girl was, just sitting there. But that was something he was never going to admit. Not to his wife and certainly not to that poor lass. He didn't want her to think that he hadn't meant to help her, that he couldn't even remember making the offer.

'So?' Bertha was leaning towards him. 'What did happen to my pork pie and sausages?'

'It—it wasn't Tony,' Eddie stammered. 'It was me. I—I was hungry. In the night.' He wasn't used to telling lies. That was yet another thing he hadn't known he was capable of doing.

'If you expect me to believe that, Eddie Appleyard, you're even dafter than I thought you were.' She paused and her small, piercing eyes were boring into his soul. 'Is she still here? Is she still in the hayloft?'

Now he could answer honestly and even Bertha could detect the note of truth. 'No, she isn't.'

'Well, good riddance is all I can say. And if that's the truth, Eddie, then we'll say no more about it. And now I've got work to do even if you haven't.' She levered herself up and turned away, leaving her husband sitting at the table, his head still in his hands, vowing that as long as he lived he would never touch another drop of drink.

CHAPTER FOUR

From the scullery the boy heard his mother's chair scrape along the floor as she got up from the table. He scuttled out of the back door. He was halfway across the yard when the collie, chained up near its kennel, barked a greeting. The boy hesitated, glanced back towards the farmhouse and then hurriedly released the dog's collar from the chain.

'Come on then, boy.' Together they ran across the yard and out of the gate. In the gathering dusk the boy began to run up the track, the dog loping at his side. At the top of the hill Tony stopped to look down to where the cottage nestled against the trees. He could see a dim glow from the windows and knew that the girl was there.

He shivered, but whether from the cold or the misgiving he felt he could not be sure. Yesterday's rain had gone and stars shone in a clear sky, the moon a gleaming orb. There'd be a frost tonight. Though he was only ten, Tony knew about the weather and the changing seasons. He bent and pulled up his knee-length grey socks. He hadn't had time to change from his short school trousers. Nor had he stopped to put on his wellingtons. His mam'd scold if he messed up the leather lace-up boots he wore for school. He didn't want to make his mother cross with him. She seemed to spend a lot of the time cross these days, but mostly with his dad. The boy frowned and chewed on his lower lip. He couldn't understand why his mam and dad argued so much. But maybe all parents did. He didn't really know. He had some school pals whose homes he sometimes visited. He went to a birthday party now and then and one or two of the boys in his class had been to Cackle Hill Farm. But he still didn't know if other mams and dads carried on at each other like his did.

A gust of wind nibbled icily at his knees and his mind came back to the girl. *She'll be cold*, he thought. Without making any conscious decision, he began to walk slowly down the hill towards the cottage.

*   *   *

Anna had lit a fire from the kindling Eddie had brought her. Thoughtfully, he had also left a box of matches. She had drunk the milk and eaten most of the loaf of bread he had brought too. The hurricane lamp he had given her hung from a hook in the ceiling, casting eerie shadows around the walls.

'I'll bring you some more bits and pieces as soon as I can and I'll start work on the repairs tomorrow. I reckon the chimney'll need sweeping an' all.'

She'd looked him straight in the eye then. 'What about your wife? I don't want to bring trouble on you, Mister. You—you've been kind and I'd like to stay here for a few days. But maybe I'd better move on when I've rested a bit.'

'No.' His retort was swift and surprisingly firm. There was no way he was going to allow this girl to be turned away, especially not just before Christmas. 'No,' he said more gently. 'I—I want you to stay. Bertha needn't know. Not if we're careful. She never comes up this way. She never'— there was a bitter tone to his words now—'goes

27

anywhere about the farm. The only time she goes out the house is to town. She dun't even use the village shop. Says she dun't want to give the gossips any more to chatter about. She—she dun't mix wi' folk easy.' He had smiled then, his eyes crinkling with a spark of mischief. 'But that's all to the good. She'll never know if I get things for you from the local shop, will she? And when I go into town next market day, I can get you some more bits of furniture.'

'Furniture? However are you going to get that past her?'

His smile broadened to a grin, his face looking suddenly years younger. 'I don't have to. The road to town runs yon side this wood and there's a track that comes round the other side of the trees to here and then on to our farm.' He gestured with his left hand in a vaguely northerly direction. 'We don't use this way, because the gate from our farm'—now with the other hand he pointed southwards—'leads out onto the road between the town and the village.'

Anna could not hide the fear in her eyes. 'So—so does anyone use this track past the cottage?'

'Not many, love. Just farm workers now and again and mebbe'—he chuckled suddenly—'a poacher or two.'

She had dropped her gaze and breathed more easily.

And now, as the early darkness of a cold December evening came, she sat huddled against the fire. He had been right. The chimney did need sweeping, for every so often smoke puthered into the room, making her cough and her eyes smart. Once that was cleaned, she would be able to build

28

up the fire to use the bread oven, and when the holes in the walls and the roof were mended she could make this a very cosy little home.

If only . . . Her thoughts started to drift but she shook herself physically and pulled herself back to the present.

It was then that she heard a scuffle outside the door from the kitchen and her whole being stiffened. It was too late to turn out the lamp and hide. She jumped at the soft tap on the door. She could not move, could not call out. She just sat there rigid with fear as, slowly, the door opened.

The boy stood framed against the darkness, blinking in the light from the lamp. They stared at one another for a moment and then the girl shivered in the frosty air coming into the room from the open door. The boy stepped inside and closed the door.

'I guessed you might be here. I came to see if you was all right. I—I thought you might be cold.'

She could see the man's features in the boy's face now; similar dark brown eyes and brown hair and a thin but well-shaped face. The boyish features would strengthen into a firm jawline and the father's kindness was already showing in the son's concern for her.

Anna summoned a smile. 'Does your dad know you've come up here?'

He shook his head. 'No.' He bit his lip and then blurted out, 'They're—they're rowing.'

Her smile faded. 'Over me?'

Tony shook his head. 'Not—not really. She thinks you've gone.' He moved closer and squatted down in front of the fire, holding out his hands to the meagre warmth the few sticks were giving. 'I'll get you some logs from the woods tomorrow before I go to school.'

'She doesn't know I'm here, then?' Anna asked softly.

He shook his head. He glanced up at her briefly and then looked back into the flames. Haltingly he said, 'I—don't reckon me dad wants her to know either.' Tony was reluctant to tell her that his father had lied to his mother over the food he had given the girl. He knew why his father had done so, but he wasn't happy about it. He felt torn between his parents. He didn't want his mam to be upset, yet he could understand why his father wanted to help this girl. What he couldn't understand was why his mother didn't want to help her too.

But Anna seemed to know, for she said quietly, 'No, I don't suppose he does.'

After a few moments Tony stood up. 'I'd better go. I've the hens to feed before I go to bed. It's one of me jobs,' he said importantly. 'And—and Mam might be looking for me.'

Anna nodded.

He hesitated a moment and then pulled a crumpled bar of chocolate from his pocket. Holding it out to her, he said, 'You can have this. It's mine. Me mam brought it for me from town. She won't know.'

Anna took it, unable to speak for the sudden lump in her throat. She had thought she had been past all feeling, past caring. Yet the actions of the farmer, and now his young son, made tears prickle behind her eyes.

'And I've brought someone to keep you company.'

For a brief moment her eyes were panic-stricken.

30

'I don't want . . .' she began, but already he had opened the door. In answer to his soft whistle a black and white collie trotted into the room and stood close to the boy, looking up at him with adoring, obedient eyes.

Tony fondled the dog's head. 'Stay, Rip. Stay here with the lady.' He glanced up and smiled at her. 'He'll look after you.'

'Won't your mam miss him?' Anna asked, torn between wanting the animal's company and yet not wanting the boy's kindly action to bring him trouble.

Tony shrugged. 'She might, but I'm just hoping she won't.'

Anna tried to raise a smile, anxious to let him know that she appreciated his gesture.

'Thank you,' she said, her voice hoarse with gratitude. She held out her hand to the dog. The animal did not move until the boy nodded and said, 'Go on.' Then Rip padded across the floor and allowed himself to be patted by the stranger. He lay down on the floor and rested his nose on his paws, but his eyes once again sought his young master.

'Stay,' Tony said firmly and though, as the boy went out of the door, the dog gave a little whine, he did not move from his place beside Anna.

'Well, now,' she said softly, stroking the dog's head, 'it looks like we're both going to sleep here on the floor for the night.'

Wrapping herself in the horse blanket she had brought with her from the barn, she lay down between the dying fire and the dog. The animal's warm presence against her back soothed her chilled limbs and brought unexpected comfort to her lonely soul.

31

CHAPTER FIVE

The dog was scratching at the door, whining to be let out. Anna roused herself from heavy sleep and dragged herself up from the floor. She was stiff and cold. The fire had died out in the night and the room, never really warmed, was now freezing.

'All right, boy, I'm coming.' She opened the door and the dog ran out. She watched him streak up the hillside towards home. She closed the door and looked around the room in the pale light of early morning. There was little she could do except wait and see if the boy came as he had promised. What was his name? Tony, that was it. Maybe, later in the day, the man would come to see her too. Maybe he would bring her food. Maybe . . . Maybe . . .

She sighed, irritated to find herself dependent on these strangers for her survival. And she was afraid too. The man seemed kind, but why was he prepared to do so much for her? He was even risking trouble within his own family. Was he expecting something from her in return for his generosity? More than just helping him with the lambing? She shuddered and shied away from such thoughts. And how safe was this place anyway? The cottage was certainly isolated, nestling in a vale and obscured from the road by the wood. And it was on the farmer's land; that would offer some protection.

But was it enough?

It would have to be, she told herself. For now at least. If she rested here for a while, then, when she was feeling stronger, she could move on. Further away. She must get further away . . .

She heard a voice outside and looked out of the grimy window. She saw Tony with the dog bounding around him, leaping up to lick the boy's face. She could see that they were overjoyed to see each other again. The boy was laughing. 'Down, Rip, down. Good boy. Good dog.'

She opened the door and stood waiting until they reached her.

'I've come to get you some wood,' Tony said, smiling at her. 'Like I promised.' His face fell a little as he said, 'I'm sorry, but I couldn't get you anything to eat this morning. Me mam . . .' He fell silent, not wanting to sound disloyal to his mother, yet wanting to help the girl. 'Anyway, Dad's milking just now, but he gave me this to bring up. He'll be up later, he said, when he comes to the sheep.' The boy held out a can of milk.

'Thanks,' she said, taking the can eagerly and drinking thirstily.

'You're hungry, aren't you?' the boy said. 'I wish I could . . .'

'Don't worry,' she said at once. 'This is lovely. Really.'

There was a brief pause before he said awkwardly, 'I'd best get you the wood. I don't want me mam to miss me and it'll soon be school time.'

'I'll come with you and then I can find it for myself.'

He led the way in amongst the trees. The girl, still clutching the blanket around her, followed. The dog ran ahead, investigating the exciting smell of rabbit.

'I should have brought a sack,' Tony said, his arms soon full of twigs and broken branches.

33

'It's all right,' Anna said, taking off the blanket from around her shoulders. She shivered as she felt the loss of its warmth. 'We'll use this.' Together they collected enough kindling and larger pieces of wood to last her the day and carried their haul back to the cottage.

They tipped it onto the hearth and Tony squatted in front of the fireplace. He began to put the twigs into the grate. 'They're a bit damp. I don't think they'll catch light.'

'I'll see to it. You'd best be off.'

He stood up, for a moment feeling suddenly shy. 'Ta-ta, then.'

She nodded and managed a smile. 'Ta-ta,' she echoed.

'Come on, Rip.'

She watched them running up the track until they disappeared over the brow of the hill.

*　　　*　　　*

The boy had been right; the sticks were too damp to catch light and after the torrential rain she doubted there'd be anything in the woods that would be dry enough. And the dry kindling that Eddie had provided that first day was all gone. So, hugging the blanket around her again, Anna decided to look around the cottage. There just might be an old piece of wood she could use. There was nothing in the other room, where damp patches marked the floor and the wind whistled in through the broken windows. But when she climbed the ladder-like stairs and stepped into the two rooms under the roof, she found the floor littered with leaves that had blown in through a

34

hole in the thatch and drifted into a corner. The leaves were brittle dry.

She filled the pockets of her coat and climbed down the ladder. Within minutes, the leaves caught light and she picked out the least wet of the twigs to pile on the top of the leaves. The fire smoked as before, but at least it was alight.

She drank the last of the milk and tended the fire. When she looked out of the window again, she was surprised to see that it was fully light, the winter sun pale in a watery sky. For a while she watched the sheep grazing on the slopes and then she saw the man coming down the track carrying a basket over one arm and two blankets under the other.

'Here we are then, lass,' he greeted her. 'I bet you're ready for this.' He held out the basket. There was bread, butter, cheese and more milk. 'Sorry it's not more. I'll go to the village shop later ... Oh, you've got a fire going. That's good.'

'Your son came up earlier,' Anna said in her soft, husky voice. 'I hope you don't mind.'

Eddie pulled a wry expression. 'I don't. But if the wife finds out—'

'You—you'd better tell him not to come then. I don't want him getting into trouble on my account.'

The man shrugged. 'I don't reckon Bertha'll guess. He roams all over the farm with that dog of his. Gone for hours sometimes. Look,' he said, returning to the matter of her welfare, 'I'll mebbe manage to bring the tractor and trailer up this way later. I can't get into town until next market day without it looking odd, but I'll see what I can find in the outhouses. There's always bits and pieces we've thrown out.'

Later that day Eddie's tractor came chugging down the track with a loaded trailer behind him and pulled to a halt outside the cottage. To Anna, who had nothing, Eddie's barn seemed to have yielded a treasure trove.

'There's a kettle, a few old pots and pans and an armchair. It was me dad's.' His eyes clouded. 'Bertha threw it out the day after he died. And I've managed to get the old feather bed down from the loft when she was in the dairy,' he added, dragging it off the trailer. 'It'll be a bit damp. You'd better let it dry out before you use it.'

Remembering her soaking of two days earlier, Anna smiled to herself, but said nothing. She was hardly likely to take harm from a damp bed, she thought. But the man meant well.

Lastly he unloaded three sacks. 'There's potatoes from our own store and a few apples. And I've been to the shop for you. You'll have to let me know if I've forgotten anything you need.'

Anna stood, shaking her head in wonder. 'It's—it's wonderful. I don't know how to thank you.'

'No need, lass. You're working for me now, aren't ya?' He glanced at her and winked. 'And I always look after me employees.'

'I'll work for you, Mister. Oh, I'll work as hard as I can, but . . .' She touched the mound of her belly briefly.

He nodded sympathetically. 'Don't worry about that, lass. We'll cross that bridge when we come to it.'

But what would happen when they did come to that particular bridge, as he put it, even the man dared not contemplate. 'And now,' he said, trying to divert their thoughts. 'I must see to me sheep.'

36

'Can I help?'

'No, no, lass. You get ya'sen sorted out. And then—well—we'll see tomorrow, eh?'

Anna nodded. 'All right,' she agreed in her low, soft voice, 'but from tomorrow I want you to tell me what needs doing. And if you don't . . .' She smiled suddenly and the man stared at her, unable to take his eyes off her. She was a pretty lass, though a bit thin at the moment to his mind, but when she smiled her whole face seemed to light up. Even so, it was not enough to drive away the sadness in the depths of her dark eyes. 'And if you don't, Mister, then I'll *find* something.'

He laughed. 'Right you are then, lass. It's a deal.'

As he drove his tractor and trailer back towards the farm to fetch bales of hay for his sheep, Eddie was still smiling.

*   *   *

The following morning Anna walked across the meadow in front of the cottage towards the next field, where she could see the sheep contentedly munching long stalks of kale. She moved stealthily. Sheep were nervous creatures, easily panicked and bunching together in the face of danger and most of Eddie's ewes would be in lamb; the last thing she must do was to startle them.

Shading her eyes, Anna glanced round the edge of the field. There were several gaps in the hedges where the sheep could easily push their way into the neighbouring field. Anna began to smile. Here was something she could do to repay the farmer for his kindness. When the tractor and trailer chugged down the track later that morning, Anna was waiting for him.

'I don't suppose you've left those holes in the hedges for a reason, have you?'

'No, lass,' Eddie said wryly. 'I just haven't had time to repair them.'

'Right, then. You can bring me a billhook and a hedge knife too. Oh, and a few stakes.'

Eddie laughed. 'You're not going to try plashing, are you?'

Anna nodded.

Now he eyed her sceptically. 'Are you sure you can do it?'

Anna gave him one of her rare smiles. 'That's for you to say when I've had a go. I'll do one small gap first and then, if you're not satisfied, you can say so and I'll let well alone. All right?'

Eddie looked mesmerized. To him hedge-laying was a skilled art and one, he had to admit, that he had never been able to master properly.

Whilst he fetched the tools, Anna chose one of the smaller holes and began to clear the hedgerow of weeds and long, dead grass. By the time Eddie brought back the items she had asked for, Anna was ready to position two stakes in the gap. Then, taking up the billhook, she chose the thickest stem she could find in the existing hedge to the right of the hole and began to chip off all its side shoots.

'I'll—er—leave you to it, lass. I'll—um—come back later and see how you're getting on. Only don't tire ya'sen, will you?'

'I'll be fine, Mr Appleyard. It's nice to have something to do.'

Concern was still plainly written on the man's face, though whether it was for the pale waif who had come into his life or for his hedge, even Eddie could not have said. He glanced at her again and now his anxiety was wholly for her, but he was gratified to see a healthy pink tinge to her cheeks this morning. And the way she was wielding the billhook showed no sign of any ill effects from the cold night she must have spent in the cottage.

'I'll be off then,' he said again, still reluctant to leave his hedge. He sighed as he turned away. *Oh well*, he was thinking, *I don't suppose she can make a much worse mess of it than I would.*

*   *   *

A surprise awaited Eddie on his return to the field with Rip trotting beside him, pink tongue lolling, eyes ever watchful and alert. They stopped before the hole in the hedge—or at least where the hole had been. The thickest stems from the existing growth had been cut diagonally a few inches from the ground to a depth of about three-quarters of the thickness and bent carefully over so that the stem did not break. The branches then lay one above the other at angles of about thirty degrees across the gap in the hedge and were neatly woven in and out between the stakes. In time, new shoots from the old wood would form a thick hedge once more. Even the top had been neatly finished off.

Eddie stood gaping. He took off his cap, scratched his head and then pulled it on again, whilst Anna stood by, smiling quietly. 'By heck, lass, it's as good as I could do. No, if I'm honest, it's better. Where on earth did you learn to lay a hedge like that?'

Anna's smile faded and she turned away, but not before Eddie had seen tears fill her eyes.

'I had a good teacher, Mister,' she said huskily. 'A very good teacher.' Then she took a deep breath and called to the dog. 'Come on, boy.'

As she bent to pick up her tools and move on to the next gap, Rip bounded alongside, leaving Eddie staring after her and then, glancing back to his newly repaired hedge, marvelling again at the young girl's workmanship.

*   *   *

Tony came each night after school to see her, always managing to bring something useful for her. And every night he ordered his dog to 'stay' with her.

'We've broke up from school today,' he told her near the end of the week following her arrival. 'It's Christmas next week.'

'Is it?' Anna said, surprise in her tone.

The boy stared at her. 'You hadn't forgotten?' he asked. To the boy, who had been counting the days, it was incredible that anyone could not know it was almost Christmas. Even his mam, who usually scorned merrymaking at other times, always loved Christmas. She had been mixing the puddings and baking mince pies all this last week. And last night she had helped him put up paper chains, looping them along the picture rail around the best parlour, which they would use on Christmas Day.

In answer to Tony's question, Anna shrugged. 'I've been travelling. I'd forgotten what date it is.'

'How long have you been travelling?' he asked with a boy's natural curiosity. 'Where d'you come from?'

Even the ten-year-old boy could not fail to

notice the fear that sprang into her eyes at his question. She bit her lip and turned away. 'Oh, a long way away. You wouldn't know it.'

'I might,' he insisted. 'We've been doing geography at school on the British Isles and learning where lots of places are. I *might* know it.' He was trying to wheedle an answer from her, but now the girl said nothing and deliberately turned her back on him and his questions.

*   *   *

A few days before Christmas Tony brought her a hot mince pie. 'Me mam's just finished baking. She didn't notice I took an extra one.'

Anna bit into the light pastry with the warm juicy mincemeat inside. 'It's lovely,' she said. 'I wish I could send a message to your mam.' She smiled and suddenly some of the pain that was always in the depths of her violet eyes, lightened. 'But I'd better not.'

Tony was staring at her. 'You're ever so pretty when you smile,' he said with the innocent candour of a young boy. 'Haven't you got funny coloured eyes? I mean,' he added hastily, 'they're nice, but I've never seen anyone with eyes that colour before.'

At once the smile fled from her face and the anguish returned. Her words came haltingly, almost as if she were trying not to speak them, but an innate politeness was forcing her to do so. 'They're the same—colour as my—mother's.' The last word was spoken in a strangled whisper and, to the boy's horror, tears welled in her eyes.

'I'll be off,' he said gruffly, pushing his hands

deep into the pockets of his coat. There was an embarrassed pause before he said, haltingly, 'I'll have to take Rip back with me tonight.'

He bit his lip. He didn't want to explain to the girl that there had been an awkward moment at home the previous evening. He had been sitting in his pyjamas in front of the kitchen range drinking cocoa when his mother, coming in from the outside privy, had said, 'Where's Rip? He's not chained up.'

Tony had felt his heart miss a beat and then begin to pound. He licked the line of chocolate from his upper lip and said, 'He—he wouldn't come home with me. He—he went off chasing rabbits, I think.'

'At this time of night? That's not like him. He's a very obedient dog usually. Specially with you, Tony. Oh well, mebbe it's not only rabbits he's chasing,' she added dryly. 'He's male, after all.'

Tony buried his nose in his mug to finish his drink. Then he stood up. Going to his mother, he put his arms around her and gave her an extra tight hug, trying to assuage his guilt at lying to her. 'Night, Mam.'

She had kissed his hair and patted his back. 'Night-night, love.'

Now, in the cottage, he commanded, 'Come on, Rip. Home, boy.'

The dog wagged his tail, but made no move to follow. Instead, Rip glanced at Anna and then sat down.

Tony slapped his own thigh. 'Come *on*, Rip.'

The dog flattened his ears and lay down, crawling on his belly, not towards his young master, but towards the girl.

Now it was the boy who had tears in his eyes. 'He's *my* dog,' he said. 'Not yours. I only lent him to you.'

'I know you did,' Anna said quietly, her own misery forgotten for the moment. 'Rip is confused, that's all.' She bent and stroked the dog's head and he licked her hand. 'Good dog. Go with your master now, boy. Go with Tony.'

As if understanding he had been released from any obligation, Rip sprang up, barked and ran to the boy, leaping up to lick his face. Tony knelt and put his arms around the dog, hugging the wriggling body to him. Without another word, he turned and began to run up the hill, the dog racing ahead and then coming back to him.

Anna heard the boy's joyful laughter and the dog barking. As she closed the door against the dusk of approaching evening, she was already missing Rip's comforting presence in the cottage.

CHAPTER SIX

Anna did not see the boy for the next three days, but each morning, when she opened the side door of the cottage to visit the privy, a small pile of wood was neatly stacked against the wall just outside. Later in the day Eddie would come to check on his sheep and would bring her food.

'All right, lass?' was his usual greeting and, as he left, he would say, 'Now, don't you go overdoing it, love.' It was the closest he ever came to referring to her advancing pregnancy.

Anna was surprised how much she missed seeing

Tony, but there was plenty of work for her to do. She was kept busy collecting more wood to keep her fire burning through the cold nights and cleaning the inside of the one room in the cottage. She swept the floor and cleaned the windows and scrubbed out the bread oven. But, apart from the brief visits from Eddie and Rip, she saw no one. She had thought that solitude was what she wanted. She had believed she wanted to hide herself away from the world and all its cruelties, yet the farmer's kindness, and especially the boy's, had melted her resolve. Besides, she reminded herself, she had been desperate. Standing in the marketplace that night with nowhere to go, no money and hunger gnawing, she had known she could not hold out much longer.

If the man had not brought her to this place that night, she doubted she would still have been alive by now. When she felt the child within her move, and in the moments of despair that still racked her, she wondered if it wouldn't have been for the best if she and the child had not survived. But the tranquillity of this place was already seeping into her wounded heart and bringing her a measure of peace. She was not happy—she doubted she would ever feel real happiness again—but she was no longer in the depths of misery. The instinct to survive was strong again within her. And now she had a place to stay. It was only when darkness closed in and she was alone in the cottage that the fear threatened to overwhelm her once more. Maybe she should ask Eddie for strong bolts for the two doors into the cottage. Perhaps then she would feel safe. . .

*   *   *

'I bet you thought I'd forgotten all about mending the walls,' Eddie called to her one afternoon, as he climbed down from his tractor and went to the trailer behind it to unload tools, wood and what looked suspiciously like a pile of wet mud.

Seeing her looking at it with a puzzled expression on her face, Eddie said, 'It's subsoil. I dug a hole ovver yonder near the stream. It's just right for this.'

Anna leant closer. 'What are all the bits in it?'

'Chopped-up pieces of barley straw. Now, all we need to do is mix it with a bit of sand and water and we'll be ready.' He smiled at her. 'Good, ain't it, when you can provide your own building materials? And it dun't cost me a penny,' he added, to reassure her that her presence in his cottage was not costing him a fortune.

Fascinated, Anna stood watching him nailing the thin laths of wood into place and then plastering the mud mixture onto the wooden framework.

'I could do that,' she murmured, after watching him for a while.

He glanced up at her. 'Now, leave me summat to do, lass, else I shall start to feel I'm not needed.'

'Oh, you're needed, Mr Appleyard,' she murmured softly, thinking what might have happened to her by now if it hadn't been for this kind and generous man.

'Tell you what,' Eddie said. 'You'll be able to do the whitewashing when the mud's dried enough. How about that?'

By the time dusk came creeping across the field, the other downstairs room was already

45

weatherproof.

'Joe Wainwright's promised to come early in the New Year to see to the roof,' Eddie said, straightening up to ease his aching back. 'That should make the upstairs rooms habitable if you should want to use them.'

Silently, Anna thought: *I won't be here by then*, but she did not want to seem ungrateful. Instead she asked, 'Do you think you could spare some whitewash for the inside walls? I hate asking for anything—you've been so good, but—'

'Course, lass. I should have thought of it mesen.'

'And—and could I have a snare? I could catch rabbits in the woods then.'

Now Eddie looked doubtful. 'I'm not too keen on setting traps or snares for wild creatures, love. I don't like to think of poor animals suffering, you know?' He pulled off his cap, scratched his head and then replaced his cap. Anna was beginning to notice that this was a habit with him when he was perplexed or anxious, or maybe even embarrassed in some way. 'Oh, I know I'm a farmer and I raise animals to be killed for meat, but that's done in a humane way.'

'I'm sorry,' Anna said swiftly. 'I shouldn't have asked.'

*   *   *

On Christmas Eve, in the late afternoon, there was a knock at the door. Anna's heart beat faster and her throat was dry as, standing in the shadows, she edged close to the window to see who was standing outside. When she saw the slight figure of the boy, she let out the breath she had been holding and

46

opened the door with a genuine smile of welcome that widened when she saw the expression of apology on his face.

'I'm sorry,' he blurted out.

'Whatever for?' Anna said, pretending not to understand and, so that he would not have to explain his earlier childish petulance, she added swiftly, 'I know you can't come every day to see me.' She pulled the door wider, inviting him inside. 'But it's nice to see you when you can.'

She became aware that his coat was bulging, as if he was carrying something clutched to his chest.

'I've brought you a Christmas present,' he said.

'You shouldn't have . . .' Her voice faded away as she realized that the 'something' he carried was wriggling and pushing its way out from beneath his coat. A tiny wet nose appeared and then the silky black and white head of a collie puppy.

'Oh!' Reaching out with trembling hands, she whispered, 'For me? Is it really for me?'

The boy nodded, grinning broadly now, his earlier awkwardness forgotten. 'Me dad knows this farmer whose bitch had puppies a while back. It's all right. It's ready to leave its mother.' He handed the squirming creature to her.

Anna held the puppy against her breast and stroked its head, whilst it licked at her hand. 'Oh thank you, Tony, thank you,' she murmured. 'He's lovely.'

'You'll have to think of a name for him and when he's bigger you can train him to be a good sheep dog. Rip is,' he added proudly. 'Me dad trained him. He'd tell you what to do.'

For a brief moment, the girl's eyes clouded and seemed to take on a faraway look.

'What are you going to call him?'

Without even stopping to give thought to her choice, she said at once, 'Buster.'

'Buster,' the boy repeated, trying out the name aloud. Then he grinned and nodded. 'Yeah, it's a nice name. Buster. I'll bring you an old basket out of the barn tomorrow and—'

'It'll be Christmas Day. You mustn't come tomorrow. Your mam—' Her voice trailed away.

'Well, as soon as I can then.'

Rip was barking outside the cottage and the boy said, 'I'll have to be off.'

The puppy made all the difference to Anna. He demanded her constant attention and his antics brought the long-forgotten smile more readily to her mouth.

*　　*　　*

Tony landed with a thump on the end of his parents' double bed. 'Wake up. Wake up. It's Christmas Day.'

There were grunts and groans from both his mother and father.

'Whatever time is it?'

'It's not light yet. Go back to bed for a bit. There's a good lad.' Eddie was burrowing further beneath the covers, trying to recapture sleep.

'But I want to open my presents.' A plaintive note crept into the boy's tone. 'Don't you want to see me open my presents?'

Bertha roused herself and threw back the covers. 'Course we do, love. Come on, Eddie, stir ya'sen. T'ain't Christmas every day.'

She pulled on her old dressing gown and pushed

48

her feet into well-worn slippers. 'I just 'ope Father Christmas has remembered to bring me summat an' all.'

'Oh Mam,' Tony laughed. 'There isn't a Father Christmas.'

His mother pretended to look scandalized. 'What do you mean? Course there is. Who else do you think brings you all them presents? Enough to fill a pillowcase?'

Tony grinned and bounced up and down on the end of the bed. 'You do, Mam.'

'Well, I believe in Father Christmas,' she declared, her slippers flapping across the linoleum-covered floor. 'Not much else to believe in,' she muttered in a low voice so that the boy would not hear. 'Come on, then. Let's go an' see what he's left you.'

As the woman descended the stairs, grunting with each heavy tread, the boy scrambled to the top of the bed. 'Dad, Dad!' he whispered urgently. 'What about the girl? She'll be all alone. And it's Christmas. Are you going to see her today?'

Eddie yawned and stretched. 'I'll try, lad. But don't you go. Not today. Your mam'll want you to stay here today.'

'I took her the puppy. She—she was ever so pleased. I could tell. She'd got tears in her eyes. But pleased tears. Not sad tears.'

'Had she, son?' The man put his hand on the boy's shoulder. 'I'm glad. The little chap'll be company for her, won't he?'

'Well, yes.' The boy was not convinced. 'But it's not the same as being with other people and having presents to open and a nice dinner and . . .' His voice trailed away as he thought about their own day ahead here in the cosy farmhouse. It was a stark contrast to the draughty cottage and the meagre fare that Anna would be facing.

Eddie patted his son's shoulder again and said, 'Run along. I'll be down in a minute. I'll see what I can do later.'

The next few hours were spent happily. Even Bertha was delighted with the gift that Eddie had bought her, a warm dressing gown and cosy slippers. Luckily, she couldn't know that, as she slipped them on and paraded around the parlour, his thoughts were not on her, but with the lonely girl in the cottage over the hill. Hidden in the barn were some clothes for her. Useful, serviceable clothes and not new, but his desire to see her face when he presented them to her, the delight he hoped to see in her expression was in the forefront of his mind. But he played the part of dutiful husband and doting father. The latter was not difficult, for Tony's pleasure in the day was obvious and even Bertha had gone to a lot of trouble over the Christmas dinner. Goose and all the trimmings followed by Christmas pudding and brandy sauce.

But all the time he was eating it, Eddie was wondering how he could take some to the girl. He didn't guess that, as they sat side by side at the table, his son was worrying about exactly the same thing.

*   *   *

In the afternoon Tony played with his new toys whilst Eddie helped Bertha wash up. It was the only day in the year when he lent a hand in the kitchen.

50

'You've spent your morning cooking for us, love,' he always said. 'It's only fair I give you a hand to clear up. Not much of a Christmas Day for you otherwise, is it?'

Later, as Bertha played a noisy game of Snap with Tony, Eddie said, 'I'd better nip out and check the animals. Feed Duke and Rip. I reckon they deserve a Christmas dinner an' all.'

'There's some scraps on the side for the dog,' Bertha said absently and then shouted loudly, 'SNAP! You missed that one, Tony. You weren't watching.'

'Sorry, Mam,' the boy mumbled and looked down again at the cards, but not before he and his father had exchanged a meaningful glance.

This time it was Tony who shouted loudly, 'SNAP!' Now he was happy to pay full attention to the game for he knew from the look that his father was going to take a plateful of Christmas dinner to the girl.

CHAPTER SEVEN

In January the weekly ration of fresh meat for each person was cut yet further. And there were gloomy predictions that there would soon be a cut in the bread ration, with no hope of any increase either in eggs, bacon or fish.

'You'd've thought they'd be increasing rations now, not cutting 'em further,' Bertha grumbled. 'The war's been over two years come May.'

But Eddie was more philosophical. 'That's one advantage of living on a farm,' he told Anna later

51

and winked conspiratorially as he smuggled more food to her without Bertha knowing. 'Always a bit extra for us that no one need know about.'

The girl was staring at him, a stricken look in her violet eyes.

'I'm sorry, lass,' Eddie said hastily. 'I didn't mean to worry you.'

As she turned from him, she lifted her hand in a gesture of reassurance. 'It's all right. It's just . . .' But she did not finish her sentence and moved away, leaving Eddie staring after her with a puzzled expression. He waited for her to turn back again, to say more, but no explanation was forthcoming.

What on earth could he possibly have said to make that look of fear leap into her eyes once more?

Eddie sighed. The lass was a mystery and no mistake.

*   *   *

Towards the end of January, freezing weather gripped the whole country in its icy fingers. Power failures plunged towns and villages into darkness, whilst the temperature dropped lower and lower.

Cackle Hill Farm had its own generator, but Eddie was concerned for the girl in the cottage. Every few days he took a bag of coal with him on his trailer, hidden beneath the feed for his sheep.

Anna looked out of the cottage one morning to see a slate grey sky. She lifted her face and sniffed the air. *Snow*, she thought. *There's snow coming and a lot of it.*

'How many sheep have you got?' she asked Eddie later when he came on the tractor with bales of hay for his flock.

'About fifty. Why?'

'I reckon we're in for some snow, Mr Appleyard.'

Eddie glanced at the laden sky and then at the girl. 'Aye,' he agreed, marvelling at her knowledge. 'I was thinking the same mesen.' Just who was this girl, he was wondering, and where had she come from? She was certainly knowledgeable about the countryside and about farming. The image of her hedge-laying was in his mind. She was looking about her now, glancing over the sheep, which were grazing with placid contentment unaware of the threatening weather. Eddie was sure that the girl was thinking the same thing he was—his flock ought to be under cover before the snow came. It was the most animated he had seen her, the most conversation they had had. Even over the hedging, she had not been quite so interested, so concerned, so—alive!

He smiled, thankful to see the change in her. 'Call me "Eddie". Everyone does. Meks me feel old to be called "Mester Appleyard".' For a brief moment she looked uncertain, as if, suddenly, her growing trust in him had been threatened. He saw her glance at him and he couldn't mistake the suspicion in her eyes. And something else too. Could it possibly be fear? Hastily, he added, 'Only if you want to, of course. Mebbe I ought to call you "Miss Woods". But to hear mesen called "Mester Appleyard",' he went on, trying to make a joke of it, 'meks me think me dad's come back.'

Her expression lightened a little and there was even the ghost of a smile as she said softly, 'No, no. "Anna" is just fine . . .' There was a long pause before she added almost inaudibly, 'Eddie.'

'Now, about these sheep,' Eddie said, deliberately changing the subject, his gaze roaming over the nearby slopes, 'we could be in real trouble if the snow comes. We're due to start lambing any time.'

Horrified, Anna stared at him. 'As early as this?'

Eddie nodded. 'I usually plan it to start in February, with a batch of about twenty.' He tapped the side of his nose. 'Then I can get them to market by late June or early July when the prices are good. The rest lamb in March and April. Those lambs get the clean grazing, the new grass that year. Then I can sell them any time I want or keep a few to add to my own flock.'

Anna smiled and began to say, 'That's what—'. She stopped and bit her lip. Sensing her thoughts were again turning to a troubled past, Eddie tactfully hurried on. 'They lamb outdoors unless the weather's bad, then, I take them down to the barn. But as soon as the lambs are strong enough, I bring 'em back to the field.' He paused and then laughed wryly. 'Course, some of 'em are awk'ard beggars and drop too early. That's when we end up in your cottage.'

'It must be a busy time for you,' she murmured, her eyes still with a faraway look.

'Tony helps when he can.' He laughed. 'I forget sometimes just how young he is. He's a good lad.'

'Mm, I can see that,' Anna murmured. She did not ask if Bertha ever helped for she'd guessed the answer.

'Mebbe'—Eddie was glancing worriedly at the sky and thinking out loud—'I ought to get as many as I can of the flock down to the yard. I can't get all fifty under cover, but at least they'd all be in one place.'

'It'd certainly be better than them getting buried in the snow out here. We'd never find them. And when those that are due start lambing—'

'I'll bring Rip and Tony up tomorrow and we'll start rounding them up. One day off school won't matter.'

'There's no need to keep him off. I can help you.'

Eddie nodded. 'All right then, lass. I'll see you bright and early in the morning.'

'Eddie,' she said suddenly, as he began to climb back onto his tractor, 'leave me your crook, will you?'

He eyed her speculatively. 'Course I will. But what do you want with it? I mean, you didn't ought to be tugging about with sheep. Not in your . . .' His voice trailed away, but when he glanced briefly towards her stomach she understood. 'Now, promise me you won't.'

Touched by his concern, she smiled, though as always the smile scarcely reached her eyes. The deep sadness in them was something that haunted Eddie Appleyard even when he was not with her.

'I'd just feel better if I had one,' she answered, neatly evading giving her promise and knowing he would not deny her request.

Eddie reached into the trailer behind his tractor and handed her his shepherd's crook.

'This isn't your only one, is it?' she asked softly, running her hands lovingly up and down the polished wood.

He laughed. 'Lord, no. I've two more and Tony's even got his own little one. I had it specially made

55

for him.'

Anna closed her eyes and sighed, and when she opened them again Eddie was startled to see tears brimming. Her voice was husky as she said, 'That's nice.' Then swiftly, she turned away.

As he drove up the track, Eddie was filled with acute sadness, yet he didn't quite know why. Every so often something was said or something happened that seemed to remind the lass of her past—something that brought tears. He wished she would open up, that she would tell him more about herself. He sighed. There was nothing more he could do except look after her—no matter what it cost him.

As he drove into the yard and climbed down from his tractor, he saw Bertha standing in the doorway, her arms folded across her bosom. Scowling, she shouted, 'And what's so interesting up yon track, might I ask?'

As he walked towards her, he forced a smile. 'Me sheep,' he said and added mildly, 'Any tea in the pot, Bertha love?'

*   *   *

The snow came that night. It began stealthily, falling innocently enough at first and clothing the world in a thin, white sheet.

The following morning Eddie, Anna and Rip rounded up thirty-three sheep and drove them down to the farmyard, though Anna was careful to stay out of sight of the house. Another ten wandered down to the cottage of their own accord and sheltered near the walls or beneath the trees. By dinnertime the snow was coming thick and fast.

'There's still seven missing,' Anna panted, leaning on her crook and screwing her eyes up against the huge flakes that settled on her face. They clung to her hair and covered her shoulders.

'You go in now, love. You're beginning to look like a walking snowman. You'll be soaked through.' He didn't refer to the day he had found her and brought her home, yet it was in both their minds. She had changed even in that short time. Now she had a home, she was warm and well fed. Now she was able to laugh and retort, 'So do you.'

Beside them, Rip shook himself vigorously, the snow from his coat showering them both with even more.

'We must find them,' Anna insisted as her thoughts returned to the missing animals.

'Me an' Rip'll keep looking, but it's pretty hopeless in this lot. We can't see more than a few yards in front of our noses, never mind trying to see sheep across the field. If it'd only stop snowing, we might have a better chance.'

'But seven,' Anna said, 'that's a lot to lose.'

'I know,' Eddie said soberly, 'but think of all those we've saved. Besides, they might be all right if it stops soon.'

They both glanced at the sky and then at each other, but neither spoke. They didn't need to. The sky was so heavy with snow that it was almost like the dusk of evening even though it was only midday. They both knew that the snow would keep coming until it was ankle deep, then up to the knee and, finally, almost too deep for anyone to wade through. They were facing day after day of blizzards that would shroud the countryside and bring transport, movement of any kind, to a halt.

The lanes and then the roads would soon be impassable and only tractors or vehicles with heavy chains on their wheels would be able to move anywhere. Children from outlying areas would not get into the village school. Isolated farms and houses would be snowed in and would have to rely on their own food stores.

That first evening, when Eddie returned, wet through, aching in every limb and disconsolate because he had not found even one of his missing sheep, Bertha was already fretting. 'I'm going to be trapped 'ere, not knowing if me sister's alive or dead.'

'I'll take you into the town on the tractor, love, if it gets that bad and you're worried about her,' Eddie offered.

His wife's retort was scathing. 'Spect me to ride on that thing? I'd be a laughing stock.'

'Nobody's laughing, Bertha. We'll have to get about as best we can.'

'Aye well, you're all right, aren't you? You can still get into town of a Wednesday.' She leant towards him, wagging her finger. 'Only thing is, Eddie Appleyard, you can't drink like a fish no more, 'cos the tractor won't know it's own way home like that poor old pony.'

Eddie turned away without replying. There was no talking to the woman sometimes. He couldn't believe that she had not noticed by now—and he certainly wasn't going to remind her—that he had not come home drunk, not once, since the night he'd brought the girl home. He had kept his silent vow of abstinence, but Bertha hadn't even commented on it.

In the cottage, Anna didn't mind the weather. In fact, it made her feel more secure. No one could reach her now. No one would find her hidden away in a snow-covered cottage near the wood. And she had all the supplies she needed. In the weeks since Christmas she had built up a woodpile in the next room and, thanks to Eddie, she had a good store of tinned food in the larder. She and the puppy would be fine—the only thing that concerned her was Eddie's sheep.

Gently, young though he was, Anna had begun to train the puppy. She would whistle softly in different tones and different pitches and repeat the words of instruction that the shepherds used. When he grew bigger and spring came, then she would take him into the fields and teach him properly.

But sometimes the tears overcame her and she buried her face in his soft coat, remembering that other dog called Buster who had been hers in that other life.

The following morning Anna looked out to see a white world outside her window. But, for the moment, the snow had stopped falling. After a hasty breakfast, she pulled on her warmest clothes and the wellingtons Eddie had brought her.

'Now you stay here, warm and cosy by the fire,' she said to little Buster, who, sensing that he was going to be left alone, whimpered. 'It's a pity you're not bigger like . . .' she began and then faltered, blinking back sudden tears. Then she added bravely, 'You could be a great help today.'

With a final pat, she opened the front door. Normally, she used the door from the kitchen, but today she had another idea. At once a deluge of snow that had drifted against it during the night fell in and it took the girl several precious minutes before she could get the door closed again and then begin to dig a path away from the cottage.

'This is worse than I thought,' she muttered, resting on her spade for a moment. Digging away the snow was hard work and the ever-increasing bulge of her stomach hampered her. But the thought of the sheep buried out there in the fields spurred her on. 'Worst of it is,' she muttered to herself, 'they're such silly creatures. They might not be together. They could be anywhere.' But her words were spoken fondly. She had a great affection for sheep and it was this that was making her disregard her own safety—even the wellbeing of her unborn child—in an effort to save the rest of Eddie Appleyard's flock.

First, she dug her way round to the back of the cottage, to find the sheep huddled against the back wall of the cottage, their long coats matted with snow.

'You poor things, you do look miserable. Come on, let's get you in the warm.' Grabbing hold of the nearest one, she began to lead it round the side of the building and in through the front door and pushed it into the empty 'parlour' of the cottage. Two had followed her of their own accord and, with three similar trips, she soon had all the sheep under cover. She counted them. Ten. Yes, she had been right. Somewhere on the snow-covered hills were seven more. Already the little room looked crowded, but Anna was determined to find the others and bring them to safety.

'Now for the difficult bit,' she murmured, taking

up the crook and plodding round to the front of the cottage.

Snow was falling again, but only light, small flakes. Even though the sky looked laden, at the moment she could still see across the fields. Anna scanned the slopes. Taking a deep breath, she pushed her way through the deep snow towards the side of the field. Sheep tended to look for shelter and when the snow began the hedgerows would be the most likely place to find them.

She had unearthed two by the time she heard a shout and looked up to see Eddie, Tony and Rip struggling to reach her.

'I thought—you promised me . . .' Eddie panted as he neared her, 'that you wouldn't do this.'

For the first time Anna laughed aloud throwing back her head, the joyous sound echoing around them. For a moment, Eddie and Tony stood looking at her and then, unable to stop themselves, they laughed too.

Anna was shaking her head. 'I didn't actually answer you.' Then she looked at him with an expression that was almost coy. 'But I expect you're used to being obeyed.' And she nodded towards Tony.

Eddie smiled, but there was a wry twist to his mouth now. 'By Tony, yes. Well, most of the time.'

He looked at the two bedraggled sheep standing miserably in the snow. 'I'm surprised they're still alive.'

'Luckily, they weren't buried very deep, but we'd better get on looking for the rest . . .'

'Oh no! You're doing no more. You take this pair back to the cottage and . . .'

Her face was suddenly mutinous. She shook her

head. 'Not until we've found the others.'

The man and the young girl stared at each other, whilst the boy looked from one to the other, watching the battle of wills between them.

'You need my help,' Anna said, her expression softening. 'Let me repay you for your kindness when I can. Please?'

He sighed. She was right. He did need her help, but he was worried about her. Even in the short time he had known her, her belly had swelled. She couldn't have much longer to go, he thought.

'Well,' he said still doubtful, but weakening. 'All right, but promise if you feel tired you'll stop.'

'Yes, I'll promise you that.'

'Right. Tony, you take these two down to the cottage . . .' Eddie said and Anna added, 'In through the front door and into the other room. The one to the left.'

Eddie stared at her. 'You've got some inside?'

She nodded. 'The ones that were sheltering at the back of the cottage.' She laughed. 'They're guests in my front parlour now.'

They worked—the three of them—until late afternoon, until all but one sheep had been accounted for.

'We'll have to leave it at that. I'll take these down to the yard if they can make it through the snow. Mebbe she'll turn up.' Eddie's thoughts were still with his one lost sheep. 'Mebbe she's wandered off and found her own shelter somewhere.' But his tone was not convincing.

'I wanted to find them all,' Anna murmured, her gaze still roaming the hillsides, but in the gathering dusk she could no longer see very far.

'We've found more than I dared to hope thanks

to you, lass,' Eddie said. 'Can you manage with those twelve? I really can't get any more into the barn.'

'It's a bit crowded, but yes. They'll be fine.'

'I'll bring some feed for them, but now into the cottage with you and get yourself dry and warm.'

'I will, but first . . .' Letting her crook fall, Anna bent and scooped up a handful of snow. Then she moulded it into a ball. 'Let's have snowball fight.' And she lobbed the ball of snow at Tony, catching him full in the chest.

For a brief moment, the man and the boy stared at her in amazement. Then, with a whoop they began to fling snow at her and at each other until a blizzard of snowballs was flying through the air and their laughter was echoing through the dusk and the gently falling snowflakes.

At last, breathless, they stopped, bending over to catch their breath. As she straightened up, Anna's laughter turned into a cry as pain stabbed at her stomach and she fell to her knees in the snow.

'What is it?'

She was bending double, crouching in the snow and groaning. 'It—hurts,' she gasped.

'Let's get you inside. Then I'll have to fetch the midwife from the village. I reckon it's your bairn coming, lass.'

She clutched his arm and looked up at him with terrified eyes. 'No—no. I don't want anyone else here. And I don't want the baby.' Her voice rose to a hysterical pitch as she gripped Eddie's arm with an intensity that frightened him. 'I won't have it. I won't.'

CHAPTER EIGHT

They helped her back to the cottage. The man was worried and the young boy's eyes were wide and fearful. All Tony wanted to do was to run as far away as possible.

'Let's get you into the warm and lying down,' Eddie said, aware of how inadequate warmth and comfort were in the snowbound, isolated cottage.

'Shall I go and get Mam?' Tony asked.

'No,' the girl cried. 'No. I don't want anyone.'

As another spasm of pain gripped her, she grasped Eddie. 'I don't want anyone else. Promise me. I don't want anyone to know I'm even here.'

He didn't answer her, but pushed open the door and half carried her inside the cottage. 'Lie down,' he commanded. His voice was gentle, but there was a note of firmness in his tone. 'Now, look here, lass. I respect your feelings. Whatever reason you've got, I know you don't want other folks around. But this is different. I can't manage on me own . . .'

'Why not? You know about sheep—about lambing . . . aah . . .' Her words ended in a cry of pain and she held her stomach.

Eddie could not help a wry smile. 'This is a bit different, love, than helping a few lambs into the world.'

'I don't see why,' she panted, as the contraction faded.

Eddie shook his head. 'I'm going to the village to fetch the midwife. I'll ask her not to say owt. Pat Jessop's a good sort.' His face sobered. 'I'd never forgive mesen, if owt happened to you—or to the

64

bairn.'

Anna closed her eyes as she whispered dully, 'It wouldn't matter. It wouldn't matter to anyone. Maybe it'd be for the best.'

Eddie took her hand and squeezed it. 'Don't say things like that, lass. It'd matter to me. To both of us.' He turned and looked at his son. 'Wouldn't it, Tony?'

The boy nodded. He was still frightened. He'd seen lambs and calves born all his young life. But, like his dad said, this was very different. At his father's next words his fears increased.

'Now, son, you stay here with Anna while I go back to the farm and fetch the tractor. I'm going to tell your mam that I've got to stay up here with the sheep. Then I'll go to the village and fetch Mrs Jessop and when I get back with her, you can go home.'

Seeing the boy's terror, Eddie put his hand on Tony's shoulder. 'Don't leave her, lad. I'm counting on you. I won't be long.'

The boy's voice trembled as he asked, 'What if Mam comes looking for me?' He put out his hand to fondle his dog's head. Rip had come to sit beside his young master, his attention divided between Tony and the boisterous puppy. Buster was leaping around him, giving excited little yelps, inviting the older dog to play. But Rip sat obediently to heel.

'She won't,' Eddie replied, trying to sound more confident than he felt. Bertha would never venture out to look for her husband, but Tony was a different matter. She just might be worried enough about him to brave the weather.

'Please, oh please, don't go,' Anna moaned, but Eddie was adamant. 'I have to, lass.'

'But it's coming. It's coming.' Her voice rose in anguish.

'No, it isn't. If I know owt about these things, you're going to be a while yet. Specially . . .' He had been going to add 'with your first', but he thought better of it. Instead, he patted her hand encouragingly and turned away. 'I'll be as quick as I can.'

He trudged back through the snow to the farmhouse.

'Where's Tony?' was Bertha's first question.

'He's all right.' Eddie managed to sound convincing and, as much as he could, he determined to keep to the truth. His lies would sound more convincing. 'We've got all the remaining sheep into the cottage, bar one. And one or two of them look as if they're going to start.' If only she knew just who it was that was 'lambing', he thought wryly. 'I'll have to stay up there for a bit, love. I've come for the tractor. I—I need some bits and pieces from the village. Anything you want while I'm going?' he added swiftly, hoping to divert her from asking too many questions about what was happening in the fields.

'No, no, I don't think so,' Bertha said abstractedly, then, returning to her main cause for concern, she added, 'You're not to keep Tony up there all night.'

'No, no, love, of course not. I'll make sure he comes home well before dark. But,' he added, with more truth than she could ever know, 'I know he's only young, but he's a great help to me.'

'You don't have to tell me that,' Bertha said and there was pride in her tone. For a moment she softened. 'You get off to the village and I'll pack you some food up now and you can call for it on your way back.'

Eddie swallowed, feeling trapped. He hadn't planned on coming back this way, but on taking Mrs Jessop further along the lane and in by the track round the far side of the woods to reach the cottage. He couldn't risk Bertha seeing Pat Jessop riding on his tractor complete with her midwife's bag. But all he could say was, 'Righto, love. That'd be grand.'

As he rode into town on his tractor, Eddie worked out a plan. *I'll take Pat straight to the cottage, then double back round by the lane and into the farmyard. That way I can collect what she's packed up for me and then go back up the track from the farm to the cottage.* It was lucky, he thought, that the lane was not visible from the farmhouse. Bertha wouldn't be able to see him going past the gate and then coming back again. Not unless she was out in the yard near the gate. And he very much doubted she would be. Not in this weather! He smiled to himself, beginning to enjoy the intrigue.

'Who'd have thought it?' he muttered aloud. 'Quiet old Eddie Appleyard having a bit of excitement in his life.'

*　　*　　*

Left in the cottage with Anna and the two dogs and with twelve sheep now huddled in the next room, Tony was mentally counting the seconds from the moment his father left.

'Can I—get you anything?' he asked tentatively.

Anna, lying quietly for the moment, with her

eyes closed, shook her head. 'I'm sorry,' she said, 'that you're having to see this. You shouldn't be here.'

Tony shrugged, suddenly feeling important. 'S'all right. I've seen lambs and calves an' that born. I know all about it.'

Anna smiled weakly. Did he? Did he really know the whole process? How a lamb, a calf, a child was conceived? Perhaps he did, she thought. He lived on a farm. Had done all his young life. He must have seen the ram in the fields with the sheep, the bull with the cows and maybe Eddie even allowed him to watch when the boar visited. For an intelligent boy it wouldn't be too great a step to imagine what happened between a man and a woman . . .

Anna groaned and covered her face with her hands, trying to keep the memories at bay.

'Is it hurting again?' Tony asked.

She let out a deep sigh and tried to relax her body. 'Not just now.'

But only a minute later she was doubled up again and thrashing about the bed in agony. Tony backed away from her, standing pressed against the far wall, wanting to run, but knowing that he could not, must not, leave her.

He had promised his dad.

Rip whined and pressed against the boy's legs. Even the puppy's lively scampering was quietened. Giving little whimpering cries, he nestled between Rip's paws.

If only, Tony agonized, she would stop crying out in pain.

*   *   *

68

Eddie banged loudly on the door of the village midwife's little cottage. Wintersby village was lucky to have a trained district nurse cum midwife living there. Not all villages had one and a trip to the market town of Ludthorpe would have been impossibly slow in this weather, even on the tractor.

The door was flung open and the tall, buxom figure of Pat Jessop stood there.

'Eddie.' She smiled in welcome. 'What brings you here? Something wrong, ducky?'

'I need your help, Pat.' At her gesture of invitation, he knocked the snow from his boots and stepped inside the door. As she closed it, he pulled off his cap.

'Slip your boots off and come into the kitchen. Tell me all about it,' she said leading the way.

Eddie and Pat Jessop, Pat Anderson as she had been then, had attended the village school at the same time. They had played together as children and Pat had loved nothing better than visiting Cackle Hill Farm and helping with the harvest or, as she had grown older, lambing time. She always said it had been that experience that had led her into nursing. Yet, because she had gone to train in the hospital on the hill in Ludthorpe and had lived in the nurses' home there, the tender romance that might have blossomed between her and Eddie had withered. Pat had fallen in love with a handsome night porter on the hospital staff and, eventually, Eddie had married Bertha. Pat's husband had been killed in the recent war and sadly there had been no child from the union for Pat to love and cherish in his memory. Her loving nature could now only

69

find fulfilment in the care of her patients and nothing gave her greater joy than bringing a child safely into the world.

'I've a bit of trouble on, Pat.' Eddie stood awkwardly in the tiny kitchen, turning his cap through restless fingers.

'Sit down, Eddie, and have a cup of tea.'

'I'd love to, Pat, but I can't stay. I need your help.'

Swiftly, he explained how he had met Anna and taken her home with him. 'Bertha doesn't know she's staying in me cottage. And,' he added pointedly, 'she mustn't.'

'Oh, Eddie,' she murmured, shaking her head at him in gentle admonishment, 'you and that big heart of yours. It'll get you into real trouble one of these days.'

With wry humour, Eddie ran his hand through his hair. 'I think it already has, Pat.'

Pat pulled a face. 'I have heard the tittle-tattle in the village. Not that I take any notice of it,' she added swiftly, 'or repeat it.'

'I know you wouldn't, Pat,' Eddie said softly.

'Anyway, right now we must think about this girl. You think she's gone into labour, Eddie?'

'I'm sure of it.'

'Just give me five minutes to put me warmest clothes on and get a few things together and I'll be with you.'

*   *   *

It had begun to snow again as they started on the journey back to the farm, which lay about a mile outside the village. Pat, muffled in a mackintosh,

70

scarves and wellingtons, sat on the mudguard over the huge back wheel of the tractor. She had dispensed with her official district nurse's uniform in favour of slacks and jumpers. She knew just how long this night might be.

Dusk was closing in as they reached the cottage, to see Tony standing in the doorway. There were tears running down the boy's face and as soon as the tractor stopped and Eddie and Pat climbed down, he ran towards them and flung himself against his father.

'Come quick. She's screaming and screaming all the time now and—and there's water and blood too—'

'Oh my God!' Eddie muttered, but already Pat was hurrying into the cottage.

'Now, ducky, here I am. You'll be all right. Let's have a look at you.'

The man and the boy stood in the shadows, feeling helpless but unable to tear themselves away.

Anna was bathed in sweat and clutching the sides of the mattress. She was crying out and writhing in agony.

'Now, now, calm down. I'm here now and everything will be all right,' Pat was saying, soothing the terrified, pain-racked young girl. Pat examined her swiftly and looked up, smiling. 'It's only your waters broken, ducky. Everything's just fine. Baby will be fine. Now, when's your due date?'

The girl's head moved from side to side.

'When did the doctor tell you your baby would come, ducky?' Pat persisted gently.

'Never—seen—a doctor,' Anna gasped. 'I don't want it.' Her voice rose. 'I don't want it.'

71

Briefly, Pat left Anna's side and crossed the small room to Eddie.

'This isn't going to be easy,' she whispered. 'She's fighting it. Send the boy home, but you'll have to stay, Eddie. I'll need you. Get that fire built up. Plenty of hot water and—' Her eyes fell on the two dogs in the corner. She pointed in horror. 'And get them out of here this minute.' At that moment bleating came from the next room and Pat's eyes widened. 'Oh, Eddie, don't tell me! You've got sheep in there, haven't you?'

Eddie nodded.

Pat sighed and shook her head. 'Eddie Appleyard, what am I to do with you? This is hardly the ideal place anyway for the lass to give birth, but with animals a few feet away . . . I don't want her getting an infection. So,' she went on, rolling up her sleeves, 'get me a bowl of hot water and the first thing we'll do is wash in disinfectant. Both of us. Where's my bag? Ah, there it is.' As she turned she added, 'You still here, Tony? Off you go and take those dogs with you.'

Tony cast a wide-eyed glance at his father. 'I can't take Buster home. What'll Mam say?'

'Put him in with Duke. She never goes in there.'

Tony picked up the puppy. Like his father, he knew that Bertha never went anywhere near the pony unless it was safely harnessed between the shafts of the trap. Buster made little yelping noises and licked the boy's face, ecstatic to be fussed.

'Have I time to take the tractor back and pick up some food? Bertha was packing summat up for me. I—I don't want her to wonder why I haven't gone back.'

Pat could only guess at the full story from the

72

brief outline Eddie had given her, but, knowing his wife, she realized the importance of Eddie's request. 'Yes, go on, but be as quick as you can.'

Eddie put his hand on his son's shoulder. 'You run on home, son, but not a word to your mam.'

The boy nodded and turned towards the door, but before he left he gave one last glance at the girl on the bed. Then he was out of the door and wading through the snow as fast as he could. As he went, he heard Anna's last, despairing cry. 'I don't want it. Let me die. Just let me die.'

CHAPTER NINE

The birth itself was straightforward enough. The baby was small, a little early, Pat thought, but it was the girl's attitude that concerned her. Anna screamed and writhed, fighting the pain.

'When you get a contraction, you've got to push,' Pat told her, but irrationally Anna would only shout, 'I don't want it. I don't want it.'

Kindly, but firmly, Pat said, 'Well, you can't leave it in there, ducky.'

Eddie kept the fire built up and soon the room was hot and stifling. He fetched and carried to Pat's commands and, as she brought the child, kicking and screaming, into the world, he was standing beside her, holding Anna's hand and mopping the girl's brow gently.

'You've a lovely baby girl, Anna. She looks a bit premature, but she's beautiful and what a pair of lungs!' Pat laughed and held up the wriggling infant. Swiftly, she wrapped the baby in a piece of

73

flannelette sheeting. 'I'll see to you in a minute, my pet,' she murmured. 'Here, Eddie, you'll have to hold her for a moment. I must get the placenta.'

'Me?' Eddie looked startled.

'Yes, you, Eddie Appleyard. I don't see anyone else handy.'

Eddie sat down in the battered old armchair he had brought from his barn for Anna and held out his arms. Gently, Pat laid the tiny infant in the crook of his elbow and watched Eddie's face soften as he looked down at the baby girl. If Pat Jessop had not known Eddie so well that she believed every word he had told her implicitly, at that moment she could have believed that the child was indeed his. Watching his tender expression and the gentle way he held the child, as if she were the most precious being on God's earth, brought a lump to Pat's throat. There were going to be plenty of the village gossips who would believe that he was the father once this news got out. But no one would hear it from Nurse Jessop.

'Now then,' she said briskly, turning back to the new mother, who was lying quietly with her eyes closed. Anna's cheeks were red with the effort of giving birth, but it was not the colour of robust health. The young girl was very thin and Pat wondered if she would have enough milk to feed the child naturally.

'Now, Anna, you're lucky you don't need any stitches, but we've got to get the afterbirth away. I'll have to massage your tummy.' Drowsily, the girl opened her eyes and frowned. 'That hurts.'

'Sorry, love, but I have to do it.' When that did not produce the desired effect, Pat said, 'Can you cough, ducky?'

74

Anna made a little noise in her throat.

'Come on, Anna. A real good, deep cough. Right from your boots. That's it. Good girl,' Pat exclaimed as the placenta came slithering out. 'That's what I wanted. Now we'll get you cleaned up and you can rest while I wash the baby. Then you can hold her.'

Pat glanced at the girl, but she had closed her eyes again. She lay passively all the time while Pat washed her and changed the sheets, which the nurse had had the forethought to bring with her.

'It's amazing how many times I have to use me own sheets.' Pat laughed. 'And I've brought you some baby clothes too. I keep a few spares. Now, you have a little sleep whilst I wash the baby and then you can hold her.'

To Pat's dismay the only response Anna made was to turn her face to the wall.

When she had washed and dressed the baby, Pat sighed as she sat in the chair beside the warm fire, holding the child close. She brushed her lips against the tiny infant's downy hair and asked softly, 'What's going to happen to you, little one?'

The firelight was a soft glow on Pat's round face and glinted on her blonde curls, which were usually tucked neatly away beneath her district nurse's severe hat. Her blue eyes were troubled as she looked up and asked quietly, 'What's going on here, Eddie?'

Eddie moved closer to the fire to sit beside Pat. He passed his hand wearily across his forehead. 'I don't know, love, any more than you do. All I can tell you is'—he glanced across to the bed in the corner, but Anna was now sleeping—'it looks like she's run away from home. She's desperate that no one should know she's here. She didn't want me to fetch you, even though she was obviously in pain. She's terrified someone is going to find her. Her family, I suppose.'

Pat nodded and sighed. 'Same old story, I expect. She's got pregnant and her family's given her a hard time about it. She's either run away or'—her tone hardened—'they've thrown her out.' There was silence between them before Pat added angrily, 'You'd think, wouldn't you, after what we've all been through in the war, that folks would have learnt to be a bit more understanding. It breaks my heart to think of all the poor little bairns born in the war that'll never know their fathers, even some of 'em born *in* wedlock ne'er mind those that weren't. And there's a few of both sorts round here, let me tell you. Ee, what's the world coming to, Eddie? What's the world coming to?'

Eddie was silent, unwilling to admit, even to Pat, that his own wife had shown the same lack of compassion towards Anna.

'But you'd better be careful, Eddie, letting her stay here. She can only be seventeen or eighteen at the most. Legally, still a minor.'

'Well, I'm not going to report her, if that's what you're suggesting.'

'I'm not,' Pat said swiftly, 'but you ought to talk to her when she's stronger. Make her see that she should at least get in touch with her family.'

'She's never mentioned anything about her family, and when I've tried to ask her about herself she clams up.'

Pat glanced across at the bed in the corner. 'Mm. Something's not right, Eddie. Have you seen that scar on her fingers?'

Eddie stared at her and then shook his head.

Pat held up her right hand and with her left forefinger, made a slashing movement across the first two fingers on her right hand. 'She's got a nasty wound across here. A deep cut, I'd say. It's healed now, but it's not an old scar. I reckon it's been done about six or seven months ago. About the time,' she added pointedly, 'that she would find out she was pregnant.'

There was silence between them, each busy with their own thoughts, until Eddie said, 'I'd better check on the sheep.'

Minutes later, he put his head round the door. 'There's one going into labour and there's not much room in there—'

'Well, you can't bring it in here.'

Eddie shrugged and was about to disappear again when he paused and asked, 'What about you? Do you want me to take you home?'

'No, no. I'll stay here the night.' She cast a coy look at him. 'Though what it'll do to my reputation, I daren't think.'

'Well—' Eddie scratched his head.

Pat laughed. 'Go on with you, you old softy. I'm only teasing. I must stay here till morning anyway and make sure Anna knows how to feed her baby.'

'Oh, right,' Eddie said and looked relieved. He grinned at her before disappearing back into the neighbouring room.

How nice it was, Eddie was thinking as he knelt beside his ewe, to have a woman with a sense of fun and a bit of sparkle about her. Yes, that was the word he would use to describe Pat Jessop. Despite the sadness she had experienced in her own life, there was always a sparkle about her.

77

It was two o'clock in the morning before Eddie came back into the kitchen, washed himself thoroughly in the sink and sat down wearily in the chair beside the fire. 'The rest seem OK for the moment. What a day!' He leant his head back against the chair and closed his eyes.

'Sorry I couldn't offer to come and help you. It'd've been just like the old days,' Pat said softly. 'How's the lamb?'

'Fine and healthy and suckling straight away.'

'Mm,' Pat said dryly as she glanced towards the sleeping girl in the corner of the room. 'I've always said the animals can teach us a thing or two.' She paused and then said, 'Tell you what, Eddie, you nurse this little mite for a moment and I'll make us some tea and then you get a bit of rest.'

'What about you?' Eddie asked as Pat gently placed the sleeping infant in his arms.

'Me? Oh, I'm all right. Quite used to the odd sleepless night, but you'll have to take me back to the village in the morning. I've me rounds to do. In fact'—she smiled impishly—'you'd better get me back home before it's light, else there'll be gossip.'

Eddie chuckled softly, but his eyes were now on the baby in his arms. 'She's a bonny little thing, ain't she?'

'She is,' Pat agreed, once again watching the gentle expression on Eddie's face and feeling the prickle of tears behind her eyelids.

In her job, Pat Jessop rarely let her emotions get the better of her. It didn't mean she didn't care. Far from it. Her compassion was what made her so good at her job and loved by all her patients. But the whole village knew that Eddie's marriage was not all that it might have been. And Pat's tender heart went out to the man who had been her friend since childhood.

'Funny woman, that Bertha,' was what the gossips said. 'Her dad was a right 'un. Affairs? He 'ad more women than I've had 'ot dinners. And what he didn't get up to in the war was nobody's business.' Here, the storyteller would tap the side of his nose and nod knowingly. 'Black market. Mind you, if you wanted owt, you knew where to go. There wasn't much that Wilf Tinker couldn't lay his hands on.'

'Where is he now then? Dead?'

'Oh no.' The teller would warm to his tale, saying triumphantly, 'He's inside.'

'Never!'

'S'right, but the family don't want folks to know. As if we don't all know already.'

'What happened?'

'It was near the end of the war. Several of the farmers were having ducks pinched in the night. Course, good source of food, weren't it, on the black market? Well, Wilf's driving his old van one night along a country lane in the middle of nowhere when the local bobby stops him. "I ain't no ducks," Wilf ses straight away and then, of course, the bobby looks in the back of the van and finds half a dozen of the little beggars. Still alive, mind you, in a sort of coop and covered over with sacks to muffle the quacking. Daft part about it was'—at this point the storyteller would be almost overcome with mirth—'the bobby'd only stopped Wilf 'cos one of his headlamps was showing a bit too much light. He weren't even looking for ducks.'

All this ran through Pat Jessop's mind as she watched the infant lying in the strong arms of Eddie Appleyard. She felt guilty that she had played a part in his present unhappy marriage. Much as she had adored her husband and never once regretted falling head over heels in love with him and marrying him, she did regret that this had perhaps precipitated Eddie into taking up with Bertha Tinker. If only he hadn't, she reflected, then maybe now . . .

'Here's your tea, Eddie,' she said, placing it on the floor beside him. 'Let me have her.' She held out her arms once more for the child. 'Drink that and then get your head down for an hour or two. You're going to have a few busy days and nights ahead of you.'

*   *   *

In the early hours, before it was quite light, Pat woke Anna.

'I'll have to go soon, ducky, and I want to make sure you know how to feed the little mite.' Whilst Anna made no effort to resist Pat unfastening her clothes and putting the baby to her breast, she made no attempt to hold the child against her. She refused even to put her arms beneath the baby to support it. The baby girl nuzzled against the reluctantly offered breast but made no attempt to suckle.

'They sometimes take a bit of time to learn how to do it. Come on, love. You must hold her. She can't do it all on her own.'

But the girl lay with her head turned to one side,

80

her eyes closed, and refused even to look down at her child.

Pat sighed but continued to support the child, holding her so that the tiny mouth felt the red nipple. After what seemed a long time to the man watching, the baby began to suck.

'There's a clever girl,' Pat talked soothingly to the child. 'That's wonderful. Sometimes they take a lot of coaxing,' she told the new mother, 'but this little one knows what's good for her. Don't you, my precious?'

Eddie looked on, glancing anxiously from child to mother. It was all right whilst Pat was here, but what was going to happen once she had to leave? Would the girl go on rejecting the child? He knew what to do in the animal world when the mother acted this way, but if it came to dealing with a human being he was lost. He thought about the night Tony had been born. Pat had brought him into the world too and he remembered Bertha's arms reaching eagerly for her son. Whatever else she might be, Eddie could not fault Bertha as a mother. The only sad thing about it was that whatever love Bertha had to give was centred upon the boy and there was none left for her husband.

Pat lifted the baby away from Anna and immediately the infant opened her mouth and began to yell.

'My, my, you're letting us know you like it now you've got the hang of it, aren't you?' Pat laughed and put the baby to her mother's other breast.

Still Anna made no move to look down at her child and Pat and Eddie exchanged a worried glance.

At last the baby's hunger was satisfied and she

fell asleep.

'There now, Anna, you can go back to sleep again. You must mind you get plenty of rest. I think she's going to be a very demanding baby. But you're young and strong and you'll cope as long as you're sensible and take care of yourself as well as the child.'

Anna lay with her eyes closed. She made no sign that she had even heard Pat, let alone understood what she was saying.

As the light of dawn filtered into the cottage Pat wrapped the child and laid her in the deep armchair. 'She'll be safe there till you get back, Eddie.' She cast an anxious glance back towards the bed. 'I'm worried about that lass, though,' she said quietly. 'I think I'll ask the doctor to take a look at her. If he can get out here in all this lot.'

Eddie nodded. 'Whatever you think best, Pat. But once I've taken you back, I shan't leave her for long. I might have to go down to the house . . .' They exchanged a look. 'But I'll come straight back.'

'Fetch me again tonight, Eddie.'

'If you're sure?'

Pat nodded firmly. 'I am. Besides by the look of some of those ewes in there, you could use another pair of hands.'

*   *   *

Eddie returned to the cottage later, bringing the puppy back with him from the stable, just in case Bertha heard its yapping and decided to investigate. As he opened the door, he found the baby crying again, but Anna had made no effort to

82

get up from her bed. She was just lying there with her eyes closed, a tiny frown furrowing her brow as if the noise was irritating her.

At once the puppy trotted across the floor and, taking little runs, tried to jump up onto the bed, barking excitedly. Anna opened her eyes, leant down and lifted it onto the bed. She fondled its silky ears and even smiled gently at it. Eddie watched in disbelief to see that the girl could fuss a dog and yet turn away from her own child. Determinedly, he crossed the room and lifted the puppy from the bed and carried it to its basket in the opposite corner.

'Stay,' he instructed sternly. The little thing whimpered, but lay down obediently, its nose resting on its paws, its eyes large and appealing.

Then Eddie picked up the child and carried her to the bed. 'This is the one you should be taking notice of. You must feed her, love. You're all she's got. Come along now.'

But Anna turned her face towards the wall again and refused to answer.

'Look, lass. I don't want to have to do what the midwife did—' He bit his lip at the thought of having to put the child to the mother's breast himself. He took a deep breath. 'But I will, if you force me to it, 'cos I'm not going to stand by and see her go hungry.'

Suddenly, she turned her head to face him angrily. 'I don't want it,' she cried out passionately above the noise of her child's crying. 'I *hate* it. I don't care if it dies. And me along with it. Just leave us. Let us both die. It'd be for the best.'

Appalled, Eddie stared at her. Then he said firmly, 'This little mite doesn't deserve to be

83

spoken about like that. *She's* done no wrong.' He couldn't prevent the obvious emphasis, but immediately he regretted his words.

Anna raised herself on one elbow. For the first time there was real spirit in her tone. 'What right have you to judge me? You don't know the first thing about me. You don't know what happened.'

'Then tell me.'

'It's none of your business.' She lay back down again. 'I don't know why you're bothering with us, anyway. Just let us be.'

'If I just "let you be" as you put it, you'll let this little one die, won't you? And then you'll be in trouble yourself.'

'No, I won't,' she muttered. ' 'Cos I won't be here either.'

'Don't talk silly, Anna,' Eddie said. 'Sit up and feed this little one. Come on.' His tone was authoritative now, but still it had no effect. The girl turned her whole body away from him and her child and lay on her side facing the wall.

Eddie sighed and laid the baby back in the big armchair. There was nothing else for it. He'd have to feed the child himself the way he sometimes fed motherless lambs.

For the rest of the day Eddie tended the baby and his sheep. He warmed milk on the fire and dipped a teaspoon in boiling water to cleanse it. Then, when it was cool enough, he sat with the child on his knee and painstakingly spooned the milk into the baby's mouth.

He kept his eye on Anna, but spoke to her only briefly to give her some food.

'Anything else you want?' he asked abruptly. Anna shook her head, unwilling to meet his gaze.

It wasn't that he was deliberately punishing her, it was just that he didn't know how to deal with her callous treatment of the child. To see her fondle the puppy but turn her back on her baby had made him angry.

Late in the afternoon another ewe gave birth to a healthy lamb. Eddie placed the newborn creature to the mother's teat and at once the lamb began to suck, the mother patiently giving herself to her young.

From her bed, Anna heard the bleating and could picture the scene—the new mother and her offspring. When Eddie came back into the room, Anna had raised herself on one elbow and was looking across the room towards her own child, lying quietly now in the chair.

She glanced briefly at Eddie, but then lay down again and closed her eyes. She was sore and ached all over. And she was tired, so very, very tired. All she wanted to do was lie here and not have to move ever again. For months she had tried to ignore the inevitable. And since Eddie had brought her to this cottage, she had begun to feel that, perhaps, she could begin to live again, that the nightmare would begin to fade. But now, after the birth, she would have a daily reminder. Every time she looked at the child, the memories would come flooding back. Anna was fighting an internal emotional battle that the man could know nothing about, nor even begin to guess at.

CHAPTER TEN

That evening Eddie again fetched Pat Jessop from the village on his tractor.

'I hope, for your sake, nobody sees us,' Pat said.

Eddie shrugged. 'They'll just think I'm taking you to some outlying place 'cos of the weather.'

'Which you are,' she smiled. 'Just as long as they don't guess exactly *where* it is you're taking me. Anyway, how is she?'

Pat's face became anxious as Eddie explained what he had been obliged to do to feed the child. 'She doesn't want owt to do with the bairn, Pat. I'm worried sick.'

Pat put her hand briefly on his arm. 'Don't worry, Eddie. If the worst comes to the worst, I'll bring the child back here and look after it myself. I've a good neighbour who'd look after her whilst I'm out on my rounds. She's seven of her own.' Pat laughed. 'She'd hardly notice another one to feed. Jessie'd take it all in her stride.'

Eddie smiled briefly, but said, 'Well, I hope it won't have to come to that.'

'I hope so too. Come on, we'd better get back there and see what this night brings.'

To their disappointment, it brought no change in Anna's attitude. True, Pat was able to make her feed the child, but she could not coax Anna to hold the baby nor even to look at it properly.

In the early morning Pat found herself in the neighbouring room, delivering a lamb whilst Eddie attended to another ewe.

In the cosiness of the cottage, cut off from the

rest of the world by the swirling snow outside, Eddie and Pat smiled at each other. 'It's just like when I used to come and help you and your dad when we were little, Eddie.'

Eddie's dark eyes held her gaze in the flickering light from the hurricane lamp. Her lovely face glowed in the soft light and her gentle eyes held such compassion, such understanding and, yes, love. He was sure he could see love in her eyes. 'Aye,' he said softly. 'I remember.' He sighed and murmured, 'Oh Pat, if only—'

She touched his arm. 'Don't, Eddie,' she whispered, a catch in her voice. 'Please don't say it.'

They gazed at each other for a long moment, each knowing instinctively what the other was thinking, before Pat stood up and deliberately broke the spell.

But it was a moment between them that she would cherish.

*   *   *

When Eddie and Pat left just before dawn, the cottage was quiet. Slowly, Anna sat up and looked across to where her daughter lay. The child was quiet now, full of her milk, which, the midwife had told her, was going to be plentiful.

'You must drink plenty of milk yourself and eat well,' Pat had urged her and had left a bowl of cereal and a glass of milk beside the bed. 'And please, ducky, try to feed the bairn yourself.'

'It—hurts,' the girl had said. She had touched her own breasts. 'They're hard.'

'It's the milk coming.' Deviously, and keeping her tone deliberately casual, Pat had added, 'It would help that feeling if you fed her.'

But, yet again, Anna had turned away. Now, in the stillness of early morning, she lay back and drifted into sleep again but was awakened by the door opening very quietly. For once, she could not even summon up the terror that usually assailed her. She just lay there keeping her eyes closed. Whoever it was, she had not the strength to do anything about it. Just as before, she had not had the strength . . .

She winced, screwing up her eyes tightly to block out the terrifying memories.

Tony tiptoed across the floor, pausing to look down at the baby lying fast asleep in the chair. Then he came to stand by the bed.

'Are you all right?' he whispered, afraid to wake her if she was sleeping.

Anna nodded, but did not speak. She did not even open her eyes.

'Where's me dad?'

Again, there was no answer.

He tried again. 'Is it a boy or a girl?'

Silence. A little more loudly he repeated his question.

Anna licked her dry, cracked lips. 'A girl.'

'What are you going to call her?'

Anna let out a long, deep sigh that seemed to come from the very depths of her being. 'I don't know,' she said dully.

'You'll have to call her something,' the boy said practically and wrinkled his brow thoughtfully, as if the whole burden of naming the child rested with him. Perhaps it did, for the mother was uninterested. 'What about Alice?' he ventured. At school, the teacher had just been reading *Alice's*

Adventures in Wonderland to the class. It was the first name that came to his mind.

There was no response from Anna. 'There's Rose or Janet or Mary . . .' He ticked the suggestions off on his fingers, naming the girls in his class. At last, as if wearying of his persistence, Anna opened her eyes and said, 'Maisie. Her name's Maisie.'

'Maisie,' the boy repeated, sounding the name out aloud. 'Maisie Woods. Yes, it sounds nice. I like it.'

The child began to whimper and Tony grinned. 'See, she knows her name already.'

Very gently, he picked up the child and carried her to the bed. 'She wants her mummy, don't you, Maisie?'

He tried to lay the child in Anna's arms, but she made no move to take her. 'Come on,' he said a little impatiently. 'She's hungry. She wants feeding.'

Anna stared down at the child. The baby's crying ceased for a moment. Dark blue eyes stared at her mother. Whether or not the tiny infant could really see her, Anna did not know, but it seemed as if she could. The baby's face worked, stretching and grimacing.

'Look, she's smiling at you,' Tony said, his knowledge of human babies too sketchy to think otherwise.

Slowly, tentatively, Anna slipped her left arm beneath the baby's head. With her right hand she gently pulled down the shawl and looked upon her daughter for the first time.

*   *   *

When Eddie returned to the cottage, Anna was feeding her daughter and Tony, without a shred of embarrassment, was sitting on the end of the bed watching her. To the young boy, it was perfectly natural to see a mother feeding her young.

Eddie felt relief flood through him. Only later would he learn that it had been his son's prompting that had finally broken down Anna's defences.

He came towards the bed, smiling. 'All right, lass?' Anna looked up, managed a weak smile and nodded.

'I've brought a few things to stock up your pantry.' He glanced at Tony. 'You'd better get back home, lad. Your mam knows I'm going to be up here for the next few days. With the sheep,' he added pointedly.

The boy stared at him for a moment, then looked away. He understood his father's unspoken insinuation. 'Can I—can I come up each day? I shan't be going to school 'cos of the roads, but I can get up here, specially now your tractor's made some tracks.'

'Only if your mam ses you can.'

The boy nodded eagerly. 'She'll want to send you some food anyway.'

Eddie put his hand on Tony's shoulder. 'Now, you look after your mam. Let me know straight away if she needs owt. All right?'

The boy nodded, grinned at Anna and then reached out and gently touched the baby's head. ' 'Bye, Maisie,' he whispered softly.

As he left, Eddie asked, 'Is that her name? Maisie?'

Anna's voice was husky. 'Yes. Tony—wanted me to decide on a name.'

Quietly, Eddie said, 'It doesn't matter yet, but you do know you'll have to register her birth, don't you? It's the law.'

Anna looked at him with startled eyes. 'How— how would I have to do that?'

'Go into town and—'

'Oh, I couldn't.'

'But you must register her.'

Her eyes were wide with fear. 'I couldn't go into town.'

Eddie sighed and let the matter drop for the moment. Perhaps he could get Pat to deal with the problem.

*   *   *

Pat beamed with delight when she entered the cottage that evening to find Anna sitting up in the bed, cuddling the child to her breast. She stamped the snow from her boots and shook her coat.

'It's snowing again,' Pat remarked as she crossed the room towards Anna. Making no direct comment about the change in the girl, she merely enquired, 'All right, ducky?'

Anna nodded. 'Thank you,' she said huskily, 'for all you've done.'

Pat shrugged. 'It's me job, love.' But the look in Anna's dark eyes told the midwife that she understood Pat Jessop had done far more for her than was usual.

'Now then,' Pat said briskly, 'we'll banish Eddie to the other room while I help you have a good wash. I've brought you some clean sheets and a nightie. And there's some clothes for the bairn. Now, off you go, Eddie, and see to your sheep.' Pat smiled at him and flapped her hand to dismiss him.

Eddie grinned as he closed the door behind him, marvelling at how Pat Jessop got her own way without even raising her voice. With her merry face and good-humoured banter, people just did as she asked them without arguing. He shook his head thoughtfully, unable to prevent himself once more comparing Pat's methods to his wife's sharp, demanding ways.

With a minimum of fuss, Anna was soon washed and lying in a clean flannelette nightdress between crisp, sweet-smelling sheets. Then Pat turned her attention to the baby. For a while, Anna lay watching her bathing the child in a tin bath that Eddie had brought from his barn, murmuring endearments to the wriggling infant all the while.

'You're a lovely little thing, aren't you, my precious. With those big eyes and such a lot of pretty hair.' Pat glanced up at Anna and smiled. 'I think she's going to be a real carrot top, love. Just look at her pretty hair.'

Anna's eyes widened and her lips parted in a gasp. With a noise that sounding suspiciously like a cry of despair, Anna turned her back on them both and buried her head in her pillow.

Pat watched her, biting her lip and frowning worriedly. *Now what have I said?* she thought.

She laid the child down in the deep armchair and went towards the bed. Touching the girl's shaking shoulder, she said softly, 'I'm sorry, love. I didn't mean to upset you. Would you like to tell me about it?'

The girl's only reply was to shake her head.

Pat sighed. In all her years of experience, she had never come across a case like this before. She'd dealt with mothers who had rejected their children initially, but once they came around, as she had believed Anna had done, then they didn't often lapse back into withdrawing themselves from their child. Yet now, it seemed, she had unwittingly touched some raw nerve that had made this girl turn her back on her child once more.

She patted the girl's shoulder again, feeling powerless. It was a feeling she did not often experience and certainly did not relish. She liked to be able to help people and, most of the time, she did. 'I'm a good listener, love. And I never judge folk. Whatever it is that's upsetting you, it'll not be anything I've not heard before. So, if you ever want a kindly ear, you know where I am. Your secret—whatever it is—would be safe with me.'

The girl's shoulder was rigid beneath Pat's touch and she made no movement, gave no sign that she had even heard the nurse's words.

*   *   *

Later, when Anna had fallen into a restless sleep and the baby was quiet, Eddie and Pat sat before the fire.

'I said summat to upset her, Eddie,' Pat whispered. 'Just as she seemed to be coming round an' all. I could kick mesen.'

'What did you say?'

Pat sighed and shook her head. 'I was just talking to her about how pretty the child is. With big, dark eyes and that she's going to be a redhead.'

They sat in silence for a moment before Eddie said thoughtfully, 'Perhaps it reminds her of someone. Someone she'd rather forget?'

93

Pat stared at him. 'Oh. The—the father, you mean?'

Soberly, Eddie nodded. He opened his mouth to say more, but at that moment there was scuffling outside the back door.

With a worried expression, Eddie got up, 'This can't be Tony. Not at this time of night. Surely—'

As he moved across the room, the door was flung open and a rotund figure, wrapped in thick clothes and covered in snow, stepped into the kitchen. Behind her came a much smaller figure, a figure that scurried into the room and flung itself against Eddie.

'I tried to stop her coming, Dad. Really I did,' Tony cried, tears running down his cold face and mingling with the snow.

Eddie put his arm about the boy, 'It's all right, son. It's all right,' he said gently, as he looked up to face his wife.

CHAPTER ELEVEN

Bertha's glance took in the girl in the bed, now awakened and sitting up, her eyes fearful. The commotion woke the baby, who began to wail, and Bertha's face contorted into a look of loathing. She swung round and, with surprising agility, flew at her husband, her arms flailing, her hands reaching to slap and punch and scratch. He tried to defend himself as her blows rained upon him, whilst Tony pulled at her coat, crying, 'Mam, Mam, don't. Please, don't.'

Pat hurried forward to intervene, but Bertha

shrieked, 'You keep out of this, Pat Jessop. I might 'ave known you'd be in on this.' Then she raised her hand and dealt her husband a stinging blow on his cheek that sent him reeling. Before he had time to recover his senses, Bertha had whirled about and was moving to where the child lay, her hands outstretched, her eyes murderous.

Pat moved, but there was someone even quicker than she was. Anna flung back the bedclothes and seemed to fly across the room. She snatched up her child and hugged her close. 'Don't you touch her. Don't you dare lay a finger on her.'

Her eyes blazing, she faced the irate woman and even Bertha faltered in the face of the lioness protecting her young.

'Bertha, please—' Pat began, but Bertha now turned and vented her anger on the midwife.

'I told you, keep out of this. You've done enough. I suppose you know all about his goings on, do you? And if you know, then the whole village'll know. Aye, an' half Ludthorpe too, I shouldn't wonder.'

'You've no cause to talk to me like that, Bertha.' Pat bristled. 'And you're not being fair to Eddie—'

'Oho, "Eddie", is it? Summat going on between the two of you, is there?' Her face twisted into an ugly sneer. 'Now the war's over you'll have to look a bit nearer home for fellers, won't you?'

Pat was furious. 'How dare you—?'

'Oh, I dare all right. It was common gossip about you cycling up to that RAF camp *and* afore your husband was killed, an' all.' Her mouth twisted and she flung her arm out towards Anna. 'You're no better than that trollop there, Pat Jessop, so don't try to play the innocent with me.'

95

Pat was shaking her head sadly now. 'You're not right in the head, Bertha. Do you know that? You're twisted, saying such things. I'm a district nurse, for heaven's sake and the camp was in my district.'

Bertha's mouth curled with disbelief. 'Expect me to believe that? They'd got their own doctors and nurses. So why would they need your'—she paused deliberately—'services?'

'Oh, there's no reasoning with you, Bertha. I was often called to the families of RAF personnel who lived near the camp. And I'll tell you something, whether you want to hear it or not. I don't care what you say about me, but you've no call to make such horrible insinuations about Eddie.' Pat shook her forefinger in Bertha's face. 'You've got a good man there, and you're a fool not to see it.'

'How would you know?'

'Come off it, Bertha. I've known Eddie all me life. Do you really expect me to call him "Mr Appleyard" now? 'Cos if you do, then you've another think coming.'

All the time the heated exchange was taking place between the two women, Tony had clung to his father. Anna clutched her baby to her, patting the child's back and trying to soothe her crying.

'If you're so clever, then, Nurse Jessop, p'raps you'd like to tell me what's really going on then with this girl here?'

'Like he told you, Bertha. She was in the marketplace in town with nowhere to go and he took pity on her. That's all.'

Bertha snorted. 'If you believe that, then it's you that's the fool. Not me.'

She turned and held out her hand to her son.

96

'Come on, Tony. You an' me's going home. You're not to come up here again. You hear me?'

Tony cast a helpless glance at his father. 'But—but we haven't told him why we came.' He glanced nervously at his mother, yet he was determined to speak out. 'It's the sheep in the barn. There's one or two of them dropping their lambs. And one—well—you ought to come, Dad.' His voice petered away as his mother added, 'Oh, he's far more important things to do up here, Tony love. I see that now. And I also see why you tried to stop me coming.'

The boy hung his head and shrank against his father, but Bertha was holding out her fat arms towards her son. 'But I don't blame you, lovey. It's not your fault. You're not old enough to understand. Come on, love. Come to your mammy.'

Eddie gripped the boy's shoulder understandingly and then gave him a gentle push. 'Go on, son,' he said quietly.

'But what about the sheep, Dad?'

Eddie nodded. 'I'll come down.'

With obvious reluctance, the boy moved towards his mother. She put her arm about his shoulders and drew him to her. Her eyes narrowed as she said, 'You and your carryings on, Eddie, are one thing, but involving your own son in your lies and deceit is quite another. I'll never forgive you for that. Never.'

And then she was gone, out into the wild night, dragging the boy with her and leaving the three adults staring after her, mesmerized and beginning to wonder if it had all really happened.

'I'm so sorry,' Anna began. 'It's all my fault. I

97

should never have let you bring me with you that night. I'll go.'

Eddie spread his hands in a helpless gesture. 'You can't go anywhere in this lot, love.' He sighed heavily as he sank into the armchair, weary and dispirited. He dropped his head into his hands as he muttered. 'Wait till the weather improves and you're feeling stronger, then we'll see.'

The truth was that, deep inside him, he didn't want her to go anywhere. Eddie wanted Anna to stay right here in his little cottage.

Pat seemed to recover her senses. 'Get back into bed, love. Here, give me the bairn. There, there,' she crooned as she took the crying child into her arms. 'All that shouting's upset you, hasn't it, my little love? There, there. It's all over and your mammy's going to feed you now.'

Anna climbed back into the bed and soon a comparative peace was restored as the infant's cries were silenced while she sucked hungrily. But the cosy, intimate atmosphere of the little cottage was gone, spoiled by Bertha's bitter wrath.

When mother and child were sleeping, Eddie and Pat sat before the fire, their heads close together.

'What are you going to do, Eddie?'

Eddie closed his eyes and sighed wearily. Then, as the baby stirred and gave a little snuffling sound in her sleep, he smiled. He seemed to straighten up as he glanced towards Anna lying in the bed. 'D'you know,' he said, as if he was as surprised as Pat to hear himself saying the words, 'I reckon I'm going to stand up to Bertha for once in me life.'

Pat touched his hand. 'Good for you.'

'The lass and her bairn can stay as long as they

98

want. If—if she wants to go'—Pat saw a fleeting expression of disappointment in his eyes—'then— so be it. But if she wants to stay, then she can.' He stood up and pulled on his coat. 'I'd best be off and see to me sheep.' He paused at the door and turned to say solemnly, 'There's one thing Bertha was right about, though.'

Pat raised her eyebrows. She couldn't think of a single thing that the vitriolic woman had been right about.

Eddie went on, 'Tony. I shouldn't have involved him. I'll have to tell him not to come here any more.'

Pat smiled as she said softly, 'You can try, but I don't think either you—or Bertha—will be able to stop him.'

*   *   *

The snow ceased at last, but then came the thaw and, with it, the danger of flooding to the surrounding district.

'You can't stay here. You'll have to go into the village,' Eddie told Anna. 'Pat's said she'll have you and the bairn. I'll take you—'

'No!' Anna's voice was sharp and determined. She was up and about now and able to care for herself and her child and even the puppy, but she was not yet fully recovered from the birth and had not ventured outside the cottage except to visit the privy. 'We're going nowhere. Not yet, anyway. Not until I'm well enough to move on. To get right away.'

Eddie spread his hands. 'But this cottage lies almost at the lowest point in the vale. The stream will overflow. There's no doubt about that happening, and when it does the water could back up as far as here. It'll get into the cottage—'

'Then we'll go upstairs.'

'You can't do that. The whole place would be damp. You wouldn't be able to keep the bairn warm. You can't light a fire up there.'

'Can't you bring me a paraffin heater, or something?'

'I could,' Eddie agreed reluctantly, 'but it would hardly keep you warm enough up there.'

'We'll be fine.'

'You might be, but what about the baby?' He eyed her thoughtfully. She seemed to have come round now and to be caring for her child properly. Pat had no worries, but Eddie couldn't stop the dreadful suspicion that the girl was just biding her time and that perhaps she still hoped something would happen to the child. To both of them, if it came to that. He lay awake at night, alone now in the spare bedroom to which Bertha had banished him, thinking of the young girl in the cottage and wondering . . .

'Maisie'll be fine,' Anna was insisting now. 'I'll keep her warm.' She must have seen the anxiety in his face, for she added, in her soft, husky voice, 'I promise.'

*　　　*　　　*

As the snow melted and the earth began to show through in brown patches, it was still too wet for the sheep to find grazing, even though they were out on the hillside again. Each day Eddie brought hay for his sheep, but each night Anna still found them huddled against the cottage wall, as if asking to be let in. And each night she would open the door wide and usher them into the room, comforted by the sound of their soft bleating in the middle of the night.

'The stream's overflowing like I said it would. I've brought you some sandbags, but I don't reckon it'll hold the water from getting into the cottage.'

Anna nodded. 'I saw. I went out for the first time today. I took Buster for a walk.' She laughed. 'But he doesn't like getting his paws wet.'

Eddie smiled, though the worry never quite left his eyes. 'He's only little.'

'I've got everything ready in the room upstairs.'

'I'm sorry now that I didn't get Joe Wainwright up here to the roof afore Christmas.'

Anna shrugged and smiled. 'One room's all right. That's all we need.' She glanced at him, teasing. 'I wasn't thinking of taking the sheep up there an' all.'

Eddie laughed. 'No, I don't think they'd manage to climb the ladder. Not even with Rip barking at their heels.' He watched her for a moment. It was the first time that Anna had said something light-hearted and now he saw that she looked better—calmer, he thought, and not so afraid.

'Are you happy here?' he asked before he stopped to think. To his chagrin, the smile faded from her face and the haunted look was at once back in her eyes. She returned his gaze, but avoided answering his question directly.

'I'm very grateful for what you've done for me, Eddie.' Suddenly, she was on her guard again as she added, 'I'll—I'll always be grateful to you, but I can't stay here for ever.'

'Why? Why not, love? You said you'd nowhere to go.' He paused, then when she did not answer he pressed on. 'Or is it different now you've had the bairn? Is that it? Are you going home—?'

Almost before the words were out of his mouth, she had spat back. 'No, no. Never.' Then she faltered. 'I—I have no home.'

'All right, lass, all right.' He spread his hands, trying to placate her. 'I didn't mean to upset you and I'm not trying to pry. It's just that'—he took a deep breath—'it's just that I'd miss you if you did go and—and—well—' He was floundering now and the words came out in a rush. 'If you really haven't anywhere special to go, you're welcome to stay here.'

'What about your wife?' Her unusual dark eyes were regarding him steadily.

He shrugged. 'She's said no more about it. The only thing she has done is to stop Tony from coming to see you.' He forbore to tell Anna that his wife had also banished him from her bed. Not that it was any great loss. She had not allowed any 'marital relations', as they called it, for years, he thought bitterly. The only thing he did miss was the warmth of her bulk next to him on a cold night. But a brick heated in the oven, wrapped in a piece of blanket and shoved into the bed was a good substitute! Now he smiled mischievously. 'But I don't expect for one minute that she'll be able to stop him sneaking over the hill to see you now and again. That lad will find a way, if I'm not much mistaken.'

Anna's small smile chased away some of the guarded look on her face. 'Well,' she said slowly, 'I'd like to stay for a while longer, but I don't want

102

to cause you any more trouble.'

'You won't,' he said briefly and silently added to himself: *No more than I'd already got afore you came.*

CHAPTER TWELVE

The snow continued to melt and the rushing stream became a torrent, which overflowed its banks and flooded the land. Nearer and nearer it crept to the cottage and Anna was obliged to move upstairs, though she could wade through the water if she needed to in her wellingtons. Eddie helped her take her bedding up the narrow ladder and lift the armchair onto the table, so that it would not get soaked.

'I still wish you'd go and stay with Pat Jessop. She asked about you again yesterday.'

'That was kind of her,' Anna said carefully. 'But we'll be fine up there, specially now you've brought us that little stove. As long as I can keep Maisie safe and warm and fed, we'll be all right.'

'But can you?' Eddie asked worriedly.

Anna regarded him steadily. 'If I can't, Eddie, I promise you I'll give in and let you take us to Nurse Jessop's.'

'That's all right then, lass.' He smiled with relief. 'And now I'd better get these sheep onto higher ground.'

'How's the lambing going?' Anna asked. 'I wish I could be more help to you.'

'Considering what we've had to cope with, very well, really. I've still several ewes to drop, but I've already got a good few healthy lambs.' He raised his hand. 'Must get on, lass. See you later.'

' 'Bye,' Anna murmured as she watched him whistle to Rip and begin to round up the sheep that had been her companions for several days. She was sorry to see them go.

*   *   *

The water was now lapping at the walls of the cottage and against the sandbags across the thresholds. As Anna sat on the floor at the top of the ladder with the puppy beside her, the water began to seep into her home. Buster yapped excitedly, as if he could drive back the thing invading the cottage. They watched tiny rivulets creep beneath the door and spread out, until the whole of the earth floor was covered. And still the water kept coming.

She felt a moment's panic, imagining it rising so high that it engulfed the whole cottage and drowned them.

And suddenly she wanted to live. She no longer felt the craving to lie down and let a welcome oblivion overtake her. Now she had something, or rather someone, to live for. She had another human being dependent upon her. She hadn't wanted the child. It had grown within her against her will and she had hated it. Hated the thing inside because of how it had come to be there.

But now the child was no longer an 'it'. Maisie was a tiny human being in her own right, already with a character that was evident when she bellowed for attention. Anna smiled fondly as she glanced over her shoulder to where her child lay sleeping in a Moses basket that Pat Jessop had brought. Where had she heard the phrase 'They bring their love with them'? Well, it was certainly true of her Maisie. Now Anna loved her daughter with a fierce, protective passion. And, ironically, it had been Bertha Appleyard who had made her see that.

If only—Anna's face clouded—the child had not been born with red hair.

She glanced down again at the water, still rising below her. Rationally, she worked out that, because of the lie of the land, the water could not possibly rise above a certain depth. Up here, they would be quite safe.

That night Anna lay down on the soft featherbed mattress on the floor and cuddled her child to her.

Though the water lapped beneath them, she felt safer than she had done for weeks. Cut off from the outside world by the flooding, no one could find her.

*   *   *

'Still visiting ya little bastard, are ya?'

Eddie sighed deeply and cast a sideways glance at Tony sitting at the table, head bowed and toying with the food on his plate.

'Bertha, the child's not mine. How many more times—?'

Bertha snorted. 'She's got brown hair. Just like you. I saw that much that night.'

Holding onto his patience with a supreme effort, Eddie said, 'No, she hasn't. It's red. Ginger. And her eyes are blue.'

'That's nowt to go by. All newborn babies have

blue eyes.' She nodded knowingly. 'Its eyes'll be brown and its hair'll go darker. Like yours.'

Bertha pursed her small mouth until it almost disappeared into her fat face. She banged Eddie's dinner onto the table in front of him and then took her place opposite, beside Tony.

'Don't you worry, love.' She patted her son's arm. 'You've still got me, even if your dad is so taken up with his new daughter that he hasn't any time for you now.'

'That's not true, Bertha—'

Bertha's tone was vitriolic. 'Isn't it? You're off up that track two or three times a day and you don't come back for an hour or more. And don't try telling me you're with your sheep all that time, 'cos most of 'em are down here in the barn or the yard. I bet you're off up there to watch her feeding her kid. Getting an eyeful, are ya? Disgusting, that's what you are.' Her mouth twisted. 'Disgusting.'

Tony's head hung lower as he felt the colour creep up his own face. He'd watched Anna feeding little Maisie. He'd not thought it wrong. So was he 'disgusting' as well, then, in his mother's eyes?

He'd not go to the cottage again, he vowed silently. He didn't want to upset his mam—didn't want her to think that about him. And he didn't want to see the baby any more. Not if his dad was going to love her more than him. Yet he liked going to see Anna and the puppy, and the baby, too, if he was truthful. He'd helped name the little girl. He'd begun to feel she belonged to him a little bit as well. But his mam was so angry. Angry at his dad, angry because the girl was even there. It seemed to him that she hated Anna and the little baby. But he still couldn't understand what his mam meant when she said the baby was his dad's.

The young boy, with a tumult of emotions going on inside his head that he couldn't really understand or rationalize, pushed the food around his plate and chewed each mouthful round and round, unable to swallow for the lump in his throat.

*   *   *

'You all right, lass?' It was Eddie's voice shouting through the front door.

Anna climbed down the ladder and stepped into the water. She pulled open the door and smiled a welcome. As Eddie stepped inside, she said, 'We're fine. Managing to keep warm and dry.'

'Pat wants to come and see you. Check on you and the bairn, but—'

'Tell her not to worry till this lot's gone. We're all right. Honestly.'

Eddie nodded, but the worried look never left his eyes.

'There's something else, isn't there?' Anna said.

Eddie smiled ruefully. 'I don't think Tony'll be coming to see you any more. His—his mam's put a stop to it.'

'Well, I expected that. I'm sorry, though. I'll miss him.'

'Aye, an' I reckon he'll miss you. He keeps asking about you and Maisie, but—' His voice trailed away.

'But what?' Anna prompted.

Eddie sighed. 'Oh, nothing really.' He didn't want to tell Anna about the full extent of Bertha's spite, though he knew she would guess most of it.

Her presence in the cottage was causing Eddie Appleyard all sorts of problems that he had not foreseen when he had brought the girl home that night. He hadn't known what he was doing, he thought wryly, in more ways than one!

But, despite it all, not for one moment did he regret that Anna had come into his life.

CHAPTER THIRTEEN

It was late the following afternoon when Anna heard movement outside the cottage and then someone hammering on the front door at the bottom of the ladder. She climbed down and stood near the door, but did not open it.

'Who is it?' she called.

'Me,' came Tony's voice. She pulled open the door, rippling the water further into the cottage.

The boy was breathless from wading through the flood to reach her.

'What are you doing here? You shouldn't—'

'Me dad sent me,' he interrupted. 'He ses can you come down to the farm? He needs help and he ses I'm not big enough to do it.' For a moment, the boy's mouth was a disgruntled pout and there was resentment in his eyes as he looked at her, as if she was personally to blame for taking the place he believed was rightfully his. 'He's got two ewes dropping at once and they're both difficult. He needs help and I can't get to the village—'

'Of course I'll come, but I'll just have to get Maisie wrapped up warm—'

'Dad said not to take her.' His head drooped

sulkily. 'I—I'm to stay with her, he said.'

Anna bit her lip, uncertain whether to trust the boy in his present mood, though she really had no choice. Eddie Appleyard had been good to her. In fact, he had probably saved her life and that of her child. She couldn't refuse his plea for help.

'All right then. She's just been fed, so she'll be all right for some time and she's asleep. But don't touch the stove, will you?'

'Course I won't,' he said, vexed that she could doubt his common sense.

She followed him up the ladder and dressed herself quickly in the warmest clothing she had, then, with a last glance at her child, she descended the ladder again and left the cottage. Once out of the water, she hurried up the track towards the farm. She was gratified to find that she had almost recovered from the birth of her child. She was not quite as strong as normal, but youth had helped her to heal quickly.

She paused at the top of the hill to look down at the farm below her. In the low-lying parts of the land, water stood in small lakes, and as she set off down the track she could see that part of Eddie's yard too was under water. As she waded through it to reach the barn, she glanced apprehensively towards the farmhouse, hoping that Bertha would not catch sight of her.

She reached the huge barn door, pulled it open and stepped inside. There were two makeshift pens at one end with straw bales where Eddie could attend to the ewes in labour. Anna pushed her way through the flock, patting a head here, stroking a woolly back there until she reached him.

'I've got a bad one here,' Eddie said. 'Breech

and I reckon it's twins.' Then he nodded towards the ewe in the next pen. 'I want you to have a go at that one. The forelegs are presented but there's no sign of the head. Do you know what to do?'

Anna nodded. 'I think so. Push it back very gently and try to manipulate the head into line with the forelegs?'

Eddie gave a quick smile. 'That's it. Your hands are smaller than mine. Tony tried, but his wrist wasn't quite strong enough.'

As she squatted down beside the ewe, Anna smiled ruefully. 'He's not very happy at me taking his place.'

'I'll talk to him later. At the moment I've more to think about than Tony having a mardy.'

There was silence between Eddie and Anna as they struggled to help the ewes. The only noise the bleating from thirty or so sheep.

'There!' Anna said triumphantly, as the lamb slithered safely from its mother. Swiftly she cleaned its mouth. 'It's not breathing, Eddie.' But without waiting for instruction, Anna bent her head close to the tiny creature and blew into its mouth. After a few attempts she looked up, smiling. 'It's fine now.'

'Well done, lass. Mind you dry it well and don't forget to see to the navel.'

'How are you doing?'

'Not good. I think I could lose this ewe. She's quite old and, like I thought, it was twins. I've got them both and they're OK, but she's not cleansing properly.' He shook his head sadly and ruffled the sheep's coat. 'Poor old lass. You've given me a lot of healthy lambs, though, in your time, haven't you?'

'Mine's all right. She's cleansed and I've checked

her udders. Do you think she'd take one of those lambs?'

Eddie looked doubtful. 'I'd sooner rear these by the bottle and let her feed her own. One strong lamb's much better than two weaker ones. Mind you,' he said, scratching his head thoughtfully, 'I don't know how I'm going to cope. I've two lambs in the house already and Bertha won't have owt to do with them. Tony's been looking after them, but now the snow's gone he'll have to go back to school. The lane to Wintersby village isn't too bad with flood water.'

'I could take them home with me,' Anna offered.

In the warm cosiness of the barn, they looked at each other. In the soft glow of the lamplight, Eddie marvelled at the girl's beauty. Her eyes were dark pools and in the light from the lamp her skin was a golden colour. And, it was not lost on either of them that she had referred to the tumbledown cottage as 'home'. Tremulously, Anna smiled. 'I've nothing else to do—apart from looking after Maisie—and I could manage to carry them up the ladder.'

'Well, if you're sure, it would help if you could take at least one. I'll bring you bottles and everything you'll need for feeding.'

He glanced at the ewe near Anna. 'Tell you what,' he said, suddenly coming to a decision, 'Let's risk it. She's young and healthy. Let's try her with one of 'em and then you can feed the other. If we can get hers and one of these twins to suckle, we might trick her into thinking she's had the pair of them.'

Eddie picked up one of the lambs and passed it over to Anna, who rubbed some of the adoptive mother's afterbirth fluids over the orphan. She gave it to the ewe to lick first and kept the animal's own offspring back from her until she had accepted the other lamb.

'That's it,' Eddie murmured, not needing to give advice and amazed, yet again, at the young girl's knowledge. *She's been brought up on a farm*, he thought briefly. *She must have been. And she's been taught well.*

It wasn't until late at night that both lambs were suckling contentedly. Anna stood up and eased her aching limbs. She glanced towards the other pen, an unspoken question on her face. Eddie shook his head. 'Gone, I'm afraid,' he said of the ewe and sighed.

'I'm sorry,' she said. Then she glanced around the barn. 'If there's nothing else I can do, Eddie, I'll be getting back. Maisie must be hungry by now and—'

'Another minute won't hurt, love. Here, sit down and have a drink first. There's a flask of tea I brought out somewhere. Ah, here it is. I reckon we've earned this.'

They sat side by side, leaning against a bale of straw, and sipped the warm, sweet tea gratefully.

'What a night,' Eddie murmured. 'I couldn't have managed without you, lass.'

'We've still lost a ewe, though,' she said sadly.

'Aye, but I'd likely have lost more if you hadn't been here.' He bit his lip, wanting to ask her about her past, wanting to ask how she knew so much about sheep, but he held back the words, knowing that if he so much as mentioned the subject, she would withdraw into silence.

Anna was sitting watching the newborn lambs, a

112

gentle smile on her face. 'Isn't it wonderful—?' she was beginning when the big door of the barn opened and they looked up to see Bertha standing there.

'Eddie? Where are you? Oh, there you are. What do you mean by keeping Tony up all night?' At that moment, she became aware that it was not Tony sitting beside Eddie, but the girl. 'You! What the hell are you doing here?' She glanced around the barn. 'And where's Tony?'

Eddie sighed and struggled to his feet. Wearied by the night's events, the last thing he needed was a confrontation with Bertha. But there was no way out this time. Flatly, he said, 'We've had two difficult births and Tony couldn't help so I sent him to fetch Anna.'

'Oh aye,' Bertha said sarcastically. 'Any excuse.'

'It's not an excuse, Bertha. It's the truth. She's saved me a lamb and possibly a ewe as well, to say nothing of getting this ewe to adopt—'

'Never mind all that. Where's Tony?'

'Looking after Maisie.'

'Maisie?' Bertha glanced around the sheep. 'Which one's Maisie?'

Eddie almost laughed aloud, but the thought of what was going to come in the next few seconds killed his laughter. 'Maisie is Anna's baby.'

For a brief moment Bertha stared at him in disbelief. 'You—you've sent him up there to look after this trollop's bastard?'

'Bertha—' Eddie began, but his wife was in full flow. 'Well, that takes the biscuit, that does. I've heard it all now. I must be the laughing stock of the village. You and your carryings on. For two pins I'd pack me bags and go.' She wagged her forefinger at

113

Eddie. 'And take Tony with me. But I'm not going to, 'cos that's just what you'd like me to do, isn't it? And then you could set up home with your fancy piece here. Well, you aren't going to get what you want, 'cos I'm staying put. I'm not going to see my son done out of his rightful inheritance. Oh no!'

'Bertha, you've got it all wrong.'

'Oh, I don't think so. I'm not blind. But you've a nerve, Eddie Appleyard. Parading your love child for all the world to see as if you're proud—'

'The child isn't his,' Anna said huskily. 'What he's told you is true. He'd never met me before that night he brought me here. Why won't you believe him?'

Bertha stepped closer and thrust her face close to Anna's. ''Cos I know men. Dirty buggers. Only after one thing.' She prodded a vicious finger into Anna's stomach. '*You* ought to know that.'

Even in the half-light, Eddie could see that Anna's face had turned white.

'That's enough, Bertha. There's no call to say such things to Anna.'

'I've every right. She's no better than a whore and a marriage-wrecker and, mark my words, if the old customs still survived, I'd have her ran-tan-tanned out of here. Yes, that's what I'd do, I'd get the whole village up against her.'

'I'll go,' Anna murmured and picked up the lamb.

'Yes, you go. Get out of my sight and off my boy's land. The quicker you and your bastard leave the better.'

'You'd best go on home,' Eddie said in a low voice. 'I'll bring all the paraphernalia you'll need for feeding.'

114

As Anna moved away towards the barn door, she could feel the woman's malevolent gaze following her like a knife in her back. And as she hurried across the yard and up the track, her heart was pounding. *We'll go*, she promised herself. *As soon as the flood waters have gone and the weather improves, we'll go.*

It wasn't until she reached the cottage that she began to breathe easily again.

Tony was peering down from the upstairs. 'What happened?' he asked eagerly. 'Is everything all right?'

Huskily, Anna told him, 'I'm afraid we lost a ewe, but she gave us two healthy lambs. Here.' She began to climb the ladder, holding up the lamb. 'Take this one. We managed to get the other ewe, which only had one lamb, to take one of the orphans and I'm going to look after this one.'

Tony took the lamb and held it close. 'Why?' he asked and his eyes were belligerent once more. 'I can look after it. I've already got two at home.'

'That's just it,' Anna said reasonably. 'You've got enough to cope with and you'll be going back to school soon.'

The boy pulled a face but could not argue.

As she stepped off the ladder, the puppy sprang up from his place by the Moses basket, where he had been sleeping, his nose resting on his paws. He galloped across the floor, sliding and tumbling in his anxiety to reach her. He jumped and made little yapping sounds of pleasure.

Anna smiled down at him and fondled him, but her attention was on Tony as she watched him cuddling the newborn lamb. 'They're still your lambs,' she said softly, 'not mine.'

He shrugged and tried to say with grown-up common sense, 'They'll be going for slaughter as soon as they're old enough anyway.' But there was a tremble in his voice that the young boy could not hide. 'Dad always tells me I shouldn't treat them like pets. We're farmers.'

'That's right. Rip's your pet, but—'

'Not really. He's a working dog.' He nodded towards Buster, still jumping and barking excitedly. 'He's growing, isn't he?'

Anna nodded. 'Yes, and he'll be a working dog too, but it doesn't mean I can't fuss him now and then.'

'You'll have to start training him soon, then,' the boy said, knowledgeably.

'I already have.'

Tony's eyes widened. '*You* have? You know about training sheepdogs?'

Suddenly, the wariness was back in Anna's face and she turned away from him. 'A bit,' she said shortly and then deliberately changed the subject. 'Now, we'd better get somewhere sorted out for this little chap to sleep. Let's go and look in the other room.'

They inspected the other upper room together, but both declared it far too cold and draughty for the young lamb.

'We'll all stay in here,' Anna declared. 'And keep each other warm.'

*　　　*　　　*

The weather improved at last, the flood waters drained away and Pat Jessop was able to cycle from the village to see Anna. She came up the lane and rode boldly through the farmyard. Leaving her bicycle propped against the barn wall, she took her bag and climbed the track to the top of the rise and down the other side to the cottage.

'I'd like you to see the doctor. Maisie ought to be checked over and you certainly should be.'

'We're all right—' Anna began at once, but Pat interrupted firmly. 'I wouldn't be doing my job properly, love, if I didn't insist. Now, do you want to go into town or have him come here?'

Her eyes wide with fear, the young girl looked around her, as if casting about for some way to escape. 'I—'

'Look,' Pat said gently. 'Why not let Eddie take you into town next market day? You've got to register the child anyway. You must do that. It's the law.'

'I—I know, but—'

'I'll come with you, if you like.' Pat chuckled. 'I'd quite like a ride in Eddie's old pony and trap again. It wouldn't be the first time.' Her tone grew wistful. 'Mind you, it was a different pony in those days.' Then she became businesslike once more. 'I'll speak to Eddie, and if it's a nice day next Wednesday we'll all go. I'll make an appointment at the doctor's for you and we'll go and see the registrar too.'

There was no getting out of it. When Pat Jessop was in her most persuasive mood, there was no arguing with her.

Anna sighed. 'All right then.'

Pat beamed. 'Good. I shall look forward to our little jaunt. And now I must go. See you next week.'

Pat was already late for her rounds that morning. The cycle ride out to Cackle Hill Farm would put

117

another hour on her routine, but she was not ready to leave yet. There was someone else she wanted to see first.

*   *   *

Pat knocked on the back door of the farmhouse, summoning her most forbidding expression. It was not an easy thing for the district nurse to do, for she was a buxom, pleasant-faced young woman with a ready smile and a teasing, jovial manner. Her long blonde curls were tucked up neatly beneath her cap and the navy blue uniform gave an impression of a severity that was not really part of her nature, though she could, when necessary—as she had been that morning—be firm and persuasive with her patients.

'Oh, it's you,' Bertha said unnecessarily when she opened the door.

'Yes, it's me, Bertha. Can I have a word?'

'What about?'

'Oh things,' Pat said airily evasive. 'How about a cup of tea? I'm parched. It's a long ride out here.'

'It's not a cafe. I haven't time to be making tea.'

'Oh come on, Bertha, there's a dear. Surely, we've known one another long enough—'

'Oh aye, we know enough about each other not to need cosy chats over my kitchen table.'

But seeing that the nurse was not to be budged, Bertha turned away, muttering, 'Oh, come in then, if you must.'

Pat stepped into the warm kitchen, drew off her gloves and held her hands out to the roaring fire in the range. How different was this kitchen to the meagre surroundings in the little white cottage over the hill. Yet Pat could feel that there was already far more love in the tumbledown haven near the woods than there ever would be in this house.

For a brief moment she wondered if Bertha was right. Was there an affair going on between Eddie and the girl? Perhaps the child *was* his. But then she dismissed her fanciful notions as being just that. She had seen them together and whilst there was no doubting Eddie's concern for Anna's welfare, it seemed to be no more than that.

But who knew what the future might bring? For a moment she felt a pang of sympathy for Bertha, who was at this moment banging cups and saucers onto the table with bad grace.

'This is very kind of you, Bertha. It's cold riding about the countryside on that bike in this weather.' But Pat's words were only greeted with a belligerent glare.

When the tea was ready, they sat down together on opposite sides of the table.

'What is it you want, then? Come to talk me round about that little slut up yonder?' Bertha jerked her head in the direction the cottage lay. ' 'Cos if you have, you're wasting your time.'

'Not really, Bertha,' Pat said, taking a sip of tea and then placing her cup carefully onto its saucer. She looked up and held Bertha's gaze. 'I just wondered what you know about her.'

Bertha shrugged her fat shoulders. 'Nowt. Nor do I want to.'

'Why not?' Pat's question was direct and pointed.

'Why d'ya think?'

Pat leant ever so slightly towards her. 'I don't

know, Bertha. That's why I'm asking you.'

Bertha clattered her own cup into its saucer. 'It's obvious, ain't it? She's Eddie's bit on the side. He's got her into trouble and she's coming knocking at his door. And him being the soft fool he is—'

Pat was shaking her head, unable to believe the tirade of abuse coming out of Bertha's mouth. 'Bertha, your Eddie's not like that.'

'How do you know?' Bertha's retort was like a whiplash. 'Men are all the same. Only after one thing. And even when they've got it on tap at home, it's never enough.' Her small mouth twisted into a bitter sneer.

Pat was appalled at what she was hearing. Eddie's home life must be far worse than she had imagined. Whether or not Eddie had looked for comfort elsewhere, Pat couldn't be sure, but she knew one thing now.

If he had, she wouldn't blame him.

She stood up, unwilling to listen a moment longer to Bertha's twisted logic. The whole village had known for years that Bertha's father had been a 'ladies' man'. Pat had grown up hearing the gossip, witnessing the men's nudges and winks and the women 'tut-tutting' in sympathy with his poor wife. But what she hadn't realized was the terrible effect her father's philandering had had on the young Bertha.

'Do you know something, Bertha? I feel sorry for you. Really I do. But you're a fool. You've got a good man in Eddie Appleyard. There's never been a hint of gossip about him and other women that I've heard. And, believe me, in my job I'd hear it. I carry a lot of secrets for folks round here. And that's what they'll always remain. Secrets. But I'm telling you now, Bertha, Eddie's a good man and I believe him. He felt sorry for that lass and tried to help her.' She leant towards Bertha to emphasize her point. 'And that's all.'

Bertha heaved herself to her feet. 'Get out of my kitchen, Pat Jessop. You're another of his fancy women. Oh, don't think I don't know that you an' him went together afore you found yourself a better catch. And now your husband's dead, you're trying to worm your way back in with Eddie. Well, you won't get the farm. I'll tell you that. I'm his wife and all this'—she waved her arms to encompass the house and all the land that lay around it—'will one day belong to my son.' She jabbed her finger into her own chest. '*My* son.'

Pat shook her head. 'Oh Bertha,' she said sadly, 'is that all poor Eddie is to you? A good catch?'

Bertha's eyes narrowed. 'I told you, get out of my kitchen, Pat Jessop.'

Pat pedalled away from the farm with a heavy heart. *Poor Eddie*, she was thinking. *Poor, poor Eddie. And that poor lass, too*, for she was sure that Bertha Appleyard was just biding her time and that one day, when the opportunity came, she would cause that poor lass a whole barrowload of trouble.

CHAPTER FOURTEEN

'I don't want to go. I don't see why I have to go.' Anna's face was mutinous. 'The baby's fine. You've said so yourself. And so am I. We don't need a doctor.'

Pat was patiently adamant. 'But *I* need you to

see a doctor. If there was anything wrong, then I'd be for the high jump. You wouldn't want me to lose my job, would you?'

If Pat had hoped to appeal to Anna's sympathy, she was sadly mistaken. 'It wouldn't have anything to do with you. Nobody knows about me. Nobody knows I'm here.' She paused and, almost accusingly, added, 'Do they?'

'No.' Pat was holding onto her patience. 'But like I said, if there was anything wrong and you had to see a doctor—or even go to the hospital—well, questions would be asked.'

Anna frowned. 'What do you mean "wrong"?'

'I like to have a newborn baby checked thoroughly. And only a doctor can do that properly. And you should be checked too, particularly when a doctor didn't attend the birth.' Pat forbore to add: *Especially when the birth happened in such a squalid place.* Instead she added, 'Besides, you've got to register her.'

Anna's frown deepened, but at last she muttered, 'All right, then.'

So on market day the following week Eddie took Pat, Anna and the child into the market town of Ludthorpe. The baby was snugly wrapped in shawls and her mother held her close for extra warmth.

'We'll have to go in the trap,' Eddie had said. 'I've got to save me petrol for the tractor.'

Above the rattle of the wheels, Pat chattered merrily.

'This is a treat and no mistake. I can get some shopping that I can't manage on my bicycle.' She smiled saucily at Eddie. 'We'll have to do this more often, Eddie.'

He smiled, but did not answer her.

From the moment they had climbed into the trap outside the white cottage, Anna had seemed ill at ease. As they came down the hill towards the church with its tall spire and turned right along a street that widened out into the marketplace, Pat noticed that the girl's nervousness was increasing. Her eyes were wide and dark with fear and her hands trembled. They passed through the busy marketplace and in front of the low, whitewashed Shepherd's Crook. Eddie glanced at it with nostalgia. He'd had some good times in there. He'd had some good pals and he missed their friendly company on market days, but he had kept his vow. He would never again get sow drunk.

Pat put her arm around Anna's shoulders. 'It's all right, love. I'll come in with you, if you want me to.' With kindly bluntness, she added, 'You're not the first to have a bairn with no dad around and you'll not be the last neither. There's just one thing, though. You do know that you can't put the father's name on the birth certificate when you're not married.' She leant a little closer. 'I presume you're not married to the father, are you?'

Anna shook her head with a vehemence that surprised both Pat and Eddie, who was listening. 'No,' the girl almost spat. 'No, I'm not.'

'Well then,' Pat went on placidly, giving no sign that she had noticed the girl's agitation, 'in that case, you have to register the child in your surname. That's all.'

'I—know,' the girl whispered, but Pat could see that she was still disturbed.

'Mr Bowen's not going to judge you. He's just there to do his job.'

Anna hung her head, her dark hair falling down

123

like curtains on either side of her face, hiding her expression. Above her bent head, Pat and Eddie exchanged an anxious glance. Then Pat pulled a face and lifted her shoulders in a gesture of bewilderment.

When Eddie pulled the trap to a halt outside a tall, stone-clad building with pillars on either side of the huge oak door, Anna was still white-faced and trembling. When she walked into the registrar's dingy office, she almost turned and ran.

'Go on, love. It'll be all right.' Pat gave her a gentle push. 'I'll be just out here if you need me.'

Mr Reginald Bowen was a bent, wizened little man with a wrinkled, unsmiling face. He frowned at her over small, steel-rimmed spectacles and his beady eyes seemed to bore into her soul. She felt that he could read her innermost secrets.

But Anna's first impression was wrong. When the registrar spoke, his voice was gentle. When he moved forward and ushered her to a seat in front of his desk, his manner was kind. As she sat down, Anna looked into his face, close to her now as he bent forward and, with a hooked finger, gently pulled aside the shawl so that he might see the child.

'So this is your little one.' Mr Bowen smiled and all the deep lines on his face seemed to curve upwards so that his whole face seemed to be smiling. His beady eyes were no longer fearsome, but twinkled with pleasure. 'What a little treasure. A girl, is it?'

Anna nodded.

'Well now.' Mr Bowen straightened up and went round to his own side of the desk. He pulled a notepad towards him and, pen poised, glanced up at her. His 'official' face returned and he looked severe once more. Anna was still a little nervous, but no longer frightened of what she must do. It had to be done, for the sake of her child.

'I must ask you a lot of questions,' the registrar explained, 'but I want to reassure you that whatever you tell me is in the strictest confidence.'

Anna bit her lip and nodded.

'There now, shall we begin?'

The child's Christian name, date and place of birth were quite easy to answer, but when it came to Anna's details she hesitated and bit her lip. Mr Bowen glanced up.

'Don't be shy, my dear. I can assure you that nothing can shock me. I've seen and heard it all.'

Have you? Anna wanted to cry. *Is there no story you could hear that wouldn't shock and disgust you? Perhaps if you heard what happened to me . . . ?*

Softly, Mr Bowen interrupted her thoughts. 'I take it you're not married?'

Anna shook her head.

'Then we must register your little girl under your surname. We cannot put the father's name on the certificate unless he is here. Are you in touch with the father? Could he—er—be persuaded to come with you?'

Harshly, Anna said, 'I don't want his name on it.'

'I see,' the man said. He cleared his throat and added, 'Have you any identification with you? Your own birth certificate?'

Again, Anna answered with a mute shake of her head.

'Your identity card then or your ration book?'

He bent his head, preparing to write again, but when she did not speak, he looked up once more.

125

Anna was staring at him, her face devoid of colour. Nervously, she ran her tongue around her mouth to moisten her dry lips.

'Y-yes,' she stammered as, with a trembling hand, she pulled the documents from her pocket and held them out to him.

'Ah,' Mr Bowen said as he perused the papers. 'Woods. I see your name is Annabel Woods.'

Anna nodded. Hoarsely, almost as if she were dragging out the words, she said, 'But—but I'm called Anna.'

'Well, that seems to be in order, my dear,' Mr Bowen said, handing the documents back. Anna almost snatched the card and book from his fingers and pushed them deep into her coat pocket.

'So now we can register your little one. Maisie Woods? Is that it? No second name?'

Anna stared at him for a moment and then said slowly, 'Yes. Maisie Patricia. After Mrs Jessop. She's been—very kind.'

Mr Bowen smiled and, for the first time, Anna understood the expression 'wreathed in smiles'. All the lines in his face seemed to join together in one huge smile. 'She's a lovely lady. She'll be tickled pink.'

*   *   *

Registering both herself and her child at the doctor's surgery was easy, especially as now she had Pat's comforting presence beside her. The receptionist accepted their names as Annabel and Maisie Patricia Woods. Only one moment gave Anna a brief scare.

'We might need to see your birth certificates at

some point,' the woman said, 'but it doesn't matter today.'

Anna breathed again. She turned to Pat, who was now standing by her side. 'I hope you don't mind. I called her after you.'

'Oh ducky . . .' Pat said and squeezed her arm. As Mr Bowen had predicted, Pat really did turn pink with pleasure.

The doctor was young, a junior partner in the well-established practice in Ludthorpe.

'I think you'll get on better with Dr Mortimer,' Pat had told her. 'Dr Jacobs is an old dear, but a bit crusty, if you know what I mean. He's an ex-army doctor and not ever so good with babies and children. He's a big man and his handlebar moustache frightens the little ones.' Pat laughed merrily. 'And the not-so-little ones sometimes, too. But Dr Mortimer's a dear.'

The young man's fresh face beamed as Pat ushered a nervous Anna into the surgery. He bounced up from his chair and sprang around the desk to shake Pat's hand. 'Nurse Jessop. Lovely to see you. Come in, come in. How kind of you to bring me a new patient.' And he smiled at Anna and held out his arms to take her baby. 'Now, let's have a look at little Maisie, shall we?'

Swiftly and expertly, he examined the baby, taking time to murmur endearments to her and even to tickle and play with her so that he gained her confidence. 'Well, she's fine,' he said straightening up at last. He turned towards Anna. 'And how's the new mother coping? Any problems.'

Anna bit her lip, glanced nervously at Pat and then shook her head.

'I need to examine you, Mrs Woods. If you like

to undress behind the curtains and then—'

'No!'

There was a startled silence and Pat looked up from where she was redressing the baby. 'It's all right, Anna. I'll be here.'

Avoiding their glances, Anna shook her head. 'I'm fine. I don't mind you looking at the baby, but I don't need—'

'It really is advisable, Mrs Woods—'

'Stop calling me Mrs Woods,' Anna snapped. 'It's Miss—'

There was an awkward silence and then, to their horror, Anna burst into tears. 'I'm so sorry. I—I didn't mean to be rude. It's just—I'm so frightened.'

'Frightened?' The young doctor was genuinely distressed. 'Of me?'

Anna's voice was muffled by her tears, but they both heard her whisper, 'Of you touching me.'

Again, the doctor and Pat Jessop exchanged a glance. A look that said: *There's something going on here that we don't know about.*

'I'll be right with you, love,' Pat tried to reassure her. 'I'll even hold your hand, but the doctor must examine you internally to make sure—'

'Internally?' Anna almost shrieked. 'Whatever for?'

'To make sure everything's as it should be. It is important both for now and for the next time you have a child—'

'There won't be a next time,' Anna interrupted bitterly. 'I'll make sure of that.'

Again a look passed between the doctor and the district nurse, but neither of them said anything.

After a great deal of gentle persuasion, for both

128

doctor and nurse could see that the girl was genuinely terrified, Anna gave her reluctant consent. The examination was difficult. Despite the doctor telling her to relax, Anna tensed every muscle against him. But at last he said, 'Everything seems to be fine.' He could not stop himself adding, 'Physically.'

Anna took no notice and pulled on her clothes quickly, but Pat gave a little nod of agreement.

There was something upsetting this poor girl and she meant to find out what it was. She had grown fond of Anna and she could understand now why the kindly Eddie Appleyard was still taking such risks to help her. There was just something about the girl. Even Pat couldn't put her finger on quite what it was. Anna was a strange mixture of vulnerability and feistiness. *But for some reason*, Pat thought, *she makes you want to put your arm round her and take care of her.*

Pat acted out the thought, putting her arm about the girl's shoulders. 'Let's get you home now. Eddie'll be waiting and, if I know babies, it won't be long before Maisie here starts to let us know she's hungry.'

As she led the girl from the room, Pat glanced back over her shoulder. 'Thank you very much, Dr Mortimer.' She gave a brief nod to the young doctor that said silently: *I'll look after her.*

The doctor smiled but his glance, following the young girl, was full of concern. He wished the girl would stay, would allow him more time to talk to her. He was sure she needed help. He knew he could give it. But it was obvious she couldn't wait to get away from his surgery. The young man sighed as he promised himself that the next time he saw

Nurse Jessop on her own, he would ask her about the mysterious Anna Woods.

*   *   *

'You're home from market early. Couldn't ya find a doxy today?' Bertha paused significantly. 'Or don't ya need one now you've got a live-in trollop just over the hill?'

Eddie had dropped Anna and the child off at the end of the track on the far side of the wood.

'Are you sure it's not too far for you, lass? Carrying the little 'un an' all?' he'd asked, but Anna had shaken her head. 'It'll do me good.'

'I know of someone who's not likely to need their pram any more. I'll see if I can get it for you,' Pat offered.

'I can't pay for it—' Anna began, but Pat laughed. 'It's had seven bairns in it. It's that battered I don't reckon Mrs Dawson'll want anything for it.' Hastily, before Anna might think she was being treated like a charity case, the district nurse added, 'But I'll ask her. We'll do it proper.' Pat waved. 'See you soon, love. Now, Eddie, you'd best get me home. I've still got patients I must see today.'

How different was Pat's attitude towards the young lass, Eddie was thinking now as he faced his wife. He couldn't help comparing the fat, blowsy woman before him, with her small, mean mouth and beady, suspicious eyes, with Pat's warm friendliness and ready laugh.

For once his anger bubbled to the surface. 'Give it a rest, Bertha,' he snapped. He spun round and left the house, slamming the back door behind him.

So, Bertha thought, her eyes narrowing, *I was right. That little trollop is still in the cottage. Well, Mr Eddie Appleyard, we'll have to see about that, won't we? But I'm patient. I can wait. I can bide me time. I can wait years, if that's what it takes. But one day, oh yes, one day. There's summat funny going on there with that little madam and one day I'll find out what it is.*

CHAPTER FIFTEEN

By the time the snow and the flood waters were gone, Anna had begun to feel a little safer in her hideaway home. Until Joe Wainwright arrived to repair the roof.

Anna saw a lorry chugging towards her down the track from the farm. At first she thought it was Eddie, but as the vehicle drew nearer she realized that the driver was a stranger.

The lorry halted in front of the cottage and now Anna could see the name painted along the side. *Joe Wainwright, Builder.*

The man climbed stiffly out of the cab. He was small and stocky and dressed in corduroy trousers and jacket with a red neckerchief tucked into his striped shirt. He was very bow-legged and walked with a rolling gait as he came towards her, holding out his callused hand in greeting. His face, with three or four days' growth of stubble, was swarthy and lined. Anna couldn't help staring at him as she put out her hand, a little nervously, to shake his.

Joe laughed. 'Aye, I know I'm a funny little feller. I couldn't stop a pig in a passage, could I,

131

lass? But I'm good at me job, else Eddie wouldn't have asked me to come and look at that there roof.'

He squinted up at the holes in the thatch. 'Aye, that's no problem. We'll soon have you all shipshape, lass.' His glance rested on her once more. He gave a little nod. 'So you're the one all the village is talking about, a' ya? The one Eddie Appleyard's moved into his cottage? A bonny 'un an' all.' Joe looked around him, his sharp eyes searching. 'And ya've a babby, ain't ya?'

Anna felt a prickle of fear. It was the first time her privacy had been invaded so boldly. Pat's questioning had been probing, certainly, but it had been done with a feeling of genuine concern. This man was just plain nosy.

'I have,' Anna said shortly. 'But it's not Mr Appleyard's bairn, if that's what folks are saying.'

Unabashed, Joe wheezed with laughter. With blunt honesty, he said, 'Aye well, lass, that's what they *are* saying.' He winked. 'You should hear the owd beezums in the village. Clackety-clack, their tongues are going. Like me to set 'em straight, would ya?'

Anna shrugged. 'I don't care one way or the other. *I* know the truth and so does Mr Appleyard.'

She wondered how the village had heard of her existence in the secluded, tumbledown cottage. Her mouth tightened involuntarily. There was only one person, other than the Appleyard family, who knew she was here. Pat Jessop. And to think Anna had allowed herself to trust the nurse.

Joe interrupted her thoughts. 'Aye, but his *wife* dun't, does she?'

Incredulous, Anna stared at him. 'Are you telling me that it's her spreading the gossip?'

He rubbed his fingers on the bristly growth on his chin. 'Well, who else could it be? No one else knew you was here. 'Cept their lad, Tony.' He gave another wheezing laugh. 'And I don't reckon it's the sort of thing he'd tell his schoolmates, do you?'

Anna chastised herself inwardly. She had been wrong to accuse Pat. Thank goodness it had only been in her mind and not spoken aloud.

'Where've you come from then?' Joe's prying was not finished.

'That's my business,' Anna snapped, hoping that she could offend him just enough to stop his questions but not enough to prevent him mending the roof. But it was impossible to offend Joe Wainwright. His skin was as thick and impervious as the leather on his boots. He just laughed and countered with another question. 'And are you staying here then?'

'Not for long. Now,' she added, trying desperately to steer the focus of his attention away from her, 'would you like a cup of tea and a slice of currant cake? I've just managed to master the bread oven.'

'I wouldn't say no, lass. I wouldn't say no.'

*   *   *

Joe Wainwright was, as he had said, good at his work. In a few hours the thatched roof was repaired.

As he climbed down his ladder, he remarked, 'I see you've had a bit o' trouble with that there wall. Eddie mend that himself, did he?'

'Yes.'

'Ah well, 'spect he has to watch the pennies like

133

the rest of us. Specially with Bertha Tinker for a wife.' He sniffed contemptuously. 'By, she's a shrew and no mistake. Just like 'er mother. No wonder poor old Wilf Tinker used to look elsewhere for 'is comforts.' He gave a huge wink and tapped the side of his nose as he added, 'If ya know what I mean.'

For once, Anna could not stop a twinge of curiosity. She did not venture any questions, but Joe needed no prompting and she made no attempt to stop him. 'Mind you,' he went on, warming to his subject as he found a new ear to listen to his gossip, 'he's a bit of a lad in more ways than one, is Wilf. Ended up in the nick, he has.'

Anna's eyes widened, but still she ventured no comment.

'Aye, black market in the war, y'know.'

Anna bit her lip.

'Course, lots o' folk dabbled a bit in a harmless sort of way. Most of us got away wi' it.' He winked again, indicating that he, Joe Wainwright, had not been above making a bit on the side. 'But poor old Wilf Tinker was 'is own worst enemy. Couldn't tell a lie, see. Not a convincing one at any rate and o' course when he was faced with the law . . .' He shrugged and spread his hands. 'They saw right through 'im. Pity, really. He's not a bad sort in lots of ways. He certainly wasn't a real crook, if you knows what I mean.' He nodded knowingly. 'There was some hard nuts in the war, lass. Real spiv types that'd sell their granny if they thought they could get a bob or two for her.'

A shudder ran through Anna and she felt suddenly sick. She turned her head away before Joe should read her expression.

'And this Wilf Tinker was Mrs Appleyard's

father?' she asked, recovering herself.

'Tha's right. Him and his missis had two lasses. Bertha and Lucy. Lucy did well for herself. Married an office worker and lives in Ludthorpe. Quite the lady, Lucy is. I reckon poor old Bertha envies her. Though give me Eddie Appleyard any time. He's all right, is Eddie. But I dun't reckon I need to tell you that, lass, do I?'

Anna turned back slowly to meet his steady gaze. 'No, Mr Wainwright,' she said. 'You don't.'

*   *   *

By shearing time Maisie was out in the bright, early summer days, sitting up in the deep, black pram that Pat had brought for her.

'Jessie Dawson doesn't want owt for it.'

Anna had eyed the district nurse sceptically. 'Are you sure?'

'Course I am.' Pat laughed. 'Mind you, I had a job to get her to part with it. She shed tears as I wheeled it away. "All my bairns have been in that pram," she said.'

Anna frowned. 'Are you sure she won't want it again? I mean, she sounds very fond of children. She might—'

'I'm sure Jessie'd love another half-dozen given the chance. But she won't have the chance, love. She had to have a hysterectomy after the last baby.'

Anna put her hand onto the well-worn handle. The pram sagged down at one corner where a spring had weakened.

'It's a bit battered, ducky, like I told you.'

'It's fine.' Anna smiled as she rocked the pram gently. 'Maisie will love being outside.'

135

The local farmers all helped one another at certain times of the year: haymaking, harvest and, for those who kept sheep on the Wolds' hills, shearing. But with Eddie's small flock, only Sam Granger, an acknowledged 'dab hand' at shearing, would come. And, of course, Joe Wainwright, who seemed to turn up at every event, would no doubt be there.

On the day before shearing was to begin in the yard at Cackle Hill Farm, Anna wheeled Maisie into the warm sunshine and parked the pram just outside the gate in the fence surrounding their home. She glanced back towards the cottage garden with a small stab of pride. Despite her intention to leave as soon as she could, she had not been able to stand the sight of the neglected garden. In front of the cottage, she had scythed the small patches of grass and was able to keep it short now with a battered old lawnmower that Pat had brought her.

'I've treated myself to a brand-new one,' the nurse had said, beaming. 'I've got quite a big lawn and this one was too much like hard work. But you're young and strong. You'll cope with it.'

Anna had weeded the flowerbeds and now Canterbury bells, cornflowers and convolvulus sprouted happily, whilst lupins and irises were just coming into flower. At the side of the building, there had once been a square of kitchen garden. Whilst Anna was adamant that she would not be here long enough to enjoy the fruits of her labour, she had nevertheless cleared the ground and planted onions and lettuce.

'Why don't you plant cabbage and caulis?' Eddie had suggested in March. 'And what about runner

136

beans and . . .'

'It's not worth it,' Anna said quietly. 'I won't be here to enjoy them.'

Eddie's face fell.

'Unless you'd like me to plant them for you?' she added.

Eddie shook his head. 'No, lass,' he said heavily as he turned away. 'Don't bother.'

But she had dug the kitchen garden over anyway and now, unearthed from the choking weeds and nettles, a rhubarb plant flourished in one corner flanked by two gooseberry bushes.

Buster, usually so boisterous, sat by the pram whenever Maisie was outside, as if guarding the child. Today, however, Anna had other work for him.

The sheep had all been washed in the stream a few days earlier in time for their fleeces to dry in the summer sunshine. It had been hard work, for the sheep hated being plunged into the water and had fought and struggled. Panting and soaked through, Anna and Eddie had laughed at each other.

'You look like a drowned rat,' she had giggled.

'So do you,' he had countered, grinning. 'Go on home. Go and get dry.'

'Why don't you come too? There's a sharp breeze. You'll be chilled by the time you walk back to the farm.'

'Aye, mebbe you're right.'

They walked together towards the cottage, Eddie pushing the pram containing a sleeping Maisie.

'D'you know,' he mused. 'I don't reckon I ever pushed our Tony in his pram. Not once.'

137

Anna laughed softly. 'Not reckoned to be man's work, eh?'

'Wouldn't have bothered me,' Eddie said and there was a note of regret in his tone as if he thought he might have missed a special moment.

As he manoeuvred the pram through the back door, Anna said, 'I'll get a blanket for you. Could you set up the clothes airer? And get those wet things off.'

Eddie grinned. 'Yes, ma'am.'

Anna changed into dry clothes in her bedroom and Eddie sat wrapped in a blanket whilst his wet garments steamed in front of the fire. Anna handed him a cup of hot cocoa and sat down beside him.

'A good job done.' She smiled.

Eddie glanced up to meet her eyes. As he took the cup, their fingers touched briefly. 'Aye lass,' he said. 'A good job done.'

They sat together in companionable silence and even when his clothes were dry enough to put on Eddie seemed reluctant to leave.

He paused in the doorway on his way out and said softly, 'Thanks, lass, for everything.' Very gently, he touched her cheek and then turned and walked away up the slope.

'Oh, Eddie, what a lovely man you are,' Anna whispered to herself as she watched him go. For the first time in many months she suddenly realized that she had not been afraid to be alone with a man.

And now the day for shearing was almost here. Anna surveyed the sheep contentedly grazing in the field near her cottage. Then she shaded her eyes and looked up to the top of the rise, where she could see Tony standing looking down the track

138

towards her. Rip was sitting obediently beside him. She had often seen the two of them at the top of the hill, but not once, since the day he had been sent by his father to fetch her to help with the difficult birth of twin lambs, had the boy visited the cottage.

Now she saw him glance, just once, over his shoulder as if checking to see if anyone was watching him. Then suddenly he launched himself down the hill, running pell-mell towards her, Rip bounding along at his side barking joyfully.

The dog reached her first and jumped up to lick her face. Then Rip capered with the half-grown puppy. Anna held out her arms and, as Tony flung himself into them, she lifted him bodily off the ground and swung him round.

'Oh, I've missed you,' she said impulsively as she set him on the ground and breathlessly they leant against each other, laughing together. She pulled back and held him at arm's length. 'You've grown. I'm sure you've grown.'

Tony grinned. 'Nah.'

'You have, you have,' she insisted and then laughed again. 'But if you haven't then come and look at Maisie. She certainly has.'

As he reached the pram, Tony gasped. 'Oh. She's sitting up and she's smiling. Really smiling now.' He held out a finger to her. The baby gripped it and tried to pull it towards her mouth, but the boy laughed and gently eased it from her grasp. 'No, no, dirty.'

Maisie blinked at him. Her smile faded. Her chin quivered and she began to whimper, huge tears welling in her dark brown eyes.

'Oh don't. Don't cry, little Maisie. I didn't mean

to make you cry, but my finger's mucky.' He leant towards her and tickled Maisie until she chuckled once more.

Watching the young boy's tenderness with her child, Anna felt a lump come to her throat.

'Come on,' she tried to say briskly, though she didn't quite manage it for her voice was unsteady. 'We've work to do.'

CHAPTER SIXTEEN

'Sam's coming tomorrow to start the shearing,' Tony said. 'And Dad says he wants you to come down to the yard and wrap the fleeces for him.' The boy put his head on one side and regarded her thoughtfully. 'Do you know how to do it?'

Anna closed her eyes for a moment as the memories came flooding back, threatening, not for the first time, to overwhelm her. She knew just how it would be. The yard alive with activity: sheep bleating, men laughing and ribbing one another, yet all the while the fleeces would be falling from the sheep as if by magic under the expert hands wielding the shears. She opened her eyes again, but, not trusting herself to speak, she merely nodded.

'We've to round up about half the flock tomorrow morning. Joe Wainwright comes an' all. He cuts all the clags off and opens up the necks for Sam. We do about half the flock one day and the rest the next.'

'Oh.' Anna raised her eyebrows. 'I'd have thought an expert shearer could do your dad's flock

140

in a day.'

Tony grinned. 'He could easy, but he doesn't start till midday. Ses he likes the sheep to have the sun on their backs for a while. Makes the shearing easier, he ses.'

Anna smiled, for a moment her thoughts were far away once more. 'So it does,' she murmured. 'I'd forgotten that.' Then she brought her wandering mind back to the job in hand. 'So, are you coming to help me round them up in the morning?'

Tony nodded. 'I'll be here early.'

The following morning Anna and Tony worked together, leaving Buster sitting beside the pram. For once, the little dog was restless, wanting to join in the rounding up. At last, unable to sit still any longer, he bounded across to Rip, startling the five sheep the older dog was guiding up the track. Anna and Tony burst out laughing, imagining they could see an aggrieved look on Rip's face.

'Just look at him,' Tony spluttered. 'He looks like me dad when I've done something daft.'

'I know just what you mean. He looks as if he's saying, "Look what you've done. Now I've got to start all over again."'

'And poor Buster hasn't a clue what he *has* done.'

'Here, boy. Here, Buster,' Anna called and the young dog came slowly towards her, head down in apology. But Anna fondled him. 'It's all right, but you've got to learn. Now, stay.'

The dog lay down whilst Anna, holding the crook that Eddie had lent her, moved to the right and began to whistle to Rip. With a series of shouted instructions and whistles, they rounded up the five sheep again.

'Yan, tan, tethera, fethera, pethera . . .' she murmured to herself as her eyes misted over once more. But Tony had heard her.

'Oh, you can count like the shepherds, an' all.'

'What?' Anna turned startled eyes upon him, hardly realizing that she had spoken aloud. 'Oh—er—yes.'

'Then you can teach me. Dad only knows "yan, tan, tethera", then he forgets. How far can you count?'

'Only to about twenty . . .'

'That'll do.' Tony grinned.

Anna smiled. 'You follow Rip up the hill and see he gets them into the barn whilst I get the next lot. And I'll try to get this little rascal to do as he's told.' She turned towards the young dog. 'Come on, Buster. High time you learned to earn your keep.'

*   *   *

Anna felt very nervous about going down to the yard. If it hadn't been for the fact that she owed Eddie Appleyard so much, she would have stayed in her little haven, safe from inquisitive eyes. But, she sighed, she had no choice. So she put Maisie in the pram with a bottle for her feed and set off up the track. Joe Wainwright and a man Anna had not met before were already at work in the yard.

Eddie made the brief introduction. 'This is Sam, Anna.' Eddie made no reference to the baby in the pram, which she had parked at the edge of the yard.

'Morning, lass,' Joe greeted her cheerfully, but Sam glowered briefly at her and then turned his back.

As she was making ready the table where she would lay the fleeces to wrap them, Joe came and stood beside her. 'Tek no notice of old Sam, lass. He's got a daughter of his own about your age. And he's a better guard dog than Eddie's sheepdog ovver yonder.' The man gave a wheezing laugh. He leant a little closer. 'Won't let the poor lass even speak to the young fellers, ne'er mind walk out with any of 'em.'

Anna's mouth tightened as she glanced towards Maisie sitting contentedly in her pram. 'He doesn't approve of me, you mean.'

Quite unabashed, Joe nodded. 'Summat like that, aye, lass. But you mark my words, he's stacking up a barrowload of trouble for 'issen. The more you try to keep 'em tied down, the more they'll try to slip the leash. 'Tis only nature, lass, 'tis only nature.' Joe laughed again and leant closer to whisper, 'But what he forgets is that some of us round here have long memories. When he was a young feller his wife's father went after him with a shotgun one night.'

Anna turned to stare at Joe.

'You've heard of a shotgun wedding, lass, ain't ya?'

Anna nodded.

'Well, that was a real one, an' no mistake, 'cos their first bairn was born only six months after they was wed.' Joe winked and tapped the side of his nose. 'So Sam's the last one to be disapproving, ain't he?'

Anna said nothing, but let her head drop forwards to hide her face. Then she felt Joe's friendly hand rest briefly on her shoulder. 'Chin up,

143

lass. You'm got a lovely babby there. Be proud of her.'

Then he turned and walked away, but the man's bluff kindness had brought tears to her eyes.

The men worked hard, with Anna alongside them pausing only to feed and change Maisie and to grab a quick bite to eat herself. She watched in admiration as Sam tipped each sheep onto its rump. So sharp were his blades and so experienced his hands that he didn't even seem to work the shears, but swept the blades down with long easy strokes, deftly turning the animal so that the fleece came off in one whole piece. Then it was Anna's turn to pick up the fleece and take it to the slatted table. Taking it by the hind legs, she flung it upwards and outwards, as if shaking a rug, so that dust and loose fibres floated around her. Then she picked off all the bits of briar and grass that still clung to it. She folded the flanks towards the centre to form a rectangle and rolled the fleece from the back end up towards the neck, where she drew out the neck wool to form a tie long enough to encircle the rolled fleece and tuck back in under itself.

All afternoon she worked steadily, until Eddie called a halt and Bertha appeared in the yard carrying drinks for the workers. Anna turned away, but not before she had seen the look of fury on the older woman's face.

It was late in the evening when Anna climbed the track wearily, with scarcely the strength left to push the pram up the slope. Even when the shearing was done for the day and the men had gone, the work was not finished. The sheared sheep had to be driven back to the field and the next lot brought down to the farm for the night, ready for shearing the following day.

'Dad, Dad,' Anna heard Tony shouting. 'There's three lambs can't find their mothers. They're crying.'

The high-pitched bleating of the lambs as they darted from one ewe to another, unable to recognize their newly shorn dams, was pitiful. But Eddie only chuckled. 'It's all right, lad, I'll make sure they've found the right ones afore I leave them. But you run on home now. Ya mam'll be wanting you away to your bed. And you too, Anna, you take that little one home. You look all in, ya'sen.'

'Goodnight, then, Eddie. I'll see you in the morning.'

'Goodnight, lass. And thanks for all your help today.'

Anna smiled and turned away. As she entered the cottage, she leant a moment against the closed door, glad to be back in her little sanctuary. And yet it hadn't been a bad day. Despite Sam's obvious disapproval and Bertha's malevolent glare, Joe had treated her kindly. It had been a good day.

There had only been one moment that had caused her anguish, but no one could have guessed. At least, she hoped no one had noticed that for a moment her heart had seemed to rise into her throat and her hands had trembled.

Joe had unwittingly brought about the stab of fear. He had been admiring Sam's skill at shearing and had commented lightly. 'You remind me of a young feller that lives over Lincoln way. By, I've never seen a better shearer in me life. Like a knife through butter, it is, to watch him and he never leaves so much as a nick on the sheep. But blessed

145

if I can remember his name.'

'I bet you mean Jed Rower,' she heard Sam say. 'I saw him at the show one year. You'm right, he's a clever feller . . .' The two men had continued their chatter, whilst Anna froze for a moment and then her heart began to pound. Her hands were trembling as she carried the next fleece to the table, her face flushing bright red. Biting her lip, she tried to concentrate on the wrapping, but she did it so badly that she was obliged to unfold it once more and begin again. No one seemed to notice and gradually her heartbeat returned to normal and she tried to squash the thoughts that mention of the name had evoked.

But now, in the stillness of the cottage, those thoughts refused to be ignored.

I must go, was all she could think of. *I'm still not far enough away. Once the shearing's finished, I must move on.*

CHAPTER SEVENTEEN

'You coming with me into town?' Eddie asked Anna as they stacked the rolled fleeces into the back of his trailer to take into Ludthorpe. She shook her head. 'No—I—er—I've things to do.'

'All right, then, lass. I'll see you later. Anything you want bringing?'

Anna's heart beat a little faster and her hands were clammy. She didn't like deceiving Eddie, who had been so kind to her, but, as soon as he had left the farm heading towards the town, she intended to leave too, but in the opposite direction. She dared

146

not tell him, dared not say goodbye, for she knew he would try to persuade her to stay. And he would probably succeed. She would leave via the village, Anna decided. She would call in to say her farewells to Pat and to leave a message for Eddie with her. She could even write him a note . . .

'We'll have to dip in about a fortnight's time . . .' Eddie was saying as he climbed up onto his tractor.

Startled from her own thoughts, Anna said, 'What? What did you say?'

'I said, we'll have to dip all the sheep in about a fortnight.' He smiled down at her. 'I'll need your help then all right, lass. Tony's not strong enough to manage them when they struggle . . .'

Anna stared up at him. Oh no, it wasn't possible. Quite unaware of her plans, Eddie had innocently presented her with yet another reason for her to stay longer.

'Oh, er, right,' she murmured and silently promised: *Two more weeks, then. Just two more weeks and then we'll go.*

*   *   *

Anna stood at the top of the rise, watching the lorry taking a batch of the lambs to market manoeuvre its way out of the gate of Cackle Hill Farm. Beside her Maisie lay asleep in the depths of the black pram, blissfully unaware of her mother's inner turmoil. The young woman smiled gently, though tears prickled her eyes. She couldn't help it. It was not the way of a true farmer. Though never cruel to any animal, nevertheless proper farmers were unsentimental about the need to slaughter the livestock they had so carefully reared. But Anna had not been able to stop herself becoming fond of the woolly little creatures that gambolled and leapt about in their joy at just being alive.

Once she had known that kind of joy.

Her gaze roamed over the slopes of the surrounding fields, vibrant in their summer colours. Below her in the cottage garden splashes of colour vibrated against the darkness of the trees beyond, stately white foxgloves, purple lupins, and pink petunias and even a few early red roses. She wished she could plant more flowers in front of the cottage and there was room in the vegetable patch at the side to plant potatoes, carrots, beans—enough to provide for herself and Maisie for months. She could make it into a real home. She already had, really. She could be content here, almost happy. Anna bit her lip. But it was futile to make such plans.

She couldn't stay here. They had to move on. It wasn't safe. She must get as far away as possible. There were too many people now who knew she was living here. Pat Bishop, Joe Wainwright, the doctor and the registrar in the town and, more recently, the vet and then the men who had come to help with the shearing. And it had been then that she had realized she was still not far enough away. The list of those who now knew where she was was getting far too long, to say nothing of the gossips in the village who knew all about her presence in Eddie Appleyard's shepherd's cottage, even if they had never seen her. The more who knew, the more likely it was that word might get back . . .

And most dangerous of all was Bertha, whose malevolent gaze seemed to follow her everywhere.

It was time to go. The dipping was done, the lambs all gone. Now would be a good time to leave.

Her mind made up, Anna turned her back on the idyllic scene and determinedly pushed the pram down the rough track towards the cottage that had been her haven for the past few months. She would go, she resolved, and go now before she could change her mind.

Back at the cottage, she began to gather her belongings together, her own and Maisie's clothes and food for the journey, piling them all beside the pram. Then she stood looking down at the heap. There was far too much to fit on the pram. Its already sagging springs would never take the extra weight. And there was too much for her to carry. Maybe if she put some in the pram and made up a kind of bundle she could carry on her back . . .

From outside, the sound of Eddie's tractor came closer.

'Oh no!' Anna breathed and hurried outside to forestall him coming into the cottage. He was back earlier than she had thought. She had taken too long to get ready.

He drew to a halt and switched off the engine. Climbing down, he came towards her, smiling. 'Well, lass, that's another lot gone and I got a good price.' His grin widened. 'I'll be able to give you a bonus on your wages.'

Anna smiled tremulously and walked away from the door, trying to keep a distance between him and her home. But her ruse was not working.

'Where's Maisie?' He moved towards the back door.

'She—she's asleep,' Anna said desperately. 'Don't wake her. She's teething and—and she's not sleeping very well.'

This was not strictly true. The child was indeed teething, but she seemed to be having little trouble.

'She's very lucky,' Pat had told Anna on her last visit, adding with a laugh, 'and so are you. Most kiddies have an awful time and so do their mothers. Being kept awake half the night isn't any fun for baby or mother.'

'Oh.' Eddie stopped at once. 'Poor little mite,' he said sympathetically. 'I remember Tony crying a lot when he was teething. I used to rub a little whisky onto his gums.' He grinned. 'But don't tell Pat I told you that, will ya?'

Anna tried to smile, but it was a nervous, half-hearted effort. Eddie didn't seem to notice. His gaze was roving over the outside walls of the cottage. 'You know, this could do with a lick of lime wash—'

At that moment, much to Anna's chagrin, they heard Maisie wail.

Eddie's face brightened. 'She's awake. Now I can see her.' He was in through the back door before Anna could stop him.

She sighed and followed him. He was standing quite still, staring down at the pile of their belongings beside the pram. Slowly he turned to look at Anna, disappointment and concern on his face.

'What's this? You—you're not thinking of leaving, love, are you?'

Silently, Anna nodded.

'Aw, lass, why? What's wrong? Is there something you need? What is it? Tell me and I'll get it.'

Anna shook her head. 'It—it's not that, Eddie.

You've been wonderful, so good. Too good—'

He stared at her for a moment and then closed his eyes and groaned. 'Aw, lass, you're not thinking I'm going to want summat in return. Aw, lass, don't ever think that. Not of me.'

'No, no, Eddie,' she reassured him swiftly. 'It's not that. Truly. That—that never entered my head.'

He eyed her sceptically. 'Didn't it?' he asked gently. ' 'Cos it has into other folks' nasty minds.' His voice dropped to a whisper. 'Even me own wife's.'

'Well, maybe at first,' Anna admitted. 'But not now. Not since I've got to know you. You're just a very kind man, Eddie Appleyard.'

For a moment there was silence between them as they gazed at each other. At last Eddie cleared his throat, but his voice was still husky with emotion as he asked, 'Then why, lass?'

Maisie's wailing grew louder and before she answered him, Anna moved to the pram and picked up the child. Resting her baby against her shoulder, Anna patted her back soothingly. Maisie's cries subsided to gentle hiccuping.

'I have to move on. I have to get further away.'

'Why? What is it you're afraid of? *Who* are you afraid of? You've been here months now and no one's come looking for you. Or has summat happened I don't know about?'

Anna lowered her eyes, not daring to meet his steady gaze. Hating herself for lying, she shook her head.

'Then why, lass? You're safe here.' When she did not answer, he added, 'Aren't you?'

Anna closed her eyes and let out a deep sigh. Flatly, she said, 'I don't know. I—I just feel that the further away the better.'

'Further away from where exactly?' Again there was no reply from her, so he prompted gently. 'Won't you trust me enough to tell me that at least?'

In a husky, reluctant whisper she said, 'Lincoln.'

'Lincoln?' Eddie almost laughed. 'Why, that's miles away. No one's going to find you here. To folks from the city, this is the back of beyond.'

Anna smiled thinly but said nothing.

'So will you stay, lass? At least a little longer? It'll be haymaking afore we know it and then harvest . . .'

'And then it'll be winter and I won't be able to go,' she said.

Eddie grinned ruefully. 'Aye, so it will, lass. So it will. You see right through me, don't ya?' They smiled, understanding one another. 'So, will you stay, love? Please say you will.'

With a jolt Anna saw that there were tears in his eyes. A lump grew in her own throat so that she could not answer. Instead, slowly, she nodded.

*   *   *

Anna and her daughter were still there through haymaking and into the harvest in the heat of August. It seemed as if half the village turned out to help the local farmers get in the harvest.

'It's always happened round here. It's a sort of custom, but more so in the war,' Pat told her. 'With a lot of the fellers away, we had Land Army girls here and the local women helped an' all.' She laughed. 'I reckon we all got to enjoy it.'

'Did—did Eddie have Land Army girls here?'

152

Anna asked.

'Oh yes,' Pat said. 'Most of the farmers did. Some of the girls even stayed on. One girl married a local lad and stayed.' She nodded towards a pretty, fair-haired girl. 'That's her. That's Phyllis. Nice lass, she is. You'd like her. Why don't you let me introduce—'

'No,' Anna said swiftly. 'No, thanks.'

Puzzled, Pat glanced at Anna but said no more. Anna was staring across at Phyllis, almost as if she recognized her and yet she had refused to meet her. In fact, she refused to meet anyone, refused even to try to make friends. Pat sighed. Anna was a funny lass and no mistake.

As Eddie towed the last of the wagons behind the tractor to his stack yard, Pat said, 'There, that's Eddie's all safely gathered in. We've just Ted Bucknall's to do now and that's the harvest home. There'll be a harvest supper in the village hall then. You'll come, won't you?'

Anna shook her head.

'But everyone will be there—'

'No!' Anna was adamant. 'I—I can't.'

Pat sighed as they walked together back towards the farm. 'You will have to mix with folk sometime, love. You can't keep yourself a recluse.' She laughed and nudged Anna's arm. 'They'll be calling you a witch soon.'

Anna smiled wanly.

'And what about Maisie? She needs to play—'

'I play with her.'

'But she needs to be with kiddies of her own age. She needs—'

Anna stopped and turned to face Pat. 'I know you mean it kindly, and I'm grateful, really I am,

153

but I can't mix with folk. And—and I can't let Maisie either.'

'She'll have to when she gets to five years old and has to go to school,' Pat said bluntly. 'You've got to face that, Anna, because it's a fact and you can't get away from it.'

Now Anna smiled. 'I know that, but we'll be miles away from here by then.'

*   *   *

On the evening of the harvest supper, Anna sat alone on the grass outside the little white cottage, watching the sunset. She drew her knees up, wrapped her arms around her legs and rested her chin on her knees. It was so quiet, so still, so peaceful . . .

As the sun dropped lower, emblazoning the western sky with red and gold, Anna dared to feel happy for the first time. The feeling of contentment came stealthily, unbidden, and yet she hardly dared to acknowledge it, to believe that she could ever feel secure and . . .

She heard a movement and jumped, glancing round to see Eddie standing only a few feet from her.

'Sorry, lass,' he said softly. 'I didn't mean to startle you.'

He came across the grass and sat down beside her. 'Lovely sight, ain't it? A Lincolnshire sunset. Nowt to beat it. "Red sky at night, shepherds' delight".'

They sat in companionable silence. For a while, it seemed as if there was no one in the world but them. Then, quietly, Eddie began to talk. 'You

154

must wonder why me an' Bertha ever came to get married.'

'It's not my business, Eddie,' Anna said, not sure she wanted to be the keeper of his confidence. It bound them even closer.

'You might have guessed'—he smiled ruefully—'that once upon a time I carried a torch for Pat Anderson. Sorry, Jessop she is now.'

'I could see there was a closeness between you,' Anna murmured.

Eddie sighed. 'But she left the village. Went to be a nurse in Ludthorpe and met this handsome young feller at the hospital.' There was no bitterness or jealousy in Eddie's tone, just sadness. 'Couldn't blame her, I suppose. He was a really nice feller.'

'And you started seeing Bertha?'

Eddie gave a short laugh. 'Sort of. She came to work here at the farm. My mam and dad were still alive then, but getting on a bit. Mam needed help in the house and with the dairy work. She was a kindly old dear, my mam.'

'That doesn't surprise me,' Anna said, before she could stop herself.

His eyebrows raised in question, Eddie glanced at her. Anna laughed softly. 'You must take after her, Eddie.'

He smiled and gave a little nod. 'I'd like to think so.' He paused as if lost in thought for a moment. 'Anyway, me mam felt sorry for the Tinker family, specially the youngsters, and when Bertha left school she offered her a job here. And, of course,' he added pointedly as if it explained everything, 'she lived in.'

Anna could imagine how it must have been. A

young man, disappointed in love, and a young girl thrown together. Maybe, then, Bertha had been prettier than she was now. Maybe she had fallen in love with Eddie . . .

But Eddie had no such illusions. His next words dispelled Anna's romantic hopes. 'The Tinkers always had an eye for the main chance and my dear wife was no exception. She set her cap at me and I, like a fool, fell for it.' He sighed heavily. 'It wasn't so bad in the early days, I have to admit. She was good to me mam and dad, nursing them in their final illnesses. I'll give her that. But then, after Tony was born, it was as if she gave all the love she had to give to him. So'—he turned to look at her gravely—'don't ever think, lass, that it's you who's caused trouble between us, 'cos it ain't.'

'I'm very sorry, Eddie,' Anna said huskily. 'There's no happy endings in real life are there? That only happens in books.'

'Don't say that, lass. Mebbe there's not one for me, but for you—'

Anna pursed her mouth and shook her head emphatically. 'No. Not for me either.'

There was a long silence until Eddie said, 'Then I'm sorry too, love. Very sorry.' He paused again before asking tentatively, 'Won't you tell me what happened to you?'

Anna's head dropped forward and she pulled at the grass with agitated fingers. 'I can't. It's—it's too painful.'

'All right, love. But if you ever feel the need to talk, I'm here. I'll always be here for you.'

As if pulled by an invisible string, they turned to look at each other. Hesitantly, Eddie reached out. For a moment, Anna drew in a breath and almost

156

jerked away, but then, seeing the tenderness in his eyes, she allowed him to touch her. He traced the line of her cheek with his roughened forefinger, yet his touch was surprisingly gentle.

'Ya won't leave, lass, will ya?' he pleaded softly. 'Ya'll stay here. With me.'

His face was soft in the golden glow of the sunset, his eyes dark unreadable depths, but she could hear the longing in his voice. Anna trembled. By going, she would hurt this lovely man. This man who had given her everything, yet asked nothing in return. But by staying she risked the safety of herself and her child too.

'Till spring, Eddie,' she whispered. 'That's all I can promise. Till spring.'

CHAPTER EIGHTEEN

Anna did not leave the following spring. Maisie learned to walk on the soft grass of Eddie's meadows on the hillside outside the cottage, whilst Anna helped again with the birthing and rearing of the lambs. Anna planted vegetables in the garden at the back of their home and Eddie renovated the upstairs rooms.

'Maisie needs a room of her own, now she's getting such a big girl,' he said, smiling down at the little girl, who followed him whenever she could, clinging to his legs and gazing up at him. He ruffled her coppery curls and tickled her cheek.

'Tony?' Maisie would ask day after day and Eddie would laugh. 'He's at school, lovey. You'll have to make do with old Eddie today. I know, you

157

can come and watch me do the milking.'

'No, Eddie. She's not to go to the farm,' Anna said, overhearing.

In the past year, she had seen Bertha rarely and, in all that time, had never spoken to her once. The other woman made no trouble now, but on the odd occasions that Eddie had needed Anna's help in the buildings or the yard near the house Anna had felt Bertha's malevolent glare following her.

'It'll be all right—'

'No!' Anna was adamant. 'She's not to go to the farm. Not ever.'

'Bertha wouldn't hurt her, Anna. She's got a lot of faults, but she'd never hurt a child. She loves children.'

'Even *my* child?'

'Oh Anna.' His eyes reproached her. 'She's not a bad woman. She'd not harm your little girl.' He shrugged. 'She didn't like the idea of you being here. Still doesn't, I expect.' He wrinkled his forehead. 'But she's not even mentioned you recently. 'Spect she's got used to you being here now.'

'She doesn't allow Tony to come to see us though, does she?'

Eddie smiled. 'No, but he comes anyway.'

'Not so often now and when he does he comes round by the road and the woods so that she can't see him come up the track.'

'Aye, well, I expect he's only trying to save her feelings. He's very fond of his mam, y'know.'

'Of course he is,' Anna murmured and there was a catch to her voice that Eddie couldn't fail to hear. For a brief moment, her eyes had that haunted, faraway look. 'That's as it should be.' She paused

158

and then added emphatically, 'I'm sorry, but I don't want her to go to the farm.'

Eddie sighed and shrugged. 'All right, love, if that's the way you want it.'

He patted the little girl's head and gently disentangled himself from her clinging arms. 'Ta-ta, lovey,' he murmured and then walked away from them.

Anna bit her lip. He was disappointed, she could see that, but she dared not risk Maisie going to the farm.

She could not blot out the memory of the murderous look in Bertha's eyes at the time of Maisie's birth.

*   *   *

They were still living in the cottage when Maisie reached her fourth birthday. And on that day the little girl decided it was high time she investigated what lay beyond the hill up the track from her home. By now Maisie, with her shining coppery curls and dark brown eyes, was bright, intelligent and surprisingly knowledgeable for her age, considering that she had had little contact with the world outside her isolated home.

She knew very few people other than her mother, Eddie, Tony and Pat Jessop. But now the inquisitive child was set on adventure.

'I need to fetch some water,' Anna said. 'Are you coming?'

Maisie shook her head. 'No. I'll stay with Buster.' The dog was now fully trained as a sheepdog and was every bit as trustworthy at looking after the child as he was at guarding

Eddie's flock.

Anna shrugged and set off carrying two water buckets. With narrowed eyes Maisie watched her go. When her mother was some distance away, the child went round the side of the cottage and began to climb the hill, hidden from her mother's view if she happened to glance back.

Sensing that his charge was about to do something wrong, Buster began to bark.

'Ssh,' Maisie frowned at him. 'If you make a noise, I'll shut you in the house.'

The dog whined and then leapt around her, trying to shepherd her back home as he would have done a wayward sheep. But the little girl was not as docile as the animals. She wagged her finger at him. 'Quiet, Buster.' Then she added, 'Down!' in such a firm, grown-up voice that the dog obeyed her. Panting, his pink tongue lolling, he watched her climb the hill with anxiety in his eyes. He sensed this was wrong, but he didn't know how to stop her.

At the top of the track, the child, a tiny figure now, looked back. The dog barked and stood up, but Maisie's shrill voice bounced over the breeze to him. 'Stay!' Buster obeyed, though as she disappeared over the brow of the rise he whined unhappily.

The day was bright but cold and blustery and now, in the late afternoon of the February day, Anna sat down for a few moments on an old tree stump near the stream. She looked down into the brook as it bubbled and chattered its way down the slope, past the wood and under the bridge in the lane and on out of sight. Where it went she didn't know, but she felt as if this little stretch of the stream belonged to her. She pulled her coat around her as she watched the bright water. She sighed. She loved this place and now she would hate to leave, but soon they must. This time next year Maisie would be five and, if they stayed, she would have to go to the village school.

Anna couldn't risk it. She would have to get further away. She couldn't risk even more people knowing them. People who might ask questions: teachers, other children and their parents.

She must get away, yet the thought made her feel sad. She stood up, but then, hearing the sound of a bus coming along the lane, she crouched down behind the tree stump until it had passed by. The vehicle stopped and she heard voices. As the bus drew away, she peeped round the side of the stump to see Tony walking along the side of the stream, head down and his hands thrust into the pockets of his trousers. He was whistling and his bulging satchel swung from his shoulder.

Tony, at fourteen, now attended the grammar school in Ludthorpe. Anna still remembered the look of pride on Eddie's face when he had given her the news. 'He's passed the scholarship for the grammar. Bertha dun't know where to put 'ersen, she's that pleased.'

Anna had smiled. 'And so are you, Eddie. I can see it on your face.'

'Well, course I am. Can't deny it.'

'Is Tony pleased?' Anna had asked softly.

Eddie had shrugged. 'I reckon he is, but he ses all he wants to do is follow me onto the farm. But I tell him he'll have the chance to go to agricultural college now when he leaves there. That'd be something, wouldn't it?'

Anna had nodded, happy to see Eddie so pleased and proud.

Now, as she watched Tony come towards her, Anna realized how much he'd grown and matured in the last four years. He was a young man, already taller than her and almost as tall as his father. He had Eddie's brown hair and dark eyes.

As she saw that he was alone, she rose from her hiding place and waited for him to reach her.

'Hello,' she called and he looked up and grinned at her, his eyes wrinkling in just the same way that Eddie's did.

'Thought I'd come and see Maisie on her birthday.' He dug in his pocket and pulled out a small white paper bag. 'I've brought her some sherbet lemons. It isn't much . . .' he began, 'but she likes them and I've got her a card,' he added as if in apology that his gifts weren't more.

'That's lovely,' Anna reassured him.

Tony grinned. 'Went without me dinner today so I could get her a card.'

'You shouldn't have done that. What would your mother say?'

Tony tapped the side of his nose. 'She'll not know if you don't tell her.' He laughed. 'And you're not likely to do that, are you?'

Anna laughed too. 'Certainly not. Come on,' she said, picking up the buckets. 'Let's go and find Maisie.'

'Here, let me take those,' Tony offered, but Anna shook her head. 'No, I'm fine. That satchel looks heavy enough and, besides, carrying two I'm balanced.'

As they walked back towards the cottage, Anna said, 'She's been a very lucky little girl. Pat brought her a lovely doll and Eddie has made her a wooden cradle for it. They must have had their heads together planning it.'

Tony nodded. 'I know. He's been making it in the shed for weeks. It's from both of us really, but I wanted to get her a bit of something on me own.'

Anna laughed. 'They're her favourite sweets. The only trouble is I'll have to hide them from her and dole them out one by one.'

'Why?'

'If she eats too many at once—and given half a chance she will—the lemon makes her mouth sore.'

Tony laughed too and nodded ruefully. 'Yeah, I've done that too.' As they reached the cottage, Tony added, 'Is she inside?'

'I left her out here, playing with Buster. Oh, there he is. Look, halfway up the hill.' Suddenly, there was fear in Anna's eyes. 'But where's Maisie?'

CHAPTER NINETEEN

Maisie skipped down the track towards the farm below her. There was no one about, so she climbed onto the five-barred gate leading into the yard and swung on it as she looked around her. It was lambing time; it always was near her birthday. Only yesterday a ewe had given birth in the field near the cottage. Her mother had allowed her to watch and the child had been fascinated to see a lamb sliding from its mother's tummy and within minutes stand on its own wobbly legs.

'Can we take it into the house to feed, Mam?'

she had asked.

Anna had smiled. 'No, darling. This mother can feed her lamb herself. It's only when the mother can't feed her young for one reason or another that we have to do that.'

The child was disappointed, yet glad that the lamb would have its own mother. She wouldn't like to be without hers.

Now, swinging on the gate, she looked across to the large barn in front of her. She could hear the sound of sheep coming from inside. She knew that Mr Eddie, as she called him, took as many of the sheep as he could down to the farm when they were lambing. But he had too many to house them all. He never tired of telling her that she had been born in the cottage alongside several lambs.

Her glance swivelled to the back door of the farmhouse. She ran her tongue round her lips, jumped from the gate and pushed it open. She skipped through it and across the yard. She hesitated only a moment before she raised her small fist and banged on the back door. A few moments elapsed before she heard a shuffling on the other side and then the door swung open and she was looking up into the unsmiling face of the large woman standing there.

Unfazed, Maisie looked her up and down then she smiled her most winning smile. Her dark brown eyes lit up and a dimple appeared in each cheek.

'Hello. I'm Maisie. I live over the hill in the cottage. Who are you?'

The woman gasped and blinked her small eyes rapidly. 'Well, I never did!' was all she could say.

'What did you never did?' the child asked innocently and completely unabashed.

164

'It's you.'

The child nodded. 'Yes, it's me. But who are you?'

'Who am I?' the woman repeated, rather stupidly it seemed even to the four-year-old girl. 'I'm Mrs Appleyard.'

'That's Mr Eddie's name. Are you his wife?'

Her mouth dropping open, Bertha merely nodded, dumbfounded.

'What's your first name?'

'Bertha,' the woman murmured, as if in a trance.

Maisie beamed. 'I'll call you Mrs Bertha then. I like that. It's a nice name. Mrs Bertha.' She nodded as if satisfied by the sound of it. 'Can I come in?'

Wordlessly, Bertha stood back and opened the door wider, her gaze following the child as if she were utterly mesmerized by her small visitor.

'Ooh, it does smell nice in here. Have you been baking?' The child sniffed the air appreciatively as she stepped into Bertha's farmhouse kitchen.

'Er—well—yes,' Bertha said, waddling after Maisie. Already the child had hitched herself onto a tall stool near the table and was looking longingly at the scones laid out on a wire cooling tray.

To her astonishment, Bertha found herself saying, 'Would you like one?'

'Ooh, yes please. And please may I have some raspberry jam on it? I like raspberry jam best.'

Bertha cut open a scone, spread it thickly with butter and jam on each half. 'Wait a moment,' she said, bustling to the pantry. 'I've some cream here ...'

A minute later she stood watching as Maisie bit into the warm scone, leaving a smear of jam and cream on her upper lip. 'Mmm, it's lovely, Mrs

165

Bertha. Thank you.'

'You're welcome,' Bertha murmured. She sat down, her gaze fixed on the child. So this was that girl's child. The girl that Eddie had brought home four years ago and taken up the hill to live in his cottage near the wood. She stared hard at Maisie, trying to see any likeness to her husband in the child's face. She had brown eyes like his, but there any resemblance ended. Her hair was copper-coloured, almost ginger, and her features were nothing like Eddie's.

Of course, she probably took after her mother. Bertha screwed up her eyes, visualizing the girl. She'd had black hair and unusual eyes—a deep blue, violet almost, Bertha remembered.

That meant nothing. This child could still be Eddie's.

Maisie had finished her scone and was licking her finger and picking up all the crumbs on the plate. She smiled widely at Bertha, the line of jam and cream still on her lip. 'Are you Tony's mam?'

Bertha nodded.

'He's nice, isn't he? But he doesn't come to play with me very often. I 'spect he's too busy. My mam says he is. Doing his homework and helping his dad and you on the farm.' She paused and leant across the table. 'I'm going to school next year. I'll be five then.'

'So you will,' Bertha murmured absently, her gaze never leaving the child's face, her thoughts in a turmoil.

Maisie jumped down from the high stool and came around the table to stand near Bertha. 'I'd better go home. I'm not supposed to come over the hill. I 'spect Mam'll be ever so cross.'

She smiled as if the thought didn't worry her too much.

Then she put her arms around Bertha as far as she could reach and puckered up her mouth. Bewildered, Bertha found herself lowering her face towards the child to receive a jammy kiss. She was still sitting at the kitchen table, gazing after her as Maisie skipped out of the back door and across the yard.

'Well,' Bertha murmured, 'I never did.'

*   *   *

'Where can she be?'

Anna was almost wild with panic and Tony couldn't calm her down. 'Don't worry. She'll have wandered into the woods. We built a den in there last summer. I bet she's—'

'She's not allowed to go into the woods on her own,' Anna snapped. 'There's poachers' snares in there. Anything might happen. She knows that.'

Tony glanced up the slope again, frowning. 'What's the matter with Buster? He's never moved. I'd've thought he'd have come to us.'

'Buster,' Anna called. 'Here, boy.'

The dog rose reluctantly and came towards them, head down, tail between his legs.

'There's something wrong,' Anna said, her anxiety spiralling. 'Something's happened. I know it.'

Tony fondled the dog's head. 'What is it, boy? Eh?' he murmured. 'You'd tell us if you could, wouldn't you?' He knelt in front of the animal and held the dog's head between his hands. 'Where is she, Buster? Where's Maisie?'

167

The dog barked, pulled himself free of Tony's hold and began to run up the hill. A little way off, he stopped and looked back, then ran on again. Tony and Anna glanced at each other.

'I bet she's gone up there,' Tony said. 'He's trying to make us follow him.'

Anna's hand fluttered to her mouth. 'Oh no! She would never go up there. I've forbidden her. Someone—someone must have got her.'

Tony frowned. 'Got her? What do you mean?'

Anna did not answer. She was already running up the hill. Tony followed, his long legs loping easily after her. They arrived at the top together. At once they saw Maisie skipping merrily up the track towards them as if she hadn't a care in the world.

Anna ran towards her daughter, almost tumbling in her haste to reach her. 'Where on earth have you been?' She grasped Maisie's arm roughly.

'Mam—you're hurting.'

'I'll hurt you, you naughty girl.' Anna bent and slapped Maisie's bare legs so hard that red imprints of her hand marked the child's calves. Maisie opened her mouth wide and yelled.

Watching, Tony winced as if he, too, felt the little girl's pain. Anna was still incensed, shaking the girl and shouting, 'Where have you been? Tell me where you've been.' But Maisie only wailed louder.

Tony moved forward and tried to prise her from her mother's grasp but Anna held on tightly. 'No, leave this to me. Come on . . .' She began to drag the screaming child up the track and over the hill. Maisie, tears running down her cheeks, looked back at Tony, whose tender heart twisted at the sight of her pitiful face. When they disappeared he turned and walked slowly down the hill towards the farm.

He must find his dad.

*   *   *

In the cottage, Anna stood Maisie on a chair in the kitchen, their faces on a level. 'Now, you will tell me where you've been or I'll smack you again.'

The child's wails had subsided to a hiccuping sob. 'To see Mrs Bertha.'

'Bertha?' For a moment Anna thought Maisie must be lying, but then she noticed the smear of jam on the child's mouth. 'You've been to the farm?' she asked incredulously. 'You've been inside the house?'

Maisie nodded. 'To see Mrs Bertha. She's Tony's mam. She gave me a lovely scone with jam and cream.'

The surprise was deflating Anna's anger. Whilst the child had deliberately disobeyed her, Anna knew Maisie could not be expected to understand *why* she should not go to the farm.

'Was she—was she nice to you?'

In a strangely adult manner, Maisie wrinkled her brow thoughtfully and then nodded. 'She didn't say a lot. I think she was surprised to see me.'

'I bet she was,' Anna murmured, lost for words herself. Then she pulled herself out of her stunned reverie to say, 'I'm not going to smack you again, but you've got to promise me that you will never go there again. If you do,' she warned, 'I will punish you very severely. Do you understand me, Maisie?'

The child had stopped crying, but her tears streaked her grubby face. 'Why can't I go and see

169

Mrs Bertha again? *She* didn't say I couldn't.'

Anna sighed, unable to find a plausible explanation to make the young child understand. So she resorted to the age-old decree of all parents at one time or another. 'Because I say so.'

*　　*　　*

It was later that evening when Maisie was in bed in one of the upstairs rooms that Eddie knocked on the side door of the cottage. He stepped into the kitchen and without even greeting her, he demanded, 'What's been going on?' He was frowning and his tone held a note of censure. 'Tony told me you'd smacked Maisie.'

'Huh! I'd've thought you'd've heard all about it from Bertha.'

Eddie shook his head. 'Bertha's said nothing.'

'Maisie went to the farm. If she'll do that, she might take it into her head to go anywhere. She'll be going to the village before I know it.'

'She'll have to soon enough when she goes to school.'

'Oh no!' Anna shook her head. 'We're leaving before she has to go to school. In fact, I've made up my mind. I'll help you with the lambing and then we're going.'

'And where do you intend to go, might I ask?'

'Anywhere as long as it's far enough away from— from here, so that no one knows us.' Her voice dropped as she muttered, 'There's a few too many folks around here know us already.'

'Meaning?'

Anna ticked them off on her fingers. 'You, Tony, Bertha, Pat Jessop, Joe Wainwright and the other fellers who come at shearing and harvest. The doctor in town and the registrar, to say nothing of folks in shops when I've been forced to go into them. Specially the one in Wintersby. The gossip was rife in the village when I first came here. Mr Wainwright told me so.'

Eddie's tone softened. He could hear the panic in her voice. 'You can't live on a desert island, love. Wherever you go, you'll meet other people. And Maisie will have to go to school next year. I know you're bothered about her birth certificate, but they'll ask to see it wherever you go.'

'I'll say I've lost it.'

'They'll only get you to send to the authorities for another.'

Anna stared at him. She hadn't realized that copies could be obtained so easily. She sat down heavily on a chair and, resting her elbows on the table, covered her face with her hands.

'Why can't you stay here? I don't know who or what it is you're so afraid of. You've never told me.' There was a hint of reproach in Eddie's tone. 'But no one's ever bothered you, have they? Not in four years. Surely, you can stay?'

Slowly, Anna dropped her hands and stared into his face. Even though the thought of having to leave this haven and set off into the unknown frightened her, she shook her head sadly and whispered, 'I'm sorry, Eddie, but I daren't stay here. Not now. Not any longer. Not if Maisie's going to do what she did today.'

CHAPTER TWENTY

Lambing was almost over. Only two more ewes left to give birth.

'You'll manage now, Eddie. You've been lucky this year. No motherless lambs for me to rear by hand in the cottage.' She smiled. 'Maisie's quite disappointed. She likes feeding them with a bottle.'

Eddie's eyes were anxious. 'You really mean you're going?'

'I'm sorry, Eddie,' Anna said huskily, 'but we must. I—I don't know how to thank you for all you've done for me. For us—'

'You could thank me by staying and making this your home,' he said gruffly. 'I'll even give you the cottage—and the bit of land round it—if it'll make any difference.'

'Oh, Eddie—'

'I mean it.'

She could see he did and tears filled her eyes. 'I couldn't possibly let you do such a thing. What would your wife say? And then there's Tony. It'll be his one day.'

Avoiding a direct answer about Bertha, Eddie said, 'Tony'd agree. I know he would. He doesn't want you to go any more'n I do.'

Anna touched his arm. 'You're such a kind man. I—I didn't know such kindness from strangers still existed until I came here—' She broke off and turned away as if she was afraid of saying too much. 'We're going tomorrow,' she said with a finality that brooked no argument.

They were all packed, ready for the morning, their belongings in neat bundles and loaded onto Maisie's old pram.

'You'll be able to sit on the top if you get tired,' Anna told her, trying to make it sound like an adventure. But tears spilled down Maisie's cheeks. She cried silently, making no word of complaint, no screams of protest, but her anguish at leaving the only home she had ever known was evident on her small face.

'Come on, up to bed with you. We've got a long way to go tomorrow.'

'Where are we going?'

'You'll see,' Anna said brightly, making it sound as if their destination would be a lovely surprise, but in truth she had no idea herself where they were going.

They would just set off and see where they ended up, but after four years of comparative safety, even Anna was a little afraid.

It was completely different from the last time she had run away. Then she had not cared what became of her or of her unborn child.

Now, she did care. Eddie had taught her to care again.

*   *   *

In the middle of the night, Anna awoke to a dreadful noise. Buster was barking frantically and scratching at the front door to be let out. And from outside the cottage came the noise of barking dogs and the terrified bleating of sheep.

173

'Oh no—!' She flung back the bedclothes and dressed hurriedly. She climbed down the ladder and was pulling on her warmest coat when Maisie, bleary-eyed with sleep, appeared at the top.

'Mammy—'

'Go back to bed,' Anna began and then, with only a second's hesitation, she said, 'no, get dressed. As quickly as you can and come down.'

'Why? We're not going now, are we?' Maisie's lower lip trembled.

'No, but can you hear that awful noise? There are some dogs attacking the sheep. You must run to the farm for me and knock on the door as loudly as you can and fetch Mr Eddie. Can you do that?'

Maisie nodded eagerly, turned and ran back into her room to dress, whilst Anna lit a hurricane lamp and found her crook. She opened the side door and, as the child climbed down the ladder again, they stepped out into the darkness together, Buster streaking out ahead of them.

Outside the noise was even more frightening.

'Thank goodness,' Anna said. 'They're down there towards the stream. They won't see you. Now run, Maisie. Run as fast as you can.'

The little girl disappeared into the darkness and Anna braced herself to walk towards the terrifying noise.

In the moonlight, she could see two dogs attacking one of the ewes still in lamb. Already it was overthrown and unable to rise, helpless against the snapping jaws. Buster was barking and running at them, doing his best to drive the attackers away from the sheep. His sheep. Anna moved closer and hit one of the dogs on the back, yelling at the same time.

174

The dog yelped in surprise. Intent upon their kill, neither dog had sensed her approach. The first ran a few yards and stopped, turning to stand and stare at her, panting hard. Now she lashed out at the other dog, but it jumped out of the way and turned to face her, head down and snarling.

They were big dogs, much bigger than poor Buster and in the darkness as terrifying as a couple of wolves. Crouching low, the second dog crept towards her. Buster stood beside her, growling a warning, but the aggressor took no notice of him. Anna held her crook horizontally in front of her to fend it off as it leapt up at her. She felt a sharp pain in her left hand and knew its white teeth, flashing in the moonlight, had bitten her. Now the other dog, emboldened by its companion, came closer. They lined up side by side in front of her, ready to spring. Beside her Buster whined and barked again.

'Down!' Anna cried in the firmest tone she could muster.

They took no notice and leapt in unison, but not at her. With one accord they fell on Buster, knocking him over. They attacked him cruelly, biting and tearing at his flesh. Now Buster was yelping in pain and fear. Anna hit out at the dogs with her stick and managed to frighten one away. But the bolder of the two turned and snarled at her. It grabbed her crook in its mouth, growling all the time. Gradually she drew it away from Buster, but then the other dog crept closer once more towards the injured sheepdog lying on the ground.

'No!' Anna shouted, feeling helpless to deal with both dogs at once. At that moment she heard a shout from behind her. 'Stand clear, Anna.'

She glanced back to see Eddie just behind her,

pointing his shotgun at the dog nearest to her.

'Don't hit Buster. He's on the ground.'

'I won't. Drop your crook and move away.'

Anna did as she bade him. A shot rang out. Her attacker shuddered and fell to the ground. At the sound, the other dog ran, but Eddie levelled his gun and fired again. The dog stumbled, rolled over and lay still.

Now there was an ominous silence.

Eddie threw down his gun and held his arms wide to her. With a sob, Anna ran into them and was enfolded in his safe embrace. Behind them, watching, Tony stood holding Maisie's hand. As she became aware of them, Anna drew back.

'Are you hurt?' Eddie asked anxiously.

'Just my hand. It's nothing—'

'Let's take a look—'

'No, no—' Anna pulled away from him and stumbled towards Buster, lying motionless on the ground. Maisie ran forward.

'Oh, Mammy. What's happened to Buster?'

'The bad dogs hurt him, darling.'

Maisie squatted down beside the animal she considered her pet and touched his coat. 'It's all wet, Mammy.'

'Leave him, darling. We'll carry him home in a minute.' Anna rose and moved to where Eddie was bending over his sheep. 'I don't think we can save her,' he said, 'but she's gone into labour. Tony,' Eddie looked up and called across to his son, still standing motionless a few feet away, 'help Anna take Buster back to the cottage.' His glance rested on the little girl crying beside the inert animal. 'And take Maisie away from here.'

Silently, Tony did as he was asked. He spread

out his coat on the ground and together he and Anna gently lifted Buster onto it.

'I ought to stay here and help your dad,' Anna said. She couldn't see Tony's expression in the darkness, but his voice was harsh. 'I'll come back and help him. He doesn't need you.'

Anna gasped and knew at once that Tony had read far more into the comforting hug his father had given her than had been meant.

'Tony, you don't understand—' she began.

'Don't I?' he muttered in a low voice so that his father should not hear. 'Oh don't I? Seems me mam was right all along.'

Anna shuddered and groaned. 'No,' she cried. 'It's not like that—'

'What's the matter?' Eddie's voice came out of the blackness.

'Nothing,' Tony called quickly before Anna could speak. 'I'll just help Anna and I'll come back.'

Without speaking to each other now, Anna and Tony carried Buster back to the cottage where they laid him on the hearth in front of the dying embers of the fire. Maisie knelt beside him. Now they could see that his black and white coat was matted with blood. The animal lay still, whimpering occasionally, his dark eyes wide and full of suffering.

'He's not going to die, is he, Mammy?' Maisie sobbed.

'Darling, I don't know.' Anna always tried to be honest with her child, even if the truth was painful.

Maisie sobbed louder. 'Can't we take him to the doctor?'

As if against his will, Tony's arm crept around

177

the child's shoulders. 'We'll take him to the vet in the morning.' His glance at Anna was resentful, but he still kept his tone gentle towards the little girl. 'Dad'll take him.'

Suddenly Tony got up. 'I'll go back to him.' He left the cottage, slamming the door behind him. Anna winced but Maisie, unaware of the undercurrent of emotion between her mother and Tony, continued to stroke the dog's head. 'Don't die, Buster. Oh please don't die.'

A while later Anna heard the distant sound of a single shot. Shortly afterwards, the outer door to the kitchen opened and Eddie and Tony came in.

'The ewe's dead. I had to put her out of her misery. They'd nearly torn her throat out. There was no way even the vet could have saved her,' Eddie said as he came to where Buster was lying. 'How is he?'

Anna shook her head. 'He's still alive but covered in blood.'

'Right,' Eddie said, taking charge. 'Let's see to your hand first, love.'

He rummaged in the cupboard and produced bandages and a bottle of Dettol. As he bent over her hand bathing it and applying the bandage, Anna was acutely aware of Tony's morose expression as he watched his father's tender ministrations.

'You go home, Tony, lad. Thanks for your help, but—'

'No, Dad,' the young man said quickly. His glance rested upon Anna and his eyes narrowed. 'I'll wait for you.'

*   *   *

The following morning, Eddie arranged for the vet to visit Anna's cottage. He stood by whilst the man examined the dog. 'He'll live,' the vet pronounced. 'He's been badly mauled, but with tender care he'll be fine.'

He stood up and looked about him, noticing the bundles of belongings piled high on the pram at the side of the room. 'Going somewhere, were you?'

'We—we were leaving today.'

'Well, if you were planning on taking the dog there's no way he's walking any distance for quite a while.'

When the vet had left, Maisie looked up at her mother. 'Are we staying, Mammy?'

Anna sighed. 'It looks like it, Maisie,' she said flatly.

Despite the terrible events of the previous night, Eddie could not stop his smile stretching from ear to ear.

CHAPTER TWENTY-ONE

'You've found another excuse to stay a bit longer then?'

Later that afternoon Tony stood in the centre of her kitchen, eyeing Anna belligerently.

She sighed, glancing down to where Maisie was sitting on the hearth beside Buster, lying in his basket. The little girl had not left the dog's side all day. Anna opened the front door and motioned to Tony to follow her. Once outside she said, 'Look, what you saw last night meant nothing. It's what anyone might have done in the circumstances. I'm sorry you saw it—'

'I bet you are.' The boy was disbelieving.

'It meant nothing,' she insisted. 'I'd have run to you if you'd held out your arms to me at that moment.'

'You're a bit old for me,' Tony said nastily and Anna closed her eyes, saddened to think that their friendship was at an end. Wiped out in an instant by an innocent hug of comfort between two friends.

'We're friends,' she tried again to explain. 'Your father's been very good to me.'

'Why?' Tony snapped. 'Just why did he bring you here in the first place? I can still remember how upset me mam was when he brought you home. I didn't understand it all at the time.' He paused and added pointedly. 'Now I do. She always thought there was summat more to it than he said. She even thought Maisie was mebbe his. Now—I think she was right.'

'I swear to you, on Maisie's life if you like,' Anna retorted angrily, 'that she is *not* Eddie's daughter.'

'Then whose is she? Tell me that.'

Anna's face blanched. She shook her head. 'No,' she whispered. 'I—can't tell you that.'

Tony's mouth twisted. 'You mean,' he said unkindly, 'you don't know.'

Before she had realized what she was doing, Anna's hand flew up and she smacked Tony's left cheek. 'How dare you say such a thing to me? If you only knew the truth—'

The boy had not even flinched or moved. 'Then tell me,' he persisted.

'No.' Anna stepped back as if even the thought of having to drag up the memories was abhorrent.

'It has nothing to do with you. Or'—she added with a last vestige of spirit—'or with your father.'

Tony shrugged. 'Well, if you won't tell me, you can hardly expect me to believe you, can you?'

As he began to walk away, she cried after him, 'Why can't you just trust me?'

He paused and glanced back. 'Why can't *you* trust *me* enough to tell me the truth?' he countered. 'I know I'm only fourteen, but I'm not a child any longer. I'd understand, whatever it is. Unless,' he added pointedly, 'it's because you've something to hide. Something that you're really ashamed of.'

When she did not answer, he turned and walked away, leaving Anna staring after him. *If only you knew*, she thought, *how close to the truth you are.*

*   *   *

Of course, there was no way that Anna could leave now, even though after Tony's change towards them she would dearly have loved to go. But she could not leave Buster behind and it was impossible for him to travel in his weakened state.

Mid-morning she heard someone calling outside the cottage and opened the door to find Pat Jessop with her hand raised ready to knock.

The nurse beamed at her. 'Oh, you're still here. I was so afraid you might have set off early. I didn't want to miss saying goodbye, even though I do wish you weren't going.'

Anna sighed and gestured for Pat to step inside. 'We're not,' she said and quickly explained all the night's events that now kept them here.

'I really don't see why you have to go at all,' Pat

181

said, lifting Maisie onto her lap and cuddling her. 'You're tired, my little love, aren't you?' Maisie leant against the comforting bosom of the district nurse, sucking her thumb. 'Why don't you go upstairs and have a little nap, eh?'

Maisie took out her thumb and looked up at Pat. In a serious, adult voice she said, 'I can't leave Buster. He needs me.'

'Of course he does, but your mammy's here and so am I just now. Nurses have to rest and look after themselves too, you know, else they can't care for their patients, can they?'

Maisie regarded Pat solemnly and then slid from her knee. 'All right, but you promise to look after him?'

'I promise and if I have to leave before you wake up, your mammy will stay with him until you do.'

They listened whilst the child climbed the ladder and then Pat leant across the table towards Anna. 'There's something you're not telling me that's upsetting you.'

Anna smiled wanly. 'You're too sharp by half, Nurse Jessop.'

'It's me job, ducky,' the nurse grinned. 'Besides, I'm a nosy owd beezum. Everyone in the village ses so.'

Yes, Anna wanted to say, *but they all know too that their secrets are safe with you.* She sighed. 'It's Tony,' she began and found herself confiding in the friendly woman. 'He's begun to believe his mother's vicious lies. He can't understand why I can't talk about the—the past. I just can't. Not to anyone.'

Pat touched her hand. 'Not even to me?' she asked softly.

Anna pressed her lips together and tears welled as she shook her head. 'No, not even to you,' she said huskily. 'But if I—ever did—you'd be the first. Even before Eddie.'

Pat nodded. 'Well, you know I'm always ready to listen if you ever decide you do want to unburden yourself. And I use that word purposely, 'cos it is a burden you're carrying. I can see that. A very heavy burden. And you know I'd never tell a soul—'

Now Anna smiled. 'I know.'

Pat stood up. 'I'll have to be on my way, but I'll take a look at Buster first.' She wagged her forefinger at Anna playfully. 'Just so long as you remember to tell Maisie I did so.'

A few moments later the nurse said, 'He's doing fine.' She stood up again. 'I wouldn't have wished for any of this to happen, but I have to say I'm glad you're not going.'

Anna's eyes clouded. 'We—we'll have to go this summer. Maisie will have to start school and—and they'll start asking to see her birth certificate and—'

'Listen, ducky. The headmistress of the village school is a friend of mine. And there's only her and her assistant teacher. Why don't you let me have a word with her?'

Anna opened her mouth to protest but Pat hurried on. 'No one else will ever hear about Maisie's birth certificate not having her father's name on it. Only she and her assistant need to know and I suppose the Education Offices at Lincoln—'

'Lincoln?' Anna's head shot up and her eyes widened.

Pat stared at her, her mind working quickly.

Anna, realizing she might have given away far more than she intended, floundered. 'What I mean is, why does anyone have to know anywhere else but at the school?'

'That's where the County Offices are. They're a sort of headquarters, if you like, for all the schools. But,' she hurried on, trying to reassure Anna, 'to them you're just a name on a piece of paper. But there'll be plenty of other bits of paper with only the mother's name on, believe you me.'

Anna still looked doubtful.

'It'll be the same in every county. It'd be the same wherever you went,' Pat said and was immediately sorry to see the defeated, haunted look in Anna's eyes that had been there when she had first met her return; a look that had been banished during her years of safety in the little white cottage.

Now the fear was back.

*   *   *

'So you're going to stay?'

Anna couldn't fail to hear the eagerness in Eddie's tone. She sighed and said dully, 'It seems there's nowhere any better.'

He put his head on one side. 'Is that a compliment? 'Cos it doesn't quite sound like one.'

Anna smiled apologetically and repeated what Pat had told her. 'So it seems it'll be the same wherever I go. But I just felt I wanted to be further away.'

'From where?' Eddie asked very gently, but Anna would not allow herself to be caught off guard. 'You mentioned Lincoln once. Is that where

184

you lived?'

'Just further away from this area, that's all,' Anna answered evasively.

They were silent for a moment before Eddie said, 'But you think now that it might be all right to stay here?'

'Well, for a while anyway. Pat's going to talk to her friend at the school, so maybe—' She sighed. 'Oh I don't know. Now there's Tony—'

'What do you mean?'

'He—he read the wrong meaning into you comforting me the night the dogs attacked the sheep and—and poor Buster. When I—I ran to you and you—you hugged me.'

'Ah,' Eddie breathed. 'So that's what's up with him. I'll have a word. You leave it with me. I'll put him straight.'

*   *   *

Anna never learned what Eddie said to Tony—if indeed he said anything. Over the following weeks and months, the boy did not visit the cottage, and if he came to the sheep, he skirted their home and was brusque with Maisie when she ran to him, lifting up her arms to be swung round.

'Tony won't play with me any more,' she told her mother tearfully. 'Is he cross with me?'

Anna shook her head. 'No, darling. It's me he's cross with. Not you.'

'Then why won't he play with me? That's not fair.'

'No, it isn't, but then I'm afraid a lot of things aren't fair.'

It isn't fair, Anna thought resentfully, *that I have*

to hide myself and my daughter in the back of beyond just because . . .

Her mind shied away from the bitter memories. She forced a smile onto her face. 'Don't cry, Maisie. I know, let's go and play hide-and-seek in the woods.'

The child pouted and shook her head. 'You don't do it properly. Tony plays hide-and-seek better than you do.'

Anna sighed. 'Oh well, in that case you'd better come and help me round up the sheep. And bring Buster. He's well enough now to be getting back to work. I think he's malingering.'

Maisie, always intrigued by big words, said, 'What's that mean?'

'Pretending he's still poorly when he's not.'

Diverted from her distress over Tony, Maisie fetched the dog from the kitchen. 'Come on, boy,' Anna heard her daughter say sternly to the dog. 'No more mal'gring.'

Anna smiled.

CHAPTER TWENTY-TWO

The summer passed uneventfully and it was time for Maisie to start school.

'I know she's not five until next February,' Pat said, 'but Miss Drury says she can take her at the start of the autumn term this September, if you like. I told her she's a bright little thing and—' Pat stopped, unwilling to say that she had also indicated to the head teacher that the child needed to begin to mix with other children of her own age.

'She's been well brought up,' the nurse had confided in the teacher. 'She's a credit to her mother, but she's been forced to live the life of a recluse.'

'Why?' the thin, grey-haired woman, who had devoted her life to the education of other people's children, had asked.

Pat had sighed. 'That's all part of the great secret—whatever that is. I can only guess because Anna won't trust anyone enough to divulge anything about herself or her past.' She shrugged her plump shoulders. 'That's her privilege, of course, and I respect it, but it can't be good for the child, can it?'

Edna Drury shook her head. 'No, it can't.' She pondered a moment and then said, 'Well, I can take the child in September if the mother agrees.'

Pat beamed. 'I'll make sure she does.' Now, to Anna, she finished the sentence she had begun, 'I told her she's a bright little thing and Miss Drury respects your desire for privacy. Betty Cussons will be Maisie's teacher, by the way.'

'Is she nice?'

'Lovely. She's only young and the little ones all adore her.'

So Maisie started at the village school at the beginning of September. For the first few weeks Anna met Maisie in the lane just outside the village and listened to her chatter about her day. They always walked the long way round the wood, alongside the brook and up the track to the cottage to avoid going near the farm.

'Why don't you come through the yard and up the hill?' Eddie asked Anna. 'It's much shorter and the little lass must be tired after all day at school.'

'No,' Anna replied shortly. 'I don't want her to think she can come that way. She might be tempted to try to see your wife again.' She forbore to say that Tony's offhandedness was still causing heartache to the child—to them both, if she was truthful.

But it wasn't many weeks later that Maisie said, 'I can walk home on me own, Mammy. I can walk with Geoffrey Johnson. He lives just down the lane from Mr Eddie's farm.' She leant forward as if imparting a confidence. 'He hasn't got a dad either. His dad was killed in the war. That's what Geoffrey said.' There was a loaded pause whilst Anna held her breath. She knew, even before the child opened her mouth again, what was coming. 'Was my daddy killed in the war?'

Her heart was beating rapidly, but Anna replied carefully, 'No. You haven't got a daddy.'

'Not at all? You mean, I've never had a daddy?'

Anna avoided her small daughter's trusting gaze and shook her head. 'No. There's only ever been just you and me.'

The child looked crestfallen and said in a wistful voice, 'Meg's got a daddy. He made her a swing in their garden. She said she'll let me have a go on it if I'll be her friend. She ses I can go to her house for tea. Can I go, Mam?'

'We'll see,' Anna said, but silently determined that she would have to think up an excuse. She didn't want Maisie visiting people's houses in the village. Questions might be asked. 'Now come along, we must fetch the water from the stream. It's bath night.'

Maisie jumped up and down and clapped her hands. She loved bath night on a Friday when her mother put the tin bath in front of the fire and filled it with hot water and then knelt beside it to soap Maisie's sturdy little body and wash her bright copper curls. Afterwards, dressed in a clean nightgown, she would cuddle up with her mother in the big, old armchair and Anna would tell her stories.

Her mother needed no book to read from. Anna had enough imagination to weave a magical world for the child.

'Tell me "Mr Mumble's Gold Walking Stick",' Maisie would plead and Anna would begin, making the story different each time. 'That's not right,' the child would say laughing.

'Isn't it?' Anna would pretend innocence.

'No, last time he lost it on the beach and the sea came and washed it away, but a mermaid brought it back.'

'Oh yes, well, this is a different time. This time he lost it in a snowstorm and . . .' And off Anna's imagination would lead them into another adventure.

*   *   *

It was just before Maisie's fifth birthday, when they were already busy with the lambing that Anna rose early to see the red sky of an ominous dawn. The sight unsettled her. She believed in the country sayings and feared the onset of stormy weather. But for Anna there was more to it than that. She tried to quell the memories, tried to forget her own superstition that it was not only troubled weather that such a sky foretold but something more.

She shook herself and told herself she was being

silly and fanciful.

'I can't spare the time to take you to school, so you're to walk on your own, but you come straight home,' Anna told Maisie. 'No dawdling and no going to anyone's house. You hear me?'

To Anna's relief the burgeoning friendship between Maisie and Meg had withered and died. As little girls do, they had fallen out the very next day after Maisie's conversation with her mother, but Anna was still not convinced that Maisie would be able to resist another invitation.

'And you're to come round by the wood. You're not to go through Mr Eddie's yard.'

For a brief moment, Maisie eyed her mother and then said meekly, 'Yes, Mam.'

She skipped away towards the brook, the little satchel carrying her lunch swinging from her shoulder. But if Anna had known what was already going through the child's scheming mind she would have felt even more agitated.

Later that morning, Eddie climbed down from his tractor, his face solemn. 'I don't suppose you've heard . . . ?' he began and Anna's heart seemed to leap in her chest and then began to thud painfully.

She'd known by the sky that morning that something awful was going to happen.

'What?' Her face was white, her voice a strangled whisper.

'The King's died—poor chap—in his sleep.'

Anna felt a rush of relief flood through her. She almost said aloud, 'Is that all?' but bit the words back.

'He was a good man,' Eddie was saying solemnly. 'And the poor lass that's to follow him is so young.' He shook his head. 'So very young for

190

such an awesome task.'

Now Anna could not prevent the words spilling out. 'But she's got a husband at her side to help her. She's not alone. Not like—' She bit her lip and dropped her gaze. Guilt flooded through her that she could have been so caught up in her own fears that she had not spared a sympathetic thought for the poor man and his family. She turned away, uncomfortably aware that Eddie was staring at her, shocked and disappointed.

Her words were not only lacking in compassion for the bereaved family, but were insulting to Eddie, who had done everything he could to help her.

And that, Anna thought with shame, was how she repaid him.

*   *   *

Maisie obeyed her mother's instruction for a week. Each morning she walked down the track, turned to the right and walked towards the lane with the stream on her left and the woodland on her right. Turning to the right again, she passed the wood and came to the gate leading into the yard of Cackle Hill Farm. And each evening she returned the same way. It was a long way for the little girl. She had already walked more than twice the distance it would have been if she had taken the short cut through the farmyard.

As Maisie reached the farm gate late in the afternoon of her birthday on her return from school, it was raining hard. Her footsteps slowed and she lingered in the lane near the gate. She could hear clanking sounds from inside the cowshed and wondered if Mr Eddie was in there. She glanced up the hill. Her mother couldn't see her. The cold, wet winter's afternoon was already growing dark as she glanced at the back door of the farmhouse, imagining the warm kitchen and the smell of freshly baked bread and pies and those delicious scones with jam and cream.

It was really Mrs Bertha she wanted to see, but maybe if she pretended to see Mr Eddie in the cowshed first . . .

The little girl pushed open the gate and marched boldly into the yard.

'Mr Eddie, are you in here?' she shouted, knocking on the lower part of the door into the shed. The upper part was open and fastened back to the wall, but the lower part was shut. The noise from inside stopped and she heard footsteps. Then Eddie's head peered over the half door.

'Well, well, and what are you doing here, Maisie?' His welcoming smile faded as he remembered the reason Maisie had been sent to fetch him last time. 'Has your mam sent you to fetch me? Is something wrong?'

Her curls danced as she shook her head. 'No, she doesn't know I'm here.' She pulled a face and then smiled impishly. 'I'll be in trouble if she finds out.'

Eddie chuckled. 'Ah well, I'll not tell her, eh?'

'Is Mrs Bertha at home?'

Now Eddie could not prevent the surprise from showing on his face. 'Why, yes. She is.'

'Can I see her?'

Eddie took off his cap and ran his hand through his thinning hair. 'I don't rightly know, love. I mean . . .' He faltered, not liking to intimate that the

192

older woman might not want to see the little girl against whom she still held such resentment.

'I'm all wet,' Maisie said plaintively.

'I know, but . . .' He sighed and muttered. 'I suppose it can't do any harm. Come on then, let's go and see if she's got the kettle on.'

As they walked across the yard, Maisie put her tiny hand into Eddie's large one and skipped along at his side. And that was how Bertha saw them from her scullery window.

*   *   *

'So you've come to see me again, 'ave ya?' Bertha said as the child perched herself on the stool near the table. 'After my scones, I bet.' And she ruffled the child's curls affectionately.

Eddie stared in amazement. He couldn't believe what was happening before his eyes. Bertha was actually being civil to the child. More than civil, she was being nice to her. Very nice.

Bertha's tone sharpened. 'Well, Eddie Appleyard, ain't you got work to do?'

'Yes, but—' Eddie glanced helplessly from one to the other, not knowing what to make of it. He turned and left the house, shaking his head in bewilderment. He knew his wife was a funny mixture, but this beat all.

As he crossed the yard, he passed Tony returning from the school bus. Seeing the puzzled look on his father's face, the boy said, 'Summat up, Dad?'

Still mesmerized by what he had just witnessed, Eddie shook his head. 'No, lad. At least—I don't think so.' He did not stop to enlighten his son any further and carried on walking towards the cowshed. Tony watched him go, then shrugged and went into the house.

The moment he stepped into the kitchen, he saw the reason for his father's bafflement. Tony stood in the doorway and stared. There was Maisie sitting at the table, munching a scone and chattering to his mother as if they were bosom pals.

'It's my birthday today, y'know,' she was telling Bertha. 'I'm five.'

Bertha looked up and smiled at Tony. 'We've got a visitor,' she said. 'But I don't think I need to introduce you, do I?' There was a hint of sarcasm in her tone that was lost on the little girl, but not on Bertha's son.

Tony's face coloured as he muttered, 'What's she doing here?'

'Just visiting a neighbour, aren't you, lovey?'

Maisie nodded happily, completely unaware of the undercurrent of tension in the room. 'Why don't you come and play with me any more?' she asked Tony, her brown eyes staring candidly at him.

Tony scowled and, embarrassed, glanced at his mother. But she answered Maisie. 'Tony's getting a big boy now. He's at the grammar school in the town. He has ever such a lot of homework and then, of course, he has to help his dad.'

'Oh.' The child looked crestfallen.

'But you can come and visit me whenever you like.'

'You'd best go home now, Maisie,' Tony butted in. 'Your mam'll be wondering where you've got to. She'll be worried.'

Maisie nodded and jumped down from the stool.

' 'Bye, 'bye, Mrs Bertha and thank you for the scone.'

As the child let herself out of the back door, Tony turned on his mother. 'Mam, what are you up to?'

Bertha adopted her most innocent expression. 'Whatever do you mean, Tony? What should I be up to?'

'I don't know,' he said slowly, 'but it's summat.'

'Don't talk nonsense,' Bertha said, but as she turned her back on her son she was smiling to herself.

*   *   *

'I think it's time you left,' Tony said bluntly. He found Anna busy trying to cope with a ewe and a difficult birth. It was obvious she had not noticed that Maisie had been later home than usual or that she had appeared from the direction of the farm instead of round by the wood.

Her mind still occupied with the sheep, Anna said, 'Fetch your father, Tony. I think he might need the vet to this ewe. The lamb's all right, but the mother—'

'Yes, yes, I'll get him, but did you hear what I said?'

Anna looked at him and blinked, dragging his words to the forefront of her mind. 'Leave? Now? Why?'

'Maisie was down at the farm, sitting in me mam's kitchen as large as life and twice as cheeky.'

'The wilful little—'

'Please, don't punish her. I'm only telling tales— I don't reckon to—because it's for your own good.

195

I—I—' He hesitated, not wanting to sound disloyal to his mother, yet he had this awful feeling that something was not right. 'Me mam's being nice to her and I don't know why. It's—it's not natural. Not when you know what she thinks of *you*.' His brow puckered and he muttered, 'I can't understand it. I'd've thought she'd be horrible to Maisie an' all.'

'Mm.' Anna was thoughtful too. 'So would I. Or at the very least, make it so obvious she wasn't welcome that she didn't visit again.' She eyed Tony speculatively. He was fifteen now and, in a lot of ways, mature for his age.

'Is there anything else you're not telling me?' she asked bluntly.

Tony shook his head. 'Not really. But—' Again he hesitated and Anna probed gently. 'But what, Tony? Tell me. Please.'

The words tumbled over each other in a rush. 'If she—wants to get at you, the easiest way is through Maisie, isn't it?' He ran his hand through his hair, with an action so like his father's that Anna almost smiled—would have done if their conversation had not been so serious. 'Oh, I shouldn't be saying this,' he anguished. 'Not about me own mam. She wouldn't hurt Maisie. I know she wouldn't do that but—but . . . oh I don't know what to think.'

'It's all right,' Anna said huskily. 'Don't worry. I won't be angry with Maisie, but I must impress upon her that she is not to visit the farm. And come the better weather, this year we really *will* go.'

But at the end of the month, Eddie slipped on an icy patch in the yard and broke his leg and even Tony was now forced to ask Anna to stay a while longer.

196

'He can't work for six weeks and I'd have to stay off school.' He pulled a face. 'And me mam doesn't want that. She'll see to the dairy work if you'd go down and milk the cows—'

'You mean she's agreed for me to do that?'

Unsmiling, Tony nodded and there was bitter sarcasm to his tone. 'Oh yes. Even me mam'll swallow her pride if it gets her out of doing the milking.'

*   *   *

The weeks passed. Eddie's leg mended and then it was almost haymaking, followed by harvest and then another winter was upon them. Although the passage of time did not diminish her fear, Anna began to feel secure in her little cottage haven near the woods and gradually her need to move on lessened. She knew Eddie wanted her to stay. Of Tony's feelings, she was less certain. Sometimes he would be as friendly and caring as ever. But at others he ignored their presence in the cottage for days. He was brusque with Maisie and offhand with Anna. No doubt, Anna thought grimly, his mother had been pouring vicious lies into his young ears and turning him against them. Anna couldn't blame the lad: it was natural that he would believe his mother. She no longer cared what Bertha thought about her. She rarely saw her and, for the most part, she managed to ignore the woman's malevolent presence over the hill.

But, unbeknown to her mother and even to Eddie and Tony, Maisie's visits to see Bertha continued. Not often, but now and again when there was no one about to see, the growing child

197

would skip into the yard and knock on the back door of the farmhouse.

And Bertha would smile to herself and welcome the child into her home, content to bide her time. Bitter though Bertha was, she was a patient woman.

CHAPTER TWENTY-THREE

On the last day of January 1953, Eddie said, 'I didn't like the look of the sky this morning, lass. Did you see it? A real shepherd's warning. I reckon we're in for some stormy weather.'

Anna glanced skywards and pulled a wry face. 'The wind was rattling round the cottage last night and through the trees in the wood. You should have heard it.' She smiled. 'I could almost imagine it was the sea.'

Though she could not have known it, Anna's words were prophetic.

The wind howled all day. By nightfall it had risen to gale force. Anna sat by the fire in the white cottage, a half-finished peg rug on her knee. She worked calmly at it, pulling the pieces of rag through the hessian, trying to blot out the sound of the raging storm outside. Maisie sat close to her, her brown eyes wide with fear.

'Time you went up to bed,' Anna said, but her daughter only drew closer.

'Can't we sleep down here tonight, Mam? I don't like the wind. It sounds as if it's trying to blow the thatch off the roof.'

'We're safe enough here, darling,' Anna

murmured and a small, wistful smile played around her mouth. How could she explain to her young daughter that the elements had never held any fears for her; it was only at times like these, when other people shuddered and shut their doors against the weather, that she felt safer than at any other time.

No one would venture to seek her out in this kind of weather. Anna sighed. Perhaps it was time she stopped being quite so fearful. Six years had passed and, though she had had one or two frightening moments, they had all been in her imagination. She had not been found. No one had come looking for her. Since the early days after her arrival no one had challenged her or asked an awkward question. Eddie no longer tried to probe gently. And Tony, now a tall, thin, sixteen-year-old, due to sit his O level examinations this coming summer, rarely made reference to her past life. Even Pat Jessop, still a good friend, had stopped asking. The village gossip had died down, although, on the rare occasions that Anna ventured into the village, she was still aware of the curious glances.

Maisie broke into her thoughts. 'Buster doesn't like this weather either.'

The dog, now fully grown and already a good sheepdog, huddled against their feet, whining every so often to remind them that he was there and that he needed a friendly stroke of reassurance. As Anna was bending forward to pat his head, a loud banging sounded at the back door, making Anna and Maisie jump and Buster leap to his feet and begin barking.

In an instant all Anna's resolution fled and her fear was back as strongly as ever. Maisie ran to the window and peered out into the wild, black night. Even she, young as she was, knew that her mother did not like the door opened until they knew who was standing on the other side.

'It's Mr Eddie.'

'You're—you're sure?' Anna persisted.

Maisie nodded vigorously. 'Let him in, Mam.'

Still a little reluctant, Anna shot back the bolt and opened the door, letting the storm into the warm kitchen. Eddie almost tumbled into the room and Anna had to fight the wind to shut the door. He leant against the table, bending over it to regain his breath.

'It's the sea, lass.'

'What do you mean?'

'It's breached the sea wall at Mablethorpe and other places down the coast. People's homes are flooded. There'll be a lot of folk needing help.'

'How do you know?'

'Pat told me.'

'Pat? When have you seen Pat?'

For a moment, Eddie looked shamefaced. 'I was in the village and I just called to see if she needed any help. Don't like to think of her struggling about on her bike in this weather. You know, if there was a babby bein' born somewhere—'

'I know,' Anna said softly.

'She'd got a call to go into Ludthorpe and help set up a rescue centre in the town hall.'

'You're taking her there?'

Eddie shook his head. 'No, someone's picking her up.'

Maisie was tugging at Eddie's sleeve. 'How far will the sea come? Will—will it get here?'

Despite the gravity of the news, Eddie smiled. 'I

hope not, love,' he said. 'If it did, then—'

Though the young child did not understand, Anna realized what Eddie meant. If the sea reached Cackle Hill Farm, then half the county would be under water. She put her arm round her daughter's shoulders and pulled her close. 'There's a hill or two between us and the sea. It won't reach us.'

Maisie's lip trembled. 'Are you sure?'

'Sorry, love.' Eddie put his hand on the little girl's shoulder. 'I should have realized you wouldn't understand. No, the sea won't get here. But there is something you can do'—his gaze found Anna's face—'that we can all do to help them poor folks whose homes have been invaded by the water.'

'What?' the child asked whilst Anna's heart stood still. Before Eddie put his suggestion into words, she knew what he was going to say and her fear was back one hundredfold.

Oblivious to her feelings, Eddie said, 'There'll be hundreds being evacuated. They'll need somewhere to stay. I was wondering—?'

'What about the farmhouse?' Anna's tone was sharper than she intended. 'You've plenty of room there.'

Eddie's mouth tightened. 'Bertha won't have strangers in the house—'

Anna opened her mouth to retort that, for once, she understood how his wife felt and that she too didn't want strangers in her home. Then she saw the look of disgust on Eddie's face as he spoke of Bertha. Anna closed her mouth, the words unspoken as shame swept through her.

She remembered the night he had found her, soaked to the skin, exhausted and homeless. He had brought her to his own home, given her shelter, fed and clothed her—all against the wishes of his wife. He had done all this for her and now he was asking for that same compassion from her.

Anna touched his arm. 'What do you want us to do?'

Eddie smiled. 'I knew you'd do it, lass,' he said, hoarsely. 'I knew—that whatever it cost you—you wouldn't turn your back on those poor folks.'

Anna glanced away, unable to meet his trusting gaze, feeling very guilty that she had almost allowed herself to be every bit as selfish as Bertha.

Eddie, mercifully unaware of her inner turmoil, said, 'Tony's coming with me. We're taking the tractor and trailer. We should be able to get through the water to rescue folks.'

'Can I come?' Maisie piped up. 'I want to go with Tony.'

Eddie rested his hand briefly on the child's curls. 'No, you stay and help your mammy get ready for some visitors.' He turned back to Anna. 'They'll be cold and hungry. Can you make some soup or a stew?' Anna nodded as he went on, 'And you'll need blankets. I'll see if I can get some more. I must go—'

'Eddie'—Anna grasped his arm briefly—'be—be careful.'

With a brief smile and a swift nod of the head, he was gone out into the wild night.

*   *   *

In the early hours of the morning, Anna, who had not been to bed at all, though she had at last persuaded Maisie to go, heard the sound of Eddie's tractor chugging along the track around the wood and towards her cottage. As she opened the door, the blustery wind caught her skirt and tore at her hair. On the back of the trailer, she could see Tony with a woman and two children. One was only a baby, the other a little boy about Maisie's age. As the vehicle drew to a halt, Anna reached up with welcoming hands to help down the refugees.

'Oh, you're soaked through. Come in, come in. There's a good fire and hot food.'

The little boy held out his arms to be helped down, but the woman sat still on the trailer, clutching her crying infant to her but staring straight ahead as if she was unaware of Anna's presence.

Eddie jumped down from the tractor and came to stand beside Anna.

'Poor thing,' he murmured. 'She's in shock, I reckon. Her husband's missing.'

'How terrible,' Anna said and then raised her voice, 'Come along, love. Let's get you and the little one inside.'

At last, with Tony's urging, the woman allowed him to take the baby from her and hand it gently down to Anna. Then, woodenly, the woman climbed down from the trailer and moved into the cottage. But it was as if she was unaware of anything around her. She didn't seem to be aware of her own discomfort or even to notice the crying of her baby.

Anna sat the forlorn little family before her fire, wrapped them in blankets and ladled out hot soup, thick with pieces of meat and sliced vegetables.

'I call this "full-up soup",' Anna said, trying to raise a smile from the little boy. But he was white-faced and silent, the shock and terror showing in his eyes.

Maisie appeared in the doorway, a shawl over her nightdress, her bare feet sticking out below the uneven hem. She rubbed sleep from her eyes and stared at the strangers sitting in their kitchen. Then she sidled across the room to stand beside Tony, but stared wordlessly at the young boy, who was now eating the soup hungrily.

'We're going back—' Eddie said, making for the door.

'Not before you've had a warm and something hot to eat,' Anna said firmly. 'Come on, sit down at the table. You too, Tony.'

'But—'

'No "buts". You can't help folks if you're exhausted yourselves.'

'By heck.' Tony grinned, sitting down. 'She's getting to be a right bossy boots.'

Despite the tragedy that was unfolding all the way down the east coast of Britain, Eddie managed a brief smile. 'Aye, but she's right, lad.'

They tucked into a large bowl of soup and crusty fresh bread, but within minutes they were both rising and leaving the cottage. 'We'll have to go back, lass.'

Anna nodded. 'Take care then. Both of you.'

When they had gone, it was strangely quiet in the cottage. Only the wind, still howling outside, disturbed the silence.

'What's your name, love?' Anna asked the woman, who had scarcely touched the soup. She sat clutching the blanket around her and rocking to and fro. Then she began a strange keening, a kind of dry-eyed crying.

'Don't, Mam.' The young boy stood up and put his arm about his mother. 'Dad'll be all right. The mester said he'd go back and look for him.'

But his mother just shook her head in a hopeless gesture. 'He's gone. I know he's gone.'

The boy glanced helplessly at Anna, who was nursing the baby and trying to spoon some warm milk into the little mouth, all the while wishing that Pat Jessop would walk through the door and take charge.

'What's your name?' Now Anna addressed the boy, who seemed to be recovering from their ordeal more quickly than his mother.

'Peter Warren.'

'And your mam's?'

'Clare. And the babby's called Susie.'

Without warning, the woman suddenly stood up, threw off the blanket from around her shoulders and stumbled towards the door. 'If Bill's gone, I don't want to live—'

Before Anna could reach her, Clare pulled open the door and rushed out into the wild early morning. 'I don't want to live any more,' she wailed, her words caught and tossed callously away by the gale.

'Here, hold the baby, Peter,' Anna said. 'Don't worry. I'll get her back. Stay here.'

Snatching her coat from the peg behind the door and pulling it on, Anna hurried out into the storm leaving the two children and the baby. The woman was stumbling down the slope towards the stream, her arms stretched wide, her lament carried on the wind. A loud, hopeless wailing that chilled Anna's heart.

If she reaches the water, Anna thought, *I'll lose*

her.

The stream was a rushing torrent from recent rain and a smattering of snow. The woman could be swept away. She was teetering on the bank when Anna grabbed her around the waist and unceremoniously pulled her to the ground. They rolled over and over, locked together in a desperate struggle, the one determined to end her misery, the other stubbornly refusing to let her throw her life away. They rolled over the edge of the bank and slithered into the icy torrent. The breath was knocked from Anna's body, the water gurgled in her ears, but she held on fast, her arms around the woman's waist. Suddenly Clare stopped struggling and went limp in Anna's grasp. Together, they were carried a few yards, bumping along stones and rocks on the bed of the stream.

Then Anna surfaced, gulping in air. Somehow she gained a foothold and dragged herself to the edge, lugging the dead weight of the woman with her. Panting, she lay on the sloping bank, half in, half out of the water. And still Anna held on to her burden. Gasping, she struggled to heave herself up, but all the time she refused to let go, not even for a second, in case Clare was feigning weakness in an effort to break free when she felt Anna's hold relax. But Anna was determined not to let go.

Just as she had once been saved, now she vowed to haul this distraught and desperate woman back from the brink.

At last they lay side by side on the grass beside the stream. For a moment Anna knelt beside the prone form, bending double to regain her breath. The woman was still and silent.

'Oh no,' Anna breathed and then she screamed

and grasped Clare, shaking her. 'No! You can't die. You can't leave your bairns. Think of your children.'

And now, in that instant as she shrieked at the woman, dragging her back to life by the sheer force of her own spirit, Anna realized just what Eddie had done for her. He had saved her life—and Maisie's. And now she had the chance to save someone in return.

'I won't let you die. I won't *let* you!' But there was no spark of life. Anna felt utterly helpless. Again she shook Clare hard. Miraculously, the woman stirred and began to cough, spewing out stream water, and Anna felt tears of thankfulness.

It was several minutes before Clare was sufficiently recovered to allow Anna to half drag, half carry her across the field and back to the cottage. Maisie was watching out of the window and opened the door for them. By the look on her daughter's face, Anna knew that Maisie had witnessed the struggle near the stream.

Much later, when the boy was asleep in Maisie's bed and Clare, washed and resting in Anna's, the little girl confided, 'I didn't tell the boy, Mam. He was by the fire, holding the baby, so he didn't see. And I didn't tell him.'

Anna drew her close and buried her face in the child's copper-coloured curls. 'Oh Maisie, my precious darling,' she murmured huskily. Whilst Maisie returned her mother's hug fiercely, she had no understanding of the tumult of emotions in Anna's heart. Guilt, thankfulness and an overwhelming gratitude to Eddie Appleyard that words could never express.

A shivering Eddie and Tony sat wrapped in blankets before the fire and sipped Anna's hot soup gratefully. A restless daybreak had shown them the full extent of the disaster.

'A lot of the folks that had to be evacuated have been brought to Ludthorpe or other official rescue centres,' Eddie told her, 'but they're trying to find homes willing to take some of them in. Give them a bit more comfort, like. Poor devils.'

'There's lots of families got split up,' Tony put in. 'One poor chap couldn't find his little lad. He was—he was six.' Tony's voice broke as he glanced at Maisie and then, wordlessly, he reached out and touched her cheek. He said no more but his gesture spoke volumes.

'Is there any news of Clare's husband?' Anna asked softly.

Sadly, Eddie shook his head. Then, more briskly, he stood up and shook off the blanket. 'Well, this won't do. There's still more to be fetched to safety. To say nothing of taking feed to stranded animals.'

'You're not going back?' Anna said, before she could stop herself. 'You're out on your feet, Eddie.'

'I've got to, lass. Whilst there's folks still needing help—'

Tony began to stand up too, but Eddie put his hand on his shoulder. 'No, lad, you go home. You've done enough.'

Tony straightened up and met his father's gaze steadily. Quietly, he said, 'If you're going back, Dad, then so am I.'

Anna watched father and son standing together and marvelled at the likeness between them. Tony was so like his father in appearance; brown hair and eyes, tall and thin, but without the slight stoop that years of hard work had brought Eddie. And now the son was showing that same kindness and concern for others.

'Come on then, lad, though what your mam's going to say, I don't know.'

*　　　*　　　*

Later that night Bertha had plenty to say.

'You've done what?' she shrieked.

'Lost me tractor and trailer.'

'How on earth can you lose a tractor and trailer?'

Eddie sighed. 'It got stuck in the sand and the mud and now it's been bulldozed into the sea wall.'

'Whatever for?'

'Because they're desperate to shore up the defences and—'

'And they thought they'd use your tractor and trailer, eh?'

'No, Bertha, just listen, will you? We got stuck and they haven't time to be pulling stuff out. It's a race against time. There's an army of lorries bringing stone and slag—anything they can find to shore up the defences. And any vehicle that got stuck has ended up as part of the sea wall.'

'Just think, Dad.' Tony was laughing. 'You'll be able to walk along the sea wall and say: my tractor's somewhere under this lot.'

'You think it funny, d'ya?' For once Bertha rounded on Tony, venting her anger. 'You've not had a thought for me, 'ave ya, whilst you've been busy playing the heroes. Well, I've been worried

209

sick about you.' Her gaze rested on her son and Eddie knew that her anxiety had not included him. Now she turned to her husband. 'You'd no right to take him with you. Owt could have happened to him—'

Tony put his arm around her quivering shoulders. 'Well, it didn't. And Dad couldn't have stopped me going to help. And you'd much rather I'd've been with him, wouldn't you?'

'Yes, but—'

'Oh, Mam, don't be like this. You should have seen all those poor folks. Their homes flooded, washed away in some cases. Some of 'em had only got the clothes they stood up in.'

Bertha sniffed. 'Huh. Next thing they'll be coming round for a collection for 'em, I shouldn't wonder. Well, they'll get short shrift here now we've got a new tractor and trailer to buy.' She shrugged Tony's arm away. 'I'll get your supper. That's unless you're both off out again with the pony and trap.'

Father and son exchanged a glance. 'No,' Eddie said wearily, 'there's nothing more we can do.'

'There is one thing I'd like to do, Dad,' Tony said softly as his mother disappeared into the scullery.

Bone weary, Eddie leant back in his chair and closed his eyes. 'What's that, lad?'

'Go round all the rescue centres. See if we can find that poor woman's husband.'

Eddie opened his eyes and lifted his head. 'Clare's, you mean?'

Tony nodded. 'It's the least we can do, specially after what—' he glanced quickly towards the scullery and lowered his voice even more—'Anna

210

did.'

'Taking her in, you mean?'

'Oh no. She did more than that. Maisie told me.' Swiftly, before his mother returned, Tony explained. 'Anna saved that woman's life.'

For a moment, Eddie stared at his son and then slowly began to smile. 'Then the least we can do, son, is what you suggest.' As Bertha came back into the room, Eddie winked slyly at Tony and then raised his voice, 'D'you know, Bertha love, that was a very good idea of yours. Tomorrow we will take the pony and trap.'

His wife stared at him for a moment as if she thought he had gone completely mad. Then with a scornful snort, she banged the plates down onto the table. She turned and stormed out of the room, leaving father and son trying hard to stifle their laughter.

CHAPTER TWENTY-FOUR

The following morning, after milking and feeding all the animals, Eddie harnessed Duke into the shafts of the trap.

'We'll go and see Anna and the woman—what's her name, Tony?'

'Clare. Clare Warren and her husband's name is Bill.'

'Aye, that's right. We'll go and see them first and make sure there's nothing they want.'

'The only thing that poor woman wants is her husband back.'

Eddie's face was sober. 'Aye, aye.' He sighed.

'We'll do our best, but I don't hold out much hope. I reckon, if they'd found him, they'd have let us know.'

Tony was more optimistic. 'Oh, I don't know, Dad. They're all that busy. It's a nightmare for the authorities.'

'I suppose you're right. He might have slipped through the net and be somewhere just as desperate about his family. I wonder if that other feller found his little lad.' Eddie was suddenly still. 'He said his lad was about six, didn't he? And that little lad up yonder is about that age. You don't suppose it was him—the father, do you?'

Reluctantly, Tony shook his head. 'Too much of a coincidence, I reckon. Besides, he'd have mentioned his wife and baby, wouldn't he?'

Eddie sighed. 'Aye, I suppose so. I'm just clutching at straws, I reckon.'

Tony grinned. 'Well, just you keep clutching at 'em, Dad. Keep hoping.'

They visited the town hall in Ludthorpe and were appalled at the number of people made homeless by the disaster. Several families were frantic with worry over a missing loved one. Eddie tried to speak to the organizers about Bill Warren, but they too were now exhausted and overwhelmed.

'He's not here. That's all I can tell you, but you could try all the villages just inland from the coast. They've opened up schools and village halls to help out,' one harassed WVS lady suggested. 'But he could be anywhere. Do you know him?'

'Not exactly, but his wife's given us a good description. Tall, broad, fair hair and a little scar under his left eye from an accident when he was a kid.'

'Well, good luck. Sorry I can't be of more help.'

'You have been. You've given us more places to look for the feller. Thanks. Come on, Tony. We've a long day ahead.'

*　　　*　　　*

By milking time that evening Eddie and Tony had still not returned and, of their own accord, the cows were gathering down near the yard, their udders full and uncomfortable.

Anna, standing at the top of the rise and looking down towards the farmyard, chewed her lip worriedly. Ought she to go down to the yard and begin the milking? Two things stopped her. Bertha, of course, and the fact that Anna was uneasy around cows. In the six years she had been here, she had only helped with the milking once or twice. And even then she had scuttled into the byre and out again as quickly as she could, afraid of being kicked by a restless cow, but even more afraid of Bertha finding her. Only when Eddie had broken his leg had she felt comfortable being there.

Above the wind, she heard a distant sound and glanced to the left to see the pony turning in at the gate. She strained her eyes through the dusk of the winter's evening.

There were three figures sitting in the trap. Anna's heart leapt with hope as the three figures alighted and two—Tony and a tall, broad stranger—hurried up the path towards her. Tony spotted her and waved excitedly.

Anna felt a lump rise in her throat and tears prickle behind her eyes. 'Oh thank you, thank you,' she breathed. Then she turned and ran down the track towards the little cottage, stumbling and almost falling in her urgency. 'Clare, oh Clare, come quickly.'

The door opened before she reached it, but it was Maisie who ran out. 'Mam, Mam. She's not here. I couldn't stop her. She's gone out. Into the woods, I think—'

'No, oh no!' Anna was panic-stricken and blaming herself. She shouldn't have left Clare alone.

She caught hold of Maisie. 'Tony's coming up the track with a man and I think it's Clare's husband. Peter's daddy. Now, you stay here, darling, and tell Tony and the man to come into the woods.'

Without waiting for a response from her daughter, for Anna knew Maisie would do as she had asked, Anna ran into the wood. It was dark and cold and the wind tore through the branches overhead, making a sound like rushing water.

'This is the worst place she could have come,' Anna muttered to herself. Maybe, she thought, in her confused state poor Clare had thought the noise was the sound of the sea and she had gone towards it to search for her man.

'Clare,' she cried out. 'Clare. Come back. He's here. Bill's here.'

She was taking a chance on this being the truth, but moments later Tony and the stranger came crashing into the woods behind her. Breathlessly, Tony said. 'We found him. This is Bill. Where is she?'

'I don't know. She can't have been gone long. I only went to the top of the hill. I wasn't away more than a few minutes. Oh, I'm so sorry—'

The big man gripped her arm briefly. 'Not your fault, lass. From what this young feller tells me, you've already saved her life once. Don't blame yourself.'

Tony moved ahead shouting her name and then Bill cupped his big hands around his mouth and let out such a roar that Anna felt her ears ring.

'Clare. It's me, Bill. *Claaaare.*'

They waited a moment, listening. Bill shouted again and then they listened again.

'I heard something,' Tony said, pushing his way through the trees and undergrowth. 'I'm sure I did. This way.'

Bill and Anna followed eagerly. Bill shouted again and this time they all heard a faint cry.

'She's here,' Tony, still leading the way, shouted jubilantly, but then he stood aside as Bill rushed forward to gather his wife into his arms.

'Oh, my darling girl. I thought you were lost. I thought I'd lost all of you.'

Clare was clinging to him as if she would never let him out of her sight again. 'I thought you'd drowned. I thought you were dead. I didn't want to live. Oh, Bill, I'm sorry.'

He smoothed back her hair and between showering kisses on her face, murmured reassuring endearments. 'It's all right. I'm here now. We're all safe . . .'

Anna was standing transfixed, staring at the tender scene and feeling a mixture of thankfulness and joy for them, yet, for herself, an acute longing.

If only . . .

She felt Tony touch her arm. 'Come on,' he said softly. 'Let's leave 'em to it. They're all right now.'

'Yes,' Anna murmured. 'They're all right now.'

* * *

It wasn't until Bertha saw the reports in the local papers that she realized exactly what her husband and son had done. Eddie Appleyard was hailed as a hero for his rescue work.

* * *

Throughout the night he and his sixteen-year-old son, Tony [one of the newspapers reported], ferried people stranded by the rising water to safety. Time and again Mr Appleyard waded through icy sea water, which was sometimes up to his chest, to reach young and old and carry them out of their flooded homes. Then he drove his tractor and trailer all the way to Ludthorpe to the centre there before returning to continue the rescue. Together father and son worked tirelessly to bring people and animals to safety. It wasn't until their tractor and trailer became stranded in the sand and had to be abandoned that this courageous and unselfish pair were forced to give up and accept help themselves.

* * *

All Bertha could say was, 'And how do you think you're going to do the ploughing now?'

'I'll think of something, Bertha,' was all Eddie would say. 'I'll think of something.'

But Bertha, keeping herself to herself, had no idea what the locals thought of her husband.

'You wouldn't believe it,' a beaming Pat told Anna. 'They're falling over themselves to help. Mrs Arnold at the village shop has got a collection box on her counter for the flood victims and she ses she has to empty it twice a day. And as for Eddie, he's had the offer of three tractors and five trailers to borrow whenever he wants that I know about. And,' she added triumphantly, 'they're all talking about your brave rescue of that poor woman.'

Anna stared at her. 'How does anyone know about that?'

For a moment, Pat could have bitten her tongue off. It wasn't like her to let herself chatter so much that she was in danger of letting out secrets. But, for once, she had been so excited that Eddie's kind-heartedness had at last been recognized and then at hearing the villagers speak kindly of Anna, that she had let her tongue run away with itself. She knew very well how the news had got out. Maisie had told Tony and he had deliberately spoken of it, hoping it would cast Anna in a good light amongst the locals.

Pat wrinkled her forehead and pretended vagueness. 'Don't really know, ducky. I expect Mrs Warren is singing your praises from the rooftops. And so she should.'

'Mmm,' Anna said, eyeing the nurse suspiciously. 'Maybe.'

'Anyway,' Pat said, turning the topic of conversation, 'all's well that ends well, as they say.'

Now Anna smiled, thinking of the little family who had stayed with her and who were now happily reunited.

If only her own story could have had such a happy ending.

CHAPTER TWENTY-FIVE

'I've passed. I've passed the scholarship. I'm going to the grammar school in town. The same one Tony went to.'

Maisie danced around the table in Bertha's kitchen clapping her hands. She caught hold of Bertha and tried to make her dance too, but the woman, who had grown even larger in the last few years, flapped her hands. 'Oh go on with ya. My dancing days are over.' She sniffed and added wryly, 'If I ever had any.' Then she smiled, 'But I'm real pleased at your news, lovey. And Tony will be too.' There was a slight pause. This was the moment she had waited eleven years for. Bertha's eyes gleamed as she added, with deceptive casualness, 'To think that his sister is following in his footsteps—'

Maisie stopped, her dancing suddenly stilled. She stared at Bertha. 'What—what did you say?'

Bertha shrugged her fat shoulders. 'Surely you know you're his sister, don't you? Well, half-sister.'

As if she had been pole-axed, Maisie shook her head. 'I—I don't know what you mean? How can I be?'

'Mr Eddie's your dad, that's how.'

'But—but I haven't got a dad. Mam ses so.'

Bertha couldn't prevent her mouth twisting scathingly. 'Everyone's got a dad. Hasn't your mother even told you the facts of life yet?'

Dumbly, Maisie shook her head.

'Well, you're a big girl now and it's high time you knew. You'll be going to the big school soon and

218

you'll be laughed at if you don't know. Besides, if you learn it in the playground, you'll learn it wrong. You ought to know the truth. The whole truth. Sit down . . .' She took the girl firmly by the shoulder and pressed her onto the stool near the table. 'Let's get us a cup of tea.' Bertha's thin mouth, almost lost now between the folds of fat, smiled, and her eyes were glittering with a strange excitement. 'And one of your favourite scones. Then we'll have a little chat, eh?'

*　　　*　　　*

Maisie walked slowly up the track and over the hill, her head spinning. She forgot completely to go out of the farmyard gate and into the lane to walk the long way home, as she usually did after a visit to Mrs Bertha. This time she didn't care if her mother saw her and guessed where she had been. She didn't even care if her mother shouted at her. She would shout back. And if Anna hit her, she'd probably hit her back the way she was feeling at this minute.

Bertha had spared the young girl nothing in the end. She had begun gently enough, as if she was doing Maisie a favour. 'You know how animals are born, don't you?'

Maisie had nodded. She'd witnessed sheep and cows giving birth and had accepted it as the most natural thing in the world. 'Well, it's the same with human beings.' And then Bertha launched into an explanation of all the facts of life in the most intimate detail. By the end Maisie felt sick, but Bertha was not done yet.

'You want to be careful of men, young Maisie.'

219

She wagged her finger at the girl. 'They're only after one thing and they'll tell you all sorts to get it. Tell you they love you and that they'll marry you. But they'll never be faithful just to you. They're like animals. Like a ram amongst the ewes.'

The vivid pictures Bertha aroused in the young girl's mind made her scramble up from the table and rush outside. She had leant against the wall, breathing deeply, her eyes closed.

Inside the house Bertha cleared away the cups and saucers, smiling as she did so.

Maisie reached the cottage and entered by the back door. To her relief the kitchen was empty, so she climbed the ladder to her bedroom and lay on her bed, staring at the ceiling.

Was it really true what Mrs Bertha had told her? Was Mr Eddie really her father and Tony her half-brother? Had her mother, her pretty mother, done *that* with Mr Eddie? He was an old man in the young girl's eyes. It was disgusting. And the way that Bertha had explained it to her, it was all disgusting. Maisie groaned and turned over, burying her head in the pillow, trying to blot out the images in her mind's eye.

She couldn't ask her mother about it because Anna would then know she had been visiting Bertha and had been doing for years. And she certainly wasn't going to ask Mr Eddie. She couldn't even ask Tony. He was away at agricultural college in his final year there. He would be coming home to stay then, to work on the farm. But he wouldn't be here until the end of June or so.

Maisie sat up suddenly. There was one person she could talk to, who would understand.

Nurse Pat.

*   *   *

'Hello, ducky. This is a nice surprise. Come in.'

Pat Jessop had hardly altered in the eleven years since Maisie's birth and to the young girl she had always been Auntie Pat.

As Pat ushered her visitor into her cosy sitting room and fetched her a glass of lemonade and a chocolate biscuit, she eyed the girl worriedly. She could see at once that something was troubling Maisie.

The girl sat on the old sofa, twisting her handkerchief in her fingers, leaving her drink and biscuit untouched.

Pat sat down beside her and took the girl's agitated hands into her own. 'What is it, love? Come on, you can tell me.'

Maisie raised tearful brown eyes. 'You won't tell anyone? Not my mam? Not anyone? Promise?'

Pat's mind worked quickly. If the girl had been older she'd've guessed she was in trouble. Pregnant and scared to death. But Maisie was only eleven. It was almost impossible. Not entirely, but most unlikely. But Pat was an honest woman. Carefully she said, 'I won't tell a soul, but I might have to encourage you to tell someone else. I don't know till you do tell me. It depends what it is, but I'm trying to be truthful with you, Maisie.'

The girl nodded. Then the words came out in a rush, all jumbled up and making little sense at first. When at last Maisie fell silent, Pat swiftly pieced the sorry tale together. Her mouth was a hard line, her kind eyes unusually angry. Her wrath was not

221

directed at Maisie but at the unthinking woman who had imparted nature's most beautiful facts to a naive child in such a cruel manner. It could warp the young girl's mind for life, Pat thought, incensed by Bertha's callousness.

She sighed, knowing that she must do what she could to minimize the damage. And she must do it now.

'Now listen to me, Maisie,' Pat began in a kind but firm tone. 'Bertha Appleyard is a bitter, twisted woman.' Over the next half-hour, Pat's gentle voice eased away the girl's horror. She explained that Bertha had had an unhappy childhood because of the kind of man that her father was.

'A father is a big influence, specially on a girl and—'

Maisie raised her eyes to look steadily into Pat's. 'Auntie Pat, is Mr Eddie my father?'

'Only your mother or Mr Eddie could answer you that, but I don't believe he is. Both he and your mother always say that he found her in the marketplace in Ludthorpe just before Christmas with nowhere to go. He brought her home and gave her shelter in his little cottage. And you've lived there ever since.'

'Then—then who is my father?'

Pat took a deep breath. 'I don't know. I'm guessing that your mother wasn't married to him and that she ran away. But why she did I don't know either. Maybe one day she'll tell you. All I do know is that over the years she has tried to remain hidden away. She's terrified of being found, presumably by her family or—or your father. Several times she's talked about leaving. About getting further away.' Pat smiled gently. 'But always

222

something's happened to stop her going.'

Maisie nodded, remembering one or two of those occasions for herself.

'You mustn't believe everything that Bertha told you. There are kind men in the world. I was married to a wonderful man, but he was killed in the war. But we were happy together and—and what happens between a man and a woman who truly love each other is beautiful. Remember that, Maisie, because what I'm telling you is true. What Bertha told you is true from a—a factual point of view, but she made it sound dirty and horrible. And it isn't. Believe me, ducky, it isn't.'

*   *   *

'You evil, wicked, owd beezum.' Pat shouted and actually shook her fist in Bertha's face when the woman opened the door to Pat's banging on it. Before Bertha had time to close it again, Pat had stepped inside. 'You've bided your time all these years. Waited for an opportunity to stick the knife in, haven't you? And now you've done it.'

With troubled eyes, Pat had watched Maisie leave. She hoped she had done enough to minimize the damage to the young girl, but she doubted that Maisie would ever quite forget Bertha's tales. Pat's anger had boiled over and, before she knew what she was doing, the district nurse was pedalling furiously towards Cackle Hill Farm.

'I don't know what you're talking about and you can get out of my kitchen, Pat Jessop.' Bertha glowered at her. 'I don't want your sort in my house. You're no better than you should be. No better than that little trollop over the hill.'

223

'You're sick, Bertha. Do you know that? Sick and twisted. Oh, I know your dad gave you and your poor mam a rough time, but you've let him wreck your life. And you needn't have done because somehow, Bertha, and God alone knows how, you managed to hook yourself a decent man. A lovely man. And yet you still can't put the past behind you, can you? You've let it blight your life with Eddie and now you're trying to twist an innocent girl's mind and wreck her life an' all.'

'It's not the girl so much,' Bertha muttered and jerked her thumb over her shoulder, 'as her trollop of a mother.' She glared at Pat, her eyes full of bitterness and hatred. 'I'll swing for her one day. You mark my words. I'll swing for her.'

Pat shook her head slowly, more sad now than angry. 'Oh Bertha, why? You don't really believe that Maisie is Eddie's child, do you? He's just a kind and gentle man who helped a young lass in trouble. Look how he was in the floods. He was a hero. Can't you understand? That's just how Eddie is. He puts others afore himself.'

'He's a fool. Look after Number One, that's what I say.'

Pat nodded and glanced around her. 'Well, you've done all right for Number One, haven't you, Bertha? Got your feet well under the Appleyard table years ago.'

'Get out! Get out of my kitchen right now,' Bertha shouted, waving her arms.

'Oh I'm going. I've said what I came to say. Except,' she added pointedly, 'that I need to see Eddie and tell him what's been going on.'

Bertha's reaction was not what she had expected or hoped for. The woman merely shrugged her shoulders and muttered, 'Meks no odds to me. Tell him what you like.'

Pat's anger seethed once more. She thrust her face close to Bertha's. 'And what about Tony? Do you want him to know just what a horrible woman you really are.'

Again Bertha shrugged. 'Tony thinks same as me. He hates 'em. Both of 'em.'

'Well, there, Bertha, I think you're wrong. I think your Tony is very fond of them. Specially,' she added and she could not prevent a little thrill of malicious triumph, 'Maisie. I think he's very fond of Maisie. And I don't think for a minute that he'll like what you've done. He's got a lot of his dad in him, has Tony.'

Now the look on Bertha's face was exactly what Pat had hoped to see.

CHAPTER TWENTY-SIX

'Has the busybody nurse told you then?' was Bertha's greeting when Eddie came into the house for his dinner.

Wearily he said, 'Why, Bertha? Just tell me why you want to hurt that kiddie? You must know it's not true. She's not mine and you know it. And then to take the job upon yourself of telling her what her mother should tell her, well'—he shook his head in disbelief—'that beats all. It really does.'

Bertha turned away. For once she had no answer. She didn't care what Eddie thought of her, but her son was a different matter.

'It isn't true, love,' Eddie said gently.

He had waited in the lane, watching for Maisie to come home from school.

Maisie didn't pretend that she didn't know what he was talking about. Instead, she returned his steady gaze with her soft brown eyes that, to his sorrow, now held a more worldly look. 'Do you swear it? On—on Tony's life?' Tony was the only person that Maisie could think of on whose life Eddie would not risk tempting a cruel Fate.

Without hesitation Eddie nodded. 'I swear on Tony's life that I am not your father.' Then he smiled gently. 'Though I'd be lying if I didn't say I wished I was.'

For a moment Maisie stared at him. Then she let out a deep sigh and seemed to relax.

'There's never been anything—like that— between your mother and me.' His voice deepened. 'I am very fond of your mam, as I am of you. But I'm nearly old enough to be your *mam's* father, let alone yours. No, lass, I promise you that what my wife said is not true.'

'Some of it is, though, isn't it?' Maisie said in a small voice.

'What?'

'About—about what men—well, some men,' Maisie, remembering Pat's words, amended the sweeping statement, 'are like.'

'Ah,' Eddie said, understanding. 'That.' He paused a moment then went on. 'Well, love, I can't deny that there are some men in the world just like Mrs Bertha told you, but she made it sound as if all men are like that. You see, she was unlucky. Her father was a wrong 'un, so she thinks all men are bad. And they're not. Your difficulty, lass, is going to be recognizing a wrong 'un when you see one. But a good sort will respect you as well as love you.' He glanced down at her worriedly. She was very young to be taking all this in. Silently he cursed his wife for her vicious tongue. 'Do you understand what I'm trying to tell you, Maisie?'

'I—think so.'

'Well, when you're older and the boys start flocking round, you just come and ask me if you've any doubts about 'em.' He patted her shoulder. 'I'll sort 'em out for you.'

Maisie smiled thinly, but said nothing. How could she, an eleven-year-old child in his eyes—in everyone's eyes—tell him that she didn't want a flock of young men, as he put it, round her. There was only one boy she wanted. Only one boy she had ever wanted or would ever want.

Tony.

That was why Mrs Bertha's words had hurt her so much. The last thing that Maisie wanted in the whole wide world was for Tony to be her half-brother.

*　　　*　　　*

If Anna had known about Bertha's nastiness, more than likely she would have started to pack their belongings and threatened to leave. And this time she might have really meant it.

But for some reason that was never discussed, no one told Anna what had happened. And, unfortunately, no one thought to tell Tony either when he next came home from college.

If they had, it might have settled the turmoil in his mind about the truth of Maisie's parentage. It was something that had plagued the boy from the night that Anna had first appeared in the kitchen. A story perpetuated in his mind by his mother yet denied by his father.

Tony had never been able to decide whom he believed, and in the meantime Anna and Maisie continued to live in the little white thatched cottage near the woods.

But now Maisie never called at the farm to see Mrs Bertha.

*   *   *

In the September of 1958 Maisie started at the grammar school in Ludthorpe, travelling on the bus that trundled through the narrow lanes gathering up the children from the outlying district. As it had for Tony before her, the bus stopped for her at the bridge over the stream and she walked alongside the wood to her home.

Tony had completed his course at agricultural college and was now working on the farm that would one day belong to him. He bought himself a motorbike and even from their isolated cottage Anna and Maisie could hear the machine roaring through the country lanes, sometimes late at night. When she heard it, Anna could not resist the urge to smile. *That'll not best please Bertha*, she thought.

Maisie grew tall, slim and leggy. Coltish was the word that Pat used. The district nurse still visited the cottage as a friend. In fact, she was Anna's only female friend.

'She's going to be a real beauty,' Pat would say,

228

laughing. 'A few more curves in the right places, Anna, and you'll have 'em queuing down the track as far as the lane.'

'Not if I have anything to do with it,' Anna said darkly.

'Aw, ducky, you've got to let her grow and flourish.' Pat sighed. 'You've kept her hidden away all these years. Never let her have any friends to speak of.'

'She hasn't wanted them,' Anna retorted swiftly. 'She's quite happy with the animals. That's all she needs. We don't need people.'

'Ta very much, I'm sure.' Pat pretended to be offended.

Anna smiled and said, 'You know I don't mean you. You're not people.'

Pat laughed. 'I'm not sure if that's a compliment, but I'll take it as one.' Then she sighed again. 'But you ought to let her mix a bit more. Go to her friends' birthday parties. And as she gets older, you ought to let her go out and enjoy herself a bit. This rock and roll that's all the rage amongst the youngsters now. I wouldn't mind a bit of jiving myself.'

'And what would happen then? She'd get in with the wrong crowd and get herself into trouble.'

Pat put her head on one side and regarded Anna thoughtfully. 'Is that what happened to you?'

Over all the years, Anna had never confided in anyone about her past. And again she turned away, muttering, 'Never mind about that. It's Maisie we've to worry about.'

'Aye.' Pat nodded sagely. 'We have.' But her meaning was not quite the same as Anna's. The kindly Pat Jessop was concerned that the girl was going to be kept as a virtual recluse all her young life. It was bad enough that a lovely young woman like Anna should have chosen such an existence for herself, but to inflict it upon her daughter was little short of criminal. The youngsters of today were a different breed. They had no memory of the austerity of the war. As the Prime Minister said, they'd never had it so good. They demanded, and got, a better standard of living. As well as working, they wanted to play too. *And why shouldn't they?* Pat thought. *Why shouldn't they have a bit of fun in their youth? They'll be a long time grown up.*

She got up to leave. There was time yet for her to work on the problem, but if Anna wasn't very careful, when she was older Maisie would rebel.

And then Anna would know what trouble was.

*　　*　　*

On Maisie's fifteenth birthday Eddie presented her with a battery-operated radio. Maisie was ecstatic.

'Will it tune into Radio Luxembourg? I heard it at Sally's once. They play all the latest songs.'

'Oh, I reckon it will.' Eddie laughed and winked at Anna. 'She'll probably drive you mad playing all this rock and roll, but I thought you wouldn't mind.'

Anna did not join in. She frowned at the machine and murmured, 'Just so long as that's all she does.'

'What do you mean?'

'I don't mind her listening to the music, but she needn't think she's going to the village dances.'

The previous year the local Young Farmers' Club had started a Friday-night dance for their members. Maisie had begged to go. 'Everyone's going from school, Mam.'

'I very much doubt it,' Anna had replied shortly. 'The village hall wouldn't hold everyone from your school.'

'You know what I mean,' Maisie snapped back impatiently. 'I didn't mean it literally.' For once her soft brown eyes were sparkling with resentment. 'Why can't I go?'

'We keep ourselves to ourselves.'

'But why?' the girl cried passionately. 'Why do we have to live like this?' When her mother didn't answer, Maisie said, 'Do you know what they call you in the village? A witch.'

Anna smiled. 'I can think of worse names they could call me.'

Maisie gasped. 'But it's awful. Years ago they'd have burned you alive.'

Anna chuckled. 'But they won't, will they? And if it keeps them away from here—all the better.'

The girl stared at her. Over the last two or three years she had begun to realize that she lived a very different life from most of her schoolfriends. All her friends, if she was honest. It hadn't seemed as noticeable when she had been at the village school. Several of her classmates lived on isolated farms and the difference had not seemed so great. But now she was older and mixing with youngsters from the town, she had begun to see how odd her own life was compared with theirs.

'Ask your mam if you can stay the night at mine,' her best friend Sally had asked Maisie more than once. 'We could go to the pictures and all meet up in the coffee bar. You'd love it. It's what we do most Saturday nights.'

Maisie had shaken her head. 'She won't let me. I don't even have to ask her. I know what the answer'll be.'

'Well, try.' Sally, a good-natured plump girl with mischievous eyes and curly brown hair, had linked her arm through Maisie's. 'We'd have such fun.'

But Maisie had been right. Anna's answer was 'No'.

*   *   *

Late in the afternoon of her birthday, when she arrived home from school, Tony was waiting for her at the cottage.

'I've brought you these,' he said, handing over two magazines. 'There's some pictures of all those fellers you're always going on about. Elvis Presley, Cliff Richard and Adam Faith, is it?'

Maisie opened the pages. 'Oh, look,' she exclaimed over one of a handsome, dark-haired, moody-looking young man.

'Who on earth is that?' Anna asked.

'Elvis,' Maisie breathed. 'Oh, it's Elvis.'

Tony grinned. 'Reckon I look a bit like him, don't you?'

Maisie laughed. 'Well, a bit, but can you sing like him?'

Tony dropped the magazine onto the table. He adopted the pose of the guitar-playing idol and began to sing 'Are You Lonesome Tonight?'

Maisie laughed and clapped her hands. 'Oh you can, you can. You sound just like him.'

Tony laughed. 'I don't know about that, but I wish I had his money.'

'You wouldn't be any happier,' Anna said

232

quietly. 'Now, Maisie, take these upstairs to your room. I must get the tea.'

Maisie pulled a face, but did as her mother asked. Tony made to leave, but at the door he turned and said, 'Tell you what, I'll take you for a spin on me motorbike on Saturday afternoon.'

Before Maisie could answer, Anna said swiftly, 'Oh no. She's not going on that. Not at the speeds you go. And don't deny it, Tony, 'cos we can hear you from here roaring through the lanes. One of these day's you'll come a real cropper off that bike.'

'Oh mam, please . . .'

'No.'

'I'll be very careful,' Tony said. 'I promise.'

'Please, mam. Just once. Just for my birthday.'

Anna still looked doubtful, but relented. 'All right then. But you're not to take her far. You promise not to go too fast?'

'I promise.'

Maisie clapped her hands and rushed to hug her mother. 'Oh, thank you, Mam. Thank you, Tony.' She turned from her mother and flung her arms about his neck and kissed his cheek. Tony's face flamed and he pushed her away, but in her excitement Maisie did not notice. 'What time shall I be ready and what shall I wear?'

'Er—oh—whatever you like.' His face like thunder, Tony dragged open the door and was gone, slamming it behind him.

For a moment both Maisie and Anna stared at the closed door. Then the girl turned and looked at her mother, with wide, troubled eyes. 'What did I do, Mam? What did I do?'

Slowly, Anna shook her head. 'I don't know, love. I really don't know.'

233

On the Saturday afternoon, dressed in trousers, a thick jumper and warm coat and scarf, Maisie waited for Tony. And she waited and waited. As dusk fell, she said tearfully, 'He's not coming, is he?'

'Doesn't look like it, love.'

'Have you said anything to him? Have you put him off?'

Anna shook her head. 'No, I haven't. I admit I did think about it, 'cos I'm a bit worried about him taking you . . .'

'That's it, then,' Maisie snapped, pulling off her gloves. 'That'll be why he hasn't come. He knows you're not for it.' Then she added bitterly, 'And *she* won't be either.'

'No, she won't,' Anna said, her tone surprisingly mild. 'But I wouldn't have thought he'd've told her.'

Maisie climbed the ladder to her room and tore off her clothes. She switched on her wireless to play as loudly as possible. Then she threw herself on her bed and lay staring up, dry-eyed, at the wooden rafters of her ceiling.

I won't cry, she vowed. *I won't let him hurt me.* But with Elvis's deep tones singing 'Wooden Heart', she felt the tears welling and trickling down her temples as she lay on her back.

CHAPTER TWENTY-SEVEN

Maisie was out in the fields early the next morning. Two ewes had gone into labour at the same time and Anna could not cope alone.

'You'll have to fetch Mr Eddie, Maisie. Go down to the farm and fetch him.' She paused and added, 'Or Tony.'

'I'm not fetching *him*,' the girl replied moodily, 'but I'll go for Mr Eddie.'

'Just go, Maisie. Get someone, else we'll likely lose one of them.'

Maisie ran.

Tony was in the yard, swilling out the pigsty.

'Where's your dad?' Maisie asked, panting hard from running all the way up the track and down to the farmyard.

'He's taken Mam into town. You've heard of her sister, Lucy, haven't you?'

Anna nodded.

'Well, her sister's husband's very ill. He's had a seizure, Mam calls it, so she's gone to stay for a few days.'

When Duke had got too old to pull the trap any more he'd been 'retired' to the meadow and Eddie had invested in a small truck. But Bertha could not drive, so Eddie now had to take her wherever she wanted to go.

''Cos you needn't think I'm going on them buses. Not with all them nosy parkers. You can take me, Eddie. Every Thursday.'

'Course I will, love,' Eddie had agreed readily. He quite enjoyed a day's peace at home when

235

Bertha visited her sister, even if he did have to make two trips into town, to take her in the morning and fetch her home at night.

Today, however, there was an emergency and Lucy had sent a telegram asking Bertha to go at once.

'You'll have to come then,' Maisie said now. 'Two ewes have gone into labour and Mam needs some help.'

Tony dropped the yard brush. 'Right. Come on then.'

They hurried back up the track, Tony loping alongside her with easy strides. 'I don't know why me dad doesn't bring as many as he can down into the big barn. He did in forty-seven.' He glanced at her. 'The year you were born in all that snow. But he likes sticking to the old-fashioned way. Now, if it was me, I'd build a big barn to house 'em all every lambing time. But no. "What was good enough for me dad is good enough for me," he ses.'

Maisie glanced at Tony. He was back to his usual self this morning. 'What happened yesterday? Why didn't you come and take me out on the bike like you promised?'

Immediately, there was a wary look on his face. 'Sorry,' he said curtly. 'It—it was getting the telegram from me auntie.'

She recognized it for what it was. An excuse.

'How very convenient.' Maisie could not stop the remark and when Tony did not answer, she knew that she had hit the mark. They hurried on side by side, but now neither of them spoke.

* * *

With Tony's help, there were no problems and two healthy lambs came into the world. Anna, Maisie and Tony were standing together in the field watching the new mothers when they heard the sound of Eddie's truck drawing into the yard.

'Come on,' Tony said. 'Come down to the farm. Mam's left enough food to feed an army for a week. Come and have dinner with us.'

Anna shook her head. 'Oh no. It wouldn't be right. Knowing how your mother feels about me. About us.'

'Well, I'm going,' Maisie said, beginning to walk away. 'I want to tell Mr Eddie he's got two lambs.'

'Come on,' Tony coaxed. 'It'll be all right. And then I'll take Maisie out on me bike this afternoon.'

Anna eyed him speculatively, said nothing, but began to follow him down to the farm.

*   *   *

'Now, isn't this grand?'

Eddie was beaming from ear to ear as he spread the table with a snowy cloth and got out the cutlery from the drawer. 'She left a joint of beef in the oven that we can cut at for the week. It'll be done now. And there's veg to heat up. Isn't this grand?'

Anna had stepped nervously into the kitchen. This was the first time she had been inside the farmhouse since the night of her arrival. It had taken her a few moments to feel that she could even stay. She still wasn't quite comfortable being in Bertha's home, but she was smiling now as she helped to lay the table, guessing that this was probably the first time Eddie Appleyard had played host in his own home. Bertha never invited guests.

237

As far as Anna was aware, even Lucy and her husband had never visited the farm. As they all sat down together, Anna said, 'Well, this is a feast and no mistake.'

'Tuck in, Maisie lass, tuck in. If you're off out on that moteybike this afternoon, you'll need summat to warm you up.'

Maisie glanced at Tony, who smiled and nodded. 'Yeah. Sorry about yesterday, but we'll go after dinner.'

Maisie, ready to forgive him anything, grinned back.

*　　　*　　　*

The wind whipped through her hair and stung her cheeks as Maisie wrapped her arms around Tony's waist and clung to him.

Looking over his shoulder, she watched the lane rushing towards them and disappearing beneath the bike's wheels. Laughing, she shouted in his ear, 'Faster, Tony, faster.'

On a perfectly straight piece of lane, Tony opened up the throttle and the bike leapt forward. Maisie screamed with delight.

At the end of the lane, he slowed, turned round and roared off again back the way they had come. When they returned to the farm, they were both red-faced and laughing. But Anna was waiting for them in the yard, her arms akimbo.

'So much for your promises, Tony Appleyard. We could hear you from here. I might not know much about motorbikes, but I know when one's going too fast.'

'It was only on Long Lane. On the straight.'

'Mebbe. But there's hills and dips in the lane. What if something had been coming the other way?'

'There wasn't.' Tony was getting angry now as Maisie climbed off the pillion and he flung his leg over the bike and propped it up on its stand. He faced Anna squarely. His voice was quiet, but deadly serious. 'Do you really think I'd risk hurting her? Maisie? Of all people?' Then, slapping his gloves together he marched away from them and into the house, leaving both Anna and Maisie staring after him. The one with growing dread in her heart, the other feeling as if she was about to burst with happiness.

*   *   *

In the summer of the following year, Maisie sat her O levels and, as a special treat, Anna allowed her to attend one of the village dances with her friends to celebrate the end of the exams.

'But don't think this is a regular thing because it isn't.'

Maisie hugged her. 'No, Mam. I won't.'

Pat, who had been canvassing relentlessly on the girl's behalf for the past year, listened to the exchange. 'I'll take you into town on Saturday on the bus and buy you a pretty skirt, Maisie. You know, one of those wide ones with lots of petticoats underneath. And some nice shoes for you to dance in.'

'Oh now, I don't know about that,' Anna began. 'It'd be a waste. Like I say, this is a one off . . .'

'Oh please, Mam,' Maisie begged.

Anna sighed. 'We'll see. Now, take Buster out

239

and round up the lambs. The lorry's coming for them tomorrow.'

Maisie's face fell. She hated it when the lambs were taken to market.

As the girl closed the door behind her, Anna said, 'It's very generous of you, Pat but, honestly, she won't get the chance to wear such clothes.'

'She'll get plenty of chance when she goes away to college.'

'What?' Anna screeched. 'She's not going anywhere. She'll stay here with me and work on the farm. Eddie has already said . . .'

Pat sat down at the table without waiting for an invitation. 'Eddie will say anything to keep you here. To keep you *both* here.'

Anna stared at her and sank slowly into the chair opposite. 'Oh Pat,' she said sadly, 'not you too. You don't think there's something between me and Eddie.'

'No, I don't. I believe you. But have you ever stopped to think that Eddie maybe feels very differently? That maybe he would like there to be something between you? He doesn't have a very happy home life, y'know.'

Anna was silent, remembering the scratches on Eddie's face when she had first come here and, over the years, the odd bruise on his cheek. Even a black eye once or twice. And when these happened, Tony would stay away from the cottage for days, even weeks sometimes. Anna would guess that there had been a row between Eddie and his wife, and doubtless the cause had been her continued presence in the cottage. If so, it would throw Tony once more into a conflict of emotions—torn between his parents.

'I know,' she said flatly, 'and it's my fault. I should have gone years ago. I—we—shouldn't have stayed.'

'It's nobody's fault but Bertha's. It's certainly not yours, ducky, so don't even think it. He'd've had a rough time with her whether you were here or not.'

'Do you think so?'

'I know so. Anyway, we were talking about Maisie and her career.'

'*You* were.'

'She's a bright lass and ought to be given a chance. She wants to be a teacher and—'

Anna stared at Pat incredulously. 'She's told you that?'

Pat nodded. 'Well, yes. I thought you knew.'

Anna shook her head and said slowly and thoughtfully. 'No. She's said nothing to me.'

'I don't suppose you've given her the chance. You've just decided that she's got to bury herself away here and—'

Anna sprang up and began to pace about the room. 'You don't understand. I've got to keep her safe.'

'She's a sensible girl. She—she knows the facts of life,' Pat said, carefully avoiding referring to the unfortunate way in which the girl had learnt them. 'If I had to put money on any of the youngsters around here *not* going off the rails, it would be your Maisie.'

The compliment did not ease Anna's agitation. 'You don't understand,' she repeated. 'It's not *Maisie* herself that's the problem. It's—it's other people.'

'What other people? Her peers, you mean?'

Anna shook her head. 'I can't risk us—being—

241

found.' Then, as always when the conversation came close to matters from the past, Anna clamped her mouth shut and refused to say more.

Pat heaved herself up. 'Well, if you won't confide in me, I can't help you. But after all these years, surely you've nothing to fear now. It's sixteen years, for heaven's sake. You can't still be frightened about your family—or whoever it was—coming after you? You're not still hiding from the past, are you? Not after all this time. Surely, they'll forgive and forget by now?'

Anna swung round, her magnificent eyes sparkling with bitterness and hatred. She almost spat the words out. 'Oh, you don't know the half of it. It's me that can't forgive and forget. Me! Don't you understand?'

'How can I, ducky,' Pat said sadly, 'when you won't even tell me what happened?'

Anna turned away from her and, through gritted teeth, all she said was, 'No, and I don't intend to either. So leave it, Pat, will you? Else you and me are going to fall out.'

CHAPTER TWENTY-EIGHT

'Well, you've been and now you know what it's like. Not all it's cracked up to be, I bet. I expect you were a wallflower for most of the evening. So don't be asking to go any more.'

Maisie gaped at her mother. She had never heard Anna speak so scathingly. Not all it'd been cracked up to be! The village dance had been everything and more that Maisie could have possibly imagined.

Tony had taken her into the village, not on his motorbike but in his father's truck. When they arrived outside the hall, he got out and opened the door for her, just as if she was royalty. 'In you go then. Have a good time. I'll pick you up at eleven.'

'Aren't you coming in?' Her disappointment was obvious.

Through the darkness she heard his chuckle. 'I reckon I'm a bit old for the village hop now. I'll leave it to you youngsters.'

'Don't be silly. Of course you're not old. Auntie Pat still goes sometimes. She told me.' Maisie put her hand through his arm and tried to pull him towards the door. 'Please come in, Tony. You can go if you don't like it. But—but please just come in with me.'

Tony glanced down at the girl. In the light from the doorway, he could see that she was biting her lip nervously.

'All right then. Just for a bit, eh? But I can't do all this fancy jiving stuff.'

Maisie giggled. 'Neither can I.'

'Wait while I park the truck.'

She stood near the doorway whilst Tony moved the vehicle a little way down the road and parked it on the grass verge.

'You goin' to stand out here all night?' Chris Wainwright, Joe's son, swaggered past her on his way in. He was dressed in tight trousers—drainpipes—and a long jacket, which almost reached his knees, and thick-soled suede shoes. His black hair was greased into a hairstyle like Elvis's. But there, sadly, the resemblance ended. Chris had a large, almost hooked nose and a spotty face. But

243

he had other redeeming features. He was nice. He wasn't a bully or unkind and Maisie liked him. She grinned at him. 'I'm waiting for Tony.'

Chris's smile wavered as he said, 'Oh. He's coming, is he?'

'He wasn't. It's—only 'cos I asked him to come in with me.'

'You could have come in with me if I'd known you were coming. Anyway, I'll save you a dance.' Clowning, he said, 'Course me card's full, you know, but I'll squeeze you in somewhere.'

Maisie laughed and gave a mock curtsy. 'Thank you, kind sir.'

Chris went into the hall as Maisie turned to see Tony coming towards her.

'Who was that?' Tony asked, frowning after the disappearing youth.

'Chris Wainwright.'

'What did he want?'

'A dance later on.' Maisie laughed. 'Least I've got one.'

Maisie had more than one dance. A lot more. In fact, she hardly missed one and then only because she was completely out of breath.

Tony stood leaning on the temporary bar at the end of the big room. They were serving soft drinks only and Tony would dearly have loved to go across the road to the King's Head, but he had no intention of leaving Maisie to the tender mercies of this lot. He glanced around morosely, half envious of their youth, half disgusted at their style of dress. Fashions reached the countryside much later than in the city and the village lads were now heavily into the Teddy boy look, complete, in some cases, with bicycle chains and knuckle-dusters. One or

244

two even carried flick knives, but it was all for show—just bravado, Tony believed. He knew most of the kids here and that they would run a mile if anyone raised an 'offensive weapon' in anger. He almost laughed as he watched the boys congregating on one side of the room, the girls on the other. Every so often a brave male would leave the pack and venture across to the female herd to pick a partner. And most of them seemed to make a beeline for Maisie, he thought morosely.

Tony had attended one or two of the dances in his teens, but it had never really been his scene. He was much happier with his own company or about the farm with the animals or going over the hill to see Anna and Maisie . . .

He sighed now as his eyes still followed the whirling, laughing figure of the girl who filled his thoughts and disturbed his dreams.

If only, he thought for the umpteenth time, *I knew the truth about her.*

*   *   *

Maisie did not answer her mother, but turned away before Anna could see the defiance in her eyes. The girl had had a wonderful time, and best of all had been driving home through the July night with Tony. He'd parked the truck in the farmyard and insisted on walking with her up the track, right to the door of the cottage.

'Mam's still up,' Maisie had said as they reached the top of the rise and saw the light glowing in the cottage window.

Tony laughed. 'Well, of course she will be. It's the first time you've been out as late as this and to a dance. What can you expect?'

'Does your mam still wait up for you?' It had been a long time since Maisie had spoken of Mrs Bertha, so deep went the hurt that his mother had inflicted.

'No, not now. But she used to until I got to twenty-one.'

Maisie sighed. 'It must be nice to be older and be able to do what you want.' She was silent for a moment as they descended the slope. Then, after a pause, she said, 'I wish Mam would let me go out a bit more.'

Carefully, Tony said, 'She's worried you might get into the—the wrong company.' Silently, he sympathized with Anna. He had never experienced such a mixture of emotions as he had watching Maisie dance with one lad after another. Concern, envy and, yes, he had to admit it, jealousy. And yet he didn't agree with Anna keeping her daughter shut away from the world like a hermit.

'They're only lads from the village and one or two from town,' Maisie interrupted his thoughts, answering his comment. 'I go to school with most of them. Oh, I know they dress a bit daft. All this Teddy boy stuff. But they're harmless.'

'I know,' he had to admit, 'but your mam doesn't know that, does she?'

'Suppose not,' Maisie admitted grudgingly. She sighed heavily. 'I don't suppose she'd let me go to a show in Lincoln. Sal says Billy Fury and some other stars are coming to do a live show at one of the cinemas there in October. I'd love to go.'

In the darkness Tony grinned and, feigning ignorance, asked, 'Who's Billy Fury?'

'Oh he's smashing. Ever so good-looking. He's a

singer. Sal gave me a picture of him. I've got it beside my bed.'

'Huh!' Tony feigned indignation. 'I thought you'd've had my picture on your bedside table.'

Maisie grinned. 'I would—if you gave me one.'

After a moment's pause, Tony asked, 'Would you really like to go to see this chap then?'

'Oh yes,' Maisie breathed and even through the darkness he could hear the longing in her voice.

'Then I'll take you.'

'Will you? Oh Tony, will you? Really?'

And before he realized what she was doing, she had flung her arms round his neck and kissed him firmly on the lips. 'Oh thank you, thank you.'

'S'all right,' he said gruffly. 'You'd better get inside now. And don't tell your mam. She'll not let you go if you tell her. We'll just go. Right?'

With breathless excitement, Maisie said, 'Yes, yes. All right.' As she broke into a run down the last few yards to the cottage, she shouted through the night. 'Thank you, Tony. You're the best. Oh thank you. I love you.'

*   *   *

'I've told Mam I'm going home with Sal after school on Wednesday,' Maisie told Tony as they planned their outing.

'And I've told Dad that I can't help with the evening milking 'cos I've got to take me bike into a garage in Ludthorpe.'

Maisie's eyes clouded for a moment. 'Have you?' If there was something wrong with Tony's motorbike, the whole trip might be off.

'Course not,' Tony was saying cheerfully, 'but if

247

you can get out of school at dinnertime, we can get to Lincoln in the afternoon. You'd like a look round the shops, wouldn't you?'

Maisie's eyes shone. 'Ooh, yes, please.'

Her childlike excitement at the thought of such a simple pleasure touched Tony. Anna had no right to keep a young girl like Maisie shut away. Their life was little better than a hermit's. No wonder Maisie had rebelled at last.

'Mind you wear something warm,' he reminded her.

'I'll take my clothes to school with my games kit and hide them in my locker in the changing room.'

They grinned at each other, enjoying their secret. Now Tony had no qualms about helping the girl deceive her mother. Maisie deserved a bit of fun.

*   *   *

The following Wednesday afternoon Maisie was waiting round the corner from the school. As she climbed onto the back of his motorbike, she said resentfully, 'I thought I wasn't going to make it. Mam didn't even want to let me go to Sal's tonight.'

'How does she think you're going to get home from there?'

Maisie giggled. 'I told her I'd asked you to fetch me home.'

Tony chuckled. 'You crafty monkey. Well, I will be, won't I? We should make it back home by eleven and she need be none the wiser. Hold tight, off we go.'

For the first time in her life, Maisie was on her

way to see the city of Lincoln.

*   *   *

The shops and the hustle and bustle of the High Street entranced Maisie.

'Just look at all these people,' she marvelled, standing almost open-mouthed on the pavement. 'Wherever have they all come from?'

Tony chuckled as he held on tightly to her arm. He was afraid that she would be swept off the pavement and under the wheels of a bus, unused to crowds as she was.

'Oh, and look at the swans.' The excited girl leant over the parapet of High Bridge.

'Come on, it's time we were making for the cinema.'

As they walked along the street, Maisie saw the queue of young people, mostly girls, outside the building. Her face fell in disappointment. 'We'll never get in. Oh, Tony . . .'

'Don't worry.' Tony patted his pocket. 'I got the tickets two weeks ago. Our seats are reserved.'

Feeling important, they marched to the head of the queue. Standing on the steps outside the doors was a man who appeared to be marshalling the queue.

'Now, now, ladies,' he was saying jovially. 'No need to push. You'll all get in.' He pretended to glance down the length of the line snaking along the pavement. 'Oh I don't know, though.' He laughed loudly. 'It might be standing room only by the time we get to the end.'

'Don't matter, Mister,' someone shouted. 'Long as we see Billy.'

'Oh you'll see him. You'll see him,' the man promised. He was tall, in his fifties, and he was dressed flamboyantly like an old-fashioned music-hall star. His eyes were dark brown and the hair that showed from beneath his trilby was grey with a tinge of the ginger colour it had once been. He sported a pencil-thin moustache, which he kept stroking with the fourth finger of his right hand.

Maisie heard Tony's soft chuckle. 'He looks like Max Miller, 'cept for the 'tache.'

'Who's Max Miller?' Maisie asked innocently. The man must have heard her remark, for he smiled down at her from the top step. 'Max Miller, young lady, was one of the greatest comedians this country's ever seen. Now I could tell you a thing or two about the great Max Miller . . .'

'Ne'er mind about 'im,' a girl at the front of the queue shouted. 'When are we going to get inside? It's draughty standing out here.'

'All in good time, miss. All in good time. The doors will open in five minutes.'

' 'Ere—' The girl was still not satisfied. 'What about them? They're queue jumping.'

Tony fished in his pocket and produced the tickets and waved them. 'No, we're not.'

'What a sensible fellow,' the big man boomed and, putting his hand on Maisie's shoulder, he ushered them towards the door. As she passed him, the man touched Maisie's curls and murmured, 'What pretty hair you've got, my dear. What a lovely colour.'

Maisie smiled up at him and then followed Tony through the door and into the cinema, excitement bubbling just below her ribs.

As they climbed the steps to the circle, Maisie

giggled. 'Did you hear what that man said to me? He said, "What pretty hair you've got, my dear." He sounded like the wolf out of "Little Red Riding Hood".'

Tony laughed with her, but he glanced back over his shoulder to see the man watching them climb the stairs and his gaze seemed to be fastened on Maisie.

'Well,' Tony murmured, 'I wouldn't be too sure he isn't.'

*   *   *

The show wasn't quite what Tony would have chosen to see. One of the few males sitting amidst a crowd of screaming girls, he felt very out of place. But Maisie's delight was obvious. She screamed with the rest until she was hoarse and even Tony was forced to admit that Billy Fury was charismatic. Suddenly, at twenty-six, Tony felt an old fuddy-duddy.

At the end of the performance, Maisie pleaded, 'Do let's go round to the stage door and get his autograph. I've brought a book specially.'

'Oh I don't know. It's late now—'

'Please, please, please, Tony.'

'All right then, but we mustn't stay too long.'

Outside, special police patrols and even a police dog were waiting in case of trouble from hysterical fans. But the queue in the yard outside the stage door was orderly. This time, though, Maisie and Tony were obliged to tag on at the end of it and wait with everyone else. The minutes dragged by and no one came out of the stage door. Then there was a sudden flurry and the man who had been at the front of the building before the show emerged. A photographer was with him and at the man's direction he began to move down the queue taking pictures. 'For the *Echo*. Like to see your name in the paper, wouldn't you?' He paused every so often and jotted down a few names.

'I don't want me face in the paper,' Tony muttered. 'Come on, Maisie. It's time we were going. He's not going to come out. You can't blame him, love. He worked hard on that stage, I'll give him that.'

'Just another minute, Tony,' she begged. 'Please.'

The photographer was moving closer. 'What'll your mam say if she sees your name in the paper. She'll go spare.'

Maisie grinned. 'She'll not see it. She never takes a paper. You know that.'

'Aye, but someone might see it who knows you. What then?'

But at that moment the camera flashed and Maisie and Tony blinked. 'Now, love, what's your name,' the photographer asked, pencil poised above his notepad. 'And where are you from?'

'Maisie Woods,' she blurted out, answering his question automatically. 'From near Ludthorpe.'

'And yours, sir?'

'Nowt to do with you,' Tony growled. 'And don't you print that picture in the paper else I'll bust your camera for you. Come on, Maisie, we're going.'

Maisie smiled quickly at the young photographer. 'Sorry,' she said. 'We've got to go.'

As they began to move away, the photographer beckoned to the big man still standing in the stage door. They heard a shout and saw 'Max Miller' striding towards them. 'Wait a minute, I want a word with you—'

'Come on, Maisie,' Tony grabbed her arm. 'Run for it.'

* * *

By the time they rode into the farmyard at a quarter to twelve all hell had broken loose.

Anxiety had driven Anna to come down to the farm. The three of them—Anna, Eddie and Bertha—were standing outside the back door. It was the first time that Anna had come face to face with Bertha in sixteen years.

'Where are they? Where's Tony taken her?'

'My Tony wouldn't take that little trollop anywhere. Like mother, like daughter, I say. I heard about her at that dance in the village.' Bertha nodded sagely, her jowls wobbling. 'Making an exhibition of 'ersen. Dancing with every Tom, Dick and Harry.'

'He was taking her to Sally's house in Ludthorpe. But she should have been back hours ago. Where is he? Is he here?' Anna was close to hysteria. 'I've been on edge all day. There was a funny sky this morning. I don't like it. Something bad's going to happen. I know it is.'

'Now, now, love. Calm down.' Eddie tried to pour oil on what were becoming very troubled waters. 'Tony wouldn't let any harm come to Maisie—'

Bertha's mouth twisted. 'Oh "love", is it? Oh well, now we know, don't we?' She turned to face Anna, adding sarcastically, 'Of course he wouldn't

253

let any harm come to his *sister*, now would he?'

Anna gasped. 'His—his sister?'

'Well, half-sister?'

Anna stared at the woman for a moment and then began to laugh, but it was hysterical laughter. 'After all this time you still think that?'

Bertha thrust her face close to Anna's. 'Why else would you stay here all these years? Why else would you bury yourself away in the back o' beyond. Unless you were where you wanted to be. With 'im.' At this she jabbed her husband in the chest.

Anna, her anxiety over Maisie forgotten for the minute, shook her head sadly. 'You're mad. Eddie's just a kind man who deserves better than you—'

'Now, now.' Eddie tried to placate the two women again. 'Don't let's get into all that. It's Maisie we should be thinking about—'

At that moment they heard the distant roar of the bike and turned towards the yard expectantly as the sound grew closer and at last turned in through the gate.

Anna flew across the yard. She dragged Maisie off the pillion and fired questions at her so fast that the girl had no time to answer. Then Anna rounded on Tony.

'And as for you, don't you come near her again. Do you hear me? Not ever.'

As Anna dragged her daughter away, Maisie glanced back over her shoulder. Tony was watching her. Their eyes met and held in a gaze until, through the darkness, they could no longer see each other's face.

Eddie ran his hand through his hair and muttered, 'Eh, lad, what trouble have you caused now?'

In the doorway of the farmhouse, Bertha smiled.

CHAPTER TWENTY-NINE

'I have my reasons.'

'What? What reasons?'

'You don't need to know.'

'Yes, Mam, I do.' Maisie tried to calm the hysteria in her tone. She was trying very hard to act like an adult. 'I know I'm not a grown-up yet, but I'm not a child any longer either. Why can't you trust me?'

'Trust you? Trust you? When you do what you've done today? Deliberately disobeyed me and deceived me. How do you expect me to trust you after that?'

'Because I can't see why I have to stay shut away from leading a normal life unless you tell me why.'

Anna sat down heavily at the table and laid her head on her arms. She groaned. She was tired, very tired. All the long years of loneliness, the constant fear, which despite the passage of time seemed as sharp as ever. Bringing up Maisie alone with only Eddie and Pat Jessop to turn to for help. And living in the isolated cottage with none of the amenities that most people now enjoyed. It hadn't seemed so bad at first, when Maisie was tiny, but now she was forced to acknowledge the unfairness of their life for her daughter. It was one thing for Anna to choose to hide herself away. It was quite another for her to inflict that same seclusion on the young girl.

255

Her voice trembling, Maisie said, 'I'm sorry, Mam. I—I promise I won't do anything again. At least—not without telling you. But will *you* promise *me* something?'

Anna lifted her head slowly. 'Depends what it is,' she said guardedly.

Maisie licked her lips. 'Well, if I promise to tell you exactly where I'm going, who with and what time I'll be home, will you let me go out a bit more? I'm not asking to be out every night, not even every week. I've got my school work to do, specially now I'm in the Lower Sixth.' Then the words came tumbling out in a rush of confidence. 'Mam—I—I want to go to teacher-training college.'

'I can't afford—' Anna began, but Maisie interrupted eagerly.

'You don't have to. There's grants and things we can apply for. The careers teacher said so. And I do so want to be a teacher. The little ones, you know. At a village school like the one I went to here.' She reached across and gripped her mother's hands. 'Please try to understand, Mam.'

'We ought to go away. Get as far away as possible,' Anna murmured. 'We should have gone years ago, but . . .'

'Why, Mam? What is it you're so afraid of?'

Anna pressed her lips together and shook her head. 'I can't tell you,' she said huskily. 'Please don't ask me.' Then hesitantly she said, 'All right. If you do your best to keep your promise, you can go out now and again. But if you want to go to teacher-training college, you'll have to work hard at school.'

'That's why I wanted to stay on and do A levels.'

Maisie could have left school long before now,

but Anna had agreed to her staying on into the sixth form. It had been her way of ensuring that Maisie was at home for another two years.

As if reading her thoughts, Maisie said, 'And even then I needn't go very far away. There's a very good teacher-training college at Lincoln—'

Anna sprang to her feet. '*No, no,*' she shouted. 'You'll not go there. Anywhere but there. Anywhere.'

Maisie gaped at her. 'All right, Mam. All right. There's another year before I have to decide anyway—'

'Get to bed. It's very late. I'll never be up in the morning.'

Submissively, Maisie got up, kissed her mother's cheek and then climbed the ladder to her room, still shocked by her mother's reaction to the mention of the college in Lincoln.

Maisie fell asleep almost at once, but in the other bedroom Anna lay awake until the first fingers of dawn crept in through the window.

*   *   *

'Everything all right?' Eddie asked.

'Sort of,' Anna replied guardedly and then allowed herself a wry smile. 'You?'

'Bertha's giving Tony a hard time. She hit him. First time I've ever seen her go for him.' There was wonder in his tone.

'Oh, Eddie, I'm sorry.'

Eddie shrugged. 'Not your fault, lass.'

'No, but it is Maisie's.'

'Not really. It seems it was Tony who suggested the trip.'

'Yes, but it was for Maisie, wasn't it?' Anna insisted.

'Well, yes.' Eddie was obliged to agree.

'Has she hurt him?'

'Who?'

'Tony? Has Bertha hurt him?'

Eddie laughed. 'Oh that. No.' He chuckled. 'You should have seen it, lass. He's a strong lad, you know, and whilst I've never stood up to her'—he wrinkled his brow and rubbed his nose—'never thought about it, really. But he just caught hold of her wrists and held her. She was screaming like a banshee, but she couldn't move. And he held her like that till she calmed down. He told her, quite calmly, that he was a grown man and that he'd do what he liked and that it was nothing to do with her. I don't reckon she'll tangle with him again in a hurry.'

Eddie said no more. He did not want to tell Anna about the rest of the row that had gone on in the farmhouse the previous night.

'You'll keep away from that little slut,' Bertha had screamed at her son. 'You'll have the law on you, if you don't. You could be put in prison.'

'She's sixteen. Old enough,' Tony had goaded her.

'Don't you understand?' Bertha had screeched. 'She's your sister.'

'That's what you say.' He nodded across to where Eddie was standing in the corner of the room. 'But me dad ses different. And he should know.'

'He'd deny it. Course he would. I'm surprised that trollop over the hill hasn't had a brood of his bastards by now. All men are the same.'

'No, we're not, Mam.' Tony's voice was gentle. Now he was older he understood more about his parents' unhappy marriage, though there was nothing he could do about it. A few years earlier Eddie had explained to him about Bertha's father, about his philandering and his lawless ways that had finally landed him in prison. 'We've just got news that he's died in there,' Eddie had said, 'but it won't alter how ya mam feels about him and how it's twisted her view of all men. It's something you'll have to cope with, lad, as you get older. You're all she's ever had to pour her love into and it's going to be hard for you.'

And now Tony was facing his mother's warped reasoning. 'We're not all the same, mam. There's nowt between me and Maisie, I promise you.'

He had not added that he wished with all his heart that there could be. But always there was the spectre of their relationship hanging over him. Just which of his parents was telling him the truth?

He wanted to believe Eddie, but dare he?

'Well, I'm truly sorry,' Anna said now, dragging Eddie's thoughts back from the previous night.

'No harm done, lass,' Eddie said, managing to lie cheerfully and convincingly. 'No harm done.'

*   *   *

That evening, thirty miles away in a terraced house in Lincoln, the big man dressed like Max Miller sat staring at a picture in the local paper. 'Damn,' he muttered. 'They haven't printed the picture I hoped they would. They've put one in of the audience arriving.'

'What are you on about, Dad?' The younger

259

man stood in front of the mirror over the fireplace, combing his hair into an Elvis Presley look-alike style.

The older man smiled. 'Good job I thought to call at the *Echo* offices and get the originals of all the photos taken that night, wasn't it?'

'Whatever do you want them for?'

'I'll show you,' the man answered as he pulled several black and white photographs from an envelope and sorted though them. 'Come and look at this.'

'I'm off out. Can't it wait? I'm meeting someone.' He was dressed in a bright pink Teddy boy suit with a bootlace tie and crepe-soled shoes.

His father glanced at him. 'Bit old for dressing like that now, aren't you?'

'Huh,' the other laughed. 'You're a fine one to talk. Always dressed like something from an old music hall bill.'

'Well, that's me job, son. Got to look the part of the theatre promoter, now ain't I?'

'All right. What is it?'

'Here, look at that. Remind you of anyone?' He jabbed at one of the pictures with his forefinger. 'Her. That girl there.'

His son stared at the photograph. He glanced at his father and then his gaze went to a faded photograph on the mantelpiece of himself as a child of about twelve. He looked again at the newspaper picture as the older man said softly, 'She's got bright red hair, an' all. *Just like you.*'

They stared at each other. 'Could it be?' the son asked.

'It's possible.' He pointed again at the paper. 'And do you see what her name is? Maisie. Now that's a bit like May, isn't it?'

The younger man nodded. 'What are you going to do?'

The big man heaved himself out of his chair. 'A bit of detective work first. Then we'll see. Oh yes, we'll see all right then.'

The two men grinned at each other.

If Anna had known what was happening in that terraced house in the city, she would have packed their things immediately and fled for her life.

CHAPTER THIRTY

Two men in a red sports car drove into the yard at Cackle Hill Farm, scattering hens and sending up a spray of slurry. The big man unwound himself from the seat and the younger man jumped out agilely. They looked around them.

'Hello there,' the big man's voice boomed. 'Anyone at home?'

The yard was deserted, except for the hens and three geese that waddled away quickly. 'Knock on the door,' the older man suggested and his son strode towards the back door of the house and rapped sharply.

A moment passed and then the door opened framing the ample figure of the farmer's wife. Visitors to the farm were rare and Bertha eyed them with suspicion. 'What d'you want?'

The older man moved closer and doffed his trilby with an exaggerated show of courtesy. He fingered his moustache. 'Good day to you, ma'am.'

The younger man too made a little bow towards

her, though shrewdly Bertha felt it was all an act. An act to charm her. Well, there was no man living who could charm Bertha Appleyard.

She began to close the door. 'Not today, thank you.'

'Oh now, wait a minute, love,' the older of the two began and even had the temerity to put his foot in the door. Bertha glared at him and opened the door wider, intending to slam it against his foot. Guessing her intention, he withdrew his foot hastily. Instead, he put up his hand, palm outwards as if to defend himself. 'Wait minute, Missis. Not so hasty. We only want to ask you a few questions. We reckon you can help us.'

Intrigued in spite of herself, Bertha wavered. 'Go on.'

'We're looking for someone. A girl. Well'—he glanced sideways at his companion—'she'd be a young woman now. And she'd probably have a youngster. Anna. That's her name. Anna Milton. Do you know anyone living hereabouts with that name?'

Bertha opened the door wider and smiled. Like a spider inviting a fly into its web, she said, 'Come in, why don't you?'

*　　　*　　　*

Out on the hillside, Anna wandered amongst the sheep checking them. From time to time she paused and looked back to watch Buster trailing after her, valiantly trying to keep up.

'Poor old feller,' she murmured, bending down to stroke him. 'You're so weary now, aren't you?'

The dog, who had been their faithful companion

262

since just before Maisie's birth, was old and worn out. Both Anna and Maisie knew he could not last many more years. Maybe he had only months.

'If he starts to suffer,' Anna had explained carefully to Maisie, 'we'll have to let him be put down. It's the kindest.'

With tears in her eyes, Maisie had nodded and buried her face in the dog's coat.

Today Buster seemed slower than ever, but his heart was 'as big as a bucket', as Eddie said, and the dog was still trying to do his job.

'Come on,' Anna said, 'let's get you back inside near the fire and you can rest.'

As they made their way steadily back towards the cottage, Anna saw two men crest the top of the hill and begin to walk down the slope towards them. She shaded her eyes watching them.

Suddenly, her heart began to pound. No, it wasn't possible. No, no, *no*!

She began to run towards the cottage. If she could just get inside before they reached her . . .

'Come on, Buster. Come *on*!' But the dog was too weak. His running days were over. She stopped and picked him up. Despite his frailty, he was still heavy. Clutching him tightly, she struggled and stumbled towards the cottage, desperate to reach its safety. She was almost there, a few yards more and . . .

But the younger of the two men had broken into a run. He was gaining on her. She wasn't going to reach the door. If she had dropped the dog to the ground and run, she could have made it. But, remembering that other time, she held onto him. She couldn't—wouldn't—let the same thing happen to this Buster.

'Now, now, Anna. What's all this? Aren't you pleased to see us?'

He had reached her and was standing between her and her haven. And now the older man was near and he was barring her escape to the side door.

Anna lay Buster on the ground and stood up to face the two men. 'Leave me alone,' she spat at them.

'That's no way to greet us, Anna,' the older man said, 'after all this time. We've been worried about you. Running off like that.'

Anna's eyes narrowed with hatred. The younger man moved towards the dog, lying panting on the ground. He touched it with his foot and Buster growled.

'Still got your brave little protector, eh, Anna?' he sneered. He drew his foot back and aimed a vicious kick at the defenceless animal. Buster's yelp galvanized Anna. She flung herself at the man and began to pummel him.

'Get away. Leave me alone. I hate you. I hate you.'

He was strong and stocky and, whilst Anna was no weakling, she was no match for his strength. He held her by the wrists quite easily. She kicked his shins, but he only laughed. That awful, cruel laugh she remembered so vividly in all her dreams.

Anna began to scream, but he only laughed louder. 'There's no one to hear you, Anna.'

And all the time his father just stood watching.

At the moment when Anna almost gave up the struggle, she heard a shout from the top of the hill and saw Eddie and Maisie running towards her. The man, still holding Anna, turned.

'You get the girl,' he muttered to his father. 'I'll take care of him.'

He turned back and, raising his hand, dealt Anna a vicious blow on the side of her face, knocking her down. The blow had not quite knocked her out, but when she tried to rise she found she was so dizzy that she sank back to the ground.

'Mam!' Through the mists she heard Maisie's cry, but the girl never reached her. She was caught and held fast. 'Now, now, lass. We only want to talk to your mam and you.'

Dimly, Anna was aware that the younger of the two men and Eddie were facing each other like two fighting cocks, circling warily around each other.

The man reached into his pocket and flicked open a knife. 'No!' Maisie cried and struggled, but the big man held her fast. 'Mr Eddie, he's got a knife.'

Dully, her words registered with Anna and she tried to drag herself up. 'No,' she gasped. 'No. Please, no more.' She stumbled towards the one holding Maisie and clung to his arm. 'I'll do whatever you want. I swear it, but make them stop. Don't—don't let him hurt Eddie.'

He looked down at her upturned face, the bruise on her cheek swelling already. His lip curled sarcastically. 'Oh, so the woman was right, was she? You are his fancy piece.'

Anna shook her head, then winced as the pain stabbed. 'No—no, you've got it wrong. I—'

Her words were cut short by a terrifying yell from behind her as the younger man leapt forward, stabbing with the knife.

'No!' The cry came from both Anna's and

265

Maisie's lips at once.

But his blood was up. There was murder in his eyes. Even Eddie, quiet, gentle Eddie Appleyard's face was thunderous. 'I don't know who you are, but you're not going to come here and treat her like that—'

Sudden realization was filtering through Eddie's mind, even in this moment of danger. This, then, was what Anna had been afraid of. One glance at the face and red hair of the man facing him told Eddie all he needed to know. This was the man Anna had run from and, by the look of it, she had had good reason.

There was no denying the likeness. The man threatening him with a knife was undoubtedly Maisie's father.

'Put the knife away, lad, and let's talk this through,' Eddie said, trying desperately to instil calm into his tone, though he would dearly have liked to knock this feller into the middle of next week.

'Talk?' was the scathing answer. 'Talk? What she needs is a damn good hiding. Show her who's boss. By, I've waited years to catch up with that little madam. And now I've found her. Well, she won't escape me again.'

Suddenly he lunged forward, his knife thrusting towards Eddie. It found its mark, entering deep into Eddie's body just below the ribs. Eddie gave a low grunt and his eyes stared in shocked surprise before he crumpled to the ground.

Anna and Maisie cried out together and even the big man shouted, 'No,' as the knife went home. They heard him mutter, 'You damned fool. What do you want to go and do that for?'

His attacker was standing over the still figure, holding the knife covered in blood. Anna and Maisie tore themselves free and flung themselves down beside Eddie. Maisie cradled Eddie's head in her arms, whilst Anna tore open his clothing to see how bad the wound was. Blood spilled out drenching his clothes and hers.

'Oh Eddie, Eddie,' Anna moaned and closed her eyes.

Dimly, she heard one of them say, 'Come on, we'd better get out of here. You're a fool. You've wrecked everything.'

'He was coming for me. It was self-defence.'

'Don't talk daft. He was unarmed.' He nodded towards Anna. 'She'll tell 'em that. And the girl. Come on. Let's get out of here.'

They ran up the hill and down into the farmyard and scrambled into the car. Bertha came out of the back door. 'Find her, did you? I hope you've come to take the little trollop away—'

'Sorry, Missis. Can't stay.'

The engine burst into life. The older man reversed the car erratically and, turning it, drove at speed towards the gate. Driving out into the lane without stopping to see if the way was clear, the car clipped Tony returning on his motorbike, knocking him off balance. As the sports car roared off up the lane, Tony was thrown off his bike and onto the grass verge. His landing was soft and he was unhurt but very angry. Swearing, he gained his feet in time to memorize the number plate.

'Road hog,' Tony shouted as he stood in the lane, shaking his fist after the disappearing vehicle.

Whilst over the hill, now cradled in Anna's arms, Eddie Appleyard fought for his life.

1939

CHAPTER THIRTY-ONE

'Higher, Daddy, push me higher.'

The child on the swing, petticoats flying, swooped through the air.

Her father laughed. 'You're quite big enough to work it yourself now, Anna.' But the ten-year-old smiled winningly and the man capitulated. 'Hold tight, then.'

'Oh, Ken, do be careful,' May called anxiously, nibbling agitatedly at her thumbnail. 'What if the branch breaks?'

Ken laughed. His tall frame was a little stooped, giving the deceptive appearance of frailty. His long face was thin, with hollowed cheeks, but his grey eyes were kind and gentle. He worked in an office in the city of Lincoln and perhaps that was why his skin had a sallow look. Ken stepped back from the swing, letting it slow down of its own accord.

'Daddy?' Anna cried plaintively, but her father only laughed. 'Enough now, love. Your gran will have tea ready and then we must catch the bus back home.'

Anna pouted, but then her sunny nature drove away the brief moment of petulance. She put her feet to the ground and slowed the swing even more. Jumping up, she ran to her parents, pushing her way between them, and linked her arms in theirs.

Mother and daughter were remarkably alike, with black, curling hair and smooth skin. But their most outstanding feature was the colour of their eyes: a dark blue, almost violet. Most people, meeting them for the first time, could not help remarking on the unusual, yet beautiful, colour.

As they arrived at the back door of the farmhouse, May's mother, Rosa, met them.

'Perfect timing.' The plump, placid-faced woman beamed. 'Tea's ready.'

They sat down at the huge kitchen table, with Luke Clayton at the head whilst his wife sat at the opposite end.

'The news isn't good,' he began as he carved a huge piece of boiled ham and passed plates around the table.

'Help yourselves to potatoes,' Rosa said. 'Now, Luke, I don't want any talk of war round my table, thank you. And certainly not in front of the child.'

'I thought everything was all right now, Dad,' May put in, 'since Mr Chamberlain came back from Munich last year.'

The two men exchanged a sober look.

'That agreement, or whatever it was, wasn't worth the paper it was written on,' Luke grunted. He turned to smile at his granddaughter. 'That enough ham for you, lass?'

'Yes thank you, Grandpa.' Anna smiled at the weather-beaten face with its deep lines, at the snowy white, bristly moustache that tickled her when she kissed his cheek.

Ken turned towards his wife and touched her hand lightly. 'It was in all the papers yesterday. Hitler has marched into Czechoslovakia.'

May gasped and the colour fled from her face. 'You mean there's going to be a war?'

Again the two men glanced at each other.

May's voice rose. 'Tell me. I want to know.'

'Now, now, love,' Rosa said, passing the vegetables. 'Don't get all het up about things that

272

don't concern us.'

May rounded on her mother, anxiety making her speak sharply. 'Of course it concerns us, Mam. If there's a war, Ken might have to go.' Then, as if contradicting herself, May grasped her husband's arm. 'You won't, will you?' Clinging to any hope she could think of, she said, 'Besides, you're too old, aren't you?'

Ken cleared his throat and glanced round the table in embarrassment, wishing that his father-in-law had not raised the subject. 'There's talk of more recruits being sought to join the Territorials. I—I thought I might volunteer.'

May gave a little squeak and covered her mouth with her hand, staring with wide-eyed disbelief at her husband. 'Whatever for?' she whispered. 'Why do you want to go and do something like that?'

Luke sniffed. 'Well, if you'd take a bit of advice from an old soldier who was daft enough to volunteer for the last lot—'

'Aye, off you went to war and left me with May to bring up. She was only six when you went,' Rosa began, wagging her finger across the table at her husband. Then she smiled. 'Mind you, I was that proud of you the day we came to wave you off. Marching away to serve your country.' She shook her head, remembering. Tears filled her eyes as she murmured, 'And then, all them medals you got—'

'Well, I don't care about uniforms and medals,' May declared. 'I don't want Ken to go. He might not be as lucky as Dad.'

The unspoken words lay heavily in the air.

'Aye,' Luke said softly. 'I was lucky to come back and without serious injury, an' all. I know that.' He turned towards his son-in-law. When Ken had first started courting his daughter, Luke had not been at all keen on the young man. Ken Milton was a city lad, with no interest in the country or the farm. With an only daughter, it had been Luke's dearest wish that May would marry a local farmer who would take on Clayton's Farm in the future. But May had been drawn to city life, though how she could enjoy living in those crowded streets, which were never quiet day or night, beat Luke. Yet now, as he looked at his son-in-law, Luke felt a fondness for the lad he had not known before. Ken was a good husband to May, Luke acknowledged that. And together they were bringing up a lovely daughter, Anna, who was Luke's pride and joy.

'Don't volunteer, lad. That's my advice.' Grandpa Luke's face was unusually grim. 'Patriotism is all very well and I'd be the first to defend me country from attack—even at my age.' He shook his head. 'But volunteering gets a lot of good fellers killed. Wait till you 'ave to go and not afore. Wait till they send for you.' His tone was grim as he added, ''Cos believe me, they will. If it really comes to war, they'll have to bring in conscription—just like they had to last time.'

Anna's wide-eyed glance went at once to her father's solemn face as he rose from the table. 'I'm sorry, but I'm afraid if it does come to war, I shall go.'

At the sound of May's startled gasp, Anna turned to see that her mother's face had turned deathly white.

On the bus home, her parents scarcely spoke to each other. Her mother looked out of the window and her father stared straight ahead. Sitting on the seat in front of them, Anna shivered. The pleasure of the day had turned suddenly cold.

*   *   *

Throughout the summer, preparations for war continued in earnest. Plans to evacuate children from the cities into the countryside threw May into turmoil again. 'Not from Lincoln. Surely they won't bomb us?'

Ken shrugged. 'It's a possibility we'll have to face. There's a lot of industry in Lincoln that'll be involved in war production, I don't doubt. We could easily be a target. But promise me, Maisie darling, that you'll go out to the farm. You and Anna.' Maisie was Ken's affectionate pet name for his wife, used only in their private moments together or when, as now, he was trying to win her round to his way of thinking.

May pulled a face. 'I suppose so,' she agreed reluctantly. 'But I thought I'd got away from all that when I married you. Wearing wellies all day and mucking out the hen house. To say nothing of milking those horrible cows.'

Despite his anxiety, Ken smiled. 'Is that all you married me for? To get away from the farm?'

May laughed and teased him. 'Of course it was. Didn't you know?'

They were sitting on the battered sofa in front of the plopping gas fire, their arms around each other. Anna was safely asleep upstairs and the two adults could talk freely without fear of frightening her.

Ken's arm tightened about May's waist. 'If I do go, I just want to be sure you and Anna are safe, that's all,' he said.

'Well, there'll be plenty of work for us all to do,'

May said wryly. 'Dad was saying only last weekend that the government are offering to pay farmers two pounds an acre to plough up grazing pastures to grow more crops.'

Ken nodded. 'They're worried that food imports will be at risk if there is a war.'

'But two pounds an acre, Ken. That's a lot of money.'

Ken laughed softly. 'Like your dad always says, "It's an ill wind—"'

May was not to be diverted so easily. 'Why don't we all go? If you work on the farm, you'll not have to go to fight.'

Ken shook his head. 'May, please try to understand. I want to do my bit.'

*　　　*　　　*

People in Britain tried to carry on life as normally as possible, yet everywhere they were reminded of the threat hanging over them all. Houses continued to be built, the King and Queen embarked on a tour of North America and people still went on their summer holidays. Yet news filtered through of Hitler's treatment of the Jews in Germany and rumours began that he had set his sights on Poland. By the end of August war seemed inevitable. Clutching their gas masks and perhaps a favourite toy, thousands of tearful children began to be evacuated from the cities and towns into the safety of the country.

When the day came for Ken to leave, the railway platform teemed with men in khaki. Dotted amongst them were women in flowery dresses, wiping tears from their eyes and clinging to their menfolk's arms.

Anna stood with her parents, holding tightly on to her mother's hand. She was afraid of getting separated from them and being lost amongst the crowds.

'You do understand, May, why I have to go?'

'I still can't understand why you won't at least wait for your call-up papers—like Dad said.'

Anna heard her father sigh. 'We've been through all that,' he said, sounding weary. And they had. Even Anna knew that because she'd heard them arguing in their bedroom at night, trying to keep their voices low so that she would not hear. But always the arguments would end with the sound of her mother crying.

May was trying to be brave now. Her mouth was trembling and tears brimmed in her eyes and threatened to spill down her cheeks, yet she was still trying her best to smile. 'It's just—just—I don't know how I'm going to cope without you.'

'I know, love. But you must be strong for Anna's sake too.'

'But I'm not strong, am I?' Her voice was muffled against him. He did not answer but drew her close and then held out his arm to Anna to enfold her in a bear hug too. 'You must look after each other. And promise me, May, if we get any bombing in Lincoln, you'll go out to the farm? Go and stay with your parents. Anna can go to the village school. They take them right up to leaving age there.'

May nodded.

'Oh, Daddy.' Anna turned her dark, violet eyes up to look at her father. 'Are there going to be bombs?'

'I'll not lie to you, love. There might be. But we might be lucky in Lincoln. They'll be making for the bigger cities rather than here.'

It seemed a forlorn hope and the two adults both knew it. Ken was trying to make light of it for Anna's sake. He didn't want to frighten their ten-year-old daughter. The fact that he was leaving them and that they might have to leave their home in the city had been enough to give the imaginative child nightmares already.

As the train whistle blew, May clung to Ken. He bent and kissed her hard, murmuring, 'Oh, Maisie, my darling Maisie.' Then he was sweeping Anna into a bear hug again and she was crying against the rough serge of his coat. 'Don't go, Daddy. Please don't go.' But with one last, desperate kiss he turned from them both and was gone, lost amongst the throng climbing aboard the train.

When May and Anna returned home, the terraced house was strangely quiet without him. It took May days to stop automatically laying a place for her husband at the table and every night Anna went to stand by Ken's chair to say goodnight, only to stand staring down at the empty place.

Halfway through his training, he had a precious forty-eight-hour pass and then, later, a longer leave. The day before he had to return to his unit, Ken told May quietly, 'This has been what they call embarkation leave. I'm to be posted abroad when I get back.'

May buried her face against his shoulder and asked in a muffled voice, 'Do you know where?'

'No, love. I don't.' Ken said no more. Rumours had been rife around the camp before he had left, but no one knew for sure. And even if he had known, he would not have told May. Now he murmured, 'Don't tell Anna till I've gone. Please, Maisie.'

It was bad enough having to tell the wife he adored, but to see his beloved daughter's stricken face was more than he could bear.

It was not how he wanted to remember Anna.

Ken Milton was amongst the first British troops to arrive in France in the middle of October. At the same time, a general call-up of men over twenty years of age started and May said mournfully, 'Your daddy would have had to go now anyway.' She scrunched up the newspaper and turned to Anna, plastering a bright smile on her face. 'Perhaps he was right to go. First to go, first to come home, eh?'

*   *   *

Ken had been wrong about one thing. Children were not evacuated from Lincoln but brought to the city from other places deemed to be at far greater risk.

'Your teacher's asked us to take an evacuee,' May told Anna. Biting her thumbnail, she said, 'There's thousands arriving on the train from Leeds. It's not that I don't want to help—of course I do—but I think we ought to go out to the farm. It's what Daddy would want us to do. We'll go to Grandpa. He'll look after us.' May shuddered. 'I hate us being here on our own.'

The protest from her daughter that May had expected—probably hoped to hear—was not forthcoming. Secretly Anna was delighted. She loved her grandpa Luke and she loved the farm.

The following day May locked up the house, glancing back as they turned the corner at the top of the road. Would they ever see their home again? she was thinking, but she kept these thoughts to herself, trying to make their evacuation to the country seem like a holiday. Dragging three heavy suitcases, they caught the bus from the city centre which passed through the village close to the farm. Then they walked the last few hundred yards down the lane.

Rosa came out into the yard, her arms held wide. '"It's an ill wind that blows nobody any good",' she quoted and laughed loudly. 'See, if it wasn't for the war, we wouldn't be having you come to live with us for a while, would we?'

May glanced at Anna. Missing her husband and now having to leave her city home were causing May grief, but Anna pulled her hand from her mother's grasp and ran towards her grannie, arms outstretched.

'Can I feed the hens for you and c'lect the eggs?' she gabbled excitedly.

'Course you can, lovey.' Then, catching sight of May's doleful face, Rosa said kindly, 'Now, come along, May. This horrible war will soon be over and Ken will be safely back home. But in the meantime,' she said with a chuckle, 'I can't deny that it's lovely for Grandpa and me to have you here.'

Anna flung her arms around her grandmother's ample waist and pressed her cheek to the woman's comforting warmth. 'Oh, Grannie, I do love the farm and being here with you and Grandpa. And if only Daddy were here too, it would be perfect.'

Above the girl's head, mother and grandmother

exchanged a solemn glance.

CHAPTER THIRTY-TWO

'Anna, this is Jed Rower.' Luke pointed with a gnarled finger towards the youth standing awkwardly near the cowhouse. 'He's Bill Tomalin's nephew.'

Bill Tomalin owned the farm adjacent to Luke's farm and Anna had heard the grown-ups talking about the family.

'Poor old Bill and his missis. Lost their only son in the twenties. Measles. You wouldn't think measles was a killer, now would you? But there you are . . .' Anna remembered her grandfather talking as he carved the Sunday roast.

'Poor little mite,' Rosa had put in, bustling between the scullery and the kitchen table. 'He was so poorly. And you caught it off him, our May. Do you remember?'

May had wrinkled her forehead. 'Was that the time I had to lie in a darkened room?'

'Yes, that's it. They reckoned the illness affected the eyesight and told everybody to keep their bairns in bed and in the dark. Eh dear, what a time it was. And poor little Jack didn't get better. I remember going to the funeral. What a terrible sight it is to see a child's coffin.' The tender-hearted Rosa wiped her eyes with the corner of her apron.

'So now,' Luke had gone on, 'there's only his sister's boy, Jed, for Bill to leave his farm to. Mind you, he's a real good lad. Comes at holiday times and at weekends if he can get here. And he'll help me out if I need it.'

Now, as the two youngsters stood in the yard staring at each other, Luke said, 'Jed's left school now, Anna, and he's come to live at his uncle's. Wants to be a farmer, don't you, lad?'

'That's right, Mester Clayton. Never wanted nowt else.'

Luke beamed at him. 'That's what I like to hear.' He wagged his finger at the young man. 'And no running off to the war when you gets old enough. You hear me?'

Jed grinned. 'Oh I reckon it'll be over long before then, mester.'

'Aye well, that's as mebbe. I 'ope so, lad. I do. But these wars have a terrible habit of going on a lot longer than them there politicians reckon. Any road'—Luke turned and put his hand on Anna's shoulder—'at least this war's brought Anna and her mam to live with us for a while.'

Jed, with merry hazel eyes, fair curling hair and a wide grin, glanced at her and nodded. Anna smiled shyly and then dropped her gaze.

'Well now, I can't stand here yakkerin' all day,' Luke said. 'There's work to do.'

'Can I help, sir?' Jed asked. 'Uncle Bill said you was a bit short-handed with a couple of your regular hands going off to the war.'

Luke beamed at him. 'Ya can, lad. We've two Land Army wenches due soon, but in the meantime I'm a bit stretched. So a bit of help'd be worth a lot of pity, as they say. Now, can you milk cows?'

Jed nodded.

'Right then, you set to in there'—he jerked his

thumb over his shoulder towards the cowhouse—'whilst I get the next lot from the field. Now where's that dratted dog of mine?' He gave a shrill whistle and a black and white collie came tearing round the corner of the building, sliding to a halt in front of his master.

'Come on, dog, let's get them cows in.'

Anna laughed. 'But he's a sheepdog, Grandpa.'

Luke winked at her. 'Aye, but Buster dun't know that, does he? He just thinks he's got to round up any kind of creature. Have you seen him with the geese?'

Anna shook her head.

'That's what I trained him with. They're every bit as cantankerous and awk'ard as sheep.'

'I don't like geese. They're nasty, hissy things.'

Luke laughed. 'An' you don't like the cows 'cos they kick. What do you like, lass?'

Anna beamed. 'I like sheep.'

Luke put his arm about her shoulders. 'Right, then lass. Whilst you'm here I'll teach you all I know about sheep. How's that?'

Anna glanced up at the wrinkled, weather-beaten face. Solemnly, she said, 'I'd like that very much, Grandpa.'

*   *   *

Soon the country became resigned to being at war. Like the conflict which had begun twenty-five years earlier, it was not over by Christmas. The beginning of 1940 was a bleak time and scarcely a minute of the day went by when May and Anna were not thinking about Ken. But despite the ever-present worry, Anna blossomed in the fresh

283

air and country life. She didn't even mind the heavy snowfall that arrived in February. She revelled in tramping through the deep drifts to rescue 'her' sheep.

'Now, lass, I've got summat for you.' Grandpa Luke's blue eyes were twinkling mischievously beneath his shaggy eyebrows.

'A present?' Anna's voice was high with excitement. 'For me?'

From behind his back Luke produced a strangely shaped parcel—long and thin but wider at one end. Anna ripped away the wrapping paper to reveal a shepherd's crook fashioned in every detail to be a small replica of Luke's own.

The girl gasped with delight. 'Oh, Grandpa, it's lovely. Thank you.' She kissed the old man's cheek and was tickled by his moustache.

'There now, when you go out with Buster to fetch the sheep you'll be a real shepherdess.' Luke wagged his forefinger at her and drew his eyebrows together in mock severity. 'But there is a catch. You've got to earn the title. You'll have to learn to help with the lambing and the shearing and the dipping. Even how to count them the shepherd's way.'

Anna was nodding so hard she felt as if her head might fall off. Her violet eyes were bright. 'I will, oh, I will. I want to learn everything, Grandpa,' the young girl told him solemnly. 'I want to stay on the farm for ever. I don't ever want to go back to the city.'

Tears filled the old man's rheumy eyes as he touched her cheek. 'Aye, lass, I reckon you don't.'

Since his disappointment that his own daughter had turned her back on country life, this was more

284

than he had dared to hope for from his granddaughter.

Her instruction began that day, though at first she wasn't sure whether it was she giving Buster instructions or the dog showing her what needed to be done. But soon the two became firm friends. It was almost as if the dog now belonged more to Anna than to Luke.

'He's still a working dog, lass,' the old man would remind her. 'And you mustn't make pets of the animals.'

Anna nodded, understanding. 'We're farmers, aren't we, Grandpa?'

'That's right,' the old man said, his voice hoarse with emotion. 'That's right, me little lass.'

*   *   *

The only reminder of the war was the distant drone of aircraft.

'What's that noise, Grandpa?' Anna asked the first time she heard them.

'Planes, lass. Hampdens, so they tell me. There's an aerodrome a few miles north from here.'

'Oh.' Anna was silent for a moment and then, in a small voice, she asked, 'Are they—are they going to drop bombs on the enemy?'

'Aye, mebbe.'

'But—how can they be sure they don't drop them on our soldiers?'

Luke smiled at her, his leathery face creasing into a thousand wrinkles—or so it seemed. 'Oh, they'll mind not to do that, love. They'll be aiming for things like enemy shipping, and if they do' go over enemy territory it'll be things like bridges and railways and maybe factories that make equipment for the war.'

'That's what Daddy said the Jerries'd do to us,' Anna said. 'They might bomb Lincoln because he was sure the factories there would be making things for the war.'

'Aye well, lass, I reckon he could be right. Anyway,' he added, putting his arm about her shoulders, 'that's why you've come here. To be safe with us, eh?'

Every day Luke would give his own weather forecast and try to guess whether they would hear the planes that night. 'Just look at that lovely sunset, lass. Ain't no better sight anywhere than a Lincolnshire sunset, to my mind. Sign of good weather, that is. They'll be flying tonight.' And then, in contrast, he would say, 'Don't reckon we shall hear them planes going out tonight. Bad sky this morning. Reckon we're in for a bit of a blow.'

But sometimes he would be wrong and, distantly, they'd hear the planes going out.

Each night Grandpa insisted that everyone was silent whilst he listened to the nine o'clock news on the wireless. Anna, sitting quietly, was obliged to listen too and so picked up the war news. Some of it she understood, but in her young, logical mind she still questioned the truth of her grandfather's assurances. If both sides were dropping bombs on each other, she couldn't understand how the British, whose army was over there, could be sure not to drop them on their own men.

Every night Anna knelt on the cold floor of her bedroom and prayed fervently for her father's safe return. But when she climbed into bed at last and lay down, she felt no reassurance that her prayers would be answered.

And then, at the end of May, they all listened with horror to the news of the evacuation from Dunkirk. They glanced fearfully at one another, knowing that Ken was out there somewhere.

A week later May received the telegram, forwarded from their home in Lincoln, reporting that Kenneth Milton was missing, presumed killed.

*   *   *

'It's not fair, Grandpa. It's not fair. Why did Daddy have to get killed?'

Weeks after the news had come, Anna still could not accept it. Helping her grandfather with the haymaking, she walked beside him into the meadow to rake and toss the swathes of grass that had been cut the previous day.

In his gravelly voice, Luke said, 'Life isn't fair, lass. But we all have to make the best of it, whatever comes our way. I was in the last war. I volunteered right at the start. Just like your dad did.' Luke cast a wry glance at his granddaughter. 'He wouldn't listen to me, would he? Had to go an' do the same.' Luke's bushy white eyebrows drew together in a frown. 'Can't blame him, though,' he murmured, his thoughts far away. 'But I was lucky. I came back.'

He stood leaning on his rake, gazing into the distance as if he were seeing a ghostly regiment of long-dead comrades marching past. 'A lot of good men didn't come back. The war to end wars, they called it then, yet just over twenty years after it ended here we are plunged into another. I don't reckon them politicians will ever learn,' he ended bitterly. Then Luke seemed to shake himself and said briskly, 'This won't get the work done, lass. Come on now, put ya back into it.'

Anna spent a lot of time with her grandfather. When she was not attending the local school, she was by his side.

'She's as good as any farmhand,' Luke told Rosa. 'You should see her with the sheep.' He chuckled. 'I reckon she's given 'em all names. All thirty of 'em.'

'How did she take it when the lambs went? And does she know they've gone for slaughter?'

'She understands. I explained it all to her. Aye.' Luke gave a deep sigh of contentment. 'The farm'll be in safe hands when I'm gone.'

Rosa said seriously. 'Let's not talk about anyone else going yet. That little lass has had enough sadness in her life to last her a good few years. And as for our May . . .' Rosa shook her head and sighed. 'I don't know if she'll ever get over losing Ken.'

Luke lit his pipe and puffed at it, getting it well alight before he answered. 'She's young. She'll not forget him. Course she won't. But time is a healer, love. Given time, she'll mebbe meet someone else. Our May needs a man to lean on and I won't be here for ever.' He chuckled. 'Even if I'd like to be.'

Rosa said wryly, 'But what sort of man is she likely to find, eh? We're going to lose a whole generation of fellers again, just like we did last time. And what'll we be left with? You tell me that. The dregs, that's what.'

Luke twinkled at her mischievously. 'Well, I came back last time. Is that what I am then? The dregs?'

Rosa laughed. 'You tek it how ya like, Luke Clayton. If you remember'—she nodded at him teasingly—'I was engaged to that butcher feller just afore the last war. And he didn't come back, now did he?'

'Yeah, but if I remember you'd thrown him over before he ever went to the Front.'

They laughed together, easy in the knowledge that it was all just banter between them.

Their laughter faded and Rosa said pensively, 'It'd be nice to think that—in time—May could meet someone nice, 'cos you're right, she does need someone and it'd be nice for that little lass to have a daddy again.'

'But in the meantime'—Luke opened his newspaper and spread it wide, scanning the pages for yet more news—'she's got us.'

CHAPTER THIRTY-THREE

It was a cruel Fate that was listening at that moment to Luke's confident statement. Only three weeks later Rosa began to feel ill.

'I can't understand why I feel so tired all the time,' she said, sitting down in the wooden rocking chair beside the range after a morning's work. 'I can usually go all day without stopping, but now—'

'You're not as young as you used to be, Mam.'

'I'm only fifty-seven,' Rosa responded indignantly.

May eyed her mother. 'You've lost weight, too.'

'I always do in summer. We eat more salads an' that in the hot weather, don't we?' Rosa heaved herself out of the chair in an effort to prove there was nothing wrong with her. ' 'Spect I've got a bit of anaemia. I've had it before at this time of year.'

'Anaemia doesn't give you a pain in your tummy. I've seen you holding yourself. Look, you're doing it now.'

'It's just a bit of indigestion. Something I've eaten.'

May cast her a wry look. 'I think you ought to see the doctor, Mam.'

'Aye, sometime. I'll go when I've time.'

A week later even Luke was persuading her to go. 'I'll take you into the village mesen and make sure you do see him,' he declared. 'You're not right, woman. Even I can see that. The weight's dropping off you.'

'All right, then. I'll go.'

Luke and his daughter exchanged a startled glance. The fact that Rosa was agreeing to see a doctor was enough for alarm bells to start ringing in both their minds.

They had good reason to be fearful. The doctor sent Rosa into Lincoln for further tests and two weeks later he called at the farm.

'Run along into the yard, missy,' he said in a kindly manner to Anna. 'I need to talk to your grandpa and grannie. May'—he had known the Clayton family for years and had attended May's birth in this very farmhouse—'you stay, please.'

He sat down at the table, his face solemn as he explained gently that the consultant had found a growth in Rosa's stomach.

'We can operate, but—' His silence and the unspoken words hung in the air.

'Oh no,' May cried, her hand flying to her

290

mouth. 'Oh Mam, no.'

Luke took his wife's hand and held on to it tightly. 'This operation? If she has it, there's a chance?'

The doctor glanced from Luke to Rosa and back again. He knew them so well, knew that they were strong enough to be told the truth. He wasn't so sure about May. She was crumbling before his eyes. But then, he reminded himself, this was the second lot of terrible news she'd had in a few short months. 'Fifty—fifty.'

Rosa seemed to be taking the news calmly. 'Well, I've had a good life. And May's home now to look after her dad . . .'

'Mam,' May cried, tears flooding down her cheeks, 'don't say such things. You'll get better. You'll have the operation and you'll get better. I know you will. Oh Mam, you have to. I—I can't bear to lose you too.'

Luke walked out of the house with the doctor.

'I'm so sorry, old friend. I wish there was more I could say, more I could do.'

'You've told us the truth and now we know what we have to face.' Luke glanced across to where Anna was playing with Buster. The girl was laughing at the dog's antics, their game driving away some of the sadness from her face. 'Though how I'm going to tell that little lass, I don't know.'

'Like me to do it for you?'

Luke shook his head. 'No. Thanks, but it'll come better from me. If she sees we're facing up to it, then—'

He said no more and the doctor nodded agreement, but he was thinking that May was not going to be of much use.

As if reading his thoughts, Luke said softly, 'She's stronger than her mam, I reckon. She'll be all right. She'll be all right with me.'

Wordlessly, the doctor patted Luke's shoulder and went towards his car.

*　　　*　　　*

Rosa was called in for the operation only a week later. It was a tense and anxious time for the family and visiting Rosa in the city hospital proved difficult with the war restrictions. There was no telephone at Clayton's Farm so it was the doctor who once again brought the news.

The moment he stepped out of his car and went towards Luke, who was standing near the cowshed, the old man knew the news was bad.

Dr Phillips shook his head sadly. 'I'm so sorry, Luke. She came through the operation itself well, but back on the ward she suffered a massive heart attack. There was nothing anyone could do.'

Luke nodded wordlessly.

'If it's any comfort, old friend, the end was quick. If she'd survived and the cancer had returned, she would have had a lingering and very painful death.'

'Aye, well.' Luke sniffed hard, but was unable to control the break in his voice. 'Aye well, that's summat to be thankful for.'

The family was devastated. It was almost worse than the loss of Ken, for that had been a possibility from the moment he volunteered. But that Rosa— laughing, good-hearted Rosa—should die so quickly was hard to take.

'If only we'd had more time,' May wept. 'I can't believe it.'

Luke, though suffering his loss inside, seemed on the surface to accept the blow more easily than May. He had seen a lot more of life—and of death—than his daughter.

'You couldn't have asked for her to go on suffering. She were nowt but skin and bone by the end. You wouldn't let an animal suffer like that, lass. Now would you?'

May shook her head and murmured the very same words her daughter had used only months earlier. 'But it's so unfair, Dad. It's so unfair.'

Anna's grief was silent. She shed her tears in private, anxious not to add to her grandfather's grief or to upset her mother even more. May did her best to take over the running of the farmhouse, but Rosa, born to be a farmer's wife, was a hard act to follow.

May wept through the days. 'I can't get the Yorkshire puddings to rise like Mam did,' she moaned on the first Sunday after the funeral. 'I've burnt the meat and the gravy's lumpy.'

'Ne'er mind, love,' Luke said placidly. 'That range oven's always been a bit temperamental. Even your mam used to grumble about it. You'll soon get the hang of it, though.'

'But that's just it. I don't want to get the hang of it,' May wailed. 'I want to go back to Lincoln. I want to go home.'

Luke said nothing, but Anna had seen the deep hurt in his eyes. That his daughter should consider the little terraced house in a back street of the city to be home, instead of the farm where she had been born and brought up, cut the old man to the quick.

Anna's confidant was Jed, who came to see her

the morning after the funeral. 'I'm real sorry about your gran, Anna. She was a lovely lady. Always so friendly. And cook—by heck, I've never tasted apple pasties like hers. Even me auntie Sue can't make 'em like Mrs Clayton could.' He tried to lighten the gravity of their conversation by adding, 'But don't you tell 'er I said so, else she'll chase me with me uncle's shotgun.'

Anna smiled thinly. Then Jed, trying to draw her out, said soberly, 'It must be very hard for you. First your dad and now your gran. Difficult for all your family. Look'—he hesitated, his face reddening—'if there's ever owt I can do to help you, you've only got to say. I aren't very good with words, but—but I'm a good listener. Sometimes—well—sometimes it helps just to be able to talk about it. And maybe you can't talk about it at home because—well—they're upset an' all. I don't mean I'm not,' he went on swiftly, lest she should misunderstand him. 'She'll be badly missed round here. Everybody liked her.'

The number of mourners at the funeral had told Anna that. The line following the coffin had stretched a hundred yards or more.

'But, well—' Jed was still stumbling on, trying in his youthful way to bring comfort to the young girl, 'I weren't family.'

Anna smiled at him through her tears. 'Thanks, Jed,' she said huskily. 'You're—very kind.'

Jed became her constant companion. Luke had taught her about sheep, but it was Jed she watched hedging and ditching, he who helped her with a broody hen and watched as the eggs cracked and little yellow chicks emerged. It was Jed who showed her how to milk the cows and helped her overcome

294

her fear of their restless hooves.

'I won't ever like them as much as the sheep.' She laughed. 'But I'm not quite so scared of them now. Thanks to you.'

'You've got gentle fingers. You'd make a good milkmaid.'

Anna pulled a face. 'I'd rather be a shepherdess. That's what I really want to be.'

He took her fishing in the stretch of the River Brant that ran through both her grandfather's farm and his uncle's. And it was Jed who stood with his arm about her shoulders, comforting her whenever any of their animals were loaded into the back of the lorry to be driven to market.

'How's ya mam?' he asked gently one day.

Anna shrugged. 'She's running the house better now.' She even managed to smile. 'Her cooking's improved, but she still cries a lot.' Anna's voice broke a little as she added, 'She—wants to go back to the city.'

Jed looked down at her, his blue eyes sober. 'What about you?' he asked softly. 'Do you want to go back?'

Vehemently, Anna shook her head. 'No. I never want to go back. I want to stay here for ever and ever.'

It was the dream of an eleven-year-old child, but silently Jed prayed that her wish would still be the same when Anna was grown. 'I hope you do,' he said softly.

CHAPTER THIRTY-FOUR

Clayton's Farm, handed down through the generations from Luke's great-grandfather, was situated a few miles to the south of Lincoln. It had passed from son to son, but now there were only May and Anna to take it on should anything happen to Luke. The old man couldn't hide the fact that his dearest wish was to see them both living back at the farm for good.

'It's silly to keep paying rent on an empty house in the city,' Luke told May bluntly.

'But we'll be going back,' May argued, trying to hold out.

'Look, love,' Luke said, trying to be more gentle, 'even if you do go back to town one day'—the words were said reluctantly, but he had to accept the fact that it was a strong possibility. If his daughter had her way, she'd be back to city life in a trice—'surely you'd be better to have a fresh start in a different house? Do you really want to take that little lass'—Luke almost choked on the words—'back to a house full of memories of her daddy? Do *you* want to go back there?'

May sighed. 'I don't know, Dad. Sometimes my memories of Ken are so vivid it's almost as if he's going to walk into the room at any minute. At others, it seems as if all those years were just a dream and never really happened.'

'Well, they did and you've a lovely daughter to prove it. We've all got our memories—that's what keeps us going,' Luke said, thinking back down the years to all the happy times he'd spent with his

296

beloved Rosa. 'Hold on to them, May, don't ever lose them. But it doesn't mean we have to stop living. You've still got a lot of your life left and Ken wouldn't have wanted you to mourn him for ever. And that little lass has got all of hers to come yet. Let her choose the path she wants to take, May.' He put his head on one side and regarded her solemnly. 'I didn't stand in the way of you marrying Ken Milton and letting him take you to live in the city, even though I wanted you to stay here.'

Easy tears filled May's eyes. 'You didn't like him, Dad, did you?'

Luke sighed. 'Not at first, no, but I think it was only because I knew he'd take you away from us. Later I came to see that he was a fine young man. A good husband and father.'

'Just because he volunteered for the war—like you did years ago?' There was a bitter edge to her tone now.

Luke sighed, but was honest enough to admit, 'Well, I saw then that he had the qualities I admire in a feller. It was a pity it took a war to show me that, but that was my pig-headedness. I'll own up to that.'

So, May relinquished the tenancy of the terraced house in Lincoln and moved their belongings and bits of furniture into the rambling farmhouse.

For most of the time the war seemed very far away, with only the drone of aircraft overhead to remind them. And, of course, the rationing, as May, who had now taken over the running of the household, was ever quick to tell them. But, living on a farm, they were luckier than most. By 1942 the last of Luke's young farmhands had joined the army, leaving only Luke and an old man who had

297

worked on Clayton's Farm all his life. And even he was able to work less and less.

'Tis the arthritis in me old bones,' he complained. 'I'm not as young as I used to be.'

Despite her sympathy for the old farmhand, Anna always wanted to giggle when she heard him say that. Not about the arthritis, but about his age. Was anyone ever as young as they once were? she thought.

Jed helped whenever he could, but his uncle's farm was short-handed too.

'I don't know why they all want to go rushing off,' Luke grumbled. 'They're in a reserved occupation. Just wanting to play the hero.'

'Well, you did,' May retorted and added bitterly, 'and so did Ken.'

'Aye, you're right, lass.' The old man's eyes softened. 'I suppose I should understand better than anyone. Anyway,' he went on briskly, 'we're to have a couple of Land Army girls. Can you do with 'em in the house?'

May smiled and Luke realized how hard May was trying to be more like her mother. Rosa had wanted nothing more from life than to be a good farmer's wife. To their disappointment, Luke and Rosa had only been blessed with one child, though they would have loved more. After a difficult birth with May, Dr Phillips had warned Rosa not to have any more children. So Rosa contented herself with her husband, her daughter and the extended family of their farmworkers and all the extra help that came at haymaking, harvest and shearing. Rosa was at her happiest when she had an army to feed.

May hadn't quite got to that level yet, but she said now, 'It'll be lovely to have some young folks about the place. Company for Anna too.' *And me as well*, she thought privately.

The sight of the two Land Army girls climbing out of the back of the lorry a few days later was a welcome one for Luke; May, too, smiled a greeting, but their reasons were very different. Luke was glad to see more help arriving, even if he expected it to take a few weeks for the two girls to settle in and learn the ropes. May was just glad to see two young women nearer her own age, who looked as if they might bring a little fun and laughter to the back of beyond, which was how she thought of Clayton's Farm.

May hurried out to greet them. The girls were dressed identically in the Women's Land Army 'uniform': open-necked shirts, green pullovers, brown corduroy knee breeches, long thick fawn socks and brown brogues.

'Hello. I'm May Milton. Come along in. You must be hungry. How far have you come?'

The two girls were bouncy, bubbly and quite pretty in a brash sort of way. The shorter of the two, who had blue eyes, shoulder-length blonde hair and a round, merry face, held out her hand. 'Hello, I'm Betty Purves.'

'Better known as Purvey the Curvy, because she curves in all the right places,' the other girl said. 'And I'm Rita Mackinder.' Rita was tall with short, curly dark brown hair and brown eyes. 'The skinny one.'

May shook hands with them. 'You're both very welcome. Come along in, do.'

The girls heaved their luggage from the back of the lorry and waved a cheery goodbye to the driver.

'Don't forget the dance next Saturday, Harry,'

299

Betty called after him.

'It's a date, love.' He waved as he started the engine.

'Oh you!' Rita pretended indignation. 'How many fellers do you need? What about Douglas?'

Betty patted her long golden hair. 'Safety in numbers, pet. Come on, where's that tea the nice lady was offering? I'm parched.'

Later, when Anna and Luke walked into the house together, the kitchen was alive with noisy laughter. May, her eyes more alight than they had been for months, said, 'Oh, come and meet these two. They're a scream. They ought to be on the stage.'

When the introductions were done, Luke said, 'Well now, where are you two lasses from then?'

'Me? I'm from up north,' Betty said. 'Near Newcastle, but Rita here, she's from Sheffield. We've never been to Lincolnshire before. Neither of us.' She pulled a comical face. 'I thought it was supposed to be flat, but we tried walking up Steep Hill in Lincoln last week. I don't call that flat!'

Anna stared at the two girls, fascinated by the way they talked. She'd heard a Yorkshire voice before, but never a Geordie accent. The way Betty's lilting voice rose at the end of each sentence, almost as if she was asking a question, delighted the young girl.

Luke was chuckling. 'It's flat in the south of the county, in the fens and also along the east coast. But we've got the Wolds and the Lincoln Heights to give us a few hills.' He nodded at them both. 'Not like where you come from, I admit, but it suits us.'

Rita nudged Betty. 'It'll be safe for you.' They

both laughed and Betty's face was tinged with pink.

'We were on a farm in Derbyshire until last month and she was driving a tractor on a steep slope. Going down hill, like this'—Rita sloped her hand to demonstrate—'and ended up in the river at the bottom. The farmer weren't right pleased.'

'Remind me not to let you loose in the field that borders the Brant then,' Luke said, but his eyes were twinkling.

'You can talk, Rita Mackinder. What about you and cows then?' Betty leant across the table towards Luke and now it was Rita's turn to look embarrassed. 'I hope you've got hundreds of cows, Mister. Our Rita loves 'em. Can't *wait* to get her hands on them.' Laughing, she pretended she was milking a cow.

'We've only got seventeen now, but most of them are good milkers.'

Betty hooted with laughter and dug her friend in the ribs. 'There you are, Reet. You'll be all right.'

Mystified, Luke, May and Anna stared at the two girls. Anna was the first to realize the joke. 'She's teasing you, isn't she? You don't really like them, do you?'

Rita pulled a wry face. 'Sorry, no. I don't. I got kicked badly at the farm in Derbyshire and I've been frightened of them ever since.'

'Never mind,' Anna said kindly. 'You can help with the sheep, can't she, Grandpa?'

'Course she can, love. We don't want anyone being hurt here.'

'You'll like sheep. They're lovely and gentle.'

'You're very kind,' Rita said, serious for a moment, 'but I wouldn't want it to look as if I'm trying to get out of doing summat I'm supposed to.'

Luke laughed. 'Don't worry, lass, we won't think that of you. Besides'—his eyes twinkled—'there's plenty else you can do.'

They joined in his laughter. It was the happiest sound the farmhouse kitchen had heard in months.

*   *   *

'We're going to a dance next Saturday in Lincoln,' Betty told May. 'My feller's picking us up. Why don't you come with us?'

The two girls had settled in remarkably quickly and now everyone felt they were part of the family.

'Oh, I don't know. It—it wouldn't seem right. I— I lost my husband at Dunkirk and then my mother died soon after . . .'

Looking unusually serious, Betty said gently, 'You can't live in the past, pet.'

'Well, no, but . . . It just seems a little too soon. That's all.'

'How about letting Anna come with us, then?'

Now May shook her head firmly. 'Oh no. She's far too young.'

'Is she?' Betty sounded surprised. 'How old is she?'

'Thirteen.'

'Thirteen! I thought she was at least fifteen. She looks it.'

'She's tall for her age. She's grown even in this last year. I expect it's living on the farm. She's filled out.'

Betty laughed as she ran her hands down her own body. 'And in all the right places. I'll have a rival for Miss Curvy, nineteen forty-two, if I don't watch it.' They laughed and then Betty added, 'But,

302

yeah, you're right. She is a bit young to be going to dances, specially in the city. We get a lot of the RAF lads there.' Betty's eyes sparkled at the thought. 'Tell you what, though. We'll take her to the pictures sometime. My feller's got something to do with one of the cinemas there. He'll tell us when there's a nice film on we can take her to. You'd let her go there with us, wouldn't you?'

May nodded. 'That'd be very kind of you.'

'Oh, go on.' Betty flapped her hand at May. 'We love it here. You're very good to us and as for Pops . . .' It was the name that Betty had christened Luke. 'He's a real poppet.'

May laughed. She'd never heard her father referred to as 'a poppet' before, but the endearment suited him. Her face sobered as she said pensively, 'I wish you could have met my mother. You'd have loved her.'

Betty couldn't bear anyone to be maudlin for more than a couple of minutes, so she patted May's hand and said, 'I'm sure we would. I bet you take after her, don't you?'

May sighed. 'I really wish I did. But I—I don't think I'm quite as strong a character as she was.' She bit her lip, reluctant to confide even to the friendly Betty that she hated the life on the farm. She was only biding her time until the war was over and she could go back home.

'Must be off,' Betty said, not one for analysing life too closely. 'Mustn't keep the cows waiting. I still can't remember all their names. And as for the sheep . . . I never knew anyone to give names to their sheep before.'

May laughed now. 'We don't. Cows have always had names, but naming the sheep was Anna. She loves them.'

'And that dog, Buster. He never leaves her side, does he? He was missing the other afternoon and I asked Pops where he was. "Oh he'll be down at the school," he said, "waiting for Anna to come out." And sure enough, there he was, loping alongside of her when she rode into the yard on her bike.'

At that moment, Anna and Buster were out in the fields with Luke's flock of thirty ewes and their twenty-four lambs.

Anna stood with her hand on Buster's head. 'The lambs'll have to go in a month or two,' she told the dog sadly. 'Most of them. But I think Grandpa is going to keep three female lambs to build up his flock. That's nice, isn't it?'

Beside her the dog looked up at her adoringly, his long pink tongue lolling. He gave a little bark, as if he understood her every word. 'Come on, boy, we'd better go home. We've got those two little lambs to feed that lost their mother.'

Minutes later, Betty stood watching as Anna prepared a bottle to feed the lambs. 'You really love the silly creatures, don't you, pet?' she teased the young girl, shaking her head and pretending to be mystified. 'Can't understand why. They never do what you want 'em to do. If you want 'em to go to the right, they'll go left, sure as eggs.'

Anna only grinned as she held a motherless lamb firmly under her arm to feed it with a bottle.

'Take no notice of her,' she pretended to whisper to the lamb, but making sure that Betty heard. 'She dun't know what she's talking about.'

Betty laughed. 'You could be right there, pet. But give me a tractor to drive any day. Least I can steer it where I want it to go.'

304

Anna looked up and grinned saucily. ' 'Cept when you nearly drove it into the river last week. When you first came here, Rita said you'd done the same thing in Derbyshire.'

Betty pulled a face. 'Well, yeah, I did that time, but I didn't with your grandpa's tractor. I only got a bit too close. And don't you go telling Pops, else he'll not let me drive it again.'

Anna giggled. 'As long as you are nice to my sheep.'

Betty laughed. 'Little minx!' she said fondly and then winked. 'It's a deal.'

*   *   *

They heard the noise of Betty's feller's car even before it turned into the yard gate. The roar of an engine being driven at full speed coming closer and closer down the lane, the skid of tyres as it swung in through the gate and the squeal of brakes as it came to a stop. Luke came out of the barn and stood frowning at the sleek, open-topped sports car standing in the middle of his yard.

The driver hoisted himself up and agilely swung his legs over the low door without opening it. He came towards Luke, his hand outstretched. He was dressed in a checked suit and a trilby and sported a neat moustache.

'Douglas Whittaker, sir. How do?'

Luke took the proffered hand, but glanced down at the man's brown and white shoes. 'Not the place for those, young feller. You'll get 'em messed up.'

Douglas laughed. Although he was young compared with Luke, he was in his late thirties. He gave off the appearance of being a man of the

305

world. Luke's knowing eyes narrowed as he took in Douglas Whittaker's appearance. So this was Betty's feller. He hoped it wasn't serious. Luke was becoming fond of the two Land Army girls and this wasn't the sort of man he would like to see courting anyone belonging to him. He gave a grunt. It was nowt to do with him, he told himself sharply. 'Come along in while you wait for the lasses. 'Spect they're still titivating.'

Douglas guffawed. 'Making themselves beautiful for me, eh? That's what I like to hear.' He pulled a gold cigarette case from his pocket, snapped it open and held it out towards Luke. 'Do you smoke, sir?'

Luke eyed the long, slim cigarettes. American, by the look of them. 'Only a pipe,' he murmured. And then, remembering his manners, added, 'Thanks all the same.'

'What brand of baccy do you smoke? I can get you some.' Douglas tapped the side of his nose and winked. 'Know what I mean?'

Oh yes, Luke knew what he meant. He was a black marketeer by the sound of it. Luke had heard about the goings on, but he'd never been approached directly before.

He turned his back on Douglas as he replied shortly, 'I don't smoke a lot. I've plenty for what I need.'

This time he added no word of thanks.

As he ushered the visitor into the farmhouse kitchen, May hurried forward, wiping her floury hands on her apron. 'You must be Betty's young man. Do come in. I don't think they'll be long.'

In the corner by the range, Anna was feeding a lamb with a bottle.

'Hello, young lady.' Douglas knelt beside her and touched the animal's fine, woolly coat. Buster, sitting close by on the hearth, gave a deep-throated growl. Hearing it, Luke almost laughed aloud. *You and me both, boy*, he thought, but he said nothing.

Anna, however, spoke sternly to the dog. 'Stop it, Buster. This is Betty's friend. Naughty dog.'

Buster lay down, his nose on his paws, but he continued to eye the stranger with suspicion.

There was the sound of clattering high heels on the stairs and Betty and Rita, dressed in pretty cotton dresses, swept into the kitchen.

Douglas held his arms wide. 'Well, well. Now if that isn't worth waiting for.' His gaze swept them up and down and then his grin widened. 'But if I'm not much mistaken, you're not quite dressed yet, are you?'

Betty and Rita exchanged a glance. 'Cheek of the devil,' Betty said, fluffing her hair.

Douglas laughed, holding out his hands in supplication. 'No offence, ladies.' He fished in his pocket and pulled out two packages. 'I just thought perhaps you could make use of these.'

Tearing open their gifts, the girls exclaimed over the nylon stockings, whilst May watched enviously and glanced down at her own thick lisle ones. Betty threw her arms round Douglas. 'Oh, you darling. I might have known. There's nothing you can't get, if you've a mind, is there?' She drew back and glanced at Luke and then at May. She prodded Douglas in the chest. 'So if there's anything you want, he's your man.'

'If I'd known there was another lovely young lady, I'd have brought another pair.' Douglas gave a little bow towards May and murmured, 'Maybe

307

next time, eh?'

May smiled uncertainly but Luke's only response was to turn on his heel and leave the house.

CHAPTER THIRTY-FIVE

Douglas became a regular visitor to the farm, along with other 'followers' of the two girls. One was a very good-looking RAF pilot with wavy black hair.

'He looks like a film star,' Anna breathed, watching him with wide eyes.

'Aye aye,' Betty said, winking mischievously. 'Our Anna might only be thirteen but she knows a good-looking feller when she sees one. I'll have to keep me eye on you, pet, else you'll be stealing them from under my nose with those lovely eyes of yours.'

'Oh I reckon you're safe, our Betty,' Rita chirped up. 'Anna's got a boyfriend.'

Anna turned wide eyes on the grinning girl. 'What do you mean? I haven't got a boyfriend.'

'Haven't you? You could have fooled me. Well, I know a very nice young feller who'd like to fill the part.'

'Who?'

'Jed, of course.'

'*Jed?* But he works here. And he's heaps older than me.'

'Yeah, course he is. All of five years, but it doesn't stop him making sheep's eyes at you. Oops, sorry for the pun.'

'He doesn't,' Anna denied, but could not help blushing.

*   *   *

'You know Charlie, the pilot officer,' Betty said one evening, only a week later.

'That handsome one with black hair?' Anna asked as May looked up enquiringly.

Betty nodded, biting her lip. 'His plane never came back. Went down somewhere over the Channel, they say. The whole crew are missing.'

'That's terrible,' May said, her hand to her mouth to still its trembling. 'Oh the poor boy. He was only nineteen, wasn't he?'

Anna bent her head over the rug she was learning to make from scraps of material so that the others would not see the tears in her eyes. To think that that lovely-looking young man was now dead brought back vividly all the sadness about her own daddy.

Betty nodded. 'Yeah.' She sat for a moment as if lost in thought, then she stood up quickly, 'Still, life has to go on, pet, hasn't it? At least there's no chance of that happening to good old Douglas.'

In his chair in the corner, Luke shook his newspaper and sniffed.

'What was that, Pops?' Betty said.

'Nothing,' came the short reply. 'Nothing at all.'

*   *   *

'Are you serious about this Douglas?' Luke asked after supper the following evening.

'Me?' Betty laughed. 'I'm not serious about any feller, Pops.' She beamed at him. 'Only you, mebbe.'

309

They all laughed, but no one had missed the underlying message of Luke's question. Betty put her head on one side. 'You don't like him.' It was a statement rather than a question.

Luke shrugged but said nothing.

Betty laughed again. 'I'll take that as a "no" then, shall I?'

Now Luke muttered, 'Seems a bit of a flash type to me. What I'd call a spiv.'

'Dad!' May exclaimed, scandalized at her father's blunt remark, but Betty only grinned. 'You could say that, Pops, yes.' She winked at Luke, as if sharing a secret. 'But he's good for a pair of stockings now and again, chocolates and even a new dress when my clothing coupons run out, to say nothing of keeping me well supplied with knicker elastic.'

Luke grunted and bit hard on the end of his pipe. He tried to look disapproving, drawing his shaggy white eyebrows together, but even Anna could see that he was having difficulty hiding the amused twinkle in his eyes. He removed his pipe from his mouth and jabbed the end of it towards Betty. 'Just be careful, lass, that's all.'

'I will, Pops, don't you worry,' Betty said merrily in her lilting accent, yet there was an underlying seriousness to her tone. 'He'd have to get up early to get one over on us Geordie lasses.'

May pursed her lips and said primly, 'It sounds to me as if it's you that's taking advantage of Douglas's generosity.'

Betty's eyebrows rose and she glanced at Luke and then back to May. Betty opened her mouth to make some retort but evidently thought better of it and closed it again, but suddenly there was a pink

310

tinge to her cheeks and her eyes sparkled with anger.

'How's he come to be in these parts?' Luke put in, trying to smooth over the awkwardness. 'He's a Londoner by the sound of him, ain't he?'

'Yes. He worked in the West End theatres, but when the war started the audience figures dropped off and then the government closed all the theatres throughout the country. Course they opened up again after a few months, but even then what with the evacuation of a lot of people, the blackout and a lot of restrictions the government imposed, Dougie said it was hardly worthwhile opening. Anyway,' she went on, 'he'd got this mate in the Midlands, so he came up this way and now he's got a cinema in Lincoln and reckons he's doing very nicely, thank you.'

'You mean he owns it?' Luke asked.

Betty stared at him and blinked. 'Well, I never really asked him outright. But—well—he acts as if he does.'

Luke only reply was a disbelieving grunt.

'I think he seems rather nice,' May ventured, though she cast a nervous glance at her father. 'He's taking us all to the pictures on Friday night. He's asked me to go too.' She glanced at Betty. 'I—I hope you don't mind.'

'Course I don't, pet,' Betty said, her good humour restored. 'The more the merrier.'

It was certainly a merry outing on the following Friday evening. Douglas arrived with his usual flurry.

'I'm so sorry I can't fit you all into my car,' Douglas said. 'Maybe Anna could squeeze in the back seat, but it won't take all three of you ladies.'

'That's all right,' May said. 'We'll take the bus into town and meet you and Betty somewhere.'

'Nonsense,' Douglas retorted. 'You're our guests. You and Anna must come with me.' He turned to Betty. 'Sweetheart, you and Rita won't mind catching the bus just this once, eh?'

Betty glared at him but then, seeing the disappointment on Anna's face as if she feared the whole outing was suddenly in jeopardy, she shrugged her plump shoulders and smiled. Wagging her finger playfully at him, she said, 'Just this once then, mind.'

*   *   *

Douglas was a charming and attentive host. He took them for tea in a small cafe before the film. As they left, he crooked both his arms and offered one to Betty and the other to May. Rita and Anna fell into step behind them and, laughing, they walked towards the cinema.

As they stepped into the foyer a youth of seventeen or so was waiting for them.

'Here he is,' Douglas boomed, obviously expecting the boy to be there. 'Ladies, may I introduce my son, Bruce. Bruce, this is Betty, Rita and May. And this . . .' he gestured with a flourish, 'is May's daughter, Anna. Now I'll get the tickets. Front row circle and you two young ones can sit together.'

Bruce was thin, gangly some might have said. He had dark brown eyes and carrot-coloured hair. As often happened with his colouring, his face was covered with freckles. He grinned a welcome and nodded. 'Hello.'

Betty pulled her hand from Douglas's arm. 'I didn't know you had a son,' she said tartly. 'Got a wife hidden away somewhere an' all?'

For a moment Douglas's mask of jollity slipped. His mouth tightened and his eyes were resentful. 'For your information,' he snapped, 'I'm a widower. My wife died giving birth to our son.'

Betty, red in the face, was immediately contrite. 'I'm sorry.' She turned to the boy too. 'Oh pet, I am sorry.'

Anna's glance had gone at once to the boy. He had an odd expression on his face. He was looking at his father, Anna thought, as if he were surprised at what Douglas had said. *But surely*, she thought, *he must know how his mother died?* Feeling for him, she moved to his side and, trying to change the subject, whispered, 'It looks like you're lumbered with me. I—I hope you don't mind.'

The boy dragged his gaze away from his father, who had gone to the box office and was now leaning forward to talk to the girl behind the glass. Bruce looked at her for a moment and then grinned suddenly. 'Course not. Pretty girl like you.' He leant closer. 'You've got lovely eyes. Almost violet, aren't they? Anybody ever told you that?'

Anna blushed and glanced down. Unused to compliments from strangers, she did not know how to handle it. *He's like his dad*, she thought, envying the boy his confident manner. *He's very different to Jed.* Jed was kind and always ready to help her but he was quiet and shy. This youth was outgoing, ready to take the lead and anything but shy.

'Come on,' he was saying. 'Let's go and find the best seats.'

'But—but we haven't got our tickets yet.'

313

'Ne'er mind about that. Dad's fixing it.' He took her hand and began to pull her towards the stairs leading up to the circle. 'Come on.'

'But won't the girl inside want to see our tickets?' Anna remembered her father taking them to the pictures. The usherette had inspected their tickets and torn them in half before guiding them down the steps to their seats with the narrow beam of light from her torch. Tears threatened at the memory, but Bruce was saying, 'Nah. Me dad runs this place. The girls all know me. I'm always here.'

Her eyes wide, Anna asked, 'Does he own it?'

The boy glanced at her, seemed to ponder for a moment and then said, 'Not exactly.' He seemed to be choosing his words carefully. 'But, like I say, he runs it.'

'I see.' Anna wasn't sure she did. But she surmised that Douglas must work for the people who did own it, that he was some kind of manager.

By the time they had chosen their seats, the adults had caught up. Their faces illuminated by the light from the screen, they sat in a line in the front row of the circle, Douglas between Betty and May, then Rita, Anna and, finally, Bruce on the end of the row.

Anna leant forward and glanced along the row. Douglas was laughing again. He was leaning towards her mother, whispering to her. May was smiling and nodding. Anna leant further forward to see Betty on Douglas's other side. She was staring straight ahead at the screen with, for her, a morose expression on her face.

In the intermission between the feature film and the supporting picture, the Pathé News boomed out the latest about the war, how the RAF had begun a round-the-clock bombing campaign. Sitting two seats away, Anna heard her mother's gulp and glanced to her left to see that May's head was bowed and that she had covered her face with her hands.

'There, there, May. Don't cry,' she heard Douglas say as he proffered a white handkerchief. Then Anna saw him put his arms along the back of the seat and around May's shoulders. He now sat half twisted towards May, his back towards Betty.

Throughout the whole of the second film, Betty stared stonily at the screen, looking neither to right nor left and speaking to no one.

CHAPTER THIRTY-SIX

They left Bruce on the steps of the cinema. 'You go straight home, boy,' Douglas instructed. 'I have to take these lovely ladies home and I might be late.' Anna caught him winking at his son.

Douglas had borrowed a bigger car so that he could take them all home together. As he drove, he sang at the top of his voice, but the three women and Anna were silent. When they arrived at the farm, May, sensing the atmosphere, hustled Anna upstairs to bed, with a hurried, 'Thank you for a lovely evening.'

Rita too yawned and said, 'Well, I'm for bed too. Nighty-night.'

'Don't I even get a cup of cocoa?' Douglas asked, pretending peevishness as the door closed behind the others, leaving him alone with Betty.

Betty flung her handbag on the table, sat down

in Luke's chair by the range, kicked off her shoes and began to massage her feet. She glanced up at Douglas. 'You'll get a thick ear, m'lad, unless I get an explanation. And it'd better be good.'

Feigning innocence, Douglas said, 'Now what have I done?' Before Betty could answer, he grinned and wagged his forefinger at her. 'Oho, I do believe the lady's jealous. Just because I was kind to little May.'

'Jealous? Me? Huh, don't flatter yourself. It's nothing to do with May. It's your son I want to know about. You never told me you was married.' She glared up at him. 'That you'd *been* married.' She corrected herself, but even so her look suggested that she doubted his story. She nodded at him. 'I saw how your son looked. Surprised, that's what. As if he'd never been told. Now, sorry, but I don't believe a lad of his age hadn't been told before now that his mother had died having him. And if he hadn't,' she went on pointedly, 'then it wasn't a very nice way to break the news to the lad, was it?'

Douglas sighed and sat down opposite her. Adopting a hangdog look, he said, 'Betty, you're a woman of the world.'

Betty grimaced comically. 'Aye, aye, there's something coming if the flattery starts.'

Douglas gave an exaggerated sigh. 'Like I say, you'd understand, but I wasn't sure that May and her family would.'

Betty raised an eyebrow. 'Oh aye. It matters what May thinks, does it?'

'Not just May. All of them. You're living here and I want to keep seeing you. I want to be able to come here. And I'm not sure the old man likes me much anyway.' He laughed. 'I didn't want anything else rocking the boat.'

'So?'

'Well, it's not something a chap likes to admit. Dents the old confidence a bit. My wife left me five years ago. Ran off with some wide boy . . .'

Betty laughed inwardly. She liked Douglas. He was all right for a laugh and a good touch for the odd pair of nylons and other scarcities that made a girl's life a little easier in wartime, but she had no illusions about him. A wide boy, indeed! Seemed the former Mrs Whittaker went for the same type each time, then. For if ever there was a wide boy it was Douglas himself. Old Pops was no fool. Betty smiled inwardly. He'd sussed out Douglas Whittaker from the moment he'd clapped eyes on him.

She managed to keep her face straight but she couldn't keep the sarcasm from her tone. 'Oh, I'm sorry. Left her lad an' all, did she? Tut, tut. Some women. I don't know. Divorced, are you then?'

'Yes, yes, that's it. We're divorced.'

She eyed him shrewdly, wondering. Still, it didn't make any difference to her. She was only out for a bit of fun. She was never going to be serious about a man like Douglas Whittaker.

Now that handsome pilot officer, Charlie—the one whose plane had gone down—now she could have been serious about him, poor boy.

Betty banished the unhappy thought and smiled. 'Well, pet, I won't tell anyone. Your secret's safe with me.'

Douglas leant across the hearth and planted a kiss on her mouth. 'You're a smasher, Betty. Now, about that cocoa . . .'

317

On the following Sunday afternoon Douglas brought Bruce out to the farm. 'He's done nothing but talk about you since Friday,' Douglas whispered to Anna. 'Quite smitten, he is.'

Anna blushed. At school the girls teased each other about different boys and Anna had a crush on a boy who sat two desks in front of her. She would sit in class staring at the back of his head and daydreaming until she earned a sharp reprimand from the teacher. But now here was Bruce's father telling her that his son was 'smitten' with her.

'Don't you tell him I said so, though,' Douglas was saying. 'It'll embarrass him. You know what lads of his age are like.'

She didn't really. The older boys at school took no notice of the younger girls, though she had to admit one or two had winked at her as they passed her in the corridor. There was really only Jed and he didn't count.

'Take him and show him the animals. He'd like to have a look around,' Douglas urged. 'Now, where's Betty?'

'She and Rita have gone on a bike ride. She thought you weren't coming today.'

'Ah yes, that's right. I did say I might not be able to make it, but then I found I could.' His smile widened. 'Then I'll just go and talk to your pretty mother, shall I?'

Anna nodded as Douglas beckoned his son over. 'Now you two, off you go and enjoy yourselves. Don't do anything I wouldn't, eh?' He guffawed loudly.

He turned towards the back door of the farmhouse, where May had appeared in the doorway. Arms outstretched, he walked towards her. 'Ah, May, how lovely you look.'

Anna watched the tinge of pink in her mother's cheeks and heard her girlish, nervous laugh. 'Betty's not here . . .'

Douglas lowered his voice, but Anna's sharp ears still heard him say, 'I know. I was hoping she wouldn't be. It's you I came to see. And I had to bring the lad. I hope you don't mind . . .'

'Of course not. He's very welcome. You both are.'

Anna watched them disappear inside. Then she turned to Bruce. 'What do you want to see? Cows? Pigs? The sheep?'

The boy shrugged and kicked a stone. 'Don't mind. Let's just go for a walk, eh?'

'Right. Well, we'll see the sheep as we go. We've some lovely lambs . . .' Her face sobered. 'But they've to go soon.'

'To the market, you mean?'

Anna took a deep breath as she nodded. 'For slaughter.'

Bruce laughed and drew his hand across his throat, making a gurgling sound. Anna smiled thinly, but deep down she didn't think it was funny at all.

As they walked through the pasture, she saw Bruce eyeing the lambs. 'You've got a lot. How much do you get for each one then?'

Anna stared at him. '*I* don't know. They're Grandpa's.'

'Yeah, but you live here, don't you? It'll all be yours one day, won't it, when the old man snuffs

319

it?' He glanced at her. 'Or has he got other grandchildren?'

Anna shook her head. 'No—no. There's only me. They only had one daughter, me mam.'

'So the farm'll go to your mam and then to you, won't it?'

'I—suppose so.' Anna was hesitant. She didn't even like to think about Grandpa dying. She'd lost her father and then her grandmother so recently that the thought of another death terrified her.

Bruce interrupted her thoughts. 'You ought to be taking an interest in the place.'

'I do. I help out a lot when I'm not at school. You can watch us do the milking later, if you like.'

'Yeah, that'd be fun,' he said, but his tone sounded insincere. Almost sarcastic. Then he brightened. 'Come on, you can show me all the fields your grandpa owns.'

'There's a lot,' Anna said. 'I don't think we've time to see them all.'

There was a glint in the boy's eye as he glanced about, surveying all the land around him. 'He owns all this?' He waved his hand.

'Yes. Right down to the river.'

'The river? Great! Can we go fishing?' Now he was really interested. 'I like fishing.'

'I—I don't know. I'd have to ask Grandpa.'

'I like seeing fish wriggle on the end of me line and then—' He brought his hand down in a chopping movement, demonstrating how he killed his catch.

As they walked on, he pushed his hands into his pockets and walked with a swagger. 'I'm going in the army as soon as I'm eighteen.'

'How old are you now?'

'I was seventeen last month. Roll on next year. I can't wait to get at 'em.'

Anna glanced at him. 'Who?'

'Jerry, of course.'

'Oh.'

They walked in silence until they came to the river bank and stood looking down at the flowing water.

'I bet there's plenty of fish in there,' he said.

Anna bit her lip. 'We'll have to be getting back. It'll be teatime soon and then there's the milking.'

Bruce turned towards her and put his hands on her shoulders. He looked down into her upturned face. Then without warning, he bent and pressed his mouth hard on hers. Shocked, Anna tried to pull away, but found that he was gripping her shoulders so firmly she could not move.

'There,' he said as he drew away. 'Bet that's the first time you've been kissed properly, ain't it?'

Her mind reeling, Anna could find no words. Bruce laughed softly and, still with his arm about her shoulders, began to lead her back towards the farm.

And that was how Luke saw them as they came into the yard.

CHAPTER THIRTY-SEVEN

When Douglas and Bruce had departed in a cloud of fumes, the sound of the noisy sports car echoing long after they had roared up the lane, Luke said, 'She's too young to be having the likes of him putting his arm around her. Put a stop to it, May, or I will.'

'Oh, Dad, it's only a bit of harmless fun. He's the first boyfriend she's had.'

'Boyfriend?' Luke almost shouted. 'At thirteen? Have you taken leave of your senses, May?'

'She's just flattered by the attentions of a good-looking lad, that's all.'

Luke's shaggy eyebrows almost covered his eyes as he frowned. He bit down hard on his pipe. 'Not the only one, is she?' he muttered. Then he jabbed the end of his pipe towards his daughter. 'I mean it, May. I don't want her getting romantic notions at her age.'

May flushed and bit her thumbnail, but she argued with her father no further. Luke turned away, satisfied that he had made his point and that it would be obeyed. But if he could have read May's rebellious thoughts at that moment, he would not have been so content. As he walked away, May glared after him. *If you think I'm going to risk wrecking my chances of going back to live in the city by upsetting Douglas and his son, then you've got another think coming. I'm a grown woman and I'll bring my daughter up how I like, not how you say.*

Later, when Betty and Rita had returned and they were all seated round the supper table, Luke was still unable to get the two visitors out of his mind. 'I'd like to know where he gets his petrol from.'

Betty laughed. 'Oho, don't ask, Pops. Don't ask.' Then she winked. 'But if there's anything you want, you can be sure Douglas Whittaker will know where to get it. Only no questions asked, if you know what I mean.'

'Yes,' Luke said grimly, 'I think I do.' He glanced

322

at May, who had lowered her head when the conversation had turned to Douglas. 'You're very quiet, lass.'

Her head shot up. 'Oh. I—er—no. I mean, I didn't mean to be.' She was flustered and red in the face.

'Know what I think,' Betty said, cradling her cup in her palms. 'I reckon Douglas is sweet on our May here.'

'Oh no,' May said quickly, but her blush deepened. 'He's your young man, Betty. I wouldn't want you to think . . .'

Betty flapped her hand. 'Don't worry about that, May. There's plenty more fish in the sea. And Douglas Whittaker's no great catch.' Then, realizing how that might sound, she added hastily, 'Not as far as I'm concerned anyway. I promise you, he's just a laugh. Besides, he's a bit old for me. No offence, love.'

'None taken,' May murmured. She was older than Betty by about ten years. She was much nearer Douglas's age than the young Land Army girl. Betty's eyes clouded as she added, 'I'm not getting serious about anyone. Not while this war's on.'

'Love 'em and leave 'em, that's Betty's motto,' Rita laughed.

Betty crashed her cup into its saucer and stood up suddenly. 'It's—it's them that leave us, isn't it?'

She turned and rushed from the room. They heard the back door bang. Rita looked after her thoughtfully. 'I think,' she said slowly, 'that despite what she says she was getting rather fond of Charlie.'

May gasped. 'The—the one who got shot down?'

Rita nodded.

'Oh,' May breathed. 'Poor Betty.'

'Aye,' Luke growled at his daughter. 'And it'll be poor you, if you take up with that—that spiv!'

May hung her head.

*   *   *

Despite Luke's warning, May couldn't help liking Douglas. She looked forward to his visits to the farm and she felt more comfortable now that she knew Betty did not regard him as her boyfriend. May liked the two girls who had come to live with them and help on the farm. She didn't want to offend either of them, especially the forthright Betty, whose tongue, Luke said, could mow a ten-acre field without a scythe.

Douglas began to take May out—just the two of them—roaring off up the lane in his car. He even took her away for a weekend, staying away Friday and Saturday nights, during which time Luke glowered morosely and then refused to speak to May for three days afterwards. Douglas tried his best to win the old man over, bringing him tobacco and even a can or two of precious petrol.

'No thanks,' Luke said tersely. 'I don't hold with black market stuff.'

Douglas laughed, but shrugged. 'Don't tell me you don't get a bit of extra meat from under the counter now and again.'

'We have all we need. We live on a farm,' Luke reminded him.

'That's exactly it,' Douglas said and jabbed his finger towards Luke. For a brief moment, Douglas's grey eyes were as hard as flint. 'You're lucky, but some of us are really suffering because of the shortages. Can you blame us for wanting to make life a bit easier?'

Luke's glance travelled slowly up and down the smartly dressed man before him. He said nothing, just sniffed as if to say: *You look as if you're really suffering!* Then he shrugged. 'That's your business and no concern of mine. Just don't ask me to get involved, that's all. And don't'—now it was Luke who wagged his finger at Douglas—'involve my daughter either.'

Douglas threw back his head and laughed loudly. 'She doesn't refuse the nylons and the chocolates I bring.'

Luke turned away frowning. He was pretty sure Douglas was into the black market. Oh, maybe not in a big way. But Luke felt sure that he was on the fringes of petty villainy. He didn't like May's involvement with him or the way her eyes sparkled when she heard that noisy contraption swing into the yard.

But there was not a lot Luke could do about it.

*   *   *

When Douglas visited the farm at the weekends, he usually brought Bruce with him.

'I've brought you some chocolates,' Bruce said.

'Oh, how lovely.' Anna smiled. 'How kind of you. It—it must have used up all your coupons.'

Bruce shrugged and grinned. 'You're worth it.'

Across the yard, Anna was aware of Jed glowering at them. Hastily she said, 'I'll just take these indoors and then we'll go for a walk.'

As they strolled together by the river, Bruce took

325

hold of Anna's hand, whilst Buster ran ahead, exploring for rabbits. She felt her face glowing pink, but did not pull away. It was nice to have an older boyfriend; nice to be able to boast about him to her best friend, Jean. And walking hand in hand with him made her feel really grown up.

'Has he kissed you yet?' Jean asked eagerly every Monday morning when she knew Bruce had been to the farm.

'Oh yes,' Anna said airily, giving the impression that it happened all the time. 'And when we go for walks, we hold hands.'

Jean nudged her. 'Has he tried—well—you know?'

Anna put her nose in the air. 'Course not. He's not like that. He's nice.'

'Does he know you're only thirteen? 'Cos you look older. Mebbe he thinks you're as old as him.'

Anna shrugged. 'Dunno. But I'm not going to tell him.' They giggled together.

And now, here she was once more walking with him. Maybe there'd be even more to tell Jean on Monday morning . . .

'What have you been doing with yourself this week?' Bruce broke into her dreams.

'Oh, the usual. You know, school and helping Grandpa.'

'When are the lambs going then?' Bruce asked her as they walked through the meadow, watching the lambs playing.

'Next week,' Anna said dolefully. 'They're coming for them next Monday.'

'A week tomorrow, you mean?'

Anna nodded as she pulled her hand from his and crept towards one of the lambs suckling its mother. Neither the sheep nor the lamb moved, not even when Anna stroked the lamb. Buster trotted up and stood close by, watching. 'Come and feel their lovely coats,' Anna said to Bruce. 'Isn't it a shame they have to be—to be—?'

He moved carefully across the grass towards her, but when he was about three feet from her and the sheep, Anna heard Buster growl softly. She turned to look down at him. He was crouching, his eyes on Bruce, as if ready to spring.

'Don't be silly, Buster. It's only Bruce.'

Bruce gave a nervous laugh. 'I don't reckon that dog likes me.' He grinned. 'Reckon he's jealous.'

Anna's eyes widened as she looked at him, 'Jealous?' she began and then realized what he meant. She blushed. 'Don't be silly. You ought to make friends with him. You never pet him.'

Bruce laughed. 'I don't want me hand bitten off.'

'Take no notice of Buster. He won't hurt you. Not while I'm here anyway. But he's only doing his job.'

Bruce glanced at her. 'What do you mean?'

'It's his job to protect the sheep.'

Bruce eyed the dog thoughtfully.

'Come on,' Anna encouraged. 'Feel how soft their wool is.'

Bruce, keeping a wary eye on the dog, moved forward and bent to stroke the lamb. The lamb stopped suckling and allowed Bruce to pick it up. 'Cute little fellers, aren't they?'

Anna giggled. 'Yeah. Except that one's a girl.'

Suddenly, Buster growled again and began to bark. Frightened, the lamb bleated and struggled in Bruce's grasp. 'It's all right, boy,' he said to the dog. 'I'm not going to run off with it.' He laughed as he

327

set the young animal down on its spindly legs. 'They're heavier than I thought they'd be,' he murmured as the lamb trotted away to join in a game with the others.

'They're like children, aren't they?' Anna smiled. 'Look at them, playing just like little children in a playground.'

'Yeah,' Bruce murmured, draping his arm across her shoulders. 'But they're worth a bit more than a load of screaming kids.'

Anna said nothing. She felt uncomfortable that Bruce kept referring to how much things were worth. The sheep, the crops they were growing— even the fish in the river. Everything seemed to have a price tag as far as Bruce was concerned.

'We ought to come fishing one day,' he'd remarked. 'Me dad could get a good price for fresh fish in the markets.'

Maybe it was because his father was a businessman, Anna told herself, finding excuses for him. It was just his way, that was all.

As they began to walk back towards the farmhouse, Bruce glanced back over his shoulder. 'Yeah, your old man's got a bob or two coming his way next week when he sends this little lot to market.'

CHAPTER THIRTY-EIGHT

The following Sunday Bruce came again with his father.

'Come on,' he said, catching hold of Anna's hand. 'Me dad says I can take you for a drive in the car while he's talking to your mam.'

'Drive?' Anna gasped. 'Can you drive?'

'Course I can.' The youth swaggered. 'Come on. We'll have some fun. Get your mam to pack us a picnic hamper. We'll go off for the day.'

'I don't know,' Anna said doubtfully. 'I ought to stay and help Grandpa. The lambs are going tomorrow. I told you.'

Bruce blinked, as if he had forgotten. 'Oh. Oh yes, I remember. You said last week.' He frowned. 'Why do you have to help? What have you got to do?'

'Grandpa sometimes round them all up and brings them down to the barn. It saves time in the morning, if they're all together. Ready for when the lorries come.'

'Oh.'

'I'll ask him, though. He might not bother.'

* * *

'You're not going and that's final.'

'But Grandpa—'

'Don't argue, lass. I don't want you going in that car with him. He's not safe.'

'You can't say that. You don't know what sort of a driver he is.'

'I can make a pretty good guess. It's bad enough your mother going off in the thing wi' 'im.' He jerked his thumb towards the farmhouse. 'There's not a lot I can do about that—'

'Except not speak to her for days on end when she comes back,' Anna said rashly.

'Now, now, lass. That's not like you to be cheeky to me.'

Anna was ashamed. 'I'm sorry, Grandpa, but we only wanted to go for a picnic.'

'Well . . .' Luke was still reluctant. He didn't like Douglas or his son. But he could hardly stop the youngsters spending time together. Even though in his heart of hearts he would like to have done so. 'That's all right,' he said now. 'You can walk down to the river bank. There's some nice spots there for a picnic. Me and your grannie often used to take a picnic down there—'

He turned away abruptly and Anna gazed after him, sorry to have revived poignant memories. 'We won't be late, Grandpa. I'll be back in time to help with the milking.'

As he walked away, Luke raised his hand in acknowledgement but he did not look back.

* * *

It had been a lovely afternoon down by the river. They'd sat on a rug close together, their shoulders touching. It was peaceful and quiet.

'You wouldn't think there was a war on, would you?' Bruce said. Then he'd turned and kissed her, pressing her onto her back. 'You're lovely,' he'd murmured against her mouth. His hand caressed her waist and then moved up to her breast.

'Don't!' Anna said sharply and sat up.

For a moment, Bruce's face was like thunder and Anna felt a tiny shiver of fear. But then he was smiling. 'Sorry. I keep forgetting you're only thirteen. You look older.' He sat up too, resting his arms on his knees.

Anna was relieved, yet there was a little tinge of regret. After all, he was her boyfriend. At least,

330

that was what she told Jean and the other girls at school. He lit a cigarette and sat smoking it.

'Can I—can I have a puff?'

He turned and looked at her. 'You're not old enough to smoke'—he paused deliberately and then added—'either.'

Anna felt the colour suffuse her face and she hung her head.

She heard him laugh softly. Then he was holding out the cigarette to her. 'Here, have a go.'

She took it and drew on it. The smoke stung the back of her throat and she began to cough, feeling as if she were choking. He slapped her hard on the back.

'Don't take it down the first time, you daft thing.'

She was purple in the face and it took some moments for her to recover enough to speak. 'What on earth pleasure is there in that?' she wheezed. 'It's horrible.'

Bruce was grinning at her. 'You'd probably get to like it.' He glanced at her out of the corner of his eye. 'Given time.'

Anna had the distinct feeling that he was not talking just about smoking.

*   *   *

That night Anna was restless and sleep was fitful. She tossed and turned, thinking over what had happened between her and Bruce. She felt as if she had behaved like a silly little schoolgirl. He'd only wanted a harmless cuddle, she told herself. He would never ask her to go too far, she was sure. And now she'd probably lost him. He'd find another, more mature girl who would let him love her.

She sat up in bed suddenly. Her bedroom window faced out over the yard and she could hear Buster barking. Maybe there was an intruder. There'd been a lot of thefts from nearby farms recently. Chickens, ducks and geese, even a piglet or two, anything that would sell on the black market to give hard pressed housewives a little extra meat for their families.

Anna was about to get out of bed to wake her grandfather, when she realized Buster had stopped. She listened for a few moments longer and then lay down. It couldn't have been anything serious or the dog would still be trying to raise the alarm. Her anxieties over Bruce diverted by the brief disturbance, within minutes Anna was asleep.

*   *   *

As she stepped into the kitchen the following morning, Luke and May turned to greet her.

'What is it?' she asked at once. She could see by the look on their faces that something was wrong.

'It's Buster,' Luke began, putting his hand on her shoulder.

'Buster? Why? What's happened?' She made as if to rush outside, but Luke's hand restrained her.

'There's summat the matter with him. I don't know what. He was spark out when I went out first thing this morning, just lying in the yard near his kennel. But not inside it. Looks as if he's been out there all night.'

'He's not—. You don't mean he's—?' She couldn't bring herself to voice her worst fear.

'No, he's not dead. In fact, he's woken up, but he's staggering around. If he were a man, I'd say he was drunk.' Luke shook his head. 'But he's not right. I'll have to take him into the vet as soon as they've been for the lambs.'

'Can't we go now?' Anna was frantic.

Luke shook his head. 'No, we'll have to round up the lambs ourselves. Buster's going to be no use this morning. Ya mam's agreed that you'll have to stay off school today to help.'

'I wouldn't have gone anyway,' Anna said firmly. 'Not until I know what's the matter with Buster.'

'Get your breakfast and then go with your grandpa—' May began, but Anna was already hurrying from the house. 'I've got to see Buster.'

The dog was staggering about near his kennel looking very sorry for himself. She ran her hands over his coat and he made a half-hearted attempt to lick her.

'What is it, boy? What's the matter, eh? I wish you could tell us.'

Luke appeared and came to stand beside her, scratching his head in puzzlement. 'I can't mek it out, love. We'll have to get him to the vet. Only thing is—I haven't much petrol.'

'There's a can in the barn that Douglas left for you.'

Luke's mouth tightened. 'I'm not using that—'

Anna sprang up and caught hold of his arm. 'Oh please, Grandpa. Just this once. For Buster. Please.'

'All right.' Luke gave in, but added sternly, 'But don't you go telling that feller or his son, else he'll think he's got the better of me.'

Anna hugged him. 'I won't, Grandpa. I won't.'

333

'Now, go and get some breakfast and then join me and the girls in the fields. I need all the help I can get this morning to round up those lambs.'

*　　*　　*

'There's three missing. I know there is.' Betty was adamant. 'We've got nineteen and there should be twenty-two.'

'Are you sure you haven't miscounted, lass?' Luke said. 'The little blighters keep moving about.'

Betty shook her head. 'No. Rita helped me and we counted 'em out of this pen and into that one.' The lambs that were being sent for slaughter were all in the barn now.

'What about the three I'm keeping to rear? The ones I marked with red paint.'

Betty and Rita glanced at each other. 'There's only two in the field with red paint on their backs,' Betty said. 'But we left another female lamb there. We knew you wanted to keep three back. We started with twenty-five, didn't we?'

Luke nodded.

'So,' she went on, 'take away the three that we've left in the field for rearing and we should have twenty-two and we haven't. We've only got nineteen.'

They all looked at the lambs milling about in the makeshift pen inside the barn. There was no lamb with a red paint mark on its back.

Luke scratched his head. 'Well, I dunno. We'd better go and have a look round the fields.' Then he muttered, 'Just when we could have done with Buster.' He looked round. 'I don't suppose he's recovered enough to help us, has he, Anna?'

334

Anna shook her head. She had gone straight to look at the dog on returning to the yard. 'He's in his kennel. Sleeping.'

Luke glanced at her, then turned on his heel and left the barn. Anna, Betty and Rita exchanged a worried look and then went to peer out of the door. They saw Luke bend down and reach into the kennel. Then he straightened up and came back towards them. He was smiling. 'He's sleeping right enough. I can't understand it. There doesn't seem much wrong with him.'

'But you're still going to take him to the vet, aren't you?'

'Well—' Luke hesitated.

'Oh please, Grandpa.'

'All right then. As soon as they've been for the lambs.'

'We'd better get back to the fields and see if we can find the other three,' Betty said and laughed. 'Now I know how Bo Peep felt.'

'They'll be down a dyke side somewhere, I expect,' Anna said confidently as she and the two girls set off, leaving Luke to wait in the yard for the lorry.

But Anna was wrong. They scoured the fields and the dykes but there was no sign of the three missing lambs. Tired and dispirited, they went back to the farmyard. The lorry had just arrived and the lambs were being shepherded into the back of the vehicle. As soon as they were loaded and the lorry had trundled its way down the narrow lane from the farm, Anna turned to Luke. '*Now* can we take Buster to the vet?'

*　　　*　　　*

335

'Well, I can't find anything physically wrong with him, Luke,' the vet, who was an old friend, said. He was a portly man in his early sixties who had been the local vet for 'more years than he cared to remember', as he always said. He smiled at Anna, who was standing close by, a worried expression on her face.

'I knew it was a waste of time and petrol bringing him,' Luke grumbled.

'Hold on a minute.' The vet looked at Luke over the top of his spectacles. 'I hadn't quite finished. As I said, there's nothing physically wrong with him and without taking blood samples to prove it, I can't be sure, but I'd take an educated guess that this dog's been drugged.'

'Drugged! Who on earth—?' Luke began and then, as realization began to dawn, his mouth tightened and his eyes sparked anger. 'That explains it, then.'

'Explains what?' the vet asked.

'I sent my lambs to slaughter this morning and three were missing. Someone must have come in the night and stolen them.'

'And drugged the dog to stop him barking, you mean.'

Luke nodded. Anna pulled at his sleeve. 'Grandpa, I remember now. I should have said before, but with everything happening I forgot.'

They both turned to look at her. 'What, lass?'

'Last night. Before I fell asleep, I heard Buster barking. I was just going to get out of bed and come and fetch you but—but he stopped. Oh Grandpa, if only I'd come and woken you, then— then—'

336

Luke put his arm around her. 'It's not your fault, lass. You weren't to know. Mind you, I would have gone and had a look. Buster's a good guard dog. He only barks for a reason.' He nodded again. 'That'd be it. They'd come and drug him first, stop him barking a warning when they went into the fields to pinch me sheep. We never tie him up, you see. If he'd heard a disturbance out in the fields, he'd have been off like a rocket.'

'Sounds to me as if it was someone who knew just what they were doing,' the vet said mildly.

'Yes,' Luke said grimly. 'It does, doesn't it?'

CHAPTER THIRTY-NINE

'Dad, how can you possibly accuse Douglas of such a thing?' May was angry and tearful.

'I'm not.' The words were grudging.

'Yes, you are. You've never liked him. Just because he's smart and—and has a fancy car.'

'And dabbles in the black market,' Luke shot back. 'He admitted that himself.'

'Yes, and you weren't above using the petrol he brought you when you needed it.'

Luke said nothing but gave a low growl, sounding very like Buster when Douglas or Bruce were around. He glanced at Betty across the supper table. 'You're not saying much, lass. You know him better than any of us. What do you reckon? Am I being unfair?'

Betty regarded him with her clear, blue eyes. 'I honestly don't know. I know he wheels and deals, if you know what I mean. But I didn't think he'd

337

stoop to theft. I know one thing, though.' She glanced across at May. 'I don't know if he's stolen your sheep, but I do know he's causing trouble between you and your family. And that alone makes me sorry I ever brought him here.'

'Well, I'm not,' May said boldly and glared at her father. 'And don't you go saying anything to him, Dad. You've no proof. I look forward to him coming. And his lad. We'd be buried alive out here, if it wasn't for them coming at a weekend. I never wanted to stay on the farm. Why do you think I married Ken and moved to the city? And now, because of this blasted war, I've had to come back.' Tears of anger and frustration poured down May's face as she rushed from the room and ran up the stairs.

For the quiet, usually docile May to react in such a way shocked them all.

'Oh dear,' Betty said. 'I think she's got it bad.'

'Oh dear indeed,' Luke muttered as he got up from the table.

*　　　*　　　*

Nothing was said about the lambs when Douglas and Bruce arrived as usual for Sunday dinner, after which Douglas took May for a drive in his car and Bruce and Anna walked to the river bank.

'What sort of a price did your grandpa get for his lambs then?' Bruce asked as soon as they were alone. They walked side by side, he with his hands in his pockets, Anna with her arm through his.

'I don't know,' Anna said.

Bruce grinned. 'I thought you might be in for a bit of extra pocket money if he was feeling

338

generous.'

It was on the tip of her tongue to confide in him, to tell him that three lambs had been lost and that the vet suspected their dog had been drugged. But the knowledge that her grandfather would be angry kept her silent.

'Don't you go saying anything to either of them when they come,' Luke had demanded of them all. 'You hear me, May? And you too, Anna.'

He didn't even need to press the point home to the two Land Army girls. To May and Anna's dismay, it seemed as if he trusted the two girls more than his own flesh and blood.

*   *   *

Over the next few weeks nothing more was stolen from Clayton's Farm, but Luke heard that several of the farms nearby were missing chickens and geese on a regular basis.

'They don't take many at a time,' Jed told Luke, 'but me uncle's lost four hens now. He reckons that whoever's doing it thinks that out of fifty hens or so we won't notice a couple have gone. But it's getting regular and it always happens at a weekend.'

Luke eyed him shrewdly. 'Aye, it's when these townies come out to the countryside. You've seen the two that come to our place?'

Jed nodded, his mouth tightening at the thought of Bruce.

'I don't mind telling you, Jed lad, I'm not keen on them. Too flash for my liking, but the girls like the company.'

'I'd noticed,' Jed said dryly and Luke cast him a shrewd look.

'Ah,' he said slowly, knowingly. 'Like that, is it, lad?'

'Aye, Mr Clayton. As you say, it's like that.'

Jed turned away, but Luke watched him go and chewed thoughtfully on his pipe. Now there was a lad he'd be happy to let Anna go to the ends of the earth with. Because he knew she'd be safe with Jed and, what's more, Jed would always bring her back home.

*   *   *

'Not long now before I join the army,' Bruce told Anna towards the end of the year.

The war was now three years old and yet there was no talk of it ending soon. There had been the heartening news of Monty's triumph at El Alamein and, for once, the sound of church bells was heard in celebration. But still the fighting continued.

'I—I'll miss you,' Anna said.

'I'll be home on leave in me smart uniform. All the girls like a man in uniform.'

'I—like you anyway,' Anna said quietly and Bruce squeezed her arm. There was a pause and then she asked, 'Will you have to go abroad? To—to where the fighting is?'

' 'Spect so.'

'You will be careful, won't you?'

Bruce stopped and turned to face her. He put his hands on her shoulders and kissed her gently on the lips. 'Course I will, as long as I know you're my girl.' He raised his head and looked about him, his sweeping glance taking in all the land around them. All the land that belonged to her grandfather. Then he murmured, so low that Anna only just caught his words. 'And there's all this for me to come back to.'

*   *   *

The following spring Bruce went into the army. Anna missed him and counted the days to his next leave. When he came home he was full of tales of service life.

'The training's hard, but I love it.' He flexed his arms. 'You should see my muscles. And look—I brought this to show you.' From a sheath attached to his belt, he pulled out a long, cruel-looking weapon. 'This is a bayonet. You fix it to the end of your gun and have to run at sacks of straw and thrust it in.' He demonstrated with vicious delight. 'You have to imagine it's the enemy.'

Anna gasped, scandalized. 'They teach you to do that to someone? You could kill them.'

'That's the general idea.' Bruce eyed her scathingly. 'What do you think war is? A picnic? Living out here in the back of beyond, you're sheltered from what's really going on. Oh, you hear the planes and read the papers, but you don't know what it's really like.' His eyes were shining as he added, 'I can't wait to get out there. I just hope it's not all over by the time I get overseas. I want to get at 'em.'

Anna shuddered. He was right, she knew he was. It was people like him, with that kind of attitude, who could win the war. It needed fearless people like him, but this didn't stop her being appalled by the brutality of it. To her it seemed that Bruce was actually relishing the idea of killing.

'Of course I know what war is,' Anna was stung

341

to retort. 'I should do. I lost my dad, didn't I? But I didn't realize you had to—had to—' She gulped back the tears as the sudden, horrifying picture of her lovely father being trained in hand-to-hand fighting came into her mind.

'It's either us or them,' Bruce was saying harshly. 'You've got to get them first before they get you.'

'Yes,' Anna murmured, unable to take her eyes off the bayonet. Had her father been killed in such a way, too gentle to be the first to strike?

'I've got me own knife an' all, but it's not standard issue, so I have to be careful the Sarge doesn't see it.'

Now he showed her a short, dagger-like knife. 'This is better up close.' He made an upward, stabbing movement. 'Straight through the heart.'

'I don't want to talk about it any more,' she said, turning away.

'Hey, I'm sorry,' Bruce said at once, putting his arm around her. 'I was forgetting about your dad. I'm sorry, Anna, honestly.' He adopted a hangdog expression, like a little boy caught scrumping apples. 'Forgiven?'

Anna smiled and nodded. 'Yeah, you're forgiven.'

*   *   *

Even though Bruce was away, Douglas still came every weekend, bringing nylons, chocolates and flowers for May and for Betty and Rita too. He still brought Luke's favourite brand of tobacco, but the old man refused to touch it.

It was lambing time again, and after school and at weekends Anna was out in the fields or in the barn with her grandfather and the two Land Army girls.

'Do you know,' Betty said with a comical expression, 'if anyone'd've told me before the war that I'd be sitting in a barn in the middle of the night, dressed in these awful clothes, helping bring lambs into the world, I'd've said they'd gone off their rocker.' Luke, Rita and Anna laughed, but Betty added seriously, 'But I'll tell you something, I wouldn't have missed this for the world.'

There was a cosy intimacy in the warm darkness of the barn. Strangely, the feeling was still there even when they were out in the bitter cold when sheep gave birth in the fields. The four of them were united in helping the ewes and preserving the young, fragile lives. Three lambs had to be suckled by hand and Anna had charge of these in the big farmhouse kitchen. Luke taught her how to feed the lambs with a bottle and keep them warm near the huge range. One ewe, the mother of twin lambs, had died and another had rejected her offspring.

'Isn't it sad,' Betty remarked, tears in her eyes as she stroked the soft wool of the little creature's coat, 'when a mother rejects her own?'

Anna held the lamb close and laid her cheek against its woolly warmth. 'I'll look after you,' she whispered. 'I'll look after you all.'

CHAPTER FORTY

Life on Clayton's Farm went on much the same through the seasons; lambing, shearing, haymaking, harvest and then the autumn threshing, ploughing and seeding. And then the whole routine began again. By this time, it was obvious to them all that it was May that Douglas now came to see, not Betty. Luke tolerated his visits, always hoping that something would happen to put a stop to them. He hoped that petrol would get even scarcer, but the 'wide boy' never seemed to go short of anything.

The happy atmosphere of the farmhouse was irrevocably torn asunder the Sunday evening just after the New Year of 1944 when May arrived home after a weekend with Douglas in the city, her eyes sparkling like the huge diamond on her fourth finger.

Luke took one look at the ring, glared at Douglas and then stormed out of the house, slamming the back door with such force that the whole house seemed to rattle.

Douglas laughed. 'Oh dear, I don't think my future father-in-law likes me.'

May tucked her arm through his and gazed up adoringly at him. 'Don't worry, he'll come round. Anyway, we won't be living here, will we?'

Her eyes still shining, May turned to Anna. 'Darling, we'll be going home. When Douglas and I are married, we'll be going back to live in Lincoln.'

For a moment Anna felt sick. It wasn't that she didn't like Douglas, she did, but not enough for him to take her father's place.

'You mean—we're going back to—to the house we had in Lincoln?'

'No, no, of course not. I gave up the tenancy on that. No, we'll be going to live in Douglas's house.'

Douglas came towards Anna and put his arm about her shoulder, squeezing her to his side. 'We'll get a new house for the four of us. And you can help us choose it. Now, that'd be nice, wouldn't it?'

Anna's gaze was on her mother's face. 'But what about Grandpa? We can't leave him all alone here.'

'He's got Betty and Rita.'

'Yes, but when the war's over, they'll be going home. They won't want to stay here.'

For a moment, May's face clouded. 'Oh, I hadn't thought of that.' She glanced at Betty and Rita, who, up until this moment had remained silent. 'I thought you liked it here. I thought you'd be staying.'

The two Land Army girls glanced at each other and then shook their heads. 'We do like it,' Betty said, 'more than we thought we would, I have to admit that. But no, once this lot's over, we'll be going home. I—I miss my family.'

'Me too,' Rita said quietly.

'Oh.' May was crestfallen.

Douglas hugged her. 'Don't worry, darling. The old man will be all right. He'll get a housekeeper and there'll be plenty of men coming back from the war looking for work. He'll be fine.'

Anna bit her lip, torn between concern for her grandfather and the delicious thought of seeing Bruce every day. And yet the farm was where she belonged. She took a deep breath and before she really knew what she was doing, she said, 'I'll stay with Grandpa.'

The look of relief on Douglas's face was obvious, but May was still worried. 'But you're only a child—'

'I'm not. I'll be fifteen in a few weeks. I think I can leave school at Easter. Old enough to get a job. Well, this will be my job. I'll work for Grandpa and look after him.'

May bit her lip and murmured, 'I'll talk to Dad. I really wanted to go back to the city but I suppose we *could* all live here—' Her voice trailed away in disappointment.

After Douglas had left, Betty said sharply, 'I wouldn't bank on it, if I were you. I don't think Pops will ever come round to liking Douglas.'

Helplessly, May spread her hands. 'I can't see *why*. Douglas has been nothing but generous.'

'That's maybe it,' Betty said. 'He flashes his money about and your dad doesn't like the fact that Doug is probably dealing just outside the law.'

'Is he?' May asked ingenuously. Betty shrugged her plump shoulders and said, 'I wouldn't like to ask. Dougie's got a bit of a temper on him if he's crossed.'

May's eyes widened. 'Has he? I've never seen it.'

'Well, you wouldn't, would you?' Then she added ominously, 'Not yet.' She shook her head. 'I'm sorry to say it, May, but you know me. I've got to say what I think and I think you're making a big mistake. Dougie's all right for a bit of fun, like I've always said, but that's all. Marrying him might be the worst thing you've ever done.'

May gave a nervous laugh. 'You're only jealous.'

'No, I'm not, May,' Betty said seriously. 'Not a bit. Look, me an' Reet care about this family. We're very fond of all of you and I just don't think he's right for you. That's all.'

May's lips were tight as she said, 'Well, let me be the best judge of that.'

Betty stood up and shrugged. 'Have it your way then, but don't say I didn't warn you. Come on, Reet, let's give Pops a hand.'

The two girls left the room and May and Anna were left staring silently at each other. May's wonderful news had not been met with the delight she had hoped for.

*　　*　　*

Two days later at breakfast, Luke made a startling announcement. 'If you marry that feller, May, I'm changing me will.'

Betty got up from the table. 'If you want to discuss private family business, me an' Reet—'

'Sit down,' Luke said sharply. 'You might as well hear it. If this war goes on much longer, it might even concern you, in a way. As I was saying, I'll change me will and leave it all to Anna. But'—he turned towards his granddaughter, his shaggy white eyebrows meeting in a frown—'there's a condition. You will have no more to do with that son of his. That Bruce. I won't have'—Luke glanced around the table now, prodding his knife in the air—'either of them getting their hands on my farm. You hear me?'

May was sitting with her mouth wide open, stunned by the depth of her father's dislike for her fiancé. Betty and Rita glanced uncomfortably at each other, but said nothing. Only Anna cried out, 'Oh, Grandpa, don't you like Bruce?'

'No, I don't like either of them. And that's the truth. So'—he rose and rested his hands on the table, leaning forward—'it's up to you now. I've said me piece and I'll say no more. If you want to marry that—that wide boy, May, go ahead. But you won't get my blessing—or the farm. And you, Anna, there'll be a condition in my will that you

347

only get it if you don't marry Bruce Whittaker.'

As the door closed behind Luke, May whispered, 'Can he do that? Can he put that sort of thing in a will? About Anna, I mean?'

Betty shrugged. 'I don't know, but he's going to try. That's obvious. Come on, Reet, we'd better get working.'

Once again, May and Anna were left staring helplessly at each other across the table.

*   *   *

The happy atmosphere at Clayton's Farm was gone. Luke only spoke to May when it was absolutely necessary, and then in clipped tones. On the surface he treated Anna no differently, yet the girl could feel the tension, knew that he was waiting for her to discuss the matter further with him; waiting for her to give him her promise.

Bruce was due home on leave for the weekend and this time Anna had no compunction in pouring out the whole story to him. She knew May would have told Douglas by now.

'That's blackmail,' Bruce said. 'I hope you're not going to take notice of the silly old fool.'

Despite her anguish over her grandfather's ultimatum, Anna felt a thrill run through her to think that Bruce thought so much about her that he didn't care whether she inherited the farm or not. His next words took away some of that thrill. 'You could always contest the will when the time came. You're his only relative, aren't you?'

Anna nodded.

'Well, then you could always say he was going senile when he made it. I think you'd have a pretty

348

strong case.'

Anna gasped. 'I couldn't say something like that about Grandpa. Specially when it's not true.'

Bruce shrugged and said callously, 'He wouldn't know, would he? He'd be dead by then.'

*   *   *

As they returned to the farmyard hand in hand, Douglas roared in through the gate, bringing his car to a squealing halt. May, breathless and laughing, allowed him to help her from the car.

'Anna, come and help me get the tea ready.'

'We'll stay out here and have a smoke. I know the old man doesn't like cigarette smoke.' Douglas laughed. 'I don't want to upset him any more.' He held out his cigarette case to Bruce, who took one and lit it.

As Anna and her mother moved into the house, May glanced back. 'Isn't it nice to see father and son getting on so well?' she said wistfully and Anna knew she was thinking of the growing rift between herself and her own father.

'Don't worry, Mam. Maybe Grandpa will come round once he sees how happy you are with Douglas.'

May sighed. 'Perhaps you're right. He didn't like your daddy when I first met him, but he came round in the end. But—but this seems different. I've never seen your grandfather so—so determined. No, Anna, I don't think he will ever come to like Douglas. If I marry him and you continue to see Bruce, we'll lose the farm. Somehow, my father will see to that.' Then her glance went to the window as she watched Douglas talking to his son. 'But Douglas has told me I'm not to worry about it. He's not bothered. He can provide for all of us, he says.' Her cheeks were pink with pleasure as she added shyly, 'It's me he wants, he says, not the farm.'

Anna, too, glanced out of the window, watching Douglas lean nonchalantly against his car whilst his son was talking earnestly to him, his head bent towards him.

'What do you think they're talking about?'

May smiled. 'I don't know, but it looks pretty serious. Maybe they're planning to buy that house in Lincoln Douglas has promised.'

'Mmm,' Anna said thoughtfully. 'Maybe.'

*   *   *

Douglas and Bruce left just after ten. 'I'll have to get the lad back home. He has to be up early in the morning to get back to camp.' He guffawed. 'Can't have him going AWOL.'

By half past ten everyone was in bed in the farmhouse; the only being left awake was Buster on guard outside in the yard.

Anna was drifting into sleep when the sound of barking startled her into full wakefulness. This time, she did not hesitate but sprang from the bed and, barefoot, rushed along the landing to knock on her grandfather's bedroom door.

'Grandpa, Grandpa—Buster's barking.'

'Right, lass,' her grandfather's voice sounded through the door. 'I'm on me way.'

Anna rushed back to her bedroom to pull on trousers and a warm jumper over her pyjamas. By the time she emerged again from her room, her

350

grandfather was halfway down the stairs and Betty, Rita and May had appeared at their bedroom doors.

'What is it?'

'What's the matter?'

'It's Buster barking. Maybe it's those poachers again.'

'Right,' said Betty. 'Let's get 'em.'

Downstairs they found Luke opening the back door, his twelve-bore shotgun in his hand.

'Oh, Dad, do be careful,' May cried.

Luke turned briefly. 'You stay here. All of you.'

'I'm coming with you,' Betty said firmly and Rita and Anna said in unison, 'So am I.'

'All right. But keep well back. I don't want to shoot you by mistake. But I mean to get these beggars. Whoever they are,' he added grimly.

They stood together in the yard for a few moments, listening, until their eyes became accustomed to the dark. Buster had now ceased barking and came to stand beside his master. Briefly, Luke fondled the dog's head and murmured, 'Good boy. Good dog. Quiet now.'

Now they could hear the squawking from the henhouse.

'It could be a fox,' Rita whispered.

'Aye,' Luke said grimly, 'but Mr Fox is still a poacher.'

Luke moved forward, the others following, but keeping their distance as he had instructed. The noise of the terrified hens got louder as they neared the henhouse. Luke raised his gun and pointed it to the sky. Then he fired it, the report echoing through the night.

The girls, standing near the corner of the barn,

saw two shadowy figures moving near the henhouse. One was running away, climbing over the fence and into the lane, but the other was crouching low and coming straight towards Luke.

'Stop or I'll shoot,' Luke said and lowered his gun.

The figure spoke, but the girls were too far away to hear what he said. They heard Luke say, 'You!' before the man reached him, knocked the gun aside and punched the old man viciously in the stomach. Luke groaned and slumped to the ground.

'Grandpa!' Anna cried and began to run forward, Betty and Rita close behind her.

The attacker stood over Luke for a second, his face masked by a balaclava. Then he turned and ran across the grass towards the fence, whilst Betty blundered after him, shouting obscenities.

'You bastard. Wait till I get me hands on you. Hit a poor old man, would you?'

But he was too fast for any of them. He vaulted the fence and when, panting, Betty reached it, she could only hear his feet pounding down the lane, receding into the distance. Moments later, she heard the sound of a vehicle's engine and knew that they had escaped.

Furious that she had not at least been able to catch up with one of them, Betty returned to where Anna and Rita were crouching beside Luke. Anna was crying, saying over and over, 'Grandpa. Oh, Grandpa.'

As Betty reached them, Rita stood up and began to run towards the barn. 'I'm going for the doctor, Bet. He's been stabbed. Get May—'

For a moment Betty could not move. She gazed

down at the inert form. 'Stabbed?' she repeated stupidly. Anna's hands were moving over Luke's body. 'He's bleeding. There's blood everywhere. Oh, Betty, do something. Please, do something!'

Galvanized, Betty leapt forward and began to run towards the house. 'I'll get your mam and a torch. We need some light—'

May was waiting anxiously, hovering near the back door.

'Your dad's been hurt. Stabbed,' Betty said briefly. 'Bring a torch and a towel. I'll get some blankets off my bed—'

May, too, repeated incredulously, 'Stabbed?'

'Yes. Hurry. Reet's gone for the doc.'

Betty, with May hurrying after her, returned to Anna to find the girl still weeping over the still form of the old man.

'Now, now,' Betty said kindly. 'Crying won't help him. Come on, love, stop that noise.'

'Oh Betty, I—I think he's dead. I—I've tried to feel his pulse and—and I can't find one.'

'Course he isn't, love.' But when Betty shone the torch into Luke's face and saw his wide, staring eyes and his mouth gagging open she knew the girl was right. She went through the motions of feeling for a pulse, first in his wrist and then his neck. She even put her cheek to his chest, desperate to hear the merest flicker of a heartbeat. There was nothing.

Slowly Betty stood up and took hold of Anna's arm. 'Come on, love,' she said quietly. 'There's nothing more we can do.'

'What? What do you mean?' May's voice rose hysterically.

'I'm so sorry, May. He's dead.' Betty put her

other arm around May and tried to lead them both away, but May fought her off and fell to her knees beside her father. She rocked backwards and forwards and then bent her head and kissed his cheek. Anna looked down once more and then buried her face against Betty's comforting shoulder.

At last May stood up. 'Can't we carry him into the house? We—we can't leave him here.'

'Better not move him, love,' Betty said. 'Not till the doctor and the police have seen him.'

'The police?'

'It's a police matter now, May. Your father's been murdered.'

May closed her eyes and groaned whilst Anna sobbed into Betty's shoulder.

*   *   *

There was no sleep to be had for anyone the rest of that night. May sat in the kitchen, dry-eyed now, a wooden figure at the table, her arms resting on its surface, just staring into the distance. Anna curled up in her grandfather's chair near the range, alternately crying and raging against whoever had done this dreadful thing.

'All for a few hens,' she kept saying angrily. 'His life for a few miserable hens.'

May said nothing, whilst Betty made endless cups of tea and Rita looked after the doctor and then the village bobby, who had come to the farm on his bicycle.

'Bad business, this,' he said, sitting at the table in front of May and opening his notebook. 'I'm sorry to put you through this, May, but I'll have to ask you some questions.' He glanced round the room, intimating that he would need to question them all.

'Can't it wait?' Betty asked tartly. 'You can see what a state they're both in.' Then she muttered, 'The state we're all in, if it comes to that. Me and Reet were very fond of old Pops.' Tears filled her eyes, but she dashed them away impatiently. It was no time for her to indulge in tears. She had to be strong for the others. Later, in the privacy of the room she shared with Rita, she would weep for the old man, but for now . . .

'I'm sorry, miss,' the policeman, Reg Hamlin, was saying, 'but statements are best taken as soon as possible after the event. I've had to send word to my superiors in Lincoln. It'll be out of my hands soon, but they'll expect me to have made a start. Besides'—he glanced sympathetically towards May and Anna—'I'm a friend of the family, like, and I thought they'd rather talk to me than a stranger.'

'But they can't think properly.'

'Things can always be altered later, but it's best to make a start now,' Reg said with kindly firmness, 'while it's all still clear in their minds.'

One by one he listened to what they had to say, but the sum total of all their statements didn't amount to anything very helpful.

Reg left as a red dawn was breaking over the farmhouse.

CHAPTER FORTY-ONE

Of course there had to be a post-mortem and an inquest, the outcome of which confirmed that Luke

355

had been stabbed with a knife or similar weapon by 'a person or persons unknown'. Hearing it, Anna shuddered, remembering the bayonet that Bruce had shown her.

Douglas had arrived as usual the following Sunday and was appalled to hear the news. 'Darling May,' he said, taking her into his arms, 'you should have let me know. I would have come at once. You need a man at a time like this.'

May clung to him and Anna turned away, wishing that Bruce had come with his father. She could do with a strong shoulder to cry on too. But his brief leave was over and he had had to report back to camp.

Sensing her feelings, Betty hugged her. 'Chin up, love. Pops wouldn't have wanted you to grieve for too long. Once they've let us bury him—'

'Oh Betty, don't. I can't bear to think of him being put in the cold earth.'

'He'll be next to your gran though, won't he? He'll be with her now. And he'd want to know that you were carrying on the farm. For him. You will, won't you?'

'I—don't know what Mam wants to do. She's never liked the farm, so now . . .' Anna's voice trailed away sadly.

'You don't mean she'll sell it?' Betty was shocked.

Anna shook her head miserably. 'I don't know what she'll do.'

If, at that moment, they could have heard the conversation between May and Douglas, they would have been even more uneasy.

'Don't you worry about a thing, May. I'll see to everything. Just tell me what you want doing, darling, about the funeral, I mean, and I'll arrange it all.'

'Oh Douglas, you are good. I don't know what I'd do without you.'

'You won't have to do without me, May. I'll stay here with you, if you like.'

'Would you? But what about your work?'

'I'll have to go back into town tomorrow and sort out a few things, but if I can arrange it, I'll stay the rest of the week and help you. I—er—take it you'll have to see your father's solicitor?'

'I hadn't thought about that, but yes, I expect so—. Oh!'

'What? What is it?'

'I wonder if he changed his will like he threatened.'

Douglas forced a laugh. 'Surely not. I thought that was just an idle threat to make you throw me over.'

May shook her head and said soberly, 'My father never made idle threats.'

Douglas's face darkened and there was a glint of anger in his eyes. 'I didn't think he would move so fast—' Hastily, he altered his words, 'What I mean is, I didn't think he'd really carry out his threat. Not against his own daughter.' He thought for a moment and then said, 'But if he has, he'll have left it to Anna instead, won't he?'

'Maybe.' May was still doubtful.

Douglas's face cleared. 'There you are then. It's the same thing. She can't run it, though, can she? She's only fifteen. The best thing you could both do, May, is to sell the farm and come and live with me in Lincoln.'

'He—he might have put in some clause that it

can't be sold. He threatened to leave it to Anna on the condition that she had no more to do with—with Bruce.'

Now Douglas could scarcely hide his anger. In a tight voice he said, 'Did he, indeed?' But he forced himself to smile and to say in a tender tone, 'Then the sooner you find out just how things stand the better. I'll take you into the city with me tomorrow and you can call and see the solicitor. How's that?'

'Oh, Douglas,' May breathed and said again, 'I don't know what I'd do without you.'

*   *   *

Bruce wangled compassionate leave to attend the funeral.

'I had to tell a little white lie to get here,' he told Anna. 'I said it was my stepmother's father.' He laughed. 'Mind you, by the look of them'—he nodded to where May was walking down the church path, clinging to Douglas's arm—'it doesn't look as if it'll be long before she really is.'

Anna said nothing. The day, for her, was a tumult of emotions. She had lost her beloved grandfather and it seemed only yesterday that she had lost both her father and her grandmother. And whilst Anna could see that her mother needed Douglas's support, she was uncomfortable when she remembered that Luke had disliked the man so intensely that he had threatened to cut his own daughter out of his will.

Nor had he approved of the young man walking at her side, taking her cold hand in his and squeezing it sympathetically. Anna sighed as she and Bruce fell into step behind her mother and

Douglas to follow the coffin into the church. After the funeral, she knew the solicitor would be coming to the farm to read the will in keeping with the old-fashioned custom. Maybe then they would learn just how deep Luke's resentment had gone.

Betty and Rita were walking behind her and Bruce, and behind them it seemed as if half the local population had come to Luke Clayton's funeral. Even Reg Hamlin, in plain clothes, was standing to one side watching all the mourners.

'I shall be there,' he had told May and Betty the day before when he had visited the farm, 'with my Inspector. I'd be attending old Luke's passing anyway, but I shall be in a semi-official capacity.'

'Why?' May had asked.

'It's just possible that the killers might be there.'

'Really?' Betty had put in. 'Then I'll keep me beady eye open an' all, pet.'

*   *   *

Several people returned to the farm for sandwiches and cups of tea, with something a little stronger for the men.

'You can't have a wake without a drop of the hard stuff,' Douglas had told May. 'Leave it to me.'

As the mourners began to drift away, Douglas said, 'Bruce and I should go too, May. That solicitor chappie looks to be getting a bit agitated. We'd better let him have his bit of the limelight.'

'Oh Douglas, don't go. You've every right to stay. You're—you're my fiancé.'

Douglas patted her hand. 'No, May. I don't want to intrude. You can tell me later. I'll run Bruce to the station but I'll come back tonight. That's if you want me to?'

'Of course I do. And will you—will you stay?'

Douglas put his arms round her and held her close. 'Of course I will, darling.'

'And we'll make ourselves scarce, too,' Betty said. 'This is family business.'

The solicitor's clipped tones butted in. 'No, Miss Purves and Miss Mackinder too. I shall need you to be present.'

The two Land Army girls exchanged a puzzled glance, then shrugged and sat down at the table, where the solicitor, Mr Davey, had already seated himself at one end and was setting out his papers in front of him.

'We'll go, May,' Douglas whispered and kissed her cheek. 'Chin up, darling. It'll be all right. I know it will. 'Bye for now.'

As the solicitor's voice droned through all the legal jargon of the will, the nub of Luke's wishes became clear. Although no mention was made of either Douglas or Bruce Whittaker by name, Luke's suspicions had overshadowed his thinking and his decisions. The will had been made and signed only a month earlier.

The solicitor laid down the paper. 'To sum up briefly,' he said now in his own words, 'Mr Clayton has left two thousand pounds to his daughter, May Milton, together with bequests of two hundred pounds each to Miss Purves and Miss Mackinder. The remainder of his estate is to be held in trust for his granddaughter, Anna Milton, until she attains the age of twenty-five.'

'Twenty-five!' May cried, her voice high-pitched with indignation. 'Why twenty-five for Heaven's sake? Why not twenty-one?'

'Mr Clayton felt that twenty-five was a more mature age for such decisions.'

The three women and Anna glanced at one another. May turned towards Mr Davey. 'So what you mean is that he's turning me out and expecting Anna to live here on her own and run the farm until she's twenty-five?'

'No, no, my dear lady. The reason he has, er'— the man cleared his throat in obvious embarrassment—'bypassed you and left everything to his granddaughter is that he believed you intend to marry quite soon.'

'Ah, now we have the real reason.' May's eyes glittered with anger now.

'He also mentioned to me,' the man went on calmly, no doubt used to being in situations where the dear departed's will did not meet with unmitigated delight from the rest of the family, 'that you had never had much interest in the farm, but, he said, he believed that his granddaughter did.' He fixed May with a beady look. 'Is that so, Mrs Milton?'

May was flustered now. 'Well, yes, I suppose so. But I'm his daughter. I have a right—'

Mr Davey shook his head. 'I'm sorry, dear lady, but his wishes are crystal clear and the will is solid. I helped draft it myself.'

'And you mean we can't even sell the farm?'

Mr Davey shook his head. 'He appointed one of my partners and myself as his executors and trustees. When Miss Anna reaches twenty-five the farm will be hers to do what she likes with it. But until that time—' He spread his hands and his gesture said the rest.

There was nothing that could be done to

361

challenge Luke's will.

CHAPTER FORTY-TWO

'A measly two thousand pounds!' Douglas almost shouted at May when she told him the news. 'But you're his daughter, for God's sake.' Then, realizing his error, he put his arms about her. 'I'm sorry. It's not my place to say a word. But I'm so angry on your behalf. I know how dreadfully hurt you must feel. And I feel so responsible too, darling. If it wasn't for me—'

May nestled against his chest. 'It doesn't matter. I'm not interested in the farm. He knew that.'

'But he's left it so that it can't be sold, hasn't he? Left it so—so tied up—' Douglas's tone was bitter once more—'that you can't do anything with it. Not a blasted thing.' He held her away from him and looked down into her upturned face. 'What exactly are you going to do?'

'Well, for the moment,' May began hesitantly, unsure how he would greet her plans, 'I thought we could live here at the farm.'

Douglas raised his eyebrows and said sarcastically, 'Oh—and will your daughter allow that?'

May stared at him, not knowing how to react. Then Douglas laughed loudly and drew her to him again. 'Darling, I'm only teasing. Of course, you must stay here, at least for the time being. But once the war is over, well, then we'll see.'

'Why? What do you mean?'

'You don't want to go on living here for ever, do

362

you? I thought you wanted to get back to the city.'

'You know I do,' May said slowly, 'but I can hardly leave a fifteen-year-old girl living here on her own, now can I?'

'What you ought to do is to put a manager in here until such time as she can sell the blasted place.'

May gasped. 'Douglas!'

'Well, you said yourself that you don't want to stay here.'

'I know, but Anna does.'

'She's said so?'

'Yes.'

Douglas's mouth was suddenly a thin, hard line. 'Then your daughter will have to do as she's told. As you have said, darling, she's only fifteen and you, May, are her mother.'

*   *   *

'I'm not going back to the city. I love it here. It belongs to me. Grandfather wanted me to have the farm and I want to live here.'

'And you think you know all about farming do you? You think you'll be able to run this place single-handed?' Douglas sneered.

Anna faced him. 'No, of course I don't. But Betty and Rita are here for a while and—'

'A couple of Land Army girls?'

'And,' Anna continued, 'there's Mr Tomalin—Jed's uncle—at the next farm. He'll help me. He's said so. And, and—' she added in a low tone, '—there's Jed.' She wasn't so sure that she could rely on Jed's help any more. His attitude had been decidedly frosty towards her ever since Bruce and

363

she had become close.

'But you're only fifteen, Anna,' May said. 'I can't go and live in Lincoln and leave you here.' She glanced helplessly towards Douglas. 'I can't.'

'What's wrong with you and Douglas living here?' Betty asked. 'Seems to me that's the simple answer.'

Douglas shot her a vitriolic glance. 'I'm a city dweller. My work's in the city. I couldn't drive back and forth every day. It's difficult enough getting hold of the petrol to get here at weekends as it is. Tell you what, though.' His face suddenly brightened. 'Why don't we buy a place in the city? It's quite a good time to be buying. There's your two thousand pounds, May.' He took her hand and kissed it, smiling into her face. 'We could get a very nice house in Lincoln for that.'

Before May could answer, Betty put in, 'And you'd be selling your place, too, would you?' Her stare was fixed on Douglas's face. He laughed with feigned embarrassment. 'I'm afraid I've nothing to sell. Bruce and I live in rented accommodation.' He pulled an apologetic expression.

May smiled and patted his hand. 'Don't worry. At least my father didn't leave me penniless. Or homeless. We've always a home here, haven't we?'

Above her head, Douglas looked up to meet Anna's troubled gaze. 'Of course we have.' He smiled.

But the smile did not reach his eyes.

*　　　*　　　*

Without her grandfather, the farm was not the same place to Anna. Even though the work continued as before with the guidance of Luke's friend and neighbour, Bill Tomalin, she missed the old man dreadfully. Her mother, too, was unhappy. Douglas's visits were fewer. Some weekends, as he was leaving, he would say, 'May, I'm sorry, darling, but I just can't get the petrol to come all the way out here next weekend.'

When he did not come, May moped and cast resentful eyes at Anna, as if it were all her fault.

Only Betty and Rita carried on much as before, though even they missed 'Pops'.

Anna left school and began to work full-time on the farm.

'Ya'll wear a path between your farm and mine, lass,' Bill Tomalin remarked.

Anna smiled. 'I'm sorry to keep bothering you—'

'No bother, lass. Luke'd be proud of the way you're handling things. A slip of a lass like you and you're more or less running that place, aren't ya?'

Though he didn't say so outright, Anna knew he was hinting that he understood May had no interest in the farm. It had been the talk of the district since Luke's death.

Loyally not mentioning her mother, Anna said, 'I couldn't do it without Betty and Rita.'

Bill eyed her soberly. 'Aye, but they'll soon be gone, lass, won't they, when the war's over. Still,' he brightened, 'When the fellers get demobbed, there'll be plenty looking for work.'

Anna nodded. 'But how much longer is the war going on?'

Bill sighed. 'I can't tell you that, lass. I only wish I could. But I'll let you have Jed whenever I can spare him.'

If he'll come, Anna thought, but she smiled and

thanked him.

*   *   *

'I've got what they call embarkation leave. When I get back, I'll be going overseas.'

Bruce had arrived that Friday evening with his father. When he told her the news, Anna's eyes were wide with fear. 'Where are you going?'

Bruce shrugged. 'Dunno.' Then he grinned, 'And if I did, I couldn't tell you.'

'But I'll be able to write to you?'

'Yeah, course you will. I've got the address written on a bit of paper somewhere. You write to BFPO, I think it is.'

'Whatever's that?'

'British Forces Post Office. And then it gets sent to wherever we are.'

'Oh.' Anna was silent and then asked in a small, doubtful voice. 'Do you think you'll ever get it?'

'Course I will.' He put his arm around her shoulders. 'You write every week and I'll do the same. If I can, that is.' He grinned. 'But I'll be so busy sticking it to Jerry'—he made a stabbing movement as if thrusting his bayonet into the enemy—'that I might not get much time. Anyway, let's not think about that. Let's go for a walk around *your* farm.'

He laughed and, for a brief moment, Anna felt a twinge of uneasiness at his attitude, but she brushed it aside when he added, 'Come on, let's make the most of my last day.'

Despite her inner sadness, Anna was to look back on that day as one of the happiest she had spent with Bruce. He was kind and attentive, kissing her gently and holding her hand. They talked and laughed and when she shed a few tears over her grandfather, he held her close, stroked her hair and murmured words of comfort.

When Douglas and his son left late on the Sunday night, Anna clung to Bruce. 'You will take care?'

He laughed. 'Don't worry about me. Them Jerries won't get me. It's them that'll have to watch out when I get over there.' He tapped her chin gently. 'Just you remember that you're my girl. I want to know that you're here waiting for me to come home to.'

'Of course I am,' she breathed, feeling a thrill of pleasure run through her.

Douglas revved the car engine and Bruce hopped into the passenger seat. The car roared out of the gate as May and Anna stood waving goodbye. They stood there in the empty yard, listening to the sound grow fainter and fainter.

May put her arm around Anna's shoulder and drew her back into the farmhouse. 'Anna,' she began, biting her lip, 'there's something I have to tell you. Douglas wants me to go back into town with him sometimes. Not every week,' she added hastily, 'but just now and again. You don't mind, do you? Betty and Rita will be here to look after you.'

'That's fine, Mam,' Anna said brightly. But she guessed that May's visits would get longer and longer until she was hardly at the farm at all.

CHAPTER FORTY-THREE

The tide of the war seemed to be turning in favour of the Allies. At the beginning of June they had entered Rome and only days later the newsreels of the D-Day landing had given everyone new hope. The pictures of the troops landing on the beaches were cheered loudly in every cinema. And as the soldiers pressed inland, Anna wondered if Bruce was there with them. Desperately she scanned the screen for a glimpse of him, but amongst the thousands of servicemen she could not really hope to see him.

But then Hitler launched a new and terrible weapon upon the south of England, the V-1 flying bomb, and a mass evacuation of children from the target area of the pilotless weapons began again.

'Will they get here, do you think?' Anna asked fearfully.

'Don't think so,' Betty said practically. 'They haven't got the range. It's just the south that'll get it. Them poor devils in London have had more than their fair share, I reckon. Fancy having to cope with doodlebugs after all they went through in the Blitz.' She cast a wry glance at Douglas. 'Bet you're glad you moved up here, aren't you?'

Douglas put his arm around May and smiled down at her. 'It was the best thing I've ever done in my life.'

Watching them together, Anna thought: *He really does love Mam, I'm sure he does. He's so generous. Maybe Grandpa was wrong about him after all. He never stops buying things for Mam and spoiling her.*

May was always dressed in the latest fashion—thanks to Douglas. He bought material and employed a dressmaker to make dresses and costumes for her.

'My future wife's not going to be dressed in utility clothes. Mind you,' he added, winking saucily, 'I must say I like the idea of the shorter skirt to save on material.'

And he brought gifts to the farm too. The day he came with a box of oranges, the Land Army girls and Anna fell on them with squeals of glee. 'I'm not going to ask how you got 'em,' Betty declared, peeling one and biting into the segments. She closed her eyes in ecstasy. 'I'm just glad you did.'

In August Paris was liberated and everyone began to hope that soon the war would be over. Plans for a better Britain were already being talked about. New homes were to be built and a National Health Service that would bring equal health care for all was promised.

And soon, Anna prayed, Bruce would be home. She longed to see him again. She wrote to him every week, just as she had said she would. His letters were not so frequent, but she understood why and forgave him.

I reckon I'll sign on as a regular after the war, he wrote. *I love the army life.*

Anna wrote back to him in a panic. *But what about us?*

His reply was a long time coming and Anna was in a torment of uncertainty. He didn't love her any more. He'd found someone else. A sophisticated, chic French girl perhaps, like the pictures she'd seen in the magazines Betty and Rita brought

369

home.

What do you mean 'What about us?' he wrote at last. *You're my girl, aren't you? We'll get married and you can come with me. It'd be a great life, travelling all over the world. You'd love it. You don't want to live on the farm for ever. And even if you did—which I hope you won't—you won't need me around. You'll always have the faithful Jed.*

Jed had been classed as being in a reserved occupation, much to Bruce's scathing disgust.

He's yeller, he had scoffed in a letter home to Anna. *He ought to be out here getting a taste of what being a real man is like.*

As Anna had expected, May spent more and more time in Lincoln with Douglas, but they still came at the weekend sometimes and then May would stay the rest of the week with Anna, whilst Douglas went back to the city alone.

'We'll have a lovely Christmas this year,' May promised. 'The war might be over by then and Bruce could be home. We'll make it really special.'

But the war was not over by Christmas, though towards the end of November Bruce did get leave and came home for a blissful weekend with Anna.

As they said their goodbyes on the Sunday evening, Anna clung to him. 'Do take care.'

'Course I will. It'll soon be over.'

'But—but you said you might stay in the army. Did you really mean it?'

Bruce shrugged. 'Dunno yet. I might. Look, sorry, I've got to go. Dad's waiting in the car.'

He kissed her hard on the mouth and then he was gone.

*　　　*　　　*

370

The following morning Betty came bursting into the kitchen.

'There's three hens gone missing. That beggar—whoever he is—must be back again,' Betty said angrily. 'I thought we'd got rid of him. Nothing much has happened lately.'

'How do you know? Have you counted them?' Rita asked.

'I have now,' Betty said. 'I got suspicious when I couldn't find Speckly.' Betty's favourite was a black and white speckled hen.

'They could have wandered off somewhere,' May suggested. 'Laying their eggs under a hedge, I shouldn't wonder.'

Betty pressed her lips together as she shook her head. 'No. Speckly comes to me to be fed every morning.' The girl was adamant. 'She's gone, I tell you.' And she glared belligerently at May as if it were her fault. 'She'll be plucked and roasted and lying on somebody's plate now.' She glowered as she muttered, 'Somewhere in the city, I shouldn't wonder.'

'What? What do you mean by that, Betty?' May asked sharply, but the girl turned away and left the house, slamming the back door behind her.

'What did she mean?' May asked, glancing between Rita and Anna.

Rita got up. 'I'd best get on.' As she too left the house, May stared after her.

'What did Betty mean? Do you know, Anna?'

Slowly Anna said, 'I think she's hinting that poor Speckly—and probably everything else that's gone missing over the months from the farms around here—has ended up on the black market in the

371

city.'

'Well, yes, I expect it has. We all know that, but—but she seemed to be hinting at something else. Something more—'

Mother and daughter stared at each other.

'Douglas! She thinks it's Douglas, doesn't she?' May's fingers fluttered to cover her mouth. 'Oh, how could she?' Then suddenly May's eyes sparkled with anger. 'It's more likely she's got some feller in tow who's wheeling and dealing and she's supplying him with our stock. Huh! The cheek. Accusing my Douglas. She's still jealous, that's what. Just because it's me he comes to see now and not her.'

Now it was Anna who did not know how to answer.

*   *   *

May refused to speak to either Betty or Rita for the rest of the week, and by the time Douglas arrived again on the Saturday afternoon she had packed her suitcase and was waiting for him, wearing her hat and coat in readiness.

'We're going straight back to town,' she informed him before he had scarcely got out of the car.

'Why? What's the matter? Trouble?'

'I'll tell you later. Come on, we're going.'

Anna had never seen her mother so forceful. May turned briefly towards her daughter. 'I don't know when I'll be back. You'll—you'll be all right?' There was a moment's brief hesitation in her resolve.

Anna nodded as Douglas lifted his shoulders

and spread his arms in a helpless gesture. But he was laughing again as he climbed back into the car. 'Your wish is my command, ma'am.'

As they disappeared down the lane in a cloud of exhaust fumes, Betty came to stand beside Anna. Putting her arm around the young girl, she said, 'I'm sorry I've upset your mam, but I'm not apologizing for suspecting him. Have you noticed that stuff seems to disappear only after a weekend and only when him and his lad have been?'

Anna gasped and turned to face Betty. 'You mean you think Bruce was involved too?'

Betty watched her with serious eyes. Then she nodded. 'I'm sorry, pet, but—'

Anna pulled away from Betty. 'How could you? Mam was right. It's not them. It's *you*, but you want everyone to *think* it's them.'

'Me?' Betty's face was red, not with guilt but with anger. 'How dare you think that of me? Why, if Pops was still here—'

Tears glistened in Anna's eyes. 'Don't you dare even mention his name.'

'What's going on?' Rita said, coming across the yard.

Betty swung round. 'This little madam is accusing me of stealing.'

Rita's mouth dropped open. Then she laughed. 'Don't be daft, Anna. Betty wouldn't take a ha'penny that didn't belong to her. You should know better than that.'

Now it was Anna's turn to flush with embarrassment. 'All right then, but she's no need to go accusing others.'

Puzzled, Rita glanced from Anna to Betty and back again. 'Others? What others?'

'Douglas and—and Bruce.'

'Ah, well now, there you have me because I'm afraid I have to agree with her.'

Now it was Anna's turn to glance from one to the other as she said falteringly, 'You—you do?'

Rita nodded. 'Sorry, love, but yes, I do.'

Betty was gentle now as she could see that Anna was genuinely distressed and confused. 'Actually, it's more Bruce than Douglas, but I reckon his dad was in on it and all. He was the only one with the transport. Think about it, pet. We had a spate of livestock going from all the farms around here, didn't we? And then, for a while, nothing. All the time Bruce was away doing his basic training. And then when he comes home on leave—three hens go missing.'

'Bill told me yesterday that he lost a piglet last weekend an' all. Same time as our hens went. The weekend Bruce was home on leave.'

Anna closed her eyes and groaned. 'It's not true. It's not. I won't believe it.'

'I'm sorry, love,' Betty said again, 'but I think it's more that you don't want to believe it. Don't you?'

Anna was quiet for the rest of the week. She didn't ignore Betty and Rita, who did their best to act normally, but she was unhappy. She liked Betty and Rita. Her grandpa had too—he'd thought the world of them and trusted them completely. But, she remembered uncomfortably, he had not liked Douglas or his son. Anna sighed. But she loved Bruce and wanted to believe in him. He had gone away again, back abroad, and she didn't want to write this sort of thing in a letter. If only he would come home on leave again, she could sort it all out with him and prove his innocence. And Douglas's too.

The week dragged by. She missed Bruce and now she missed her mother. But for the two Land Army girls' insinuations, it could have been a happy week. Betty and Rita were good workers and despite the atmosphere between them and Anna they still carried out the work as they always had done.

Privately, Betty said to Rita, 'For two pins I'd walk out, but I'm doing it for Pops.'

'Anna's all right. I know she likes Bruce, but I reckon she's wavering.'

Betty's tough line softened. 'Poor kid. She's only young. She doesn't know what to believe.' Her tone hardened again. 'But May's old enough to know better.'

Rita laughed. 'Come on, Bet. You fell for him once.'

Betty grinned. 'Nearly, I admit it. But,' she tapped the side of her nose knowingly, 'I never let myself get so carried away that I can't suss out what they're like. And I soon started to see that Mr Douglas Whittaker wasn't quite all he was cracked up to be.' She sighed and added, 'But May—' She needed to say no more. They both knew that May was so besotted with Douglas that she could see no wrong in him.

'We ought to work on Anna,' Rita said seriously.

Betty shrugged. 'I don't expect she'll believe us. When her own mother is so taken up with the father you can hardly expect her to turn against the son, can you?'

'It's worth a try, even if only for poor old Pops,' Rita said solemnly. 'It's what he would have wanted us to do.'

The girls' plans to get Anna to see what they believed was the truth were dashed when May returned home three weeks later, flashing a wedding ring.

'We were married by special licence, Anna,' May said, her face glowing with happiness. 'I'm sorry you couldn't be there, but Douglas says we'll make it up to you. You and Bruce, next time he's home.'

'Well, that's it, then,' Betty said, folding her arms with a gesture of finality. 'You'll not be wanting us around any longer.'

'As you wish, Betty,' May said stiffly.

'Oh now, come on, Betty.' Douglas put his arm around her shoulders. She stiffened beneath his touch. 'May's told me of your suspicions and yes, you're quite right to suspect me—'

'Douglas!' May's eyes were wide, but he was laughing.

'Oh, I'm not perfect, May darling, I'll be the first to admit it and yes, I do a bit of dealing on the black market, but I wouldn't stoop to stealing. Specially not from May. I'd be a fool wouldn't I?'

'What about that lad of yours then?' Betty persisted. 'Is he pure and lily white an' all?' she added sarcastically.

Douglas was still standing with his arm draped around her. His face was close to hers. As she looked up, she was sure she saw a fleeting malicious glint in his eyes, but it was gone in an instant and she wondered if she had imagined it.

Douglas forced himself to laugh again. 'No young feller of his age is pure and lily white, as you put it, but he's not a bad lad.'

Betty moved away from him as she glanced at May. 'I still think it would be better if we left. Now you've got a husband to help you with the farm work, you won't need us.' There was the merest hint of sarcasm in her tone and everyone noticed it. Only Douglas guffawed. 'Me? Milk cows and muck out the henhouse? I think not. Besides, May and I will be spending most of our time in Lincoln. Won't we, darling? We've got a nice house in view—a semi-detached in a nice part of the city.' He turned towards Anna, as if suddenly realizing he had not included her in their plans. 'You'll love it, Anna. And we'll have your room decorated just as you'd like it.'

Anna smiled weakly and murmured, 'That's very kind of you, but I must stay here.' She turned to Betty and Rita. 'Please don't leave me. I couldn't manage on my own.' But before either of them could answer, Douglas said, 'It'd be far better if you could sell the lot. This place is a millstone round your neck. A young girl like you should be out having fun, not slaving away out here in the back of beyond. If it hadn't been for that vindictive old man, you could be well off and having the time of your life.'

Anna gasped. 'I love the farm. I'll never sell it. Never.'

Now Douglas couldn't hide his anger. 'Well, you'll be on your own then because your mother and I have no intention of living here.'

May bit her lip and glanced anxiously between her new husband and her daughter. But she said nothing. She made no attempt to deny Douglas's words.

Anna's dark violet eyes filled with tears as she murmured again, 'Betty, please don't go.'

The two older girls glanced at each other and, as

377

if reaching mutual agreement, Betty sighed and said, 'All right, pet. We'll stay a bit longer.'

As it turned out they only stayed a few more months, for in the following May the war ended and when demobilization began, as Betty had predicted, there were plenty of men looking for work.

Anna's heart sang. Bruce would be coming home and then everything would be all right.

CHAPTER FORTY-FOUR

'I 'spect we'll be going home soon, then,' Betty said.

They had all been to the street party in the village to celebrate VE Day and had returned home to the farm tired, but elated that the war was finally over.

'I don't expect they'll let us go just yet. Not till demob starts and there's fellers back home to take our places,' Rita said.

Betty nodded. ' 'Spect you're right. They'll tell us when, I suppose.'

'You'll stay till after shearing, won't you? Even if we get new fellers, they won't be as good as you.'

'Could I have that in writing please, ma'am?' Betty quipped. 'I might need a good reference when I go back home and start looking for work.'

It was Jed who took charge at shearing time.

'He's a born natural with them shears,' his uncle said proudly. 'He's won prizes for it, y'know.'

Anna was fascinated to watch Jed at work. He was firm but gentle with the sheep. There was no panic or rough handling, but his strength kept them under control as he rolled them over and began to shear, the fleece falling off.

'Like a knife through butter,' Betty, standing beside Anna, murmured. 'He's good, isn't he?'

Anna nodded. For a brief moment there was a lump in her throat. Things had not been the same between her and Jed over the last months and she missed his easy friendship.

'Yes, he is good,' she said and meant it about more than just sheep shearing. He had taught her so much, she realized. It had been Jed who had shown her how to fold the fleeces, Jed who had helped her at dipping time when she had not wanted to plunge the poor creatures right into the dip.

'You've got to do it, Anna, for their own sake,' he'd explained gently. 'You don't want to see 'em with ticks or lice or, worse still, sheep scab, do you?'

And despite the rift between them over Bruce, he was still here, still helping her, even though she had the uncomfortable feeling that he was now doing it more for her grandfather's memory than for her.

*   *   *

'I don't like leaving you, Anna,' Betty said worriedly when the day came in the autumn for both her and Rita to leave. Their former, easy relationship had never been fully restored since Betty's accusations, yet both Land Army girls were genuinely fond of Anna—and May, too, though they were exasperated by the older woman's blind

379

worship of Douglas.

'Can't she see him for what he is? A wide boy. A spiv. If only she'd listened to Pops. He knew, bless him. Oh, how I wish I'd never brought Douglas Whittaker here. I could kick myself. If I'd thought for one minute—' Betty said more than once, but never now in front of Anna. 'And what'll happen when Bruce gets home I shudder to think.'

'It's not our worry,' Rita tried to tell her.

'No, I know. But when I think about Pops—' It was all Betty needed to say for them to lapse into a sorrowful silence, until Rita said practically, 'There's nothing more we can do, Bet. Time to go home and pick up our own lives.'

And now the day had come. Their belongings were all packed and they were in the yard waiting for the lorry that was coming to pick them up. Anna hugged them both in turn, all discord forgotten. Tears were running down her face. 'I wish you weren't going. You've been wonderful.'

'I just hope these two new fellers you've got are going to be all right.'

Anna smiled through her tears. 'Well, it isn't as if I don't know them. Jed is still here'—she pulled a face—'well, now and again. And I went to school with Phil—one of the new hands—though he is a bit older than me. Grandpa knew his family, so I know he would have approved.'

There was an awkward silence as if all of them were thinking the same thing. Luke would not have approved of May's marriage or of the fact that Anna was longing for the day when Bruce returned.

Betty nodded, comforted by Anna's words. 'They do seem nice lads,' she said, 'and at least if you say Pops would have approved of *them*—' She didn't finish the sentence and what she didn't say seemed to hang in the air between them.

'Here's the lorry,' Rita said and there was a further flurry of hugs and goodbyes and promises to write. As the lorry drew out of the yard, Anna followed it into the lane and stood waving until it turned a corner and disappeared from her sight. Slowly she walked back into the silent farmhouse and wandered from room to room. She would be sleeping here alone now and, though the fact didn't frighten her, she knew she would be very lonely.

Oh, if only, she thought, *Bruce would come home.*

* * *

The months dragged on and another Christmas came and went. Whilst May and Douglas spent Christmas Day and Boxing Day with her, there was nothing festive about the atmosphere in the farmhouse.

Anna did her best, cooking a goose with all the other Christmas fare that rationing would allow, but Douglas seemed ill at ease and fidgeting to get back to town. And May too no longer belonged at Clayton's Farm—if she ever had, Anna thought wryly.

There was no word of Bruce being home on leave or even of a date for his demob.

'Do you think he's signed on? He said he was going to.'

Douglas frowned. 'He'd better not have done, else I'll have something to say about that.'

Near the time of May's birthday in May, she and Douglas arrived at the farmhouse unexpectedly one weekend.

'Come on,' Douglas said, 'pack your case. We're taking you back to town.'

'But, I can't leave—'

'Of course you can. Phil and Maurice will manage for a few days.' He smiled as he leant towards her. 'And we've got a surprise for you.'

'What?'

'Aha, you'll have to wait and see. Wouldn't be a surprise if we told you, would it?'

Anna was still doubtful, but when May said persuasively, 'Oh please come, Anna, you haven't seen our house yet,' she gave in.

'I can't stay long though. There's sheep dipping to do soon and I don't think the lads'll manage on their own.'

'We'll see, we'll see,' Douglas said and Anna saw him wink at May. As she packed an overnight bag, Anna began to feel excited. It would be nice to go to Lincoln, to go shopping. Perhaps they'd even go to Douglas's cinema together and see a film. She'd like that. Perhaps that was the surprise.

* * *

May showed her all over the semi-detached house she and Douglas had bought. Their new home was set on a road leading up the hill on the northern side of the city. Anna buried the thought that her mother's money had paid for it.

'They're lovely houses, aren't they?' May enthused, flinging open the door of one of the three bedrooms. 'And this is your room. We've had decorators in specially. Do you like it?' she asked eagerly.

382

Anna glanced around at the pink-flowered wallpaper, the pink bedspread and matching curtains fluttering at the window. 'It's—it's lovely, Mam, but—' She turned her gaze towards her mother. 'But I won't be living here. I'll have to stay at the farm.'

May flapped her hands. 'But that's only for a few years. Until you can sell it and come and live in the city with us. You might even be able to come before, if you put a manager in. Then you can get a nice job in an office and—'

Anna shook her head. 'Mam, I don't want to work in an office. I want to work on the farm. I love it there. Besides, I couldn't sell Grandpa's farm.'

'Oh, Anna, surely you're not serious? You can't really mean that you want to live out there? All on your own?'

'I won't be on my own.'

'You will be at night when the workers have gone home. And we can't keep driving out to the farm. Petrol's still in short supply, you know.'

'Bruce will be with me.'

May laughed. 'You can forget that, you silly goose. Bruce won't want to live in the back of beyond any more than his father does.' May shook her head and added bitterly, 'If that stupid old man hadn't tied everything up so tightly that we can't sell the place for years, we'd be living in clover now.'

Anna glanced around her. The words were out before she could stop them. 'You don't look to be doing so badly, Mam.'

'Anna!' May was appalled. 'How dare you speak to me like that?'

'You shouldn't speak about Grandpa like that.'

Tears filled the girl's eyes. 'He loved us. Both of us.'

May sniffed. 'You, maybe, but I'm not so sure about me.'

Appalled, Anna stared at her. 'Of course he loved you, Mam. Look how they took us in at the start of the war and—and looked after us when Daddy—'

'I know, I know, but'—May bit her lip—'I always felt that was more your grannie's doing than *his*.'

Anna was adamant. She shook her head. 'No, no, you're wrong. I know you are. He wanted the best for you. I know he did. And as for him not liking Douglas, well, maybe then it was only because he was concerned about you getting involved with someone else so soon after Daddy—'

May said bitterly, 'Oh, you don't know the half of it, Anna. How could you? I've told you before that he didn't like your father when I first met him.'

'I know, but he came round, didn't he?'

'He was against me marrying him because Ken didn't want to live on the farm. It was always because of the farm.'

'But—but he was always nice to Daddy.'

May laughed wryly. 'Oh yes, after we had you. He came round very quickly when we gave him a grandchild. He even wanted me to christen you Anna Clayton Milton, but I drew the line at that. Such a mouthful. But he was quite happy then to think that there was someone else to pass his precious farm on to.' She paused and then added pointedly, 'He was right, wasn't he?'

Anna nodded slowly and said huskily, but with a firmness that her mother could not fail to notice, 'Yes, he was.' Then she added, 'I'm sorry, Mam, I

384

didn't mean to cheek you.'

'I should think so too. Douglas was right. He said you had a stubborn streak in you. Well, my girl'—May put her hand on Anna's shoulder and propelled her from the room—'there's someone downstairs waiting to see you who might change your mind for you.'

As they stepped into the sitting room Anna gasped aloud, for standing in front of the fireplace, resplendent in his army uniform, was Bruce.

Anna flew across the room, her arms outstretched. Bruce caught her and swung her round.

'How's my best girl?' he laughed and, though both Douglas and May were watching, he kissed Anna firmly on the mouth, ignoring her blushing protest.

*　　　*　　　*

They had a wonderful weekend. Anna and May went round the city shops on the Saturday and in the evening they went to the cinema, Douglas having procured the best seats in the front of the circle.

On the Sunday May packed a picnic and they went to the Arboretum, sitting on the grass in the warm September sunshine.

'When do you have to go back?' Anna asked Bruce for the first time. Until this moment she hadn't wanted to broach the subject.

Bruce lay back and put his hands behind his head. 'Wednesday morning. Four whole days of leave.'

'You won't be going abroad again, will you?'

385

'Dunno,' Bruce said, squinting up at her. 'I told you, I thought I might sign on after the war. Well, I've made up my mind. I'm going to become a regular. I like the army life.'

'Oh, but what about—?' she began and then bit her lip.'

Bruce grinned. 'What about what?'

'Oh nothing.' She glanced away from him and pulled at the grass.

Bruce sat up. Softly, he said, 'You were going to say, "What about us?" weren't you?'

'Well,' she said hesitantly then added hastily, 'but maybe you don't want—I mean—'

'Of course I want. You're my girl, aren't you?'

Anna blushed and nodded.

'We can write to each other and when I come home on leave—'

'Never mind about that.' Douglas raised his voice and both Anna and Bruce realized that, though he had been lying back with his eyes closed, he had been listening to every word of their conversation. 'Never mind about that,' he said again, sitting up. 'What you want to do is to get married. The pair of you—'

Now May sat up. 'Oh no, Douglas. Anna's far too young. She's only seventeen. There's plenty of time—'

'No, there isn't,' Douglas almost snapped. 'This war should have shown you that, May. Youngsters have to grab their happiness. Just think about it. They haven't even got to save up for a home of their own.' He spread his hands. 'Anna's already got one. The farm. They can live on the farm. And you'—he jabbed his finger towards his son—'can forget about signing on for years. What more could you want than a life in the country? You'll be set up for life, the pair of you.'

'But you said—' May began, but Anna saw Douglas glare at his wife. 'Never mind what I said. If it's what they both want, then why make them wait, eh?'

Still May hesitated as she looked across at Anna. 'Is it what you want, love?'

'Well—' she glanced at Bruce. He was staring at his father as if he thought Douglas had taken leave of his senses.

Ignoring him, Douglas boomed, 'Of course it is,' as if the matter had been decided. 'Come on,' he said, getting up. 'It's getting chilly. Let's go home. Bruce, you help me pack up the picnic things. You two go and sit in the car. We'll manage.'

As Anna and her mother walked down the slope to where the car was parked on the road, she glanced back. Douglas was wagging his finger in Bruce's face, whilst his son stared wordlessly at his father. It looked as if Douglas was telling his son exactly what he must do and that Bruce was not daring to argue.

Later, after their evening meal, Anna managed to whisper to Bruce. 'Will you take me back to the farm tomorrow morning? I have to get back and we need to talk.'

Bruce nodded.

CHAPTER FORTY-FIVE

'You don't have to marry me, you know. Never mind what your dad says,' Anna said as they drove back to the farm.

'Who said I didn't want to marry you?'

'No one, but—'

'Well, then, what are you going on about?' Bruce snapped and Anna glanced at him and then fell silent.

They did not speak for the rest of the journey and when they drew to a stop in the yard, Bruce leapt out saying, 'I'll bring your things in. You'd better go and make sure those lads you left in charge haven't killed off half your stock.'

As Anna climbed out and began to walk towards the house, Bruce flung up the lid of the boot and reached inside. For no particular reason, she glanced into the boot as Bruce was lifting out her bag.

Beneath it, lying in the well of the boot, Anna was sure she saw two or three chicken feathers. Bruce slammed the lid. Anna stopped and stared at him.

'How've they got in there?'

'Eh? Come again?'

'Those feathers? In the boot? How've they got in there?'

For a moment, Bruce glared at her, 'I don't know what you're talking about.'

She pointed. 'In there. There's some chicken feathers.'

'Don't be daft. You're seeing things.'

'Open the boot then. See for yourself. There's definitely feathers in the boot.'

Frowning, Bruce opened the lid once more and glanced inside.

'There! Look!'

Bruce slammed the lid once more. 'So what? Them hen feathers get everywhere. So does their flipping muck. Last time I came here I got a right rollocking from my Sergeant when I got back to camp 'cos there was chicken muck on my boots.'

Somehow he had turned the accusation against her, but for the rest of the day Anna could not put the memory out of her mind. The thought that perhaps Betty had been right after all crept insidiously into her brain.

Bruce, however, seemed to have put the incident out of his mind. As dusk fell, he said, 'I'd better be getting back to town then.' He slipped his arm around her waist. 'Unless you want me to stay the night. It must get lonely for you—'

Anna shook her head. 'No, you'd better go. It wouldn't be right, you staying here. People would talk and I don't think Mam'd like it.'

'Dad'd talk her round. Oh, go on, Anna, let me stay.'

'Well, you could sleep in the spare room.'

'The spare room? I'm not sleeping in any spare room.'

Anna gasped as his meaning became clear. 'Oh no,' she said firmly now, 'in that case, you're not staying.'

Bruce let his arm fall away. 'Please yourself. There's plenty wouldn't turn down an offer like that.'

Anna gasped. 'What—what do you mean?'

Bruce grinned. 'What do you think I mean?'

'That you—you've been with other girls?'

Bruce opened his mouth to retort and then suddenly he closed it again, then frowned slightly, almost as if he realized just what he had been going to say and had caught himself just in time. 'I didn't say that, did I?'

'No, but—'

'Don't jump to conclusions. All I said was, there's plenty wouldn't turn down the offer. Right?'

'All right,' Anna said in a small voice. Once again he had gained the upper hand in an argument.

'So? Do I stay or do I go?'

This time he could not argue when Anna turned away from him. 'You'd better go.'

From the kitchen she heard the car roar off up the lane until she could hear its sound no more.

Suddenly, she felt incredibly lonely and regretted her prim refusal of Bruce's company.

*　　　*　　　*

The following morning, her eyes still heavy with sleep after a restless night, Anna went out into the yard. Clanging noises were coming from the cowshed. The morning milking was already under way.

She peeked round the door to see Jed sitting with his head pressed against a cow's side, the milk spurting into the bucket. He was whistling softly.

'Morning, Jed,' Anna said quietly, so as not to startle the cow.

Jed twisted his head sideways. 'Morning, Anna. Had a nice weekend?' The question was not quite the polite enquiry it might have been. There was a hint of sarcasm in his tone and no friendly smile to accompany it.

She gave a swift nod, but lowered her eyes. 'Everything been all right here?'

'Fine. Phil's away up the fields to check the sheep.' His reply was terse and to the point.

'I'll have breakfast ready for you all. How long will you be finishing milking?'

' 'Bout half an hour.'

She was sitting in the kitchen, cupping a mug of tea in her hands and watching Jed devour a plateful of bacon, eggs and fried bread, when Phil burst in through the back door.

'You know those lambs you kept back from going to market? To increase the stock?' he began at once. Anna turned to look up at him and Jed stopped eating, his fork suspended halfway between the plate and his mouth.

Anna rose slowly, guessing what he was going to say. 'Yes?'

'One's missing.'

Anna closed her eyes and groaned. 'Oh no!'

Jed's face was grim. Hurriedly he finished his meal and rose to his feet. 'We'd best have a good look round, but if we can't find it, I reckon you ought to report it to the police this time, Anna.'

Anna shuddered. He was right, of course, but the memory of the chicken feathers in the back of Douglas's car was all too vivid.

CHAPTER FORTY-SIX

Over the next few weeks no letters came from Bruce and Anna could not bring herself to write to him either. Perhaps their romance was over, she thought dully, almost before it had really begun.

Douglas and May came out to the farm most weekends and never left without trying to persuade her to move to the city to live with them.

'Why won't you agree to put a manager in here? That young fellow, Jed, he'd be ideal. I know he's only young but he's got his uncle close by,' Douglas said more than once, always angling his suggestions to appear as if he only had Anna's best interests at heart. 'It's no life for a young girl like you stuck out here. Living all alone. Your mother's worried sick about you. Think of your mother, Anna. You're being very selfish, you know.'

Anna said nothing but sighed inwardly. It was amazing, she thought, how both Douglas and Bruce seemed to turn everything around to being someone else's fault.

But Anna didn't want to go. Oh yes, some nights she felt very lonely, but usually she was so tired that she went to bed early and slept the sound sleep of someone who had worked hard all day in the open air. Winter had been the worst with the long dark nights, but always the memory of Luke made her determined to stay. Her grandfather had left Clayton's Farm to her. He knew she loved it and he had trusted her to carry on the family tradition. And now it was summer again, a year on from the end of the war. Things were getting better and there was plenty of work to keep her busy.

'I'll not let you down, Grandpa,' she whispered into the darkness as she lay in bed. 'I'll never sell your farm. Never.'

*   *   *

'Bruce is coming home on leave next week,' Douglas told Anna toward the end of June. Has he told you?'

'No. He—he hasn't written lately.'

Douglas frowned. 'Not written? Well, I'll have something to say about that when I see him.' He patted Anna's shoulder. 'Don't worry, love. You know what young fellers are. I expect he's not much of a letter writer.' He gave a bellowing guffaw. 'Takes after his dad.'

Anna smiled weakly.

'Tell you what,' Douglas said, 'instead of you coming into town, we'll all come out here. Make a nice change, wouldn't it, May, to have a weekend in the country?'

'Whatever you say, dear.'

Anna glanced at her mother, but May avoided meeting her daughter's eyes. Anna made up her mind to try to speak to her mother alone. There was something different about May. She looked on edge, nervous and agitated, and every time Douglas spoke to her she seemed to jump. She was wearing more make-up than usual, Anna noticed, the powder plastered thickly onto her cheeks. May had always spurned artificial aids, Anna thought, remembering how proud her mother had been of her smooth, flawless skin. A good face cream and a touch of pale pink lipstick was all she'd ever needed had been her proud boast. But now the make-up was thick and poorly applied. And, Anna noticed, May's thumbnail was bitten down to the quick.

But during the day Douglas never left May's side and Anna had no chance to speak to her mother alone. As the car sped away that evening, Anna had the irrational feeling that Douglas had stayed close to May deliberately. He had been his usual charming and attentive self, but there was something more. Something that Anna could not quite put her finger on . . .

*   *   *

On the following Friday Anna threw open the windows in the room that had once been her grandparent's bedroom and also in the tiny spare room.

'He can sleep here,' she muttered. 'He's not getting into my bed, whatever he thinks.'

She put fresh linen on the beds and a posy of flowers in the main room to greet her mother.

'Is *he* coming?' Jed asked morosely as he ate his ploughman's lunch sitting at the scrubbed table in Anna's kitchen. His eyes followed her busy movements between table and range as she prepared a special evening meal.

'Who?' She looked up, startled.

'Him? Bruce whatever-his-name-is?'

Anna tried to hide her smile, but unsuccessfully. It sounded for all the world as if Jed was jealous. 'He's on leave, but they're all coming.' She giggled. 'My reputation will be quite safe.'

Jed glowered at her and bit deeply into his bread

and cheese.

A few moments' uncomfortable silence went by before Jed blurted out, 'Are you serious about him?'

It was on the tip of her tongue to say, 'What's it to do with you?' but something in his tone stopped her. They'd been friends ever since the day her grandfather had introduced him to her when she had come to live on the farm with her mother at the beginning of the war. Lately their easy friendship had been strained, but now he sounded like the old Jed.

She sighed and sat down opposite him. 'To tell you the truth, Jed, I don't know. Not now. A while back, I would have said "yes" straight away, but now—'

Jed's tone became gentle as if he sensed her dilemma and really wanted to help. 'I'm always here if you want to talk about it.'

Anna felt a lump in her throat. 'Thanks,' she said huskily. There was silence between them once more, but now it was a companionable one. 'Have you got a girlfriend, Jed?'

'Oh, dozens of 'em,' he said airily. 'They're queuing up, y'know.'

Anna laughed. 'I can believe that.'

Jed's smile faded as he regarded her seriously. 'I was only joking. No, Anna, there's no one.' As she met his steady gaze across the table, Anna felt a shiver run through her. She was not so naive now that she didn't recognize the look in his dark eyes.

She had not been mistaken earlier. It had most definitely been jealousy in Jed's tone when he had spoken of Bruce.

'Here we are then,' Douglas boomed as he offered his hand to May to help her from the car. Anna hurried forward. She glanced briefly at Bruce as he sprang from the back seat, but it was to her mother she went with her arms outstretched. She kissed May's cheek and then stood back to look at her. May's smile was tremulous and there was a wary look in her eyes. She met Anna's gaze and glanced towards her husband, then swiftly back to Anna. The girl had the strangest feeling that her mother was trying to tell her something. Trying to warn her, almost.

Anna linked her arm through May's and drew her towards the house, promising herself that during this weekend she would definitely get her mother on her own and find out what was troubling her. Because she was sure now that something was bothering May.

'Hey, don't I even get a kiss after all this time?' Bruce spread his arms wide.

'Later,' she teased, forcing a gaiety that she wasn't feeling, 'when there's not so many people about.'

She was uncomfortably aware that not only were her mother and Douglas there to see, but that Jed was watching from the cowhouse door.

'I'll look forward to it.' Bruce pretended to leer.

'Come along in,' Anna chattered brightly, trying to hide her disquiet. 'I've cooked you a meal and we'll have it in the front room as a special treat. I've even lit a fire. It's still cold in the evenings, isn't it, even though it's June?'

The two men were not following them into the

house but had remained standing by the car. Douglas was gesticulating and almost shaking his fist in Bruce's face. A few fractured words and partial sentences drifted across the yard to her, but made no sense.

'. . . all this . . . make her . . . just do it . . . think of . . . I'll take care . . . as I say . . .'

But Anna's mind was on her mother so she paid no heed to whatever the argument was between father and son. As she drew her mother into the kitchen, she asked quickly, 'Are you all right, Mam? You don't look—well.'

May glanced nervously through the kitchen window, but already Douglas was moving towards the back door. 'I'll tell you sometime. Not now.' Suddenly she gripped Anna's hands and whispered urgently, 'Be careful, Anna, oh, do be careful . . .' May's voice faded away as Douglas came into the kitchen, rubbing his hands together and moving towards the table laden with roast leg of lamb, fresh mint sauce and steaming vegetables.

'Now, isn't that a welcome sight? Beats life in barracks any day, doesn't it, boy? The sooner you get yourself demobbed and back here the better.' He turned and winked at Anna. 'You've got everything very nice, love, and this dinner looks a treat.'

There was a tense atmosphere around the dining table with only Douglas keeping up a hearty attempt at conversation.

Bruce kept his head down, almost shovelling the food into his mouth.

'Where's your manners, boy?' Douglas berated him. 'You've not been brought up to eat like a pig. Is that what they teach you in the army?'

May picked at her main course and refused the pudding. As she rose at the end of the meal to help Anna clear away, Douglas's hand shot out. 'Let the youngsters do that. Let's you and me go for a little walk in the moonlight, eh?'

May bit her lip, glanced anxiously towards Anna, but said meekly, 'I'll get my coat.'

'And you, m'lad'—Douglas jabbed his finger towards Bruce—'can stay and help Anna with all this washing up.' Then he bent towards his son and mumbled something close to his ear that Anna couldn't catch.

As they worked together side by side in the scullery, Bruce said, 'I'm sorry I haven't written.' He sounded so genuinely contrite that Anna glanced over her shoulder as she stood at the sink, her hands deep in the washing-up water. He looked like a naughty little boy who had been caught scrumping apples. She smiled. 'Me too. I—I didn't know what to say after—last time.'

Bruce flung down the tea towel and, standing behind her, he put his arms about her and nuzzled her neck. 'I know. I'm sorry. Am I forgiven?'

She felt the familiar thrill of excitement surge through her as she turned and put her hands about his neck, oblivious to the fact that she was dripping soapsuds onto the back of his uniform.

'Of course,' she said huskily.

His mouth came down hard upon hers, so hard that it bruised her lips. 'I want you, Anna. Oh, how I want you.'

CHAPTER FORTY-SEVEN

When her mother and Douglas returned from their walk, Anna and Bruce were sitting before the dying embers of the front-room fire, with Buster lying on the hearth rug between them. As May and Douglas came in, the dog raised his head and gave a low growl. Sitting beside him, Anna stroked his silky head soothingly and shushed him.

'Look at this pair of lovebirds,' Douglas laughed. 'Sitting here in the dark. They've been too busy to light the lamp.' He chuckled suggestively.

'I'll do it,' May said and reached up to lift down the lamp that hung from a hook in the ceiling.

'Leave it, love,' Douglas said, giving an exaggerated yawn. 'I don't know about you, but I'm for bed anyway. Must be the country air. Night, you two. Come along, May.' As if confident of her immediate obedience, he turned and left the room. May hesitated, glancing meaningfully at her daughter. Anna scrambled up from the hearthrug.

'Do you want some cocoa, Mam? I'll make some.'

'No—' May began and then changed her mind. 'Yes. That would be nice, dear. 'I'll—er—come and help you.'

As they passed through the narrow hallway towards the kitchen, they heard Douglas shouting from the top of the stairs. 'May? Are you coming, May?'

'We're just going to make some cocoa. I'll—I'll bring you some up.'

'Never mind about cocoa, May. Come on up to

399

bed.' There was a slight pause. 'Now!'

Anna gasped and opened her mouth, but her mother put her fingers to her lips and whispered, 'Don't say anything, Anna. Please. I must go. We'll talk tomorrow.' Hurriedly, she kissed her daughter's cheek and turned towards the stairs, calling, 'Just coming, dear.'

Anna returned to the front room, concerned for her mother.

'I thought you'd gone to make cocoa,' Bruce said.

'What? Oh, sorry. Mam changed her mind. She's gone up. Do you want some?'

'No.' Bruce grinned and got up, moving towards a cupboard in the sideboard. 'I'd like something a bit stronger. Now'—he was bending down opening the door of the sideboard—'if I remember rightly, the old man kept a bottle of whisky somewhere in here. Ah yes.' He lifted out a bottle triumphantly. 'Here it is.' Then he reached for two of her grandmother's best cut-glass tumblers from the shelf above the sideboard. 'Want some?'

'No, thanks.' Anna gave a shudder. 'I don't like the stuff.'

'How do you know? I bet you've never tried it.'

'I have,' she said, with a wry smile. 'When I was quite little I drank some from that very cupboard and made myself terribly sick. I can't even bear the smell of it.'

Bruce laughed as he poured himself a generous measure. 'Come on, try a bit. You might like it now you're grown up.'

'No, thanks.'

She sat close to Bruce on the sofa, resting her head against his shoulder whilst he drank. 'Mind

400

you, I'd have preferred a beer. Have you got any?'

'No. I never thought. Sorry.'

'Well, just mind you get some for next time I'm home on leave.' He tweaked her nose playfully and she laughed.

There was silence between them as Bruce seemed to concentrate more and more on drinking. He had refilled his glass three times when Anna said, 'I'm going to bed.'

Eyes half closed, Bruce took another swallow and nodded.

'Night, then,' she said. 'Come on, Buster. Let's put you out and lock up.'

The dog rose obediently, but followed her with his tail between his legs. At the back door, he refused to go outside. Anna laughed. 'I've spoiled you, haven't I? Letting you sleep on my bedroom floor when no one else is here.'

The dog gave a knowing bark, as if he knew exactly what she was saying and then, to prove it, he turned and scampered towards the stairs, bounding up them and into her bedroom. Anna gave in, hoping that her mother wouldn't find out. Besides, it would create far more commotion to try to drag the dog down the stairs again than to let him stay.

Anna was just drifting off to sleep when she heard Buster's low growl. She sat up in bed and heard the familiar squeak of the doorknob. The door opened slowly and Buster's growl grew louder. The door stopped moving, as if whoever it was coming in, had heard the dog and had hesitated.

Anna's heart was thumping. 'Who is it?'

She heard the door click shut and soft footsteps

going along the landing towards the tiny spare bedroom. She knew it had been Bruce coming to say goodnight.

She snuggled down, smiling to herself. Tomorrow night she would make sure that Buster slept in her room again.

'Good boy,' she whispered into the darkness and heard his soft, answering whine.

*   *   *

The morning milking had been done and the breakfast laid by the time that any of her bleary-eyed guests appeared.

'Oh, pour us a strong cuppa, Anna love,' Bruce said, sitting down at the kitchen table and dropping his aching head into his hands.

Jed, sitting on the opposite side of the table eating his breakfast, eyed him disgustedly.

'And you can take that look off your face, mate. Ain't you ever had a skinful?'

'Oh aye, more 'n once,' Jed said airily, 'but I can hold me liquor. Thought you army wallahs could an' all.'

'I could drink you under the table any day,' Bruce sneered.

'Betcha,' Jed muttered, through a mouthful of egg and bacon.

'Right, you're on. Tonight, down the pub.'

Jed's eyes sparkled as he nodded. 'Betcha ten bob I'm the one carrying you home.'

'You're on.'

Anna banged the cup and saucer down on the table in front of Bruce. 'Haven't you both got summat better to do with your money than drink

402

yourself senseless and then lose ten bob into the bargain?'

Bruce grinned up at her. 'I shan't lose ten bob. I'll be winning it.'

'Huh!' Anna gave a snort, exasperated with them both. She turned on Jed. 'I'm surprised at you, Jed. And don't think you can be late for morning milking tomorrow.'

'I won't be.' He grinned at her and added saucily, 'Boss.'

'Oh, you!' Anna flounced out of the kitchen, leaving each young man to savour the thought of beating his rival.

*   *   *

Anna was busy all the morning and had no chance to speak to her mother alone. She paused only once when passing through the yard, amused to see that Bruce was trying to make friends with Buster.

'Here, boy. Here, look what I've got for you. A nice piece of meat.'

She chuckled softly to herself. *Bruce is trying to befriend my guard dog*, she thought, *in the hope that he'll let him into my room tonight.*

And in the afternoon, when Bruce said, 'Let's go for a walk,' she agreed readily. 'We'll take Buster. He could do with a long run.' She whistled, but there was no answering bark, no sound of paws scampering towards her.

'Where is he?' Anna murmured, glancing round the yard.

Bruce laughed. 'Looks like he's gone for his own long run. Come on. Let's not waste time looking for him. He'll be somewhere chasing rabbits.'

It was a beautiful, peaceful afternoon as they walked along, their arms around each other. Beneath the shade of two tall trees, they stopped and Bruce turned to take her into his arms.

'I reckon you're even prettier than I remembered,' he said and kissed the tip of her nose. 'I'm going to give that Jed a run for his money tonight. Let him know you're my girl. He can keep his eyes off you.'

Anna laughed aloud. 'What, Jed? Don't be daft.' But she couldn't help a faint tinge of pink coming into her cheeks.

'Well, just you remember if he starts anything, you're my girl. And you can tell him that. Mind you, I reckon he'll get the message tonight, after I've finished with him.'

She laughed again. 'You're as daft as each other. The pair of you. Besides, Buster will look after me. He's my guard dog.' It was an oblique reference to the previous night and for a moment Bruce drew back and looked straight into her eyes. 'Yes, he is, isn't he?'

*　　　*　　　*

'Where the devil is he? Where's Bruce?' Douglas ranted after tea.

'He's gone down to the pub,' Anna said.

'The pub? When he's got a lovely girl like you here sitting on her own.' Douglas's mouth was a grim line. 'I'll have a word or two to say to him when he gets back.' He frowned. 'That lad's getting out of hand since he's been in the army. Thinks he can disobey me.'

'Why?' Anna asked innocently. 'Did you ask him

to stay in tonight?'

'What? Oh—er—no. Not exactly, but it would only have been polite when he's your guest and he has only one more day here.'

Anna shrugged. 'I don't mind.'

'Well, you should,' Douglas snapped. Then he forced a smile. 'What I mean, love, is don't you want to see as much of your young man as you can?'

'Of course I do, but I know how young men like their pint.' She forbore to tell Douglas about the wager between Bruce and Jed. It would only cause more trouble. 'I'm sure he won't be late,' she added, placatingly. *Now I'm doing it,* Anna thought. *I'm doing just what Mum does. Trying to keep the peace. Trying to keep Douglas happy.*

'He'd better not be,' she heard Douglas mutter beneath his breath. Then he seemed to recover his good humour as he said, 'How about a game of rummy? May, find the cards.'

'Yes, dear,' May said and got up obediently.

CHAPTER FORTY-EIGHT

Anna awoke with a start to find a hand covering her mouth. She tried to call out, to scream, but the hand stifled any sound other than a noise in her throat. She flailed wildly, clutching at her assailant, trying to wrestle him off her.

'Shut up, you idiot. It's only me.' Bruce's voice came out of the blackness. 'If you don't make a noise I'll take my hand away.'

Alcohol fumes were wafting in her face, making

her feel sick. She stopped struggling and lay quiescent. Slowly Bruce removed his hand and she breathed more easily. 'What do you think you're doing?' she hissed angrily, but kept her voice low. She had no more wish to wake her mother and Douglas than he had.

Bruce was pulling at the bedclothes, trying to climb in beside her. 'No!' she cried. 'Don't! Go away. Go back to your own bed—you're not getting in here.' Her voice rose in fear.

At once his hand was clamped back on her mouth. And then, suddenly, she felt something cold and sharp against her neck. 'Shut up,' he slurred. 'Just lie back and enjoy it. You know you want it.'

No, no, her mind screamed, but she was unable to utter more than a guttural noise.

'Lie still and stop struggling, or you'll get what that blasted dog of yours got.'

Now her eyes were becoming accustomed to the gloom. In the moonlight she could see his shape above her, but not his features. Buster? What had he done to Buster? She thrashed her head from side to side, tried to hit him, but now he was pinning her down, his whole body weight on top of her.

Anna tried to resist him, tried to throw him off, but he was too heavy, too strong. She couldn't breathe, couldn't summon up an ounce of strength now. Then she managed to get her left hand free and she tried to claw away his hand, but her fingers touched the cold thin thing that he was still holding against her neck. She winced as pain shot through two of her fingers. And then, in her mind's eye, she saw the bayonet he had shown her that day down by the river. Bruce was holding the long, sharp blade close to her throat and threatening to do to her what he had done to her dog. *Oh Buster, Buster! Where are you? What has he done to you?*

Bruce was flinging the bedclothes off her now and pulling up her nightgown. Then he was lying on top of her once more and she could feel his nakedness next to her trembling skin. Then, with his knees, he spread her legs wide and thrust himself into her. She felt a searing pain and tried to cry out. His fingers, still pressing on her mouth, slipped between her teeth and she bit down hard. He gave a yelp and reared up above her. He raised his hand and dealt her a blow across the side of her face that almost knocked her senseless.

But she was still aware of the pain in her groin that went on and on as he rutted like a ram at a ewe.

* * *

She must have blacked out completely for when she became aware of the pain once more he was gone. She was lying uncovered on her bed, shivering and weeping uncontrollably. Stiffly, feeling as if she had been battered, Anna crawled off the bed and lurched to the dressing table. With shaking fingers she managed to light a candle. She held it up and looked down at herself in horror. There was blood everywhere, on her nightie and on the bed. Most of it seemed to be coming from the deep cuts on her fingers. Sobbing, she pulled open a drawer and found a handkerchief to bind round her hand.

Aching in every part of her body and bent almost double, she shuffled to the door. She was about to open it and call for her mother when she realized that Bruce could be still out there—waiting for her. Instead, she dragged a chair across to the door and wedged it under the door handle. Then she staggered to the washstand and, setting the candle down, poured cold water into the bowl. She washed herself between her legs, trying to cleanse away the stickiness and the smell of him. She scrubbed herself until she was sore, but however hard she tried she could never wash away what Bruce had done to her.

Anna lay huddled in her bed for the rest of the night, alternately sobbing and falling into nightmarish sleep, only to wake with a start, imagining his weight on top of her and breaking into a cold sweat of fear and loathing. As dawn filtered into her room, she hauled herself off the bed and staggered towards the full-length mirror in the door of her wardrobe. A pathetic sight met her eyes. The left side of her face was swollen, her eye almost closed. Blood spattered her nightdress and drenched the handkerchief around her fingers. Bruises on her arms and legs pained her, but the worst pain was the dreadful soreness between her legs and in her groin.

Once more she tried to wash herself, whimpering like a whipped animal. It was time to get up, to start the day. She should be downstairs by now in the kitchen, stoking up the fire in the range, getting the breakfast . . . But Anna could not bring herself to leave her room. She lay on the bed again, her knees drawn up to her chin, arms wrapped around herself, shivering and cowering in fear as she heard footsteps hurrying along the landing and stopping outside her door . . .

When May opened the kitchen door, she looked round in surprise. No cheerful fire burned in the range's grate. There were no breakfast dishes on the table, no smell of frying bacon. The room was cold and empty. She crossed to the back door and opened it. She stood listening. From across the yard she could hear clattering in the cowhouse. Morning milking was under way. She turned back, pulled on a pair of wellingtons that stood in the scullery and crossed the yard.

Resting her arms on the lower half of the stable door, she called, 'Morning, Jed. Is Anna here?'

Jed glanced up from his place beside a cow. May was startled by the look on his face. The young man was unusually pale and there was distress in his eyes and a tightness round his usually laughing mouth. He rose, put the bucket of milk at a safe distance from the cow's restless feet and came towards her. As he came closer, she could see that his left eye was half-closed and an ugly bruise was swelling around it. His lower lip was cut.

'Whatever—?' she began but Jed interrupted, 'I haven't seen her, but I need to as soon as I can. I knocked on the back door earlier, but there didn't seem to be anyone about. I thought she—she'd maybe slept late.' His mouth seemed to tighten even more. 'I thought mebbe she—she's with him.'

He made no effort to hide the resentment in his tone.

May stared at him. Trembling, she asked, 'What—what do you mean, Jed? With him?'

He sighed and then said, 'We had a stupid bet on

409

last night. Him and me—that we could drink each other under the table. Well, it got a bit nasty. He was saying things about Anna—things I didn't like and then we got into a fight.'

'Over Anna?'

Jed lowered his head and mumbled, 'Well, yes.'

'Is that why you wanted to see her?'

Jed shook his head, his eyes sad. 'It wasn't to do with that. I've found Buster.'

May smiled. 'Oh, she will be pleased. She was worried last night. He'd run off and . . .' Her voice faded as she realized that Jed's expression was grim. Her hand fluttered to her throat. 'What? What is it?'

'He's been killed. Someone's—knifed him.'

'Killed?' May's voice was a squeak.

Jed nodded. 'Yes. It looks like he's been stabbed,' he said slowly, his dark gaze fastened on May's face.

May gave a little cry of alarm. 'Oh no!' she breathed.

No words were needed. They were both remembering the result of the post-mortem on Luke Clayton.

Killed by person or persons unknown, stabbed with a knife or similar weapon.

'I must go and find her,' May whispered. She stumbled away, back across the yard and into the house.

Wrenching off her boots, she ran through the kitchen, up the stairs and along the landing. Outside Anna's room, she paused a moment to catch her breath, leaning against the door jamb. Then she tried the doorknob. It turned, but the door would not open.

410

'Anna,' she cried, hammering on the wood. 'Anna, open the door.'

*   *   *

Anna heard her name being called as if from a distance. Then she became aware of a banging on her bedroom door. For a moment she cowered lower beneath the bedcovers, but then, as the voice penetrated her distraught mind, she realized.

'Mam! Oh, Mam.' She struggled off the bed and stumbled across the room, pulling away the chair so that the door opened at once and May almost fell into the room.

'Anna, what—?' May began, but as she saw the state of her daughter, she staggered and would have fallen had not Anna reached out and caught hold of her. They clung together until May led her gently to the bed and made her sit down.

'The door,' Anna whispered hoarsely. 'Shut the door.'

May did so, once more inserting the chair under the knob as Anna had done. Only then did Anna breathe more easily. May came and sat beside her and enfolded her in her embrace, rocking her to and fro like a small child. 'Oh, my darling, what have I done? What *have* I done?'

Anna lifted her tear-streaked face to look into her mother's. 'It's not your fault.'

Tears were running down May's face too now. 'It is. It is. If I had only listened to your grandfather. He knew, didn't he? He could see what they were like.'

'What—what do you mean?' Anna asked huskily. 'They?'

411

'Bruce did this to you, didn't he?'

Anna nodded.

'Did he—I mean—?'

Anna squeezed her eyes tightly shut, trying to blot out the nightmare. She nodded. 'He held a knife to my throat.' She held out her hand, still with its rough, blood-soaked wrapping. 'I—I tried to fight him off, but I cut my fingers on the—the blade.'

Her mother gave a deep-throated groan of despair. 'Oh, my darling, my baby.' They clung to each other, seeking solace, but there was none they could give each other.

CHAPTER FORTY-NINE

'What did you mean when you said Grandpa knew what "they" were like?' A little later, when they had hugged each other and tried to reassure each other, Anna was calmer.

Silently, May drew back from her and pulled up the sleeves of her blouse. Anna gasped as she saw the bruises on her mother's forearms, one purple, a recent injury, and two now yellow and fading.

Anna gasped. 'He—he hits you? Douglas?'

May nodded. 'When something doesn't suit him.'

'I knew there was something wrong. I knew it. But I could never seem to get you alone to talk to you. He always seemed to be in the way.'

May nodded, tears in her eyes. 'I know. He made me promise not to tell you. Told me that it would be the worse for me—and for you—if I did. But I was going to tell you, if only we could have had a few moments alone.'

'How long has it been going on?'

'It started just after I'd bought the house. He was fine before we got married and afterwards, until—until . . . Oh, Anna, I gave him all of the two thousand pounds your grandfather left me. After that, once he'd got it all, he—he started being nasty. Oh, what a fool I've been.'

'What are we going to do?' Anna whispered.

May sighed, shrugged helplessly and said, 'I don't know.'

'Leave him. Come and live here with me. Oh Mam, come home.'

'He'd never let me alone, Anna. He swore he'd never let me go. I married him, didn't I?' she added bitterly.

They sat together until they heard footsteps pass by the bedroom door and go downstairs. They held their breath.

'That's Douglas going down for his breakfast,' May whispered. 'He'll get a shock, won't he? No fire, no dutiful wife waiting to serve him.'

'You'd better go down. I don't want him going for you again because—because of me.'

At that moment a bellow came from the bottom of the stairs. 'May? Where are you?'

May jumped at the sound, but did not get up at once. 'What are you going to do? Do you want me to stay here with you? I'll see if I can get them to go back to town without me.'

'I want to get in the bath, then I'll come down. Where's—where's Bruce?'

May shook her head. 'I don't know.' Now she did stand up and held out her hand. 'Come on, I'll help you into the bathroom and make sure you've locked the door before I go down.'

*   *   *

'Where on earth have you been, May? And where's my breakfast? Where's Anna?'

Her anger emboldened May to say, 'You might well ask where Anna is.'

Douglas frowned. 'What do you mean by that?'

'Your precious son forced himself on her last night. He raped her, Douglas, there's no other way to put it. Your Bruce raped my little girl.'

Douglas stared at her for a moment and then threw back his head and laughed. 'That's my boy. I never thought he had it in him to go through with it. So that's why he went to the pub—to get a bit of Dutch courage.'

Now it was May's turn to stare at him, aghast. Her voice trembled as she said, 'What do you mean "go through with it"?' You can't mean—oh you can't—that he—that you *planned* it?'

'Well, not rape exactly, only that he should seduce her.'

'Why? In God's name—why? She liked him. She really liked him. But now—'

'Mmm.' Douglas's eyes were calculating. 'Yes, I see that. Maybe he's gone a bit too far.'

'A bit too far?' May's voice rose hysterically. 'Do you have any idea what it means for a woman to be violated like that? Especially a young girl. A *virgin*!'

'Oh, come now, May. Don't be so melodramatic. She's led him on. You can't deny that. And when a young feller's blood is up—'

'How dare you? How dare you suggest that it's

414

Anna's fault?' she screamed.

Now Douglas's eyes were glittering. 'Oh, I dare because that is what happened.' He grabbed her by the shoulders, his strong grip bruising her. 'Do you hear me? *That is what happened.*'

May gasped and stared up at him with wide, frightened eyes.

'And now,' he said ominously, 'they'll have to get married, won't they?'

'Married?' May's voice was a squeak. 'Oh no. Not now. She'll not marry him now.'

'Oh, but she will, May,' Douglas said calmly. His quiet tone was far more menacing than if he had been shouting. 'Anna will marry Bruce and then, one day, this farm will be his.'

May felt as if the breath had been knocked from her body. 'No,' she managed to gasp at last. 'Never! Over my dead body.'

Douglas laughed, but without humour. 'And even that, my dear May, can be arranged.'

At once the vision of Buster's still form came into May's imagination and then a more horrifying picture pushed its way to the forefront of her mind.

The memory of her father, Luke, lying on the ground, stabbed and bleeding to death.

May closed her eyes and groaned. 'Oh no! No,' she moaned more to herself than to the man who still held her in his grasp. 'Don't let it be true. Not that. Oh please, not that.'

Douglas let go of her suddenly so that she staggered and almost fell. She put out her hand and steadied herself against the kitchen table.

'Now, how about getting me some breakfast and when Bruce and Anna show themselves, we'll begin to make arrangements. Maybe we can get a special licence. If not, then it will have to be the next time he comes home on leave.'

May moved woodenly towards the range and took up the frying pan, wishing she had the temerity to hit him over the head with it. But she didn't. She was weak. She despised herself now. It had been her weakness—her need to have a man to love and protect and care for her—that had led her beloved daughter and herself into this mess.

She cooked breakfast for Douglas, wishing she had rat poison handy. Douglas sat at the table and opened his newspaper as if nothing untoward had happened.

'Thank you,' he said sarcastically, as she banged the plate of eggs, bacon and fried bread in front of him. He glanced round the table. 'Where's the tomato sauce?'

Obediently, May fetched it from the pantry. She poured a cup of tea for him and one for herself, but couldn't bring herself to eat anything. Revulsion against this man and his son choked her.

The kitchen door opened and a tousle-headed, yawning Bruce appeared. 'Morning,' he muttered and dropped into a chair at the table.

May stared at him in astonishment, then crashed her cup into the saucer. Bruce winced at the sudden noise and, frowning, glanced up.

'Do you have to make such a noise?' he grumbled. 'My head's fit to burst.'

May gaped at him. 'I don't believe this,' she murmured. Was she dreaming? Was this all some terrible nightmare that no one else but herself was experiencing? But no, it was true. At this moment Anna was in the bath trying to scrub away all traces of her attacker—the young man, who sat so calmly before her now, waiting for his breakfast . . .

May sprang to her feet. 'How can you sit there,' she shrieked, 'as if nothing's happened?' She shook her head in bewilderment as Bruce gaped up at her, uncomprehending. 'Don't tell me you can't remember? That you were so drunk—?'

'Can't remember what?' Bruce glanced at his father. 'Do you know what she's on about?'

'It seems,' Douglas drawled, 'that Anna is accusing you of raping her last night.'

Bruce stared at him. He opened his mouth to say something, but at that moment the door opened and all eyes turned to see Anna standing there.

For a moment, they all seemed turned to stone. The bruise on the side of Anna's face was swollen and darkening and the two fingers on her left hand were wrapped in a clean white handkerchief.

May moved suddenly and rushed to put her arms around Anna and draw her into the room. 'Come and sit down, darling.'

Stiffly, her gaze fastened on Bruce's face, Anna moved across the room and stood on the hearth rug. Facing the two men defiantly, she said, 'Leave this house. Both of you. My mother's staying here with me and—'

As if catapulted, both men sprang up and faced them.

'Oh no, she's not,' Douglas said.

'Mam,' Anna said quietly, 'go and fetch Buster.'

'Oh darling,' May said tearfully, 'I can't. He— Jed found him. Someone killed Buster.'

Briefly, Anna's gaze swivelled to look at her mother. 'Killed him? How?'

'With—with a knife.'

Anna stared at her and then slowly her gaze

417

came back to Bruce's face. 'You! You killed him. Didn't you? Didn't you?' Suddenly Anna launched herself at him, her arms flailing, but Bruce caught her easily and held her wrists. She kicked out at him, catching him on the shin, but he wound his leg around her and brought her down in a crude tackle. He pinioned her arms to the floor and straddled her body. 'Want some more of what you had last night, do you?'

'No, no,' May shouted, trying to pull him away from Anna, but now Douglas grasped May from behind, pinning her arms to her sides and holding her fast. Tears coursed down May's face. 'Anna, Anna—' she cried, watching with horrified eyes whilst her daughter struggled to throw Bruce off her, but he held her easily, laughing cruelly. 'Yeah, go on, struggle all you like. You won't get the better of me.' He glanced round to look triumphantly at May and his father. 'We've got you both just where we want you now, haven't we?'

Whether it was because Bruce relaxed his concentration for a brief moment or because Anna made one last superhuman effort, but somehow she freed her leg from beneath him, bent her knee and, pressing her foot and elbow against the floor managed to roll him over. Without waiting for him to recover from her surprise move, she brought her knee up viciously into his groin, so that Bruce gave a cry of pain and doubled over, writhing on the floor.

Anna scrambled to her feet and turned towards her mother.

'Leave me,' May gasped. 'Don't worry about me, darling. I mean it. Just go. Go on. Run, Anna. Get away from here. Run, Anna, just *run* . . .'

418

1963

CHAPTER FIFTY

'Who on earth were those two lunatics? They knocked me off my bike,' Tony asked his mother indignantly.

Bertha smiled. 'Oh, we had a very nice chat.'

Tony looked at her in surprise. '*You* did? You've been chatting to complete strangers?'

Bertha nodded, looking very pleased with herself.

'Who were they?'

'A father and son called Whittaker.' Her smile widened maliciously. 'They came looking for someone. I'll give you three guesses who. Did you see the younger feller?'

'Not really. It was all too quick. I just saw two men in the car. I got their number plate, though. Reckon I'll have a word with PC Jenkins—'

'I wouldn't, because they might be doing us a big favour.'

Tony eyed her. It was a long time since he had seen his mother with a gleam in her eye. She was excited about something.

Tony frowned. 'What's going on, Mam? And what do you mean "they came looking for someone"?'

'Exactly what I say. The younger feller—well, the older one too mebbe, though his hair's grey now—but the younger feller had bright red hair. Copper coloured. *Just like the girl's.*'

Tony stared at her. 'You mean—Maisie?'

'Course I mean Maisie. What other little trollop around here has red hair?'

'They came looking for Maisie?'

'Well, I suppose it was more *her*, Anna. They didn't even know about Maisie. Didn't even know Anna had been pregnant. Thrilled, the young feller was, to think he was a dad. And the old one kept saying, "I've got a granddaughter. Just think, I'm a granddad." Of course, they wanted to see them straight away . . .'

'And you told them?' Now Tony was incredulous.

'Course I did . . .'

Tony's face was thunderous. 'Why, Mam? When you know that's who she must have run away from? That's who she must be so frightened of.'

Suddenly, Bertha's expression was ugly. 'Why should I care? Why should I protect her? Your dad's fancy piece . . .'

The truth was filtering through Tony's mind now. He pointed accusingly at his mother. 'You've lied to me. All these years you've tried to make me believe that—that Maisie was *his* child and my *half-sister*. But she wasn't, was she, Mam? 'Cos now you're saying that this red-haired feller that turned up today was her dad.' He paused a moment and then added again incredulously, 'Why, Mam? Why?'

Now Bertha was truculent, trying to justify herself. 'Well, I thought she was. Men are all the same. Why else would he have brought the little trollop home with him that night if he wasn't getting his oats there? Or at least hoping to. All right, mebbe Maisie isn't his, but I bet they've been at it all these years since.'

Tony's last glance at his mother, before he turned and left the house, was a mixture of contempt and pity.

422

As he began to walk up the track, he saw Maisie running pell-mell towards him, her hair flying, her skirt above her knees.

'Tony, Tony, hurry—' Even before she reached him he could see that she was crying hysterically. He caught her and held her. 'What is it? Is it your mam? Did those two men frighten her?'

'No—yes—it's worse. Your dad. He—he tried to defend her and one of them had got a knife—' Maisie could say no more as sobs racked her.

'Oh my God,' Tony breathed. 'Is he hurt?'

Maisie could only nod. Releasing her, Tony began to run up the track, pausing only to say, 'Go to the house. Use the phone. Get help.'

Maisie rushed into the house, ignoring Bertha, and grabbed the phone.

''Ere, 'ere, what do you think you're doing, miss?' Bertha protested, but the girl, still crying, ignored her. With shaking fingers, she dialled Pat's number. The district nurse was the only person she could think of to ring. She was certainly the nearest. The ringing tone seemed to sound in her ears for ages, until Pat's breathless voice said, 'Hello. You just caught me. I was on my way out. Who is it?'

'It's Mr Eddie . . . I mean, this is Maisie. Mr Eddie's been hurt. Stabbed—' Dimly the girl heard the listening Bertha cry out.

'I'll come at once,' was all Pat said.

Maisie replaced the receiver in its cradle and turned to face Bertha who was staring disbelievingly at her.

'What do you mean stabbed?'

Now that Pat was on her way, Maisie was managing to control her hysteria. Pat would help

Mr Eddie. She was a nurse. If anyone could save him, it would be Pat.

'Those two men. They grabbed me mam and me and Mr Eddie tried to help us. The younger one had a knife. He went for Mr Eddie and—and stabbed him in the stomach.'

Bertha felt for the edge of the table and sat down heavily, staring unseeingly ahead. Maisie turned and left the house, running back up the hill.

Left alone, Bertha sat motionless. What had she done? she asked herself silently. She had sought to wreak revenge on Anna and her daughter. She had waited years for the right moment and when the two strangers had turned up on her doorstep, looking for Anna, Bertha had believed they had been heaven-sent. And now her husband was lying injured, possibly fatally.

Reluctantly, the bitter, twisted woman was forced to face the truth. All those years ago Anna had obviously had good reason to run away. Bertha could make a good guess at why. So, when he brought her home, Eddie hadn't known her. It was the truth he had told her. It was just him being kind. She thought back down all the years. He had always been kind. It was his nature. Look how he'd rushed to help all those folks at the time of the floods. He'd had no need. They were nothing to him. But that was Eddie.

He'd never said an unkind thing about her father, not even when Bert Tinker had been sent to prison. Throughout their marriage, he had never raised his hand to her, not once, yet she had given him cause. Oh yes, she had given him cause all right. He'd done his best to be a good husband, but she'd not let him. And now . . .

424

Bertha dragged herself up.

For the first time in many years she would have to climb the track and go over the hill.

*   *   *

Pat arrived, breathless and anxious in the yard. Flinging her bicycle against the wall, she dragged her medical bag from its strap on the back of the bicycle and ran up the hill.

Arriving at the top, she saw the sorry scene below her and, though her heart would not let her believe it, she knew already that Eddie was gone. She could see Anna cradling him in her arms, her head bent over him, whilst Tony, who was standing close by, held Maisie, trying to comfort her. A few steps away from the group stood the lonely figure of Bertha, isolated and cut off from the others.

Pat's fears were justified. When she knelt beside Eddie, she knew before she even touched him, that he was dead. Sadly, she looked up to meet Anna's tear-filled eyes and shook her head.

She was aware that Bertha turned and walked away.

*   *   *

They had to leave Eddie lying there until the police came and, even then, they were allowed no more to do with the body. It was too big an incident for the local bobby to handle. An Inspector came from Ludthorpe and, later, a Detective Chief Inspector from Lincoln. There seemed to be policemen everywhere, searching the ground minutely, taking statements from Anna, Maisie and Tony. And from

425

Bertha.

Anna told them briefly all the events that had led to her flight from home. 'I was a coward,' she said flatly. 'She told me to go, to run—and I did, but I left my poor mother to take the brunt of their fury. God knows what happened to her. I expect they killed her too.'

The Sergeant taking her statement said, 'What do you mean, love, "killed her too"?'

'Someone killed my dog, Buster, that night. I suspect it was Bruce and—and then I realized that he—probably helped by his father—had been the poacher and that they'—she swallowed painfully—'had probably killed my grandfather.'

The officer's face was grim. 'Well, if it's any consolation—and I don't suppose it is—we'll get 'em. Oh, we'll get 'em, sure as eggs is eggs. And we'll investigate everything you've told us. Specially the bit about your granddad.'

Anna regarded him with such pleading in her dark, violet eyes that even the tough Sergeant was moved. 'Could you find out about my mother? Please?'

'I'll do what I can, love. Now, give me any addresses you know.'

'There's the farm.' She gave the address. 'And there was a house in Lincoln.' She paused frowning, but little by little she remembered the road and then the number.

'We'll check that too,' the Sergeant promised. He was about to put away his notebook when Anna added, 'And then there's the cinema, of course.'

Maisie, who was hovering nearby, and the Sergeant spoke at the same time. 'The cinema?'

Anna nodded. 'Yes, Douglas had something to

do with running one of the cinemas in the city.' She wrinkled her forehead. 'I can't remember what they called it.'

Maisie gave a little cry and clapped her hand over her mouth, her eyes wide as she stared at her mother. 'It must be the man who saw us at the ABC cinema. That's where we went in Lincoln to see Billy Fury. Oh, Mam, it's all my fault.'

CHAPTER FIFTY-ONE

Maisie was inconsolable at the thought that her disobedience had brought about such tragic consequences.

Anna tried to comfort her. 'It's not your fault, darling. I should have told you everything, then you would have understood. You're old enough now. I shouldn't have kept you locked away for years. Or myself, for that matter.' She sighed. 'I should have faced things a long time ago.'

Even Tony, who was distraught and grieving too, tried to reassure Maisie. 'I'm as much to blame. I knew your mam didn't want you going out, specially not to Lincoln, yet I took you there.' He paused and scratched his head in a gesture so like Eddie's that Anna felt a lump in her throat. 'But the only people who are really to blame,' Tony went on, his tone hardening, 'are Douglas Whittaker and his son.'

'My father.' Maisie wept. 'Fancy having *him* for a father.'

Tony tried to smile, though the sadness never left his eyes. 'That's not your fault either. And you've got Anna for your mother. You couldn't have a better mother than her. Now, come on.' He shook her gently by the shoulders. 'You've got to be strong. And the best thing you can do for your mam now is to help us find *her* mam.'

*   *   *

'They've caught them,' Tony told Anna and Maisie two weeks later, 'trying to leave the country.'

Anna nodded. It was a hollow victory; it couldn't bring Eddie back, or her grandfather, or compensate for the lost seventeen years of her life. 'I've been such a coward, hiding myself away all these years. Not even caring enough to find my own mother.'

'You were only seventeen or so when you came here, weren't you? You shouldn't blame yourself.'

She smiled tremulously at him. 'You're just like your father, Tony,' she told him huskily. 'So kind. You're still trying to comfort us even when you must be hurting so dreadfully.'

Tony's voice was unsteady. 'I'll take that as a compliment, shall I?'

Anna nodded. 'Oh yes. Most definitely. I—I've never met a nicer man than Eddie. Only my own father and grandfather came close.' There was a pause before Anna asked tentatively, afraid to hear the answer, 'Have the police said any more to you about my—my mother?'

Tony shook his head. 'They wouldn't tell me, would they? They'd come to you.'

Anna sighed deeply. 'I suppose so. I did so hope that . . .' Her voice trailed away. Then more firmly she asked, 'Would you do something for me?'

428

'Of course.'

'Would you ask PC Jenkins what's happening? Actually, he might tell you more readily than me. You're not so closely involved. He might just tell you something that he wouldn't want to tell me.'

Tony nodded. 'I'll try.' He was about to turn away when he paused and said quietly, 'Poor Pat's taken my dad's death badly, hasn't she?'

Anna nodded. 'I—I think she loved your father. I think part of her always had done from the time they were young.'

Tony's mouth hardened as he said, 'I wish me mam was half as upset. I don't think she cared about him at all. Her only worry is whether she's been left the farm.'

Anna gasped, shocked that Bertha could be quite so heartless. Even after all she knew about her, she hadn't expected that. 'Has he left a will?'

Tony nodded. 'We've an appointment at the solicitors in Ludthorpe tomorrow. Wish me luck because if it's all in her name, I don't reckon I'll be staying.'

'Oh Tony, don't say that.'

'I mean it. For years, Anna, I've tried to understand her, to stand by her, even side with her against me dad sometimes, although I never liked doing that. But do you know, she's misled me all these years.' His gaze met Anna's steadily. He hesitated, wondering whether now was the time to speak out. Anna looked puzzled, so he took a deep breath and plunged on. 'She always said she believed that Maisie was my father's child and that Maisie was my half-sister. Anna—I hope you won't be angry—but my feelings for Maisie aren't a brother's. It made me feel'—he paused again

429

searching for the right word—'dirty. Unnatural. Wicked.'

'Oh, Tony.' There was no anger in Anna's tone, only sadness. Now she understood his strange, erratic behaviour. He had been suffering a turmoil of emotions caused, so unnecessarily, by his mother's lies.

'I promise you,' she said softly, 'on Maisie's life that she is not your half-sister.'

He nodded. 'Oh, I know that now.' He smiled ruefully. 'And if I'd been sensible about it, I'd have asked you before. And believed you. But when your own mother drills it into you from the age of ten or so that you were—you were—that you and my father . . .' He faltered.

Anna smiled sadly. 'I know,' she said. 'I know.'

Tony pulled off the cap he was wearing, ran his fingers through his hair and then pulled the cap on again. 'Of course, I don't know how Maisie feels about me,' he said. 'It might all be hopeless anyway.'

'She's very fond of you.'

'I know, but I have to remember that she's not mixed with other fellers much. Only the lads at school.'

Anna grimaced. 'That's my fault.'

'Oh, I didn't mean—' he began, but she held up her hand. 'It's all right, Tony,' she said. 'It's the truth. And as for Maisie, just give her a little more time, eh?'

He smiled. 'I seem to have been waiting for ever for her to grow up.'

They smiled understandingly at each other.

'Well,' he said briskly. 'This won't get the work done. I'd better go.'

'Good luck for tomorrow,' she called as he turned away.

Over his shoulder he grinned. 'I might need it because I could be gone by tomorrow night.'

As he walked away, Anna murmured, 'Me too.'

*   *   *

Eddie's will contained a shock for Bertha, a pleasant surprise for Tony and a different kind of shock for Anna.

'He's left the farm to me,' Tony told her happily as he held out an envelope to her. 'And the solicitor's sent you a letter.'

Anna eyed the long legal envelope suspiciously. 'Me? Why me?'

'Go on, open it. You'll see.' The young man could hardly contain his excitement, his obvious pleasure.

Anna rubbed her palms down the sides of her skirt, feeling suddenly nervous. Yet, by the look on Tony's face, the letter didn't contain bad news. Surely Tony wouldn't be throwing them out of the cottage? Not after what he had said about his feelings for Maisie. And yet . . .

Tony could contain himself no longer, couldn't wait for her to open the letter and read the news for herself. 'He's left you this cottage and a bit of land round it.'

Anna stared at him. 'Me? Oh no, he can't do that.'

'Well, he has,' Tony was grinning from ear to ear. 'And it's all legal and there's not a thing anyone can do about it.'

'Do you mind?' she asked swiftly.

431

He laughed. 'Course not. I'm delighted. It means you'll stay here.' He paused, realizing that the capture of the two men Anna had feared for years meant that she was now free to go wherever she chose. She might want to leave. 'You will stay, won't you?'

Anna smiled and reached out to take the envelope. 'Of course, only—' She stopped, afraid that what she had to say would hurt him. 'I must let Maisie have more freedom. It's time she spread her wings. You do see that, don't you?'

A fleeting look of pain crossed his face, but he nodded. 'I've always thought,' he said carefully, 'that if you let birds fly free, they'll come home all the more readily. I think it applies to people too, don't you?'

How sensible Tony was, Anna thought. She nodded. 'We'll have to let her decide.'

'I know,' he whispered. 'I know.'

She touched his arm. 'It'll come right. I know it will.'

He smiled, but the doubt was still deep in his eyes.

Changing the subject Anna asked, 'What about your mother?'

Tony shrugged. 'She's hopping mad, of course, but I think deep down she half expected it. He's left her some money and I've to pay her a monthly allowance—which I would have done anyway,' he added hastily.

Anna nodded. 'So she's staying on the farm?'

Now Tony laughed. 'Oh no. She's packing her belongings this very minute. She can't wait to get away. She's moving into Ludthorpe. Going to live with her sister for a start.'

432

The smile began slowly on Anna's mouth, spreading until it lit up the whole of her face. Now she could open the envelope. Reading the words of Eddie's generous and, yes, loving gesture, Anna felt a happiness and contentment flooding through her that she had never expected to feel ever again. Although her feelings were tinged with sadness that her current fortune had come about because of Eddie's death, she knew he would want her to be happy. It was all Eddie Appleyard had ever wanted for her.

There was only one cloud in her otherwise clear blue sky.

What had become of her mother?

CHAPTER FIFTY-TWO

PC Jenkins wheeled his bicycle down the track towards the little cottage. He leant it against the wall and knocked on the door. While he waited for an answer, he looked about him. Sheep grazed on the slope of the field in the sunshine. It was an idyllic scene and he wished he had better news for the young woman who was now opening the door to him.

Anna smiled a welcome. 'Come in, Mr Jenkins. You must have known I've got the kettle on.'

The constable stepped into the kitchen, laid his helmet on the table and sat down whilst Anna mashed the tea and set out home-made biscuits on a plate.

'I'll come straight to the point, Anna. We've been making enquiries about your mam, but we can't—at the moment—trace her.'

Anna sighed and sat down. She busied herself pouring the tea, but could not hide her disappointment. 'Well, I'm sure you've done your best. I can't ask more than that.'

'Oh we're not giving up. Be assured of that. Besides, we're still building a case against the two we've got in custody.' His eyes narrowed. 'From the bit you were able to tell us, it seems there's a lot more wants looking into.' He nodded knowingly. 'A lot more.'

Anna looked him straight in the eyes. 'Tell me honestly—do you think she's dead?'

He sighed. 'I don't know, love, and that's the truth, but we want to find out anyway. If she's alive, she could help us with our enquiries.' He smiled at the use of the official-sounding term. Then his expression sobered. 'If she's not, then we shall be making enquiries into the nature of her death.'

Anna nodded, unable to speak for the lump in her throat. It was defeatist, she knew, but knowing the Whittakers as she did, she could hold out no hope that her mother was still alive.

'There's one thing we did find out that might interest you. That cinema you thought he owned or at least managed—'

Anna looked up. 'Yes?'

'Seems he had nowt to do with it at all. I've talked to the chap who runs it and he remembers him well. "Oh him," he said. "That fly-by-night! He's nothing to do with this place and never has been. He fancied himself as something of an entrepreneur or whatever they call it. Reckoned he knew all the stars and used to stand outside the front there when there was a big name appearing here, making out he knew them and that it was all down to him that they'd come here. And he used to chat up the girls in the box office to get the best seats in the house. Lots of folks thought he owned the place. Oh yes, I remember Douglas Whittaker all right," he said, "I'd like to get me hands on him myself."'

Anna tried to smile, but her thoughts were still on her mother.

PC Jenkins must have read her mind for he touched her hand and said softly, 'Don't give up hope yet, love. We'll keep searching, I promise you.'

*　　　*　　　*

Eddie's death had hit Pat Jessop hard. She had stood close to the graveside during his interment, weeping openly, not caring who saw her. Beside her stood a grim-faced Maisie.

Anna stood alone beneath the shadow of a tree some distance from the other mourners around the grave. She had slipped into the back of the church at the last moment, quietly and unobserved. But Maisie had had no such compunction. Boldly, she had marched into the church to sit beside Pat. She had walked out with Pat and followed the coffin to watch it being lowered into the earth. Her eyes were dry, but bright with anger, her mouth tight. Though her arm was linked through Pat's, it was Tony's face that Maisie's glance sought constantly.

Tony was standing, white-faced, beside his mother, his mouth set in a hard line. Only his brown eyes showed any sign of the tumult of emotion raging inside him. Deliberately he avoided meeting Maisie's eyes, even though he could feel her glance upon him.

His overriding emotion was anger. Anger that his father should have been killed. Why should a kind, considerate man like Eddie Appleyard have his life snatched away so violently by a vicious thug?

But there were so many other emotions struggling within him. He felt sorry for Maisie—her natural father had been the one to take the life of the man who had been more than a father to her. And for Anna now there was understanding. Her fear had been justified. Yet he couldn't help wishing that she had had the courage to confide in his father and him too. Perhaps if they had known all about it, they could have prevented the tragedy.

And his mother. Oh, what about his mother? His loyalty and, yes, his love for his mother was being sorely tested now that he knew her part in the terrible events. Her vindictiveness towards Anna had led to his father's death.

And he felt guilt too. Guilt because, even in the midst of his grief, his heart was leaping with joy at the knowledge that Maisie was not his half-sister.

It had been difficult to assess Bertha's feelings that day. She had stood at the side of the grave, her face expressionless, and afterwards she had got into the funeral car with her sister, Lucy, and been driven back to Ludthorpe, offering no refreshment back at the farm. It had been left to Anna to invite Tony and Pat back to the little cottage, the cottage that was now rightfully hers.

Pat had sat outside the front door, an untouched cup of tea in her hands, just staring across the fields towards the sun as it began to sink in the sky.

Anna sat down beside her. 'He loved this view.'

'He loved a lot of things. He loved this farm, his land, his son and, once, I suppose—', there was a strange reluctance in her tone as she went on—'he must have loved Bertha.' She paused and then said quietly, 'And he loved you, Anna.' As Anna opened her mouth to protest, Pat hurried on, 'Oh, I don't mean in the way Bertha accused him of. No, as a dear friend, or even a daughter perhaps. The same way he loved Maisie. Do you know what I mean?'

Anna, tears choking her throat, nodded.

Then, quite simply and without any shame, Pat said, 'And I loved him and in *exactly* the way Bertha thought.' She sighed. 'Such a pity he never knew.'

Huskily, Anna said, 'I think he did, Pat. I'm sure he did.'

Pat smiled through her tears as she whispered, 'I hope so.'

*   *   *

Life settled into a new routine. Bertha was gone and Tony now lived alone in the farmhouse, though he seemed to spend far more time with Anna and Maisie in the little cottage than he did in his own home.

'We need more help on the farm and'—he smiled ruefully—'I need some sort of a housekeeper, or at least someone to come in to cook and clean for me. And to wash and iron my clothes. I'm beginning to smell.'

Maisie pretended to sniff the air. 'No worse than usual,' she quipped.

'Well, I could do that,' Anna said, but Tony shook his head. 'No, you've enough to do about the

437

farm and when you get back here. Specially looking after madam here. That's a full-time job.'

'Ta very much,' Maisie tossed her curls and pretended indignation. 'You know what you need?'

'What's that?'

'A wife.'

'You could be right. You applying for the job then?'

The banter was spoken light-heartedly, yet Anna was aware of an undercurrent between them.

'Who me?' Maisie feigned astonishment, her eyes wide. 'What makes you think I want to bury myself here? My teachers say I've already got enough qualifications to get into teacher-training college.'

'Is that what you want to do?' Anna asked.

Questioned directly, Maisie faltered. 'I'm thinking about it? I want to get my A levels first, though.'

Anna glanced at Tony. His eyes were lowered and she could not read their expression, but by the slump in his shoulders she knew that Maisie's words had dashed his hopes even further. But, strangely, Maisie did not look exactly ecstatic about her own tentative plans either.

I wonder, Anna thought.

*   *   *

Anna was sitting outside the front door of her cottage, watching a glorious sunset. The sun slipped down slowly, streaking the sky with burnished gold. Maisie had taken her homework— reading two chapters of *Pride and Prejudice*—to sit beside the stream. Anna could just see her, on the bank, head bent, engrossed in her book.

Something, she wasn't sure what, perhaps a movement or a slight sound, made her look to her left, up the hill. Tony was walking towards her. He waved and she lifted her hand in response.

He reached her and sat beside her. For a few moments they watched the sunset together in silence. Then he said gently, 'Anna, there's someone to see you.'

She turned, a moment's fear leaping into her eyes before she remembered. There was no longer any need to be afraid. All the years of hiding were over.

'Who?'

Tony glanced up the track and Anna followed his line of vision. Coming down the hill was the slight figure of a woman. Anna's heart seemed to stop and then began to thud erratically. She rose slowly, her gaze still on the figure coming closer and closer.

Then she gave a cry, held out her arms and began to run up the hill.

'Mam! Oh, Mam!'

CHAPTER FIFTY-THREE

There was so much to say and yet, for the moment, they could say nothing.

'I'll go and tell Maisie,' Tony said tactfully. 'We'll give you a few moments.'

As he turned away, Anna cried, 'Oh, Mam, can you ever forgive me?'

'It's you who need to forgive me, Anna.' Easy

tears welled in May's eyes and, in spite of her obvious joy at seeing her daughter again, she still seemed anxious and unsure.

'But I left you with—with them. I ran away,' Anna insisted.

'When I told you to run, I didn't mean you to go right away,' May said. 'Why didn't you go to Jed? He would have helped you. He was frantic when he found you had gone. And then, when we couldn't find you—'

Anna lifted her head slightly and whispered his name softly for the first time in years. 'Jed. Oh, Jed.' Her voice broke as she added, 'Mam—I couldn't. I was so—so ashamed.'

May's face was still haunted by the memories. 'If it was anyone's fault, it was mine. I should have known better. I should have listened to your grandfather. And to Betty and Rita.'

They sat down together outside the cottage, mother and daughter watching the golden sunset with their arms around one another, as if, never again, would they allow themselves to be parted.

'But you,' May went on, stroking Anna's hair tenderly, 'you were just an innocent young girl, full of romantic dreams that were smashed in a violent and terrible way. No wonder you wanted to run and hide from everything and—and everyone. Oh, Anna'—May's voice cracked—'did you hate me? Did you blame me?'

'Blame you? Oh, Mam! Never. Not for one moment. But I thought you would be ashamed of me, that it had been somehow my fault.'

'No,' May whispered. 'Oh no, it wasn't you. It was them. Both of them.'

'I felt so guilty though, and so—so cowardly,

running away like that. Just leaving you. What—' she stumbled again over his name—'what did Jed do when he found out what had happened?'

May stared straight ahead, watching the glorious colours, the blue and gold and pink, realizing that over the years since Anna had gone, she had never even noticed a sunset. Her life had been dark and gloomy and so very sad. She gave a deep sigh and said, 'Jed didn't know. I—I couldn't tell him, Anna. If he'd known and he'd caught up with Bruce—or even Douglas for that matter—there would have been murder done and an innocent boy would have gone to the gallows, or at best served life imprisonment, just because he loved you. I couldn't risk Jed knowing. So—no one knew.'

For once, Anna thought, *her mother had shown surprising strength in her decision.*

'And he—he still doesn't know?'

May turned and looked deeply into the lovely eyes of her daughter, eyes that were so like her own. 'Not all of it. Not—not why you ran away. You should tell him that yourself. But Jed knows I've found you, Anna, and he wants to see you.' She smiled. 'He would have come today if I'd let him.'

Anna closed her eyes. 'Soon,' she whispered, her heart lifting at the thought of seeing him again. 'I'll see him soon, I promise. But just now—' Her voice faded away.

'So, tell me—what happened to you, my darling? Where did you go?' May asked unsteadily. Her new-found happiness was hard to believe after all the years of anguish.

'Oh Mam.' Anna closed her eyes, trying to blot out the memories, yet they had to be relived. For her mother's sake. May had a right to know, so haltingly, she began to tell her sorry tale.

'I just ran—like you told me to. I thought about going to the city, but then, big though it is, I thought they might find me. Douglas had his cronies there and all I could think of was getting as far away as I could. So I struck across country, living rough, sleeping in barns, stealing food.' She smiled grimly. 'I had no identity card, no ration book. But I thought if I could get to the coast, maybe to Grimsby, I could stow away on a ship. It was a stupid idea, but I didn't care where I went or even what happened to me.' Anna paused, remembering vividly her feeling of hopelessness, not caring then if she lived or died. If it hadn't been for Eddie . . .

She took a deep breath and went on.

'I got as far as Horncastle and it was market day. I set about stealing some food. How I never got caught, I don't know, but I didn't. And then—then there was a young woman who left her handbag on the edge of one of the stalls whilst she moved away to look at something. Before I realized what I was doing, I'd snatched it up and walked away with it in the opposite direction. My heart was thudding. I expected any minute that someone would shout, would come running after me, but nothing happened. Perhaps part of me even wanted to get caught. I don't know. I walked and walked, never looking back, just taking the first road that took me out of the town. I didn't even know where I was heading.' Anna licked her lips and paused in telling what to her was another shameful episode in her story. 'I know it was wrong, Mam. I'm not a thief, yet after what had happened to me stealing seemed nothing.'

'No,' May said huskily, 'it wasn't wrong.' There was a pause and then May prompted. 'And what did you find in the handbag?'

Anna shook her head in wonderment. 'You'll not believe this, Mam. I could hardly believe my luck. I still felt so guilty and yet—yet it seemed—meant to happen.'

'What did? What do you mean?'

'The girl's identity card and her ration book were in the handbag. And do you know—' even now after all the intervening years there was incredulity in Anna's voice—'do you know, her name was Annabel Woods.'

May gasped. 'So—so you called yourself Anna Woods?'

Anna nodded. 'I just hope the real Annabel Woods didn't get into too much trouble. I hoped she'd be able to replace the lost items.'

Now there was a long silence between them until, haltingly now, Anna came to the part where she had been standing in Ludthorpe marketplace on a cold, wet evening just before Christmas . . .

When she had finished, Anna said, 'Now you must tell me what happened to you.'

May's voice was unsteady. 'I had to take the beatings for a while. I tried several times to get away, but he always found me and dragged me back, and then, suddenly, about two years after you'd gone, he stopped hitting me and became much nicer. Just like he had been in the early days.' She glanced at Anna as she added, bitterly, 'But there was a reason. He'd found out that if you were declared dead, then—then I was your next of kin and could inherit the farm. That's what they were after all the time. The farm. They'd planned it all.'

'So what happened?'

'At first, because we couldn't sell it, we put a manager in. The farm did well and earned quite a good living for us. But Douglas wanted the lump sum. He wanted to buy the cinema he was involved in.'

At this point, Anna interrupted her mother's tale to tell her what PC Jenkins had said.

'It doesn't surprise me.' May's mouth was grim. 'Believe me, Douglas Whittaker owned very little that had been legitimately bought, unless,' she added bitterly, 'it was something I'd paid for.'

Anna said nothing.

'When you'd been missing a few years he consulted a solicitor. But he must have been advised to wait a little longer. I think he was told that we ought to make more effort to find you first. So the farm had to stay in your name and we couldn't sell it, only continue to work it.' She sighed. 'Douglas was furious, so the beatings began again for a while. And then he stopped again, though the cruelty still continued, but it was only verbal now.'

'Only!' Anna cried.

'It—it wasn't so bad.' May tried to sound brave, but her mouth trembled. All she had ever wanted was to be taken care of, but instead she had lived with a brutal, greedy man.

'Poor Mam,' Anna murmured. Then, taking a deep breath, she asked, 'What about Bruce?'

'He stayed in the army and only came home on leave. And when he did, the conversation was always about finding you. Of course, part of me wanted you found—desperately—but on the other hand, I wanted you to stay hidden. I was so afraid

444

that if they did find you—' She needed to say no more. Anna shuddered.

'Did Douglas go back to the solicitor again?'

'Yes, and the second time—oh, Anna'—tears filled May's eyes—'I didn't really understand it all. I still don't. Douglas handled everything, but I had to swear an oath in front of an independent solicitor that I believed you to be dead and that I was your next of kin. Eventually probate was granted and—and the farm came to me.' May covered her face with her hands and wept. 'Douglas made me sell it. I lost Clayton's Farm, Anna.' She shuddered. 'Your grandfather must be turning in his grave.'

'Oh, Mam, don't. Grandpa would have understood. He loved you. He wouldn't blame you.'

'But I blame myself,' May whispered hoarsely. 'And the worst of it is it needn't have happened. Douglas didn't have the power to make me do anything, if only I'd known it.'

'What do you mean?'

May was shamefaced. 'I was never properly married to him. It—it seems he never got a divorce from his first wife. Oh, Anna, how could I have been so stupid?'

Anna did not answer her directly but asked instead, 'Who—who has the farm now?'

Through her tears, May was able to smile. 'Jed.'

'Jed!' Anna was startled. But then, as the realization seeped in, she said again, but softly now, 'Jed.'

Again there was a long silence before May asked, 'How did Douglas and Bruce find you after all this time? No one has told me.'

Anna explained that her rebellious teenage daughter had persuaded Tony to take her to Lincoln to see one of her idols.

'It wasn't their fault. I'd kept her hidden away so long without any explanation. She was bound to break out sooner or later. I see that now. I'm not really sure what happened exactly. All Maisie knows is that they were outside the cinema and a photographer took pictures of the queue. Tony thinks perhaps the picture appeared in the *Echo* complete with Maisie's name and where she lived and they came looking.' Her voice hardened. 'Of course, when they got to the farm, Bertha couldn't wait to tell them where I was. I expect she saw for herself then, the likeness of Maisie to—to Bruce.'

'Is she like him?' May asked, sounding as if she hated the idea.

Anna smiled. 'She has his red hair and his brown eyes, but, thankfully, that's the only way she resembles him.' Anna squeezed her mother's hand. 'You'll love her, Mam. I know you will.'

They glanced across the grass to see Maisie and Tony walking towards them. Anna caught her breath. Tony's arm was around Maisie's shoulder and Maisie's was around his waist. As they drew closer, Anna felt tears fill her eyes, but now, after all these years, they were tears of joy.

Tony's face was shining with happiness and Maisie was blushing as she laughed up at him.

It's all right, she thought. *Everything's going to be all right*. As they drew near, Anna, with one arm still around her mother, held out her hand towards Maisie.

'Darling,' she said, 'come and meet your grandmother.'